He drove a carriage with two smart grays. He leaned out and whisked Chrissie in before she had time to greet him. "Pull down your veil," he said, and they were off at a thrilling pace, the dust rising, and the lime trees arching above them.

"I don't care if I am seen," Chrissie said.

"That's nice, but don't let's complicate things more than necessary. How did you get out alone?"

"I had a dreadful headache all night. I even managed to look pale. I said the only thing to cure it was a quiet walk in the early-morning air. Alone. I couldn't stand distraction." She sighed a little. "They believed me."

"You don't look pale now," said Lord Monkshood.

Fawcett Crest Books
by Dorothy Eden:

☐ AN AFTERNOON WALK   24020 $2.50
☐ THE AMERICAN HEIRESS   24448 $2.95
☐ DARKWATER   23544 $2.50
☐ LADY OF MALLOW   23167 $1.95
☐ NEVER CALL IT LOVING   23143 $2.25
☐ RAVENSCROFT   23760 $1.95
☐ THE SALAMANCA DRUM   23548 $2.75
☐ THE SHADOW WIFE   23699 $1.95
☐ SLEEP IN THE WOODS   23706 $2.50
☐ SPEAK TO ME OF LOVE   23981 $2.95
☐ THE STORRINGTON PAPERS   24239 $2.50
☐ THE VINES OF YARABEE   23184 $1.95
☐ WAITING FOR WILLA   23187 $1.95
☐ WINTERWOOD   23185 $1.95

Dorothy Eden

The Millionaire's Daughter

FAWCETT CREST • NEW YORK

THE MILLIONAIRE'S DAUGHTER

THIS BOOK CONTAINS THE COMPLETE TEXT OF
THE ORIGINAL HARDCOVER EDITION.

Published by Fawcett Crest Books, CBS Educational and
Professional Publishing, a division of CBS Inc., by arrangement with Coward, McCann and Geoghegan, Inc.

ISBN: 0-449-23186-0

Selection of the Library Guild

Printed in the United States of America

26 25 24 23 22 21 20 19 18 17 16

To Dorothy Olding
for her unfailing help and encouragement,
especially with this book

Part One

The Millionaire

Chapter 1

On his way to the Academy of Music to see a performance of *Faust* (which he knew would bore him intolerably), Harry Spencer ordered his coachman to drive him uptown to the East Sixties. He had a sudden whim to pay another visit to his new house, just completed, and still unfurnished.

There would be nobody about. He could wander through the empty echoing rooms and permit himself the self-indulgence of a dream.

For tomorrow the acres of carpet and the furniture would begin to arrive and never again would this grand and beautiful house, the fulfillment of a long-cherished ambition, be empty and entirely his. After tomorrow it would be shared with servants, and after that again, a bride.

It was not too large a house. He had carefully avoided the ostentation of the Vanderbilts, with their twin mansions in the Fifties, and of other prominent New York families who still clung to the Twenties and Thirties. He had wanted something smaller and perfect. No passerby could fail to admire the portico with its slender pillars facing Central Park, the dignified façade rising only four floors and broken by beautifully wrought-iron balconies, in the style of a Venetian palace. The fortunate people who were admitted within the front door could exclaim in admiration at the yellow marble staircase, the dark paneling of the hall that was going to make such a suitable background for the pictures he intended acquiring, the suite of rooms, dining room, library and drawing room leading into the ballroom with its magnificent crystal chandeliers; the second-floor drawing room for his wife's use (he could see her there entertaining fashionable friends with hot chocolate in the mornings or reclining in a tea gown to welcome him home in the late afternoon); and the fifteen bedrooms on the upper floors, several of them complete with their own bathrooms.

Camberwell House, as he called it satirically, after the wretched suburb of London, England, from which his parents had come when he was a very small child, established him as an entrepreneur in the world of business, a shrewd man who had an instinct for what he called the day after tomorrow.

Today was not good enough. All those snobbish old families descended from the Dutch patroons might settle in enclaves downtown and think they were there forever. They were not. A rising population and what would inevitably become land hunger on an island the size of Manhattan would push building farther from the city center and higher in the air. Harry already had architects working on plans for department stores, office buildings and hotels that would rise seven or eight floors.

The day after tomorrow when Harry Spencer would be settled in Camberwell House with a wife and several children. And the shanties would have disappeared from the far end of Central Park, the park itself would be a well-kept vista of trees and gardens, and all of the Sixties, the

Seventies and the Eighties would be handsome mansions for the rich.

So this was the last time his house would echo from emptiness. Harry gave a half laugh that was more of a sigh. He found he was a little sentimental, a little reluctant to part with the dream that had possessed him for twenty years.

But there would be other dreams. He would always have a new absorbing project in view. And, he had to remind himself, there was still the vital part of this project to be completed. He was dressed for the kill, so to speak, in his tails, his gleaming white waistcoat, a white gardenia in his lapel, his small pointed golden beard groomed and shining, his blue eyes keen and alert.

Billy, his coachman, was shivering in the freezing night air. The sidewalk was slippery with ice, and the horses skidded on the frozen street as Harry stepped into his smart landau and set off in the direction of the Academy. He had arranged to meet his lawyer and friend, Ephraim de Wynt, in the foyer. Ephraim was one of the few of that powerful elite, the first four hundred, who encouraged rising men and calmly ignored less than illustrious beginnings.

People said unkindly that he himself had an eye on the quick dollar. He did not form these friendships for the pleasure they gave him, although he was reputed to have a deep and fascinated admiration for what he called the God-given talent certain men had for making fortunes. They were the backbone of America. One must never underestimate their enormous influence, even if they hadn't learned the right words to say in society or had ignorant parents hidden away in slum areas because they were uneasy or unhappy living anywhere else.

Harry Spencer, although he had a mother still living in the Bowery, had risen a good deal above this category because he had, when he liked to use it, a natural social sense, as well as the sort of blunt, stocky good looks that appealed to a number of women. He was already a personality and would be a greater one. Ephraim was going to find it amusing introducing him to the most suitable young lady to be mistress of that grand new house on Fifth Avenue.

He had one young lady in mind already. Miss Mary Ellen van Leyden. She would provide all the class Harry lacked. She was also spirited and reasonably good-looking. A little older than desirable, in her mid-twenties, he fancied, but Harry at thirty-five was no youngster. The van Leydens were a family of impeccable background who lived in a larger, shabby house on Eighth Street that had been built by an ancestor who had made a fortune in the latter part of the eighteenth century. The house was now a period piece, a part of New York history. It was a pity that it was in such a ramshackle condition. The truth was that the once-proud van Leydens had, over three generations, produced too many ne'er-do-wells and were now abysmally poor. The present owner, Robert van Leyden IV, gambled, drank, and relied on a fading charm to get him out of awkward situations.

His wife had been a Boydell from Virginia, another family that had seen better days. There were aristocratic cousins somewhere in England, but Millicent Boydell, after her marriage to Robert van Leyden, found that she was never going to make the much-longed-for trip to Europe simply from lack of money. So in spite of her connections, she withered away in the old house on Eighth Street, only occasionally giving a modest dinner party, when extra servants were hired for the evening, and her husband inevitably got drunk. The two daughters, Mary Ellen and Louisa, remained unmarried, and the son, Boydell, who unfortunately had been born with a club-foot, seemed already to be following in his father's footsteps.

It was a great shame, a great waste, and there was only one thing to be done, if it were not too late. The girls must marry money, and Boydell must work harder or find himself an heiress who didn't mind a slight physical deformity.

Ephraim, although he enjoyed the intimacy of a family friend, had no great liking for Millicent van Leyden, with her long nose and her air of superiority and fading elegance, and he despised her dissolute husband. But he was not, after all, concerned for the fortunes of the van Leydens, only for the satisfactory arrangement of his client's domestic life.

Given an entrée into society, Harry Spencer could double or triple his fortune. And that was a matter that affected Ephraim personally. He frankly enjoyed the company, and the business, of the extremely rich.

"Which one?" asked Harry, scanning the boxes. The ladies, with their fans and feathers, looked like a horticultural display formally arranged around the semicircular auditorium.

"The third box from the left with three ladies. The one in the middle is the mother. I see that they are unescorted. I know Robert van Leyden dislikes the opera, and I don't think Boydell cares for it either."

"So much the better. The ladies will be glad of some male company."

"You're right, my dear fellow. Shall we go?"

"Wait a minute. Which of the young ladies had you in mind?"

"The taller one on the right. She has her mother's long nose, but she can be as stately as a duchess when she chooses. I can imagine her coming down that fine staircase of yours." Ephraim looked at his companion. "You told me you hadn't mere prettiness as a standard."

Harry thought of the qualities he wanted in his wife and knew that good looks would have been a bonus he could hardly have expected. If the two Misses van Leyden had been raving beauties, they would have been snapped up long ago, penniless or not. That stood to reason. No, he was content to settle for quality, breeding, social eminence. After all, a man could go on having the occasional discreet affair. Not even the most innocent and protected of young women would imagine that he could have reached his middle thirties and not had his share of amorous adventures.

He believed he was prepared to settle for the elder van Leyden daughter, long nose or not. He supposed she was healthy. They'd breed children, and she would preside over his table. That would be all he expected of her. In return she could have as many luxuries as she pleased.

With a decisive gesture he put his opera glasses away.

"Then let us go, shall we?"

Millicent van Leyden, pleased for some attention, welcomed Ephraim gladly. He was an old friend. She had even toyed with the thought that he might make a husband for either Mary Ellen or Louisa. Then she had realized that he was an incurable dandy with the pernickety ways of the confirmed bachelor and an embarrassing habit of pandering to the nouveaux riches. One hoped Mary Ellen and Louisa could do better than that. If they hadn't the looks, they did have the ability to make excellent wives and mothers. It was just too bad that so far no eligible young man had been seriously interested in them.

Mary Ellen was nearly twenty-seven, Louisa six years her junior. At the ball Millicent was shortly giving for Louisa's twenty-first birthday, something had to happen. She didn't want to think she had sacrificed her diamond necklace, part of the Boydell family jewels, in vain.

In the meantime here was Ephraim with one of his outlandish rich friends, a shortish man with a small golden beard and air of overwhelming virility. Even Millicent, permanently tired from worry and hopelessness, was aware of the virility. The girls on either side of her were reacting in their usual way: Mary Ellen bridling (an unfortunate mannerism that neither her mother nor any governess had been able to eliminate) and Louisa shrinking back slightly, with her exasperating shyness.

"Millicent, my dear," Ephraim said, lifting her head in

his affected manner to kiss it. "Miss Mary Ellen. Miss Louisa. May I present my friend, Mr. Harry Spencer."

Harry gave a small formal bow to each of the ladies. He had noticed at once that Mrs. van Leyden's gown of gray satin had seen many wearings, that the elder daughter had a heavy discontented face and her white tulle was too young for her, and that the younger, who did look suitably innocent and virginal, raised her eyes only fleetingly so that he had no more than an impression of sapphire blue in a rather long, gentle face. She had a long neck, too. It was very graceful. Her hair was dark and done in a smooth coiffure, a contrast to her sister's high-piled, elaborate curls. She was obviously self-effacing and diffident. Malleable, Harry thought at once. He might not be qualified to teach his wife social graces, but he could teach her other things—if she were willing to learn.

Louisa van Leyden. He knew, with his sure instinct, that she was the one. This meeting, intended to be no more than an inspection of a possible acquisition, was suddenly surprisingly final. He would marry Louisa.

"Mr. Spencer is celebrating the completion of his new house," Ephraim was saying. "It's quite a showpiece. Isn't it, Harry?"

"Indeed," said Mrs. van Leyden politely. "And where is it, Mr. Spencer?"

"In the upper Sixties."

"Why did you build so far out of town?"

"It has a splendid view of the park. Excellent air." These people with their prejudices and their long-established habits. He was not pandering to any of them. "Perhaps you don't think it so desirable, Mrs. van Leyden. It happens to appeal to me, especially after having lived all my life in the Bowery.

"And I shall, of course, develop other areas in the vicinity," he added, as if he were speaking of doing nothing more important than tidying up an overgrown garden.

"Really!" exclaimed the elder Miss van Leyden with an air of rapt interest.

"Perhaps Mr. Spencer will invite you to see his marble staircase," Ephraim murmured. "He calls it yellow, but I prefer to say it is the color of champagne. It has that quality. The best French champagne, of course."

"Oh, Ephraim, you exaggerate so," said Mrs. van Leyden in her helpless voice.

"Do you care for the opera?" Harry asked, addressing himself to the younger daughter.

She started, realizing that he was speaking to her and that an answer was required.

"Very much, thank you. I think that Adelina Patti has a wonderful voice."

Her own voice, soft and breathless, was exactly what he had hoped it would be.

"And you, Mr. Spencer?" Mary Ellen was not going to be overlooked for her younger sister.

"I confess it goes over my head. I'm not an educated man."

"But you have come, nevertheless."

"You can try anything once, Miss van Leyden."

"I think we had better be getting back to our seats," Ephraim murmured. "The curtain must be going up in a moment."

Mrs. van Leyden leaned forward and tapped him with her fan.

"You have neglected us, Ephraim."

"I'm sorry, Millicent. May I present myself for a cup of morning chocolate tomorrow?"

"Of course. We'll be delighted, won't we, girls?"

"Yes, Mamma," said Mary Ellen, her eyes on Harry. Louisa was busy with her program. She scarcely looked up as the two men departed. Was she completely uninterested in the opposite sex? Such a thought was too macabre to be entertained for a moment.

"Well," said Ephraim, "you made an impression. Although you needn't have stated your views about the opera quite so emphatically."

"I won't pretend. I start as I mean to go on; otherwise I will find myself being dragged here every season."

"Perhaps you'll be dragged somewhere else instead. I make you a wager."

"What's that?"

"That you'll shortly receive an invitation to the forthcoming ball at the van Leyden mansion."

Harry raised his eyebrows. "Did I make enough impression for that? I thought I was firmly relegated to my right category: an upstart from the Bowery."

"Well, my dear fellow, you would mention the Bowery. However, that direct style of yours may have something to be said for it. Mark my words, you are going to be thoroughly investigated, beginning with my call tomorrow morning. That is, if you still wish me to make it."

"Certainly I do. Nothing has changed. The terms we mentioned."

"I understand. After that, I wager the ladies will take a drive up Fifth Avenue in a hired coupe, as they can no longer run their own carriage. But they will duly note the richness and tastefulness of your house. Robert van Leyden still has a friend or two in the business world who will ferret out your prospects. Yes, I fancy you'll get your invitation to the ball. I only warn you not to drink the fruit cup. Find your way into the library, and van Leyden will give you some of his best bourbon."

"Are you sure they will be so ready to accept?" Harry asked.

"Why ever not? It's their answer to a prayer. Mind you, a little wooing may be required, just for the sake of appearances. Mary Ellen is not as young as she would like to be, but I guarantee she's still a virgin."

"A ridiculous name," Harry burst out. "She's either Mary or she's Ellen. If you must know the truth, I found her terrifying. One of those man-eating orchids you find in jungles."

"Did you, by jove? But young ladies must play some

sort of courtship game. What else is there for them to do?"

"And what are they when they've stopped playing it?"

"That's a question I personally have never had the courage to find the answer to. You may have an angel or a shrew."

"For my part," said Harry definitely, "I prefer the younger one."

"Do you really! Now I never thought she would appeal to you. She hardly opens her mouth. She may even be a bluestocking. I would rather fancy she is."

"That would do me no harm."

Ephraim looked at him with disbelief.

"I never thought you'd be content to learn from a woman."

"Oh, certain things," said Harry. He seemed surprised himself. "But I'd have things to teach her, too."

"That's more like it, my dear fellow. I can't see you letting a woman get too powerful. I'd have sworn you would settle for Mary Ellen. But never mind, Louisa it shall be."

"She has that long neck," Harry murmured. "I find I like that in a woman."

"Useful for hanging diamond necklaces around, I admit. But I've known shorter necks to accommodate them quite happily. I still think Mary Ellen—"

"If it is to be either, it is to be Louisa," Harry said shortly. "Let us regard that as settled."

Chapter 2

On the day after the opera, Millicent van Leyden had one of her prostrating headaches. She lay on the sofa in the drawing room, a room on the first floor that faced the street. She had used to enjoy watching passersby, but the tree of heaven, brought back from China by her husband's seafaring grandfather, had now grown so big that it obscured the view. In the summer it turned the room into a green gloom. In winter its bare branches hung bare and melancholy or were coated with snow. It was said that when the tree was cut down, the van Leyden mansion would disappear and the family die out.

Well, the house was getting more decrepit by the year, and unless the children hastened to marry, the family was certainly doomed to extinction. Did it matter? Millicent, in thirty years of marriage to a man whom she had alternately adored and despised, did not find her loyalties committed to the van Leydens. She had remained, at heart, a Boydell. New York, or Robert with his dissolute way of life (he had the effrontery to boast that he was a man of leisure), had produced her headaches, her palpitations, the dark circles around her eyes, the petulant droop to her mouth. She never felt entirely well, and sometimes she felt it should not be expected of her to worry about the future of her children.

Nevertheless, it was becoming a matter of embarrassment that there had been no wedding in the family, with Boy approaching thirty, Mary Ellen in her late twenties, and Louisa, her baby, coming of age in three weeks' time.

Boy seemed to have the idea that his lame foot would revolt a woman and said he never meant to marry. Mary Ellen frightened off her suitors with her bossy ways, and Louisa was too self-effacing. So what was one to do?

She had had every intention of taking the girls and going for a drive as far as Central Park this morning. A brisk blow would have done them all good. They could have done a little shopping at Arnold Constable's on the way. The dressmaker, Miss Prendergast, was making Mary Ellen's ball gown from a length of sky blue satin that dear old Aunt Abigail had sent from Virginia, but yards of ribbon and lace were required. Every now and then Aunt Abigail remembered that Millicent had marriageable daughters and, owing to Robert's improvidence, too little money to equip them for the brilliant social life they should be leading.

Mary Ellen, being the elder sister, should be got off first, so the gifts were usually for her. Little Louisa, whom Aunt Abigail still thought of as a schoolgirl, would have her turn later. Which was scarcely fair when the forthcoming ball was to celebrate Louisa's coming of age, and on this occasion at least, she should have been the recipient of the blue satin.

However, white was more suitable for a young girl, and Millicent had had the idea of having her white Nottingham lace wedding gown, only slightly yellowed with age, cut down to fit Louisa. It was a beautiful piece of lace, an heirloom, and Louisa was a very lucky girl to be permitted to wear it. With her regulation eighteen-inch waist, she would look very well in the graceful clinging material.

As Aunt Abigail would agree, it might be Louisa's ball, but in reality it was a determined attempt to find Mary Ellen that badly needed beau. The girl was getting restless and touchy. Her discontent showed in her face, giving it heavy lines. The trouble was, she was too strong-minded. She had always intimidated young men. Her outspokenness, and her total lack of a dowry, left her still unasked for at twenty-seven, which was decidedly humiliating. She really needed an older man who would refuse to be dominated. If such a person could be found still unmarried.

Harry Spencer, New York's newest millionaire?

The thought had been in Millicent's mind ever since the encounter the previous evening. She had known very well what Ephraim de Wynt was up to. That man was a busybody, a matchmaker, an old woman. He lived the vicarious life of arranging other people's affairs. His action last night had brought on Millicent's headache. Her blood boiled to think that her daughters, descendants of two of the finest families in America, should be virtually held up to offer to a brash opportunist whose antecedents would certainly not bear looking into.

Nevertheless, Mr. Spencer apparently intended to conform to high standards. His appearance had been impeccable, his manners good enough, and that expensive house, even though so far out of town, could not be overlooked. If its style was too vulgar, a clever wife could moderate it. Anyway, what was vulgarity? Everyone now talked of gold plate at dinner and gold taps in the bathroom and even houses built entirely of marble.

Except the impoverished van Leydens who hid behind a flourishing tree of heaven that was visible proof of their length of tenure in the house on Eighth Street. The first van Leyden had built a farmhouse on this spot. It was his grandson who had begun ambitiously to own his own ships, beginning with a small schooner that carried sugar and rum from the Caribbean islands. Later he had brought treasures from the Orient, but there were few of those left now. Millicent remembered a small jade horse, very rare and valuable, that now stood in a glass-fronted cabinet, among other *objets d'art,* in the Astor house. She winced with humiliation every time she saw it. But it had helped to pay Boy's expenses at Harvard.

Now her diamonds had gone, as a sort of final despairing gesture, on this ball. The only comforting thing was that when she did exert herself to entertain, her friends rallied around, and the carriages rolled up to the porticoed door of the old mansion as loyally as they had done in the affluent days of the van Leydens. They were still somebody.

Or was it that people were sorry for them?

Millicent found that thought unendurable. She turned her racked head on the cushion, as she had an instant and compulsive vision of Robert sitting in the library, his handsome head lolling back in the shabby leather chair, a cigar in his hand, the decanter of bourbon at his side. He would stay there until noon, when he would put on his overcoat, its fur lining bald in patches from a thousand wearings, and stroll uptown to his club. If he were not home by seven in the evening, Boy would have to go and fetch him. Sometimes the two of them did not return until ten or later, and by then Boy, too, was flushed and limped more noticeably.

The girls were sent to bed, to be spared, if possible, the knowledge that their good-looking only brother seemed to have inherited his father's weakness. Although Boy preferred rum to bourbon.

Unfortunately, he was not interested in a career, although he had taken his degree in law at Harvard. He worked in a Wall Street office and boasted that he had no aspirations to be anything but the most junior member of the firm. The ability to work had unluckily been left out of his makeup, he said cheerfully. Neither had he any intention of taking his mother's advice and looking for an heiress to marry. The family was played out, finished. Didn't Mamma realize that?

By all means snare rich husbands for the girls, if she could. What did it matter if they made disgusting noises eating their soup if it were eaten off a gold plate? But Boy was much too old to have his life planned for him. When the girls were married and his parents dead, he would live the life of a recluse in the dear old house. The prospect appealed to him.

Millicent thought that Mary Ellen might cope with the

kind of rich husband Boy satirically described. But not Louisa. Louisa was too shy and sensitive. She must find someone of her own kind and class. With her sister married and able to entertain lavishly, this should not present the difficulty it did at the present time. Millicent found entertaining beyond her purse and an almost intolerable exertion.

Now she had to make the decision whether or not to send Mr. Harry Spencer an invitation to the ball. On the whole, one thought yes. It was what Ephraim de Wynt had intended her to do. So the man could not be too impossible. Ephraim's greed for wealthy clients did not exceed his fastidiousness.

Perhaps Boy could be persuaded to take a look at that famous house in the upper Sixties and report on it.

There was no need for this, however, for Mary Ellen had already taken the matter into her own determined hands. On the pretext of shopping, she had persuaded Louisa to accompany her, and the two of them had hired a coupe and driven the length of Fifth Avenue.

The house, Mary Ellen reported later in a vivacious voice, was splendid. Maybe a trifle smaller than one would have wished, for something so much money had been spent on, but in excellent taste. Not in the least showy.

"And in a way, Mamma, it must be fun to move out of this rut we're all in and live somewhere different. Like being a pioneer."

When she was excited, Mary Ellen looked very handsome.

"You are going to ask Mr. Spencer to our ball, aren't you, Mamma?"

"I will think about it." Ephraim had made his promised morning call and supplied her with vital information. She was still suffering from a *crise de nerfs*. Boy was so little help and Robert even less. They both thought only of themselves.

"Mr. de Wynt says he has an elderly mother living in the Bowery. The story is that she refuses to move from there."

"It's probably true."

"But what is she like?" Millicent worried. "Mr. Spencer isn't even a first-generation American. He was born in London in England. His father emigrated to New York about thirty years ago. He called himself a street trader."

"You mean a barrow boy," said Louisa. She read a great deal and could supply the most unexpected pieces of information.

"Well, I don't know what he called himself in England, but he got work in a dry goods store here and gradually got to own it. So I guess there's business brains in the family. The Civil War helped, of course. Any fool could make money selling provisions to the Yankees."

"But Mr. Harry Spencer doesn't run a store," Mary Ellen said. "He deals in real estate."

"Yes, he has more brains than his father, they say. But he keeps that little store in the Bowery for sentimental reasons. I made Ephraim tell me all this. Money or not, one must know a little about one's guests."

"So you do intend to invite him, Mamma." Mary Ellen's cheeks had an excited flush.

"Supposing," Louisa said in her quiet way, "he doesn't accept the invitation."

"Not accept!" Millicent exclaimed. "What an extraordinarily unlikely possibility."

"I just thought that Mr. Spencer looked like a law unto himself. If he comes, it will be because he wants to come. As if he were doing us a favor. Do we need favors from a man like that, Mamma?"

Millicent frowned and moved irritably.

"I must ask you not to question my decisions, Louisa."

"Let him come or let him stay away," Mary Ellen said airily. "But do let's ask him. I can't wait to give him some advice on the drapes he should hang in his front windows. A mere man—he might know about selling property, but he can't know about drapes. He really must shut out that dreary wilderness of Central Park."

"If I were you," Millicent said, "I'd wait until my advice was asked for. There's nothing a man likes less than thinking he is being managed."

"But your generation was so meek." Mary Ellen's eyes were flashing. "Ours is not, I hope. If Mr. Spencer doesn't care for my advice, it will be a pity. But I fancy he will lap it up. Like a tiger cub lapping cream."

Louisa didn't see how Mary Ellen, having reached the age of twenty-seven without having had a steady beau, could be so sure of herself. Perhaps she was right; perhaps Mr. Spencer would be humbly impressed by the interest taken in him. All the same, Louisa fancied not. She fancied Mr. Spencer would want to dictate the way the conversation went. However, she kept her mouth shut this time. Like most people too ready with advice, Mary Ellen rarely listened to it herself.

New York was accustomed to the austerity of van Leyden balls. Although the house was one of the few of that period to have its own ballroom, the atmosphere of shabbiness and decay rather canceled out this advantage. Compared to the new and costly grandeur of the Vanderbilt and the Astor mansions, the not quite sparkling chandeliers, the rickety gilt chairs around the ballroom, the hired glass and cutlery and the hired staff, the refreshments that were adequate and picturesque but lacked the piquancy and originality of those produced by a resident French chef (as was the fashion nowadays), the fruit cup instead of champagne all were a little pathetic, a little tragic.

But everyone came, of course. One would never dream of offending poor dear Millicent who had so many troubles. One shared her ardent desire to get Mary Ellen off at last. There was still time for Louisa, although remaining a spinster would perhaps not trouble her as much as it would her sister. She was so quiet, so gentle. Her pale, tranquil face was not likely to excite any great passion in any male breast. But neither would it grow bitter with the passing years. And tonight, in that madeover lace of Millicent's, she looked dignified and charming. She also knew her place. Although the ball was in honor of her coming of age, she would stay as much in the background as possible and leave Mary Ellen the limelight. Her turn would come later. If she wanted it to.

Surprisingly, however, she was not allowed to stay in the background. That newest millionaire Mr. Harry Spencer had already danced with Louisa twice and with Mary Ellen only once. Now he was bowing over Louisa again, and she was flushing, from embarrassment rather than from pleasure. She stood up with obvious reluctance, then took Mr. Spencer's arm and swept into a waltz.

One had to admit, however, that they made a nice enough couple. If there was one thing Louisa did excellently, it was ballroom dancing. And Mr. Spencer, although his figure was too short and too solid, had a certain air of arrogance that some ladies would find attractive. He had a very direct way of looking and speaking. His eyes were bright, his complexion healthy, his golden hair and beard striking. He could have been a pirate. He probably was one. Those real estate people knew how to extract money, even if not exactly at the point of a cutlass. But one thing seemed certain: he did not find this, his first ball in high society, in the least intimidating. He was enjoying himself. Somehow he gave the moldering old house a vitality it had long lacked. Even Millicent van Leyden's mouth had stopped drooping, and she was looking unusually animated. Boy was behaving impeccably, talking to the bejeweled dowagers with his special kind of wry wit. He never ventured on the dance floor. Robert had not yet reached the stage when he must be discreetly persuaded to retire upstairs. And Mary Ellen, dancing with what seemed like angry vigor, had bright patches of color in her cheeks and looked more handsome than anyone would have thought possible.

Halfway through the waltz Mr. Spencer stepped painfully on Louisa's right foot.

"I am sorry," he apologized. "Did that hurt very much?"

"Hardly at all." Louisa wriggled her numbed toes.

"Perhaps we could sit out the rest of this. I'm no performer on the dance floor, as you now have proof."

Louisa sat on the edge of one of the hired gilt chairs. She felt as if everyone in the room were looking at her, captive in the determined company of Mr. Spencer. How ever did one get rid of him?

"You lead such a busy life, Mr. Spencer. I expect you don't have time for these pastimes. Duties, I call them."

"Aren't they pleasures?" he asked, and Louisa flushed, realizing the gaffe she had made.

"I think of pleasures as things one chooses to do. As far as this ball is concerned, my parents decided it must be given whether I wished it or not. Do you see what I mean?"

"Yes, I do. All this folderol forced on you."

"I'm not ungrateful," Louisa hastened to add. "Both my sister and I enjoy dancing. Especially my sister. Wouldn't you care to—"

"No, I'll stay right here, Miss Louisa."

"But I can't monopolize you. There are people I am sure you would enjoy meeting." Louisa wished he would stop looking at her so hard. Had he no manners? She had a suspicion that he made his own. Why didn't Mamma come and rescue her? Or Mary Ellen? It was Mary Ellen who had particularly wanted Mr. Spencer invited to the ball.

"For the gentlemen who don't care for dancing," she said with a shade of desperation, "there is the billiard room."

Mr. Spencer put his head on one side, smiling in a maddening way.

"I believe you are trying to get rid of me, Miss Louisa."

"Oh, no! I mean, I only thought—I'm really a very dull person. Boy, my brother, has the van Leyden charm. Or so people say. And Mary Ellen has the vivacity. I'm just rather quiet."

"I like a quiet woman."

"But you've never married?"

"Not as yet. I had a lot of things to do first. They've kept me busy."

"One knows that. Your success, your wonderful new house."

"What did you think of my house?"

"I—How do you know I have seen it?"

"You said it was wonderful."

"Well—so Ephraim told us. Everyone says so."

"But you did take a drive up Fifth Avenue?"

"Mary Ellen and I often do that. Mamma, too; only she wasn't feeling well that day." Louisa realized what she had admitted, blushed again, and brazened it out. "I suppose since you have never married, you don't know how inquisitive women are."

"Maybe. Maybe. However, this was one occasion when I confess I hoped for a little curiosity. After meeting you at the opera, I frankly counted on you and your sister taking a drive past my house."

Louisa wanted nothing but to escape from this increasingly embarrassing conversation.

"Mr. Spencer, you really must excuse me." She consulted her dance program, holding it close to her eyes as if she were suddenly afflicted with blindness. "The band is about to stop, and I see—oh, yes, I have promised Mr. Naylor—"

"Now, Miss Louisa, don't you get involved with the son of a man who has just taken out a second mortgage on his Lexington Avenue property. Forgive my saying so, but haven't you enough of that sort of thing already?"

Louisa was outraged. The rudeness of the man! Her head rose high on her long neck.

"Mr. Spencer, I am only about to dance with Barry

Naylor. I am not embracing property or mortgages or anything else."

She paused and added specifically, "I am not even interested in money."

"Foolish! Foolish!"

"But with you it's the spur, the guiding light, the whole purpose of life. Isn't it?"

Mr. Spencer stroked his neat shining beard with a sensuous movement, as if he were stroking a cat.

"Oh, I know I'm a crude fellow. Yes, I like money. It allows you to be honest."

"Some means of acquiring it can be far from honest. I hardly know why you use that word."

"Well, let's say I would like my sons to go to dancing classes, so they wouldn't have to pretend dexterity at occasions like this and suffer the humiliation of treading on ladies' toes. I would like my daughter to have her own evening gown for her own ball. Not that yours isn't quite charming. It's a beautiful piece of lace, and age has improved it. But every inch of it wasn't cut especially for your figure, and you're pretending it was. My daughter will be able to say that the gown for her ball was specially ordered in Paris. She will never have to say she wore her mother's cut-down wedding gown."

Louisa listened in fascinated astonishment as Mr. Spencer went on. "You're pretending, too, that all this glass and china won't go back to its owners tomorrow, that this room won't look very shabby and empty when the flowers are removed, the candles blown out and these uncomfortable chairs put away. You and your family are living in a fantasy, Miss Louisa. But with money this would all be real. Do you see what I mean?"

Louisa sprang up.

"I think you are impertinent and rude."

"Oh, I agree. I told you I was a crude fellow. My grandfather was a chimney sweep. He burrowed his way down the stately chimneys of England. My father was a barrow boy in Camberwell, which is a slum area of London. I have called my house, the one you were kind enough to admire, Camberwell, because I am honestly proud of what I have achieved. I haven't had the social advantages of a van Leyden. But I have other advantages, Miss Louisa." Suddenly he smiled, and his blue eyes were brilliant. "You'll be hearing about them."

"Supposing I refuse to listen."

"I'm afraid you will have to. Human nature being what it is. I would like to think that you had a choice, and that it was favorable to me. But I doubt you will have one. Now I am going to plead a long journey home and make my farewells. My mother gets lonely since my father died. She refuses to move into my new house. She likes living above the store my father had in the Bowery. As a matter of fact, I keep the store open just because she enjoys serving behind the counter now and again. Although when she's gone, I still may keep it. It's my childhood, so to speak. Are you surprised to find me so sentimental?"

"Why do you imagine I am interested?"

He laughed suddenly, a hearty, jolly laugh, that made several people turn their heads.

"It's turned cold, all at once. I feel quite nipped. But I always enjoy a frost. It makes me feel alive." He made a small bow; then, laughing again in that uninhibited way, he wandered off, obviously meaning to take his leave.

Louisa breathed a sigh of intense relief and heard Mary Ellen hissing behind her. "Is Mr. Spencer leaving?"

"I think so."

"But it's hardly past midnight. Did you offend him? I must say, that tête-à-tête you were having—everyone was looking. It isn't done to spend so much time with one guest."

"I couldn't help it. Mr. Spencer is rude and stubborn and abominable." Louisa looked around desperately. "When do you suppose all these people will go home?"

"It's your ball. You're supposed to be enjoying it."

"I'm not, and you don't look as if you are, either."

28

"The way you monopolized that man."

"I did not. He wouldn't leave me. He trod on my toes, and had no manners—" Louisa was nearly crying.

"You little goose. You should have brought him to me. I'd have managed him. Now for goodness' sake, smile and at least look as if you're enjoying yourself. Papa has just fallen over one of the potted palms. Boy has taken him upstairs. What a night. The van Leydens' keeping up appearances!"

The next day, when Millicent van Leyden, Mary Ellen and Louisa were sitting around the fire drinking hot chocolate, a florist's box containing three dozen yellow roses arrived for Louisa. The enclosed card read: "Dear Miss Louisa, Roses like these will arrive every day until you are my wife. Your devoted admirer, Harry Spencer."

Louisa dropped the box and the card and tried to suppress hysterical laughter.

"What's the matter?" Mary Ellen asked.

"Yes, who is your beau, Louisa?" Mamma asked, giving Louisa a quick, anxious look that slid away.

Mamma was not surprised, Louisa realized. She knew!

"It's not that Mr. Spencer, surely," Mary Ellen said sourly. "It would be like him to overdo things."

Louisa said breathlessly, "He must be stopped. He says he's going to send this many roses every day. It will be like a nightmare. You have these, Mary Ellen."

"Secondhand flowers! No, thank you." Mary Ellen had picked up the card and was reading it.

"He wants to marry you!" she exclaimed.

Louisa nodded miserably. "So it seems. I shan't accept his proposal, of course, even if I run the risk of getting buried in roses." She sprang up, smoothing her skirts, alpaca and durable. This dress was three years old and would last some time longer. Although not as long as Mamma's lovely old Nottingham lace that Mr. Spencer had despised. She didn't really care to have new clothes

29

all the time, which was a thing a man like Mr. Spencer probably couldn't understand. He would imagine it to be an irresistible lure to a woman.

"It's so ridiculous," she went on incredulously. "I only danced with Mr. Spencer and talked to him last night. Under duress, I might say. I simply couldn't escape from him. Mamma, why are you looking at me like that? Did you know this terrible thing was going to happen?"

"Don't be silly, Louisa. It isn't a terrible thing, getting a proposal of marriage. I'm sure your sister will agree."

"I would accept it as quickly as it was made," Mary Ellen said unhesitatingly.

"You mean you would marry Mr. Spencer!"

"And live in that beautiful house and give the best parties in town? Oh, yes, indeed."

"But *marry*, Mary Ellen! I mean, share his bedroom, sit opposite him at breakfast, have his children. Why, we don't even know him, either of us. He's just a rich man suddenly in a great hurry to be married. Now that he has the money he wants the right wife, so he can shine in society. He hasn't even the finesse to take time in wooing her. And don't tell me there's plenty of time for that after marriage, Mamma, because I just don't believe it would work."

"You think too much, Louisa," Millicent said tartly. She adjusted her fine lace shawl with a resigned movement. Her look of faded elegance had never been more pronounced. "In this life one has to be practical. I never was, or I would have seen that your father would slowly ruin us all."

"What do you mean, Mamma? Are you actually *approving* of Mr. Spencer?"

"Well, my dear child, it seems we have no alternative. You might know that Ephraim called the other day and had a very long talk with me and your father and Boy. It seems that your father is being threatened with bankruptcy. If that happens, this house and everything in it will be sold. Imagine, the van Leyden house on the market! It would be the end of your father, and of me, too. Quite apart from how we would all live in the future. You girls would have to find positions, be governesses or something. Think of a van Leyden teaching the grandchildren of that odious Jay Gould."

"Would it matter so much?" Louisa muttered.

"Matter! When your great-great-grandfather was one of the old patroons! He built a house on this very spot. Not to mention my own family, with an ancestor in the court of Queen Elizabeth."

Louisa's heart was sinking. She had never heard her mother so eloquent or so determined. But this scheme, which had been hatched cold-bloodedly, keeping her in the dark, was humiliating in the extreme.

"So is Mr. Spencer to save the precious van Leydens from ruin?" she asked with an unfamiliar sarcasm.

"There will be a marriage settlement, of course. But certainly one of the clauses will be that our dear family home is preserved."

"In return for the sale of one of your daughters. Mamma, I never realized you cared more for a house than for Mary Ellen or me."

"Louisa!"

Louisa's lips were trembling. "But it's true, isn't it? Mary Ellen, why don't you say something? Do you like the thought of being sold, like a cow or a sheep?"

"Depends who it's to," Mary Ellen said. "That makes all the difference. Oh, don't be so dim-witted, Louisa. You must have known what was going on from the time Ephraim brought Mr. Spencer to our opera box. I certainly did. Beggars can't be choosers, even if they have blue blood in their veins." She was frowning ferociously. She squinted, as if to squeeze back angry tears. "But I wouldn't regard marrying Harry Spencer as beggary. He's so alive. He makes Boy and certain other gentlemen in our snobbish circle look pretty limp."

"Then it's a pity it wasn't you he chose."

"Yes, it was. I'd be a far better match for him than you. I'd like to tell him so."

"Then do so."

"Maybe I will."

"Mary Ellen," said Mamma, "behave yourself."

That night they talked around the dinner table in the big dining room with its early colonial furniture, its worn turkey carpet and faded velvet drapes. A portrait of Theodore van Leyden, the old patroon, with his heavy Dutch face (Mary Ellen promised to resemble him) hung over the fireplace. His wife, wearing a dark dress with an exquisite white lace collar that effectively distracted attention from her plain face, hung less conspicuously. That was symbolic of those times, Louisa thought, the wife being a person of minor importance who bowed to all the decisions of her husband.

Although if one were to believe what her own family was saying now, such conditions still existed in this enlightened age. For they were not on the side of her, their daughter, but on that of Harry Spencer, a virtual stranger. To be more accurate, they were on the side of money, and if it involved a marriage of convenience, was that so unusual? Louisa would not be the first unwilling bride. One could count numbers of girls belonging to prominent families who had made successful marriages in precisely this way. And really, someone in this family must marry.

"Anyone would think we had the plague," Papa complained. He was comparatively sober tonight and, by candlelight, looked handsome and distinguished. Louisa remembered adoring him when she was a child. It wasn't easy to stop loving someone, even when he had become a different person, with a stumbling step, blurred features and sudden wild rages. One couldn't contemplate what would happen to him if he had to leave this house. Or to Mamma, either, especially with her delicate health. She had been brought up with a strong sense of duty, and honor, and self-sacrifice, if necessary.

But surely the solution to her family problems didn't rest entirely on her frail shoulders. Need she do such a cataclysmic thing as marry a man who was not even congenial to her? Wasn't there another more likable rich man who would admire her? Must it be that brash Harry Spencer? Whatever would they talk about for the rest of their lives?

"One of us does have the plague," said Boy, in his drawling voice. He kicked his crooked foot against the table leg.

"Boy dear, your poor foot need not be the handicap you imagine it is," Mamma said. "Plenty of girls would be glad to marry you."

"And spend the rest of their lives being sorry for me? I know there are some women who thrive on that. But not for me. I'd end by strangling them." Boy reached for his glass. "No, the life of a recluse for me. I'll shut myself up and read Lord Byron's poems. But by all means marry off my sisters. What's the matter, Lou? Do you dislike your little millionaire so much?"

"No, I don't dislike him. In other circumstances I would quite like him. It was only that I had hoped to marry for love. Is that wrong?"

"Not wrong, but impractical," said Papa dismissively. "Your mother and I married to please our families. Didn't we, my dear? And it worked capitally."

But Papa was scarcely ever sober, and Mamma had her constant headaches and her palpitations. Was that happiness?

"We're not forcing you, dear," said Mamma. "We would never allow you to be unhappy. But personally I thought Mr. Spencer a perfectly charming man. I believe Mary Ellen did, too."

"Leave me out of this," said Mary Ellen tartly. "I'm not the bartered bride."

"Don't be ridiculous!" Mamma exclaimed. "Bartered bride, indeed! We must go less often to the opera."

"Fellow seemed reasonable enough," said Papa. "I had a long talk with him at my club. His intentions are honorable. Promised to get him membership at my club, for a start. Good God, when you think who gets into society nowadays. Anyway, a clever woman will soon get rid of his rough edges."

"Don't do it, sis, if you don't want to," Boy said suddenly.

"I do want to do what's right," Louisa said earnestly. "I love you all, and I want to please you and make things easier for you. But I hardly know Mr. Spencer. And all those roses! Excessiveness is so vulgar."

"But the thought is charming, you must admit," said Mamma. She was changing her tactics subtly. "And we're not here, Louisa, to persuade you to rush into marriage. Take time to think about it. Let Mr. Spencer show you over his house. Go driving with him or to the theater. Get to know each other."

"And in the meantime what happens to the bankruptcy papers?" Louisa asked.

"I'll raise a loan from somewhere," said Papa, with his easy optimism. "Don't you worry your head about that."

"If you can raise a loan, why are we having this discussion, with Mr. Spencer being held up as our only savior?"

"Hey there, don't get cynical, Lou," said Boy. "But it's true, all the same. Because nobody in Wall Street is going to trust our dear father with any more money unless this marriage is in the wind."

Papa shuffled and reached for the whiskey decanter.

"Failure," he muttered. "Should be shot."

"Robert!" Mamma put her hand over his. "If only it weren't for my weak heart, I'd go out and work myself."

"For God's sake, don't shame me, Millicent."

The little movement of Mamma putting her hand protectively over Papa's, in spite of all he had made her suffer, remained in Louisa's mind. Theirs had been an arranged marriage, they said. So was it possible that in twenty or so years she would be similarly protective toward Harry Spencer? The trouble was, he was like that heavy-faced Dutch ancestor over the fireplace; he looked much too strong and self-reliant ever to need protection from a woman.

It seemed like someone else speaking when she said, "Very well, I will allow myself to be courted. But that doesn't say that I will marry Mr. Spencer." She bit her lip in despair. "Surely there's another way. Because even if it's foolish and romantic, it really was my greatest wish to marry for love."

"There isn't anyone in love with you, is there?" said Mamma, in her sweet, insidious way.

"Except Mr. Harry Spencer obviously," said Boy dryly. "So don't despise him, Lou."

"We've never had a chance," Mary Ellen burst out with pent-up resentment. "We've always been the poor van Leydens."

"Nevertheless, you are van Leydens," said Mamma repressively. "And Boydells, too, don't forget."

"What a prize for Mr. Spencer," said Boy. "Come, cheer up, Lou. Think of the furs and jewels you'll get."

"I won't care for them. Mary Ellen would show them off better."

"That's life," said Boy. "Heavens, it's stuffy in here. Too many problems. Too much family atmosphere. I need some fresh air. I'm going down to the club."

"I'll join you," said Papa. "I'll have a game of whist. By the way, Boy, you don't have twenty dollars, do you?"

"No, Father, I don't."

"Too bad. Bit pressed."

"A familiar condition, Father."

Wrangling amiably, the two men departed shrugging off their problems as was the habit of the men in this family. Pearl came in to clear away the dishes. Mamma said she was afraid her palpitations were coming on and she would retire upstairs. When Pearl had taken out the last of the dishes, Louisa and Mary Ellen were alone.

"If Papa hadn't got twenty dollars," Louisa said, "how could we have given that expensive ball? Wasn't it crazy?"

Mary Ellen looked at her cynically.

"Didn't you know? Mamma sold her diamonds."

"Oh, no. How awful! But they were an heirloom."

"Heirlooms have a habit of disappearing in this family. Louisa, you are a little innocent. Didn't you think she would have worn them if she had them? Everyone else was swamped in jewelry."

"So therefore—"

"The ball had to achieve something for either you or me."

"I wish it had been you," Louisa said fervently.

"So do I. I wonder—" A strange look had come into Mary Ellen's eye. "Supposing you refused him, if Mr. Harry Spencer would have me instead."

Chapter 3

Percy Lund, the young and still-nervous clerk, knocked at Mr. Spencer's door.

"There's a lady to see you, sir."

"A lady? Who? Didn't she give a name?"

The improbable but hopeful thought that it might be Louisa had sprung into Harry's mind. So far, at their now regular meetings, she had been friendly in a distant way, but always withdrew behind a barrier of repressive shyness when he attempted a more intimate conversation. He didn't mind this too much. It was in accord with his idea of a lady.

It had already been made clear to him that the van Leydens would raise no objection to his marriage to their daughter, and Louisa herself had appeared to acquiesce. It was probably too much to expect enthusiasm from her as yet, but Harry was conscious of a pleasurable anticipation when Percy announced that his visitor was indeed Miss van Leyden.

He sprang up ready to embrace Louisa, but the lady who swept into the room in a determined manner lifted her veil to reveal herself as Mary Ellen.

Harry collected himself and held out his hand. He hoped his disappointment hadn't been too obvious. It would have been such a delightful surprise had his visitor been Louisa.

"Miss van Leyden! This is an unexpected pleasure."

"Is it?" said Mary Ellen uncompromisingly. "Aren't you annoyed at being interrupted in your important business transactions?"

"I'm sure you wouldn't interrupt me for any trifling reason, Miss van Leyden."

"Oh, call me Mary Ellen, do. You're going to be my brother-in-law, if not—"

Harry looked at her curiously. She seemed to be under some stress, for her color was high, her eyes gleaming.

"If not what, Miss—Mary Ellen?"

"Let's get straight to the point. I'm a great one for frank speaking. May I sit down?"

"Good gracious, yes. I should have offered you a chair."

"Well, then," said Mary Ellen, settling down and smoothing her skirts, "you must know that although my sister is prepared to marry you, to keep our dear father out of a debtor's prison, the prospect is not exactly one that appeals to her."

Harry's friendliness had chilled.

"So you want to talk me out of it?" he said brusquely.

"Oh, no. We still need your fortune. Or a part of it. You see, I am one for frank speaking. But let's admit the truth, Mr. Spencer. Your object is to acquire a wife of the correct social standing, for whatever reason: to run your house, to further your career, to give you the entrée into the right circles. It doesn't much matter who she is as long as she fulfills these requirements. I only wanted to suggest that I would fulfill them better than Louisa."

Harry was so astonished that he just prevented himself from letting out a guffaw of laughter.

"I'm sure you would fulfill them very well. But not better than Louisa, surely."

"Yes. Better. Because I would do them willingly." She stared Harry in the eye. "Louisa, as you know, is unwilling. For my part, I can't see how a man could tolerate an unwilling bride."

Harry's desire for laughter left him. He found Mary Ellen's aggressiveness, quite apart from her vanity and her insensitivity, distasteful. He could not refrain from saying, "But perhaps a bride would equally dislike an unwilling husband."

He had struck home. Mary Ellen's face went rigid with anger.

"Do I correctly understand what you mean?"

"All I mean, ma'am, is that I want to marry your sister. I appreciate your offer—I take it to be an offer?—but matters will stand as they are."

"Why, Harry Spencer, you're exactly what people say. A cold-blooded, ambitious upstart. I pity my poor sister, I pity her as much as she pities herself."

"But I love her. I've told her so. Doesn't she believe me?"

"Love! You don't even begin to know what that word means. You'll both be unhappy. And you needn't have been, you fool!"

Her angry gaze told him that he had made an enemy. He had heard that a woman scorned was no mean adversary, although he could hardly believe that Mary Ellen would be a formidable one. At the moment he was only sorry he had had to shame her. Nevertheless, she had asked for it. She had had a terrible impertinence. He was not marrying the van Leyden family, heaven preserve him. It was enough that there was an alcoholic father and an ailing mother, let alone Boy with his hated limp and now Mary Ellen cherishing a permanent grievance. He had only meant to secure Louisa for himself and plump out her impoverished family's bank account. What was so criminal about that?

"I'm ambitious like you," said Mary Ellen in a hard, grating voice. "I'd have paid for dressing. I'd have given the best parties in New York. I'd have helped you double your fortune, Harry Spencer. But no, you must choose Louisa. And she doesn't even like parties. Do you know that? So what use is she going to be to you?"

"I like a quiet woman," said Harry, giving the only answer he could.

"Now if that isn't spoken like a selfish man! She suits you, so naturally you expect to suit her. You'll break her heart, Harry Spencer, that's what you'll do. And don't come to me for sympathy when it's too late." Mary Ellen accompanied this final remark by leaving the office and banging the door. It was hardly likely, Harry thought, that he would be going to her for sympathy, no matter what the circumstances.

Louisa never knew quite at what stage she stopped resenting Harry Spencer and the dilemma in which he had placed her and began accepting him. Certainly, it was not by a spoken word. She thought the silent agreement occurred when he had been showing her his house, now sparsely furnished, but with many bare walls and empty spaces. She did not, as Mary Ellen would have done, walk about making loud suggestions. She thought the drawing room with its long windows overlooking the park a beautiful room, and she sat down on an ugly Victorian sofa and said dreamily, " I would have green walls, to bring the park into the room, and white and gold furniture, and over the mantelpiece a romantic painting."

"A portrait of you," said Harry.

She found herself giving him her first long, fearless look and thought there was tenderness as well as humor in his eyes. Suddenly she felt less oppressed. This marriage wasn't remotely what she had wanted for herself, but perhaps it would not be too impossible. She believed Harry truly did have feeling for her and no longer looked on her only as the object of another ambition.

Sitting there, Harry began talking.

"I remember my grandfather telling me stories about coming out of the dark insides of a chimney into rooms that were like palaces. He used to be dazzled, he said. Wonderful furniture and ornaments and portraits of beautiful women. He'd fall in love with them, he said."

"The women?"

"Yes. I think he thought of ruffles and lace and those pretty delicate faces when he looked at my grandmother years later. She did laundry all her life and got a crooked back from standing over tubs, and terrible red, chapped hands." Harry began stroking Louisa's fingers. "I remember their roughness when she touched me. My grandfather must have noticed that, too, and dreamed of those women he never saw in the flesh, with their red lips and white hands. He had a hard life. The soot was in his lungs by that time. I was only a little fellow when he died. Then Granny took ill and followed him within six months. Life expectancy isn't very high among the poor in England. I remember the funerals. The neighbors helped to carry the cheap coffins, and the cemetery was dripping and black. That's how I remember it. I thought of poor grandfather being buried forever in the soot he had hated. On the day after my grandmother's funeral my father suddenly said, 'Let's go to America. Let's emigrate and give the boy the chance of a future.' And so we did. I was eight years old. I remember every detail of that journey. I thought the hold of the ship was like grandfather's chimneys, black and evil-smelling. And then there was New York and the way we had to live until my father got his store started. I used to shine shoes and run errands and scrub area steps. My mother worked as a cleaning woman in the big houses on Fifth Avenue. She used to come home and tell me how the rich lived. Now some of them may be our guests in this house. But they'll have forgotten her, if they ever saw her. I mean, actually noticed her. Martha Spencer, the little Cockney sparrow."

"Harry, are you just trying to get revenge for all the things you and your family suffered? I mean, this determination to get rich and marry someone like me."

"Yes," he said. "Yes, I am. And I'm enjoying it no end."

He grinned broadly, with such good humor, that Louisa stopped being shocked and said involuntarily, "You could never have been a child."

"No. I never was. Babies are born old in those conditions. That's why I want so much for my own children. So much, Louisa. You've no idea."

She was chilled again, frightened, too. She could never live up to his expectations. Perhaps their children wouldn't be able to, either. Or supposing she didn't have children. What then? Would Mr. Spencer allow his precise plans for the future to be defeated? She had never met anyone like him, with such a strong and intense will. She was mesmerized, frightened, but in a curious fascinating way, challenged. Life with nurses and governesses, select schools, dancing and riding classes, summers on Long Island, winters in the rambling Eighth Street house, had had a secure orderliness until her teens, when Papa had begun drinking heavily and there were constant worries about money. Then she and Mary Ellen had been labeled "those two poor van Leyden girls with the lame brother" who, because they were van Leydens, necessarily must be asked to balls and parties, but who always looked dowdy, if not positively shabby. Mary Ellen's humiliation had turned into aggressiveness, Louisa's into a paralyzing shyness.

So, in a way, she could understand Harry's desire to provide a better life for his children. She would want her daughters to have a great deal. At least they would never need to experience the sorrow of knowing their mother had had to sell her diamonds to give them a ball.

That debt to Mamma, if nothing else, made it impossible to refuse Harry Spencer. She was committed now. She must put her heart into it, if she could.

They went to visit Martha Spencer, the little Cockney sparrow, in her rooms over the dry goods store in the Bowery. She was a tiny scrap of a woman, with thin fingers and long, thin feet. Her face was as alert as a bird's. She lived with a large black servant, Beulah, and deplored the fact that Harry had moved to that grand house on Fifth Avenue among all the toffs.

Her eyes missed no detail of Louisa's appearance. She was embarrassingly outspoken. "Are you delicate, my dear?"

"No. I'm quite strong."

"Don't look it. That bit of a waist. Harry wants children."

"Now, Ma—" Harry began.

"You know you do, so don't deny it. But I grant you some of these delicate-looking ladies are stronger than the plump ones. Well, it's something only the Lord knows, ain't it? All I ask is that Miss here don't come the fine lady over me."

"Ma, that's the last thing Louisa would do."

"Harry, I can speak for myself," Louisa said. "If your mother means, am I going to patronize her, that's something I have never done in my life. I wouldn't know how to."

"Well, thank the Lord for that," said Martha Spencer. "In return I won't embarrass you."

"What do you mean, Ma?"

"I won't expect to sit at your dinner table or come to your wedding. I'll expect a visit from you now and again, especially after the first baby arrives, but apart from that, I know my place."

"But, Mrs. Spencer, you must come and visit us," Louisa said. "You're Harry's mother."

The bright bird eyes softened fractionally.

"Why, I do believe she means it, Harry."

"Of course she means it."

"All the same, I won't do it. I'm content here with Beulah and a few of our old customers in the store. I don't want no Fifth Avenue house or jools. If Harry wants fine things and works for them, then he deserves them. But I'm staying right here where I'm cozy. Eh, lass? You don't take that amiss, do you?"

"I'd really enjoy coming to visit, Mrs. Spencer."

"That's right. That's what I mean. Beulah! Where's that lazy woman? Beulah, make us a cup of tea. Would you believe it, dearie. I've taught that black woman to make the best English tea in the world. Fit to be served at Buckingham Palace."

Afterward, driving home in Harry's phaeton with its sparkling red wheels, the keen wind in their faces, Harry took a hand off the reins and drew one of Louisa's hands out of her muff.

"If for nothing else, I'd love you for that, my dear."

"For what?"

"Ma spots a hypocrite quicker than anyone I know. She knew you were sincere."

"I liked her. She's real."

"Do you meet a lot of people who aren't?"

"I suppose I do, when I come to think of it."

"So do I. But they serve their purpose." He flicked the horse's rump with a whip. "Let's have a bit of speed, shall we? I feel like the devil of a fellow today."

The horse, a fast, high-stepping gray, plunged into a gallop. Houses and trees whirled by. The wheels hissed in the snow slush. Louisa took both hands out of her muff and held onto her bonnet. She was terrified and elated at the same time.

"I'm real, too," Harry shouted over the noise of galloping hooves and passing traffic. "I'm not just a dollar sign and a bottomless pocket. You'll find out. Wait till you live with me."

It was no use pleading with Mary Ellen. She flatly refused to be Louisa's bridesmaid. She simply said, "I've had enough of that sort of caper. I've followed Emily Hughes and Cassandra Meyerburg and Kate Morrison and Eveline Clancy down the aisle, and that's enough. I won't be a figure of fun."

"But this is your own sister," Millicent van Leyden protested. "How could you be a figure of fun?"

"Besides," Mary Ellen went on, as if her mother had not spoken, "I won't wear a dress paid for by that man."

"I thought you liked Mr. Spencer."

"I've changed my mind. I think he's a vulgar upstart out for all he can get, and I'm only sorry for Louisa."

Millicent sighed. "I know, dear, we all agree he's a little vulgar. He can't help that, and I must say he is learning very quickly. Papa says he's quite popular already at the Union Club, and that's no small achievement. As for being out for all he can get, he's only getting Louisa, when I'm sure he could have got a society beauty if he had looked longer. Not that I'm speaking against my own daughter; but she isn't a spectacular girl, and she really hasn't got the witty conversation a successful hostess needs. I wonder if she will ever acquire it."

"Mr. Spencer doesn't want a witty conversationalist; he wants someone he can hold under his thumb."

"My dear child, you really look quite ugly when you wear that expression. If that's how you're going to look at the wedding, then perhaps it's as well you aren't going to be a bridesmaid. Louisa will do quite nicely with the von Heffers and Madeline Earl. But do try to look cheerful on the day, whatever your feelings are. It will be enough for me seeing that your father doesn't have one of his attacks." Attacks was Millicent's polite expression for her husband's drunkenness. "I admit that none of us likes the position we are in. But if Louisa can be brave about it, surely you can. A marriage of convenience doesn't need to turn out badly," she added sententiously.

"Louisa is as meek as a mouse, that's all," Mary Ellen said. "I can tell you, Mamma, that I for one won't be visiting the Spencer household."

"Of course you will," Millicent said sharply. "Now, Mary Ellen, don't you dare provide more reason for gossip than there is already. You just behave and smile at the wedding. If you're going to glower like that, whatever hope have you got of getting a husband? You and Boy will make a fine pair."

"Moldering away with the house," said Mary Ellen. "Frightening the children. Yes, I expect we will."

"Why do you persist in calling Harry Mr. Spencer?" Louisa asked Mary Ellen. "He's going to be your brother-in-law."

"I just don't feel I can be on Christian name terms with him, that's all."

"It's very unfriendly."

"Well, listen to who's talking. Not so long ago you were paralyzed at the thought of marrying him."

Louisa was still training her mind to think only of the fuss and flurry of the wedding, of the pleasant drives she had with Harry, of their fragile but growing friendship. Of planning the furnishings for his house—her house—which was a task entirely to her liking and which she anticipated spinning out for a long time, of entertaining Mamma and Papa and Boy and Mary Ellen at Sunday dinners, of engaging servants, just three or four as she didn't intend to be an idle mistress. She had never allowed her thoughts to go into the bedroom, to that first night when Harry would expect a willing wife.

She simply couldn't imagine his strong, stocky body

45

disrobed or her own shrinking one exposed to his gaze. She only had the vaguest idea of what happened anyway. Instinct told her that this compulsory affair of the bed would be much easier with a man she loved. Although, since she had never been in love, she wasn't even sure of that. She wondered how much Mary Ellen knew about the physical side of marriage but disdained to ask her, especially while Mary Ellen was in that queer, hostile, jealous mood. She could not bear to get a scoffing answer. It was bad enough pretending that beneath the flowers and the champagne and the congratulations, this darker side of marriage did not exist.

She could never ask Mamma, who had always averted her face and whispered if this subject came into the conversation. Mamma was a deep-dyed puritan. It had occurred to Louisa that Harry's mother would be bawdily outspoken if one could have got up the courage to talk to her. But one wouldn't, of course. It would be too humiliating.

God, said Mamma, wearing her pious expression, arranged these affairs. But there was nothing in the marriage vows to say that the bridegroom should be allowed to remove the bride's nightgown. Louisa could be quite assured that she could retain her modesty.

And now Mary Ellen was taunting her because she was bravely making the best of a situation she had never expected to have to face.

"Mary Ellen, you and Harry haven't quarreled, have you?"

"Whatever makes you say that? I never see him unless he's swooning over you. I must say it doesn't suit a man like him, being sentimental. Although he does it so well, he could be on the stage."

"Are you suggesting he's acting when he says he cares for me?"

"Honestly, Louisa, can you be such an innocent? This is just a contract to Harry Spencer. He's getting what he considers a desirable property; we're getting a badly needed bank account."

The way he had drawn her hand out of her muff. She had even felt a stirring of tenderness herself. None of that had been acting, she could swear.

But she wasn't going to argue with Mary Ellen in this dour mood. Only time was going to prove which of them was right.

Ever since she had been seventeen, she had wanted so much to fall in love. Now she was terrified of going to any parties in case she met the one irresistible man and could no longer face her imminent marriage. Since it had to be, let the day come as quickly as possible, and pray heaven that if Harry were acting the devoted lover, she could do the same.

Chapter 4

Louisa couldn't pretend to be anything but the most inaudible and nervous of brides as she stood at the altar whispering her vows. Even the elegance of Madame Lucille's wedding gown couldn't give her confidence. Madame Lucille was the current fashionable designer of outfits for important brides, and Harry had insisted on her being patronized. In years to come, he planned to have his wife dressed in Paris.

Now the high-necked, tight-waisted brocade gown was stiff and uncomfortable, and the enormously long lace veil dragged at Louisa's shoulders. She had an irrelevant thought that no daughter of hers would be forced to wear a recut version of this gown for her coming of age ball, unless the incredible happened and Harry, like Papa, got into financial difficulties. Then, as she repeated dutifully "I, Louisa Boydell, take Henry Edward George Arthur" (Harry liked to maintain, with ironic pomp, that he had been named after English kings because that fictitious importance was all his parents had to give him), her wayward thoughts were on Mary Ellen, kept in bed by a mysterious fever and professing herself too ill even to wish Louisa happiness on her wedding day. She wanted to be left in a darkened room brooding jealously over the fact that her younger sister had been preferred before her. Not even a drop of champagne could she force down her aching throat. Boy was to promise to hurry home and cheer her up.

Louisa recognized mutiny when she saw it. She also recognized that Mary Ellen's strong will, always a problem, was becoming formidable. She would have to be allowed this fictional illness, but it cast another shadow over the already far from perfect day. Boy had been detailed to see that Papa didn't touch any bourbon before midday, which was difficult enough, since Papa was developing all the craftiness of the addicted drinker. Mamma had the taut lines down her forehead that heralded a headache and carried eau de cologne and other restorers in her handbag. In addition to these worries, Harry's mother, that decidedly queer woman living in the Bowery and as yet unseen by any of the van Leyden family except Louisa, had announced that she would not be attending the wedding. Her rheumatics, her message said blandly, were too bad. So that left Harry with no family and precious few friends. The rumor had got about, unkindly, that his mother was mad and locked up with a keeper. He had heard the rumor himself and given his great roar of laughter that was half amusement, half defiance. However, as Ephraim de Wynt had consented to be his best man, and a few other of his business associates had come along, things didn't look too bad. The church was filled with Fifth Avenue society. The expensive show, Louisa realized, was for them alone.

Or was it for Harry himself? He must have considered all this money well spent, for he wore a look of the utmost satisfaction. He obviously thought Louisa's over-elaborate wedding gown the very height of perfection. He whispered to her as, irrevocably married, they walked down the aisle that she looked like a princess. Was he thinking of himself in the role of one of his royal names? The way he held his head and swept his brilliant blue gaze over the fashionable audience suggested that he was.

Was it safe to realize a dream? Louisa wondered in some apprehension.

She much preferred the friendly man who had taken her on rides in his phaeton to this correctly dressed bridegroom with the inevitable white gardenia in his buttonhole. This man was a self-creation, playing a longed-for role. In a way, he was a fantasy. She was going to have to find the real man before the honeymoon was over. Or did she want to? Wouldn't their marriage be easier and more workable if she didn't probe into Harry's deeper feelings or allow him to probe into hers? Wasn't life mostly a covering up of awkward emotions? How many of the smiles of this smartly dressed throng were genuine? All the same, she did want to live honestly. She prayed she would develop a true affection for her husband.

Her husband! Dear God! She had actually allowed this to happen. If nothing else was true, the legality of her marriage was.

The reception, naturally, was at Delmonico's, and again it was all that lavish expense could make it. Louisa listened to the honeyed congratulations of the guests. Standing at Harry's side, she privately thanked Madame Lucille for the stiffly boned gown that held her upright. As Harry's transparent satisfaction grew—he surely had never set eyes on, let alone shaken hands with, such a selection of New York's privileged inner circle—she suddenly felt contemptuous of him. What sort of values were these? It had nothing to do with loving, with having children, with learning to live happily together and making a good honest life. This scene that was giving Harry such a sense of achievement was built almost entirely on the power of money. Surely that was as wrong and as treacherous as the sucking mud of a Florida swamp.

The smile on Louisa's lips grew set, her eyes glazed, as a wave of apprehension and doubt swept over her. She saw her life ahead as one of being a dressed-up doll, with Harry her master.

And all so that Mamma could indulge in her real or imaginary illnesses in comfort, so that Papa and perhaps even Boy could drink themselves to death. As for Mary Ellen, although she would no doubt consent to go on living in the family home, now blessedly free of mortgages (Harry had honored that promise already), she was never going to be the same friendly and loving sister again. Louisa sensed that in her bones. Mary Ellen was not the forgiving sort. She was going to feel forever slighted and overlooked. One suspected she was suffering also from some deeper mysterious grievance.

So was this sacrifice she had made going to be the best thing in the world for anybody?

Already Papa, released from his morning's abstention had had several bourbons. One must pray Boy would look after him. But Boy was displaying the charm that he bothered to exert only when he himself had had enough to drink. And Mamma was being the great lady, her perfect manners nevertheless suggesting hauteur and disdain, a Boydell from Virginia to whom New York society was the least bit vulgar, and her new son-in-law just tolerable.

What this lavish scene needed, Louisa thought with sudden insight, was the presence of Mrs. Martha Spencer from the Bowery, spindly, shabby, witchlike, real. Reality! That was what was needed.

In that moment she made the determination not to attempt to change Harry in any way. In spite of his over-large ambitions, he still had his own blunt, downright personality. He could learn to be suave, sophisticated, insincere, she had no doubt. But she wouldn't allow it. If ever she were to fall in love with him, he must remain himself.

Her fingers tightened on his arm in an act of possession that surprised her. It surprised him, too, for he looked at her quickly, and smiled.

"All right, my dear?"

"Fine."

"Everybody's here, aren't they? Look, there's Herbert Condon. He doesn't know it yet, but I'm going to buy his house. It's on the corner of Twenty-first and Madison. It's an area that's ripe for redevelopment. He's got so much money he'll be easy to persuade that it's more fashionable to live above the Forties. We must have him to a dinner party soon."

"Harry!"

"What?"

How insensitive he could be. He didn't even see that she was chilled by his discussion of business at his wedding.

"I don't know why you find these people so fascinating."

He grinned.

"Fascinating is the word. You don't have to love them. By the way, I don't see Mary Ellen here."

"I forgot to tell you; she's sick and feverish. She had to stay in bed this morning. Isn't it a shame?"

He gave her a sideways look that she couldn't interpret. Almost as if Mary Ellen's fever had been no secret and no surprise to him. But all he said was: "I thought it was your mother who was subject to sick headaches."

"I guess Mary Ellen might have inherited them."

"She'll probably make a miraculous recovery after the

wedding," Harry said cryptically. He was looking restless, his sharp eyes darting here and there. "When can we leave this crush?"

"Aren't you enjoying it? It's what you wanted."

"I have a promise to keep. Can you cover up all that finery in a fur cloak?"

Louisa looked puzzled. "If I had one, I guess I could."

"You have one. Billy is taking care of it in the carriage. I told my mother she would get a look at the bride."

"But I must change into my going-away clothes."

"Ma would like to see you, veil and all."

"Then she should have come to the church."

"In this mob? Can you see her? She'd be like a fly caught in a jar of honey. Now wouldn't she?"

"Louisa dear," came Mamma's drawling society voice, "you and Harry have the rest of your lives to have private conversations. Come and talk to your guests."

"We're just about to leave, Mamma."

"Already?"

"We have a train to catch later," said Harry.

"But Louisa is going to come back and say good-bye?"

"She'll do that, ma'am," said Harry. He was giving his amiable smile that held irony, not only for people like Mamma and her kind, but for himself, for wanting to be one of them and to adhere scrupulously to their customs.

"I promise to bring my wife back," he said, and now there was no irony in his voice, only a simple pride that Louisa, with an uneasy instinct for the problems of the future, told herself she must always remember.

There was a fire glowing in the fireplace in the little sitting room over the store in the Bowery. Mrs. Martha Spencer was a thin, angular cat sitting in the shadows.

She sprang up, clapping her hands, when Louisa and Harry came in. "Beulah!" she screeched. "Bring the lamps. Here's the bride."

"Since you wouldn't come to her, Ma," said Harry, "I've brought her to you."

The room was filled with the scent of hothouse lilies and orange blossom of Louisa's bouquet. On an impulse she held it toward Martha.

"Would you have this, Mrs. Spencer?"

"Don't you have to throw it to your bridesmaids? Isn't that what they do at grand weddings? Or are you aiming that I should catch it and get me another husband?"

"I think Louisa wants you to have it, Ma," said Harry. He sounded pleased.

Martha sniffed the flowers gingerly, as if they might have some deadly aroma.

"It's bad enough you wearing that sissy gardenia all the time, without having my rooms stank out." She was prickly, suspecting patronage.

"Put them in water, Mrs. Spencer," said Louisa. "The poor things are dying from my hot hands." She found, to her surprise, that she was feeling more at home in this small, dark, cluttered room than in the familiar opulence of Delmonico's. (How many weddings had she attended there, seeing the same faces, the same expensive clothes, the same smiles, the same sharp, assessing eyes?) She sat down and asked if she could take off her veil; it was nearly pulling her head from her shoulders. It had got a little muddied from Harry holding it as she had got out of the carriage. He was not an experienced bridesmaid.

Martha said dryly, "You'll expect something more of him than that, eh?" and added in pure admiration, "All of them yards of material! What they expect a small body to support. You look like the Queen of England going to be crowned. Just imagine my Harry! But then I named my sons for kings. It was all I had to give them, good proud names. I wanted six children, but the first three died. Edward, George and Arthur. So Harry got their names and their minds too, I think, all rolled into one. He's always had enough fight for four. Beulah!" she shouted again. "Hurry with the lamps."

"And the cake and the champagne," added Harry.

"Beulah's got champagne hidden in the kitchen!" Martha exclaimed.

"And on ice, I hope. We'll have a drink with you, Ma, but then we've got to hurry. Lou has to change and get back to say good-bye to her guests. It's the way things are done."

"I'm not ignorant. I know the way things are done." She suddenly gave Louisa a salacious wink. "And what will you name your first baby?"

"Give us time," Harry protested.

"No harm in thinking it out."

Beulah had come padding in carrying the lighted lamp. When she had put it on the table, she stood staring at Louisa in wonder.

"Thought an angel had come right down from heaven," she said in her deep Southern voice, and Louisa felt drawn into Martha Spencer's fantasy, seeing a dark-brown large-breasted woman like this fondling and caring for her baby. Mamma had never been allowed to have black servants in New York, because Papa was a Yankee and still associated them with slavery.

"Our baby will have a fine name," said Harry, putting his arm across Louisa's shoulders. "Lou, I think you're to cut the cake while I open the champagne."

"A party," said Martha gleefully. "I can tell you, dearie, you'll never know with Harry what's happening next. You mightn't always like what it is, but at least you won't be dull. And he'll be fair to you if you're fair to him."

The call at home was very different. Old Pearl, who was well used to being a lady's maid as well as a housemaid, helped Louisa out of her wedding finery.

"Hurry, Pearl. We're terribly late."

"Must say you are, Miss Louisa."

"We stopped to make another call. Be careful of my veil; it got a little muddied."

"Youse a married lady now, Miss Louisa."

"Yes. That's true. How is Mary Ellen?"

"Miss Mary Ellen? Well, she got up and ate half a cold chicken and a slice of blueberry pie. Seems like her sickness makes her starving. But she isn't going to die, that's for certain."

However, she seemed to have suffered a relapse, for when Louisa went to her room to say good-bye, the door was locked. A faint, weary voice from within told Louisa to go away. She was prostrated. She couldn't see anybody. Another day. . . .

"What do you mean by another day?" Louisa demanded. "I'm your sister. You can see me now."

"I'm much too ill. Just leave me alone."

"Perhaps you began eating too soon," Louisa couldn't help saying with a touch of malice.

"No, I did not." The voice from within was stronger and suddenly sharp with curiosity. "Lou, are you wearing your sables?"

Louisa felt the soft warm furs hugging her neck.

"Of course. It's very cold out."

"You're shameless! Taking all those things from that man."

The contempt in Mary Ellen's voice stung Louisa so severely that the discipline she had imposed on herself for the last weeks, particularly for today, was banished by the hot resentment that rose in her.

"Now that's not fair, Mary Ellen. That man, as you call him, is my husband. And you know perfectly well why he is. I've done this for you and Boy and our parents, and if this is all the thanks I get, I'd have been better off remaining a spinster. Like you!" she couldn't resist adding. The strain of the long day was making her spiteful, a characteristic she hadn't known she possessed. But neither had she known she could have gone so calmly through a marriage service with a man she didn't love.

Yet she knew she didn't want to change places with Mary Ellen, sulking in her room, ravaged with curiosity and jealousy.

55

"I have principles," Mary Ellen shouted harshly. "I would never marry just for money."

Louisa leaned her hot cheek against the door.

"It isn't my fault that it's this way, that I don't love him."

She heard Pearl's slow step on the worn stair carpet, and said, "I'm just coming," and turned and saw not Pearl but Harry, a square, silent figure, at the top of the stairs.

Her heart raced. How much had he heard? She didn't want to hurt him. But it was only the truth she had spoken, and that he knew already.

She lifted her chin with calm dignity.

"I'm sorry, Harry, am I keeping you waiting?"

"Not me, but that mob at Delmonico's. If we're to play the society game, we'd better play it properly."

The discipline was back.

"Of course. I'm thoughtless. You must blame me."

He took her hand to lead her down the stairs.

"I'll do that whenever you deserve it."

She couldn't read his expression. She wondered if she ever would be able to. She only knew that he, too, when he wished to, had excellent self-discipline.

Chapter 5

The carriage drew up once again. Louisa looked out, seeing a dark expanse of empty ground.

"But this isn't Grand Central Station. I thought we were catching a train."

"Sorry I deceived you. I was only putting people off. Don't want anyone nosing around here for a few days."

"We're home!" Louisa exclaimed.

He pressed her gloved hand.

"Where else should we spend our honeymoon?" His soft beard brushed her cheek. "That was nice to hear, you saying 'home.' "

"Well, it is, I suppose, although I can hardly realize it."

"For better or worse, it is. Come, they'll be waiting for us."

"They?"

"I've hired a housekeeper and a cook and a couple of maids and a butler. If they haven't lit the fire, I'll get rid of the lot of them. I say, are you upset?"

"I only thought finding servants would be my task. When we got back from our honeymoon."

"Saved you the trouble. But I didn't go so far as to get you a lady's maid. Thought you'd want to choose her yourself."

Louisa turned on him. "Harry, I must be of some *use*. I don't want a housekeeper. I'm capable of running my own house."

"Very well, we'll get rid of her. But don't let's argue on the sidewalk. It's damned cold. Are you disappointed that we're not on our way somewhere in the country?"

Louisa looked up at the outlines of the house, standing starkly alone in its lot, a block or more from any other habitation. The moon was shining with a clean cold light, blanching the windows. The front steps were glistening with frost. It was terribly cold, and she was shivering. She had imagined she would be in a warm train, the time to be alone with Harry in the bedroom still some hours away.

"You could have told me. I could have kept a secret."

"I wanted to surprise you."

"Then I am surprised. And freezing to death. Why don't you ring the bell and see if our new butler knows how to answer the door?"

"I ought to carry you over the threshold. Only this isn't a romantic wedding, is it?"

So he had overheard what she had said to Mary Ellen.

"No, Harry," she said honestly. "It isn't. On the other hand, we can pretend for the sake of the servants. I'm not very heavy, I think."

So after all she was lifted over the threshold, in a strong, swooping movement and set down in the well-lighted, warm hall. The butler, who had a jolly red face, bowed, and the four women, white-aproned, dark-dressed, bobbed to her.

Louisa mustered her dignity. She must play her part properly. She had occasionally stayed with school friends whose families boasted a butler and even footmen. It was something not unknown in the van Leyden past. Only recently had the daughters of the house polished the furniture and done a good part of the cooking. But these people standing in front of her didn't know this. At least, she hoped they didn't, because she had to be a capable mistress whom they respected.

She said in her soft voice that it was good of them to prepare the house for herself and her husband. It was delightfully warm, and wherever had all the flowers come from? She would enjoy it all tomorrow, but now she was very tired and would like to go straight upstairs.

Harry took her arm in such a proprietary fashion that for a moment she thought he was also going to carry her up the grand marble staircase.

"We'll ring if we want anything," he said over his shoulder. "Maybe a little light supper later, eh, my dear?"

"Honestly," Louisa murmured, as they climbed the stairs, "wasn't that a bit feudal?"

He grinned, well pleased. "That's only a beginning. Wait until you know what I have planned for our daughter."

Their daughter! How far did he think he could control his destiny?

"Only joking," he said, seeing her expression.

But she had a deep suspicion he was not, that Harry Spencer, born in deep poverty and deprivation, was going to acquire what he considered due him and force it on what might well be an unwilling family.

How could she have imagined his enjoyment in the exercise of power would stop with his rescue of an honored old family and his marriage to her?

The bed in the enormous bedroom had slender Chippendale posts. It was very wide; the pillows were plumped up, the bedclothes turned down. A fire glowed pleasantly in the enormous stone fireplace. Chairs were drawn up to it; a brilliant turkey rug lay across the hearth. Otherwise, the big room was sparsely furnished. It was waiting for the touches its mistress would add.

Harry ran his hand over a wall, guessing her thoughts.

"I know you're used to a house full of family mementos, generations of them. I'm not. But I think that's a challenge. Because it will be like writing on a clean slate. The beginning of the Spencer dynasty."

"Harry, don't be so pompous."

He frowned. "Is that being pompous? I just like to think of this room in thirty years' time, full of our things, our taste."

But she didn't know his taste. And she didn't want to talk about it now.

Mary Ellen's voice was in her head.

You're shameless, taking from that man. . . .

But not shameless, if you made due and just payment. . . .

"Anyway, that's why I wanted to start our marriage in this room. Because I consider this the real start of my life."

"But you started your life when you began to make your fortune. That was you more than this. Wasn't it?"

"Part of me," he acknowledged.

All of you, Louisa almost said. Talking of the grandeur awaiting your daughter when she isn't yet conceived. . . . You lay the bricks one by one on your vacant lots, don't you, Harry? I'm the first, the foundation stone on this particular lot.

Supposing you've built on a swamp. . . .

"Take off your furs, love. It's warm in here."

Love. . . . That was more natural than his attempt at sophisticated endearments. It made her think of his mother, tiny, angular, undefeatable as only those who had known true adversity were. In Harry she had four sons. Did that mean he was now four husbands. It could well be so.

"You suddenly sounded English."

"It comes out now and then. But I'm as good a Yankee as your father."

"Don't be! Don't copy."

"Why?" His frown was formidable. "Don't you want to be proud of me? Don't you think I can be as good as any Knickerbocker or whatever daft name you call them?"

"If we're to be married properly, I must know the real person you are. Which of those four sons of your mother's. Because I do want to be married properly. It would be terrible if this just remained a business arrangement."

"It isn't a business arrangement," he said shortly. "Let me take off your furs. And what about your coat and skirt? I've another surprise. Want to see it?"

"Yes," she answered nervously.

He leaped to a drawer of the massive tallboy and pulled out a handful of gleaming material.

"Think me an odd fellow if you like, but I wanted to choose what my bride wore on her wedding night." He tossed the garments to Louisa. "Put those on for me. The bathroom's in there. I'd like to undress you by the fire, but—you do what you prefer, Lou."

Masterful. Making her ignore the exquisitely hand-worked lawn nightgowns traditional for van Leyden or Boydell brides and wear this heavy satin.

Or was the word "bossy"?

"I'll go in the bathroom," she said helplessly.

It wasn't beyond her to change his taste. Wasn't that what a clever wife could do? For the expensive nightgown and the overtrimmed negligee made her feel foolish, and someone else altogether. Mary Ellen, she thought, would have looked magnificent in the smooth, gleaming satin.

She took a quick bath in the marble tub, and scented herself, and brushed out her long dark hair. But still she was unable to relax. She felt as if the frost outdoors had got into her bones.

In her absence Harry must have rung for one of the servants, for there was champagne in a bucket on the table, and long-stemmed glasses, and a dish of caviar and some thin brown bread and butter.

Harry himself was wearing a dark-red velvet dressing gown. His lips, fringed by the golden beard, curled in a small smile. He told Louisa to stand where she was, in the middle of the room, so that he could look at her. She felt like a dressed-up doll, stiff-limbed and unsmiling. And her tired eyes were playing tricks on her, for Harry seemed twice his size, a broad and powerful figure sitting there assessing his acquisition.

Suddenly he seemed to start awake and apologized for keeping her standing.

"I'm staring. I've never seen you with your hair down. Come by the fire and have some champagne. Or would you rather have it in bed?"

"By the fire, please."

Postpone the bed for a little longer. She intended to drink two or even three glasses of champagne. She had never known what Papa and Boy found so efficacious about intoxicating drinks. It was obviously something that enabled them to face life. She hoped this explanation was true, for she was very much in need of something of that kind herself.

"What are the servants' names?" she asked, to make conversation.

"The butler is Dobson. I stole him from the Bernard Crowthers. Do you know them?"

"From Park Avenue? I went to dancing class with Libby Crowther. But we didn't know them well. How did you steal their butler?"

"Offered him more money. Is there any other way?"

Louisa repressed a sigh. "And the women?"

"The housemaids are Bridget and Molly. They like to send money to their families in Ireland, so they'll work hard. The housekeeper is Mrs. Perkins—"

"Never mind about her. I don't want a housekeeper."

"The cook is Mrs. Strong. Don't say you mean to do the cooking."

"No, but I could, if necessary. Since we've been poor, Mary Ellen and I have done most of it. Of course, in our childhood, we had servants." The champagne was making her drowsy and reminiscent. "And when we visited grandmamma and Aunt Abigail in Virginia, the place was overrun with servants. Negroes, of course. Some of them asked to stay after slavery was abolished. I can't remember much about the Civil War, but I do remember Mamma crying a good deal, and once I heard her calling Papa 'a damn Yankee.' It gave me a funny feeling to see Beulah with your mother. I was thinking—if we have a child—I would like someone like Beulah. Grandmamma had a very fat nurse called Endeavor who used to look after Boy and Mary Ellen and me when we visited. Boy and Mary Ellen led her a dance, but I remember sitting on her lap and being comforted."

Harry refilled her glass, and as she sipped, the room spun gently and she felt warm and peaceful and deliciously languid.

"I promise you a Negro nurse for our first child."

"Thank you, Harry."

He was sitting beside her, his voice growling in her ear.

"You do know there's only one way to get a child, don't you?"

"Yes."

"Then come to bed."

She closed her eyes and saw, not the desired baby in her arms, but the words of the marriage contract. . . .

"To redeem the mortgage on the house on Eighth Street owned by Robert van Leyden and to provide adequately for the said Robert van Leyden and his wife Millicent for the remainder of their lives, also to see that their heirs are never in want. . . ."

What sort of want? Louisa wondered. For Mary Ellen, could it be the very thing she could never have, this man in bed beside her, divesting her of the carefully chosen negligee and nightgown. (Mamma had erroneously told her that a bride's nightgown need not be removed.)

Louisa turned her dizzy head on the pillow and gave a faint giggle.

"What's the matter, love?"

"Wondering why you spent so much on that awful nightgown just to take it off."

The voice in her ear was both belligerent and humble.

"Is it awful?"

"Just not my taste."

"I'm sorry. I see that now. I only wanted to please you."

She rubbed her cheek against his bare shoulder, intending the gesture to be comforting. Instead, it started the thing she knew so little about.

"Lou—I'll try—be gentle—not hurt."

But as he spoke, he was spreading her legs apart, lowering his heavy body on hers, crushing her breasts with his broad chest, breathing against her cheek in hot rasps. Her senses were numbed by the champagne. She couldn't resist. Anyway, she had no right to. This was the first of the ways in which she had to repay her family's debt. And even in the moment of sudden sharp pain from which she did not recoil, she had the instinct that for so strong and passionate a man Harry was controlling his impatience and being as gentle as he knew how to be.

Youse a married lady now, Miss Louisa. . . .

She opened her eyes and saw him studying her face in the lamplight.

"Are you all right, Lou?"

"Yes. Yes, fine." She was sore and bruised and smarting.

"It will get better, you know. Easier."

"Will it?"

"Yes, for sure." He muttered something about "innocent" and suddenly wrapped his arms around her and rocked her against him so that she felt like the child Endeavor had once comforted.

A random thought came to her. She must tell Mary Ellen about the efficacy of champagne if ever this should happen to her. It was better to be drunk than crying. The important thing of course was to marry a man who could afford to buy champagne. Her lips trembled with incipient laughter; then, abruptly, from exhaustion and intoxication, she was asleep.

Chapter 6

Louisa and Harry had been married for two months before Mary Ellen consented to come to the regular Sunday family dinners that Louisa had instituted.

By that time gossip and speculation had become embarrassing, as Ephraim de Wynt pointed out. Where Mary Ellen refused to listen to her mother or Louisa, or even

Boy, for whose cynical opinion she had a certain respect, she had perforce to sit and pay polite attention to Ephraim's exhortations.

Since his coup, as it could be called, in marrying Louisa to Harry Spencer, he seemed to have appointed himself more than ever the intimate friend and adviser to the van Leyden family.

Now for Mary Ellen's good he had regrettably to relay the gossip that was going about. It was said that her brother-in-law had not been overpersuasive in his attempts to get her to join the family circle. There were rumors of a quarrel and of some sort of vow Mary Ellen had made never to speak to him. It was remembered significantly that she had had to keep to her bed on the day of the wedding.

However, what was generally thought was that Mary Ellen van Leyden considered herself too grand to approve of the newlyweds, not realizing that it was she who was being left out in the cold, since fashionable New York seemed eager enough to flock to the doors of Camberwell House.

Ephraim pointed out all this to a glowering Mary Ellen. He looked immaculate and primly spinsterish, his small, well-kept hands clasped over his knees, his smoothly pink face earnest and concerned. He dearly enjoyed arranging other people's affairs. The sharp wit was kept well in control on occasions like this, and only the genuine kindness showed.

"Really, my dear Mary Ellen, your motives are inexplicable. If you refuse to see your sister—"

"I don't refuse to see her if she comes here. If she comes alone, of course."

"Exactly."

"I simply don't like Mr. Spencer. Is there any law that says I have to like him?"

"People," said Ephraim blandly, "are saying you're jealous."

The color flashed in Mary Ellen's cheeks.

"Jealous!" she exploded. "Of that vulgar upstart!"

"A lot of people like Harry. Particularly women, I believe. He's handsome in his way. Virile. And now that Louisa is taking care of the rough edges he's becoming quite a fellow. One of my successes, if I may humbly say so."

"Oh, we all know what you did that night at the opera."

"I introduced Mr. Harry Spencer to the Misses van Leyden, and he chose the younger one. Really, Mary Ellen, you're behaving like a spoiled child, and everyone is laughing at you."

"Laughing!"

"Exactly. They see through your histrionics. You're jealous of your sister. You long to see what she has done to that house, and she has done superb things already, though she isn't hurrying. A few pictures and tapestries, a little French furniture that is delightfully graceful in her drawing room. Harry admires it enormously. And she's been clever. She's made the dining room completely English, for Harry. Chippendale chairs and table and sideboard, Bristol glassware, English silver, a superb Hester Bateman epergne. Do you know about English silver, Mary Ellen?"

"No!"

"Would you have bothered to learn, just supposing you had married an Englishman?"

"Oh, Louisa's a paragon, of course. She's always tried too hard to please."

"A rather admirable characteristic in a woman. Or would you call it a failing?"

"You stop that, Ephraim de Wynt. You're deliberately setting out to annoy me. Isn't it enough that Papa comes rolling home from Sunday dinners saying his son-in-law keeps the best bourbon in New York? And Boy is talking of going into real estate, as if he knew a good building lot from a piece of swamp or wasn't too lazy to work. You've sold us all to that man, do you realize that?"

"Is that a new dress you're wearing?" Ephraim asked suavely. "And did I notice Pearl didn't answer the door today? Another servant did. Since when have the van Leydens been able to keep two servants?"

"Bother you, Ephraim, you're mischievous and conniving, and Mamma has asked you to talk to me, I know."

"Only to prevent you from being a laughingstock, my dear. Go to dinner at Camberwell House next Sunday. Otherwise people will really believe you can't forgive your sister for getting the prize you would have liked."

If only to squash such foul rumors, Mary Ellen grudgingly took Ephraim's advice.

"Ostentatious" was the word she kept using as she followed Louisa into the drawing room.

But she had to admit that it was a beautiful room with its muted blues and greens and yellows, and she was wildly jealous. She knew she would not have had Louisa's taste. She would not have had all New York exclaiming over the surprising lack of vulgarity in the Spencer house.

"I think," said Louisa gaily, "they expected us to fill the place with great heavy furniture and statues and things. I've never cared for that sort of decoration. The reason why the space over the mantelpiece is still empty is that Harry is having my portrait painted. He chose the artist himself. Someone quite unknown. That's what's nice about Harry; he remembers his own poverty and likes to help others." She dropped her brittle hostess voice and asked, "Why have you stayed away so long, Mary Ellen?"

"I didn't care to come sooner. The whole situation is too humiliating."

"I'm sorry you feel like that, especially considering that you would have been prepared to marry Harry yourself. Did you think you were fitter for the sacrifice than me?" There was a sharp gleam of humor in Louisa's eyes. She seemed to have acquired a great deal of poise since her marriage. She had begun entertaining and seemed to have a new dress on every day. She said she had found a clever young dressmaker who called herself plain Miss Jones, and now everyone was beginning to flock to her. It really was galling that shy, self-effacing Louisa was able so quickly to set fashions. It was all that expensive jewelry that Harry had heaped on her. He particularly liked her to wear sapphires to match her eyes. New York society really was slavishly in thrall to money.

"Whatever are you thinking, Mary Ellen?" Louisa was asking. "You look so ferocious. I do beg you not to be rude to Harry at dinner. He really cares about your future, you know."

"*My* future! Is he taking on the lives of the whole family? How dare he!"

"He only thinks a woman should be married. We're giving a dinner party next week and we want you to come. I've asked Gilbert Withers for you. I do hope you won't be too overbearing with him. It is your failing, you know."

She was overbearing because she couldn't help it; it was a habit too deeply formed. And above all, she didn't intend to take advice from her baby sister. But Gilbert Withers didn't seem to mind. He asked if he could call the following day. He sent Mary Ellen flowers, not all those thousands of roses Harry Spencer had sent Louisa, but a dozen American beauties, with a note saying she was constantly in his thoughts. He was a pleasant enough person, two years younger than herself, and with some ambitious prospects in business, about which he kept hinting. He intended to be a rich man.

Not what she would have chosen, but by this time she would have accepted almost anyone, because life at home was so unbearably dreary. She didn't even have housework to do now that they could afford to keep more servants. She read to Mamma, until Mamma complained that Mary Ellen's high, rapid voice brought on a headache; then she took long walks alone, window-shopping or buying flamboyant clothes (in an attempt to make Louisa look mousy in contrast). Sometimes she made calls on unmarried friends. These were getting few in number and were all a little odd in one way or another, overanxious, restless, addicted to gossip or unattractively obese. A lot of the time she just sat in her room and brooded on the unfairness of her baby sister's having so much while she had so little.

So the advent of Gilbert Withers could not have been more timely.

She was almost sure that a proposal was imminent. Excited and stimulated by the attention he paid her, her looks came back. Her only regret was that she had met Gilbert in the Spencer house, but it did have the advantage of showing Harry Spencer that she was able to attract men.

He danced with her three times at the Marcus Stones' ball, which was in itself a declaration of his intentions, and finally, half-seas over with the too freely flowing champagne (the Marcus Stones always overdid things), blurted out that he was sure that he and Mary Ellen could make a go of it.

Mary Ellen was not so eager for a husband that she could forsake certain standards. One of them was that a marriage proposal should never be made, or accepted, while the proposer was under the influence of drink. She pushed Gilbert's unsteady form gently but firmly away from her and suggested that they talk again. Tomorrow, perhaps?

"May have lost my courage by then."

"Why do you need courage?" she demanded.

He was eyeing her in a cross-eyed fashion.

"Do, you know. Besides, mightn't like you so much tomorrow."

"To be honest, I don't like you much today," Mary Ellen said.

"You don't? Then the whole thing might come apart.

That would be a pity." He lurched away, presumably to get more champagne, and Mary Ellen found Boy at her side, looking at her with his bright, derisive eyes.

"What's Gilbert doing? Drowning his sorrows?"

"What things you do say!" Mary Ellen frowned, tapping her foot. "I only hinted that I didn't care for gentlemen who couldn't hold their drink. And that's true, after all the years of Papa. I simply couldn't go through what Mamma goes through."

"One wild night doesn't make a man a drunkard."

"I know that well enough. But it's not very flattering if a man has to get drunk to make a proposal of marriage."

"Is that what he was doing?"

"I think so. Oh, bother it all! Why is nothing perfect?"

"I don't know, but your statement is unfortunately all too true. Nothing *is* perfect, and especially marrying a man set up by your brother-in-law."

Mary Ellen became very still.

"What do you mean?"

"Nothing. Shouldn't have spoken."

"You've begun now, so you'd better finish." She knew her brother well enough. "There's something you mean me to hear sooner or later."

"I wouldn't want to be bribed to marry a girl," Boy said, his black eyes gleaming pleasurably.

"Boy, you are a *devil!*"

"Why? For making me tell you?"

"If you're saying, as I suspect you are, that Harry Spencer is setting Gilbert up in business on condition that he marries me, I could kill you."

"My dear sister, you'd have heard it from someone sooner or later. You know how we all love scandal."

Mary Ellen's high color had vanished.

"How *dare* he be so impudent! Money gives him power, and he loves it because he can manipulate people. Oh, how can Louisa stand him?"

"Maybe he thought he was being kind."

"Kind! He may put food in my mouth and clothes on

my back, but he will not put a husband in my bed. Oh, men! And you're as bad, standing there with that stupid smile."

Boy's eyes were wide open and candid. He was such an actor, one might have thought he had done this just for effect, but judging by her own feelings, Mary Ellen guessed that behind his candor there was the immense resentment and injured pride of a proud family.

"I wouldn't have let you do it, old thing. Louisa might have, but I wouldn't."

"Louisa knew, too?"

"Who knows? She could genuinely have thought it was a good thing."

"For her poor spinster sister! Now I will *never* marry, I will stay in the van Leyden house, and Harry Spencer can keep me until I rot."

"I'll be keeping you company."

"And wait until I see Louisa and tell her what I think of her and her husband's scheming."

But she couldn't see Louisa the next day, for on getting up that morning, Louisa had fainted. The doctor had been sent for and prescribed complete rest and quiet. There was nothing to worry about. Out of devotion to her husband Mrs. Spencer had attempted to take on too many of the duties of a newly married woman, which was unwise when expecting a first child. Now she must cancel all her social engagements and think of the welfare of the child.

Several days later Louisa hardly heard Mary Ellen's irate mutter about a quarrel with Gilbert Withers and that she never wanted dinner partners found for her again. Very well, she agreed incuriously, not having known anything about Harry's scheme and thinking only that once more Mary Ellen had muffed her chances. Anyway, she wouldn't be giving dinner parties for some time. Wasn't it wonderful about the baby? She was overjoyed, and so was Harry.

With Mary Ellen sullen and suspicious, with Mamma, who still had feelings of guilt and anxiety about poor Louisa's forced marriage, and with Boy, who cynically never expected happiness, Louisa kept up the myth of the happy bride.

It was not the truth; nevertheless it was not totally a lie. Harry was, no doubt, as good a husband as most of her friends had got, even those who had married for love. He was a little loud and impetuous in society, but one would never want to reduce his personality by turning him into a smooth-mannered Ephraim de Wynt. He was obsessed with business. One expected this since he had been so since a child. He genuinely thought that Louisa was an understanding wife who did not expect an apology for being late for dinner, for forgetting they were to go to the theater, or to someone's party, or indeed for not arriving home until midnight. Although he was happy and intrigued to have a wife, she still came slightly behind the importance of a business deal. He did not think this unreasonable.

It was really an advantage not to be in love with him, Louisa decided; otherwise this blind side of his nature would have hurt her too much. As it was, she accepted it quietly and absorbed herself in caring for the house, which she loved and was making conspicuously her own. People talked about Louisa Spencer's blue and green drawing room and her dislike of too much ornamentation, even though she could have afforded to buy most of the contents of a royal palace had she wished. Some were already copying her, but to others the desire to display wealth in too many possessions was a temptation not to be resisted.

Louisa guessed that Harry had expected something of this showing off from her and would not have been averse to it. But since she didn't want it, neither did he. He got his satisfaction from being a guest in the great houses previously denied to him and from the financial status of the people he met. He had no polite conversation, nor did he seek to make friends. He discussed facts or was silent. He stood, a solid, self-contained figure in his correct clothes, the gardenia in his lapel, a little apart from the crowd, his expression bland, his eyes still and watchful, taking time to choose his prey. Or that was how it seemed. He confessed himself a little nervous of the restless, talkative smart women who flirted with and flattered him. Perhaps that was why he had been anxious to get Mary Ellen married. Though one could never say she had either flattered him or flirted with him.

Louisa thought that she must be pleasing Harry as a wife because, when business permitted, he was a thoughtful and generous husband. He would come home and toss her a package and say, "Wear this with your violet gown, my dear," and she would find a new necklace of amethysts or topazes, or a long gold chain studded with moonstones, or a diamond clip. Her jewel box was overflowing, and she was not a person who liked a lot of decoration. She felt overwhelmed and helpless. Perhaps she would have several daughters and be able to distribute largesse among them. She had a dream one night in which she was crying, "Chrissie will have a better wedding than me." Who was Chrissie?

No one had led her to believe that the physical side of marriage should be an exciting thing; therefore, she was not disappointed. It did get better, as Harry had promised it would. She submitted, with modesty and amiability, and it was soon over, the crushing body on hers, the heavy breathing. If Harry sensed that he was too frequently demanding, he became very gentle and held her close to him, which was the part she liked best. She could curl up against him and fall trustfully asleep.

He really was a very good husband. She knew she would never change places with Mary Ellen and that everything had turned out for the best. She looked forward to the birth of her baby with excitement and impatience.

And Harry had begun to look for a house on Long Island so that they could escape the hot New York summers. Everyone in their circle had a summer house either at Newport or on Long Island. Harry wanted one of those old Gothic mansions in Southampton that had belonged to an earlier generation of the rich. He searched and waited until just the right place came on the market, a large, sprawling building with turrets and balconies and every outrageous ornamentation the architect had been able to think of. Its appearance made him and Louisa laugh, yet the rooms were large and comfortable, and all the odd steps and stairways fascinating. What they couldn't do in the formality of their Fifth Avenue house they could do here. Harry could be as flamboyant as he pleased, and Louisa must not criticize.

There were lawns sloping down to the beach, a lake surrounded with wild vegetation, and a lot of overgrown shrubs and weed-filled borders. It was going to be a wonderful house for children with the shaded verandas, the large gardens, the stables. For Louisa it was going to be a whole new life. She had never thought she would own two houses, each in its own way so satisfying. And perhaps here, so far from New York, Harry might even forget business for a day or two at a time.

It was a lucky house, for it was after they had furnished it, in a pleasant makeshift fashion, and had the garden tidied, the shrubbery cut back, a boathouse built on the edge of the lake, and talked of who should be their first weekend guests, that Harry found Serenity.

He brought her one evening, after he had been to New York for the day. She stepped out of the carriage, a middle-aged, big-bosomed black woman, with her head in a neat bandanna, and gave Louisa a wide smile.

"Mr. Spencer aiming for me to be the baby's nurse, ma'am."

Louisa flew to Harry and threw her arms around him.

"I didn't know you had remembered."

"I remember everything, Lou. Haven't you found that out yet?"

"Yes, I have, but we hadn't mentioned—Serenity! What a lovely name. Come in, and we'll talk indoors. My husband didn't tell me he was bringing you this evening. The baby isn't due for another three months. But you can help me with its clothes and the nursery. I expect you've had a lot of experience."

"I wouldn't have hired her, otherwise," said Harry. "All the same, you must look at her references, Lou. She comes from Virginia. You may know the families she has been with."

"Miz Spencer knows the Cuspids and the de Farges, just as I know the Boydells," said Serenity calmly. "I remember you as a tiny baby, ma'am, when your mother brought you to visit with old Miss Abigail. Ain't this a fine house? Just the house for children. Yes, ma'am, I aim to be happy here. Is this where your child is to be born?"

"No," said Harry definitely. "It will be born in New York. If it's a boy, I want the pavements of New York in his blood; if it's a girl, she's to be a famous heiress."

"Oh, Harry! Isn't that a burden for a girl?"

"Not my daughter."

"Hear Harry's bought you a nigger," said Papa, refilling his glass and downing its contents in one smooth movement.

"But I thought slavery was all done with," said Mamma perplexedly. Mamma's headaches seemed to be affecting her brain. She was frequently vague and distraught and forgetful.

"It is," said Louisa. "Really, Harry has only found me a Negro nurse for the baby. I said once that I would like one, and he remembered. And Serenity is the result. She's kind and capable, and she had impeccable references. She actually knows Great-aunt Abigail. I'm very happy about her."

"Well, just don't bring her here," said Papa. "I never want a nigger in this house. All the trouble they caused.

All those fine young men who died at Gettysburg and Bull Run. I don't want to set eyes on this Serenity or any of her troublemaking race."

"You don't need to see her, Papa, unless you come up to the nursery and want to see your grandchild. Then you'll have to see Serenity, too."

"Really, Louisa, you don't need to get that uppity," said Mary Ellen. "If you aren't putting on airs these days. Talking to Papa like that."

"Papa," said Louisa, controlling her anger, "can't even run his own house, let alone mine. And as if Harry didn't—"

"I know. Support us all," Mary Ellen retorted.

"Let Lou have a bit of her own back," Boy said lazily. "She's entitled to it. She's doing all this for us, running two large houses, becoming a mother, hiring a Negro nurse. I should think she's exhausted."

"Sorry I said anything," Papa mumbled, his eyes filling with the easy tears of drunkenness. "Are you exhausted, Lou?"

"Never saw anyone look better," Mary Ellen snapped. "And why shouldn't she? She's waited on hand and foot. Exhausted! Really, Boy, when will you stop making fun of everybody?"

"Come upstairs, Robert," urged Mamma. "You need to lie down. Boy, if there were not so much bourbon in the house—" she added in a whisper.

"He would go out and get it. It's no use, you might just as well give up and let him drink Harry's liquor to his dying day."

"Which will come a good deal sooner than it otherwise would have," said Mary Ellen.

"And does that matter? Ask Papa. He'll tell you he'd rather live dangerously. Wouldn't you, Papa?"

"What's that, Boy? Are we going to the club?"

"No need to. There's another bottle here."

"Oh, splendid. I understand we have Mr. Spencer to thank—Mr. Harry Spencer. Who the hell is that little upstart? I never do remember finding out. Millicent—excuse me, my dear—feel astonishingly tired—I think I'll take a nap—right here. . . ."

Really, thought Louisa, her family was becoming impossible. Where once they had simply been impoverished but well mannered and dignified, now they were becoming monsters.

When she welcomed Harry home that evening, she suddenly lost her usual quiet self-control and burst into tears.

Harry, she discovered, didn't know how to cope with tears. He rushed to get brandy, then, when Louisa refused it, begged her to lie down. What was it? Was she ill? Was the baby coming? Was the heat too much for her? They should have stayed on Long Island for another month. Who would have known there would be this unseasonal sticky heat in the late fall?

Finally Louisa, feeling unbearably oppressed by his anxious face bending so closely over her, burst out that the trouble was his money. It was ruining her family.

"They used to be nice people," she said. "Poor, I know, but proud and self-respecting. Pride is essential to people like them. Now we've taken it away from them and they feel like objects of charity. They hate and resent it, especially Mary Ellen and Boy."

"And they're taking out this resentment on you?" Harry said shrewdly.

"I don't know. Yes, I suppose they are."

"Then you will stop visiting them, my dear."

"Oh, no, I can't do that. I still love them. And this isn't really their fault. It's the horrid influence of money."

"You will stop visiting them until after the baby is born. I won't have you upset. And if they are being so corrupted, I can always stop their allowance."

"Oh, no; then they'd starve."

"Exactly. So money can't be entirely horrid, as you say. To tell the truth, I'll be glad not to have your father lurching about my dining room on Sundays. It isn't my money that's destroying your family, Lou; it's plain weakness. Overbreeding. Too much easy living. It happens in old English families, too. It isn't a prerogative of the van Leydens."

"If you feel like that about them, I wonder that you married me. Was I young enough to be manipulated? Was that why you didn't choose Mary Ellen?"

"Perhaps. Does it matter?" He took her hand. "And it's not like you to be cynical. Let's leave that sort of thing to your brother."

"And has your manipulated wife pleased you?" Louisa could not get out of her strange, tetchy mood.

"Exceptionally. Haven't I shown you?"

"With all those presents? Yes, I suppose so."

"You know I'm not good at words. I haven't got a smooth tongue."

"You let money talk for you. I suppose all rich men do."

Harry stood up. "I'll leave you until you've rested."

"But we've only begun to talk—"

"I'm not an arguing man, Lou. You ought to know that by now. Just obey me. No more visits to your family until the baby is born. I won't risk it making its appearance among all those bad family portraits and empty bourbon bottles. It's going to be a Spencer, born in my house."

He walked away, his broad figure as arrogant as Louisa had ever seen it. She wept again, but less unhappily. She found she rather enjoyed it when Harry was masterful. And certainly she wanted her baby born in her own beautiful bedroom with its view over the park.

The trees would be bare by then. There might even be snow.

Chapter 7

~~~~~~

Robert van Leyden never saw his first grandchild because on the night of its birth he fell down the stairs and broke his neck. He had been having a drink to celebrate the arrival of a granddaughter. They had all had a glass or two of brandy, even Mary Ellen, although she said she had done so simply to keep out the cold.

It was late November, and there had been a snowfall. The tree of heaven was weighted down with snow and stood outside the front bedroom window like a small white mountain. Its ghostly light was reflected in the still and tranquil face of Robert van Leyden IV, dignified by death, no longer an object of pity and scorn.

It was just like him to escape from all their troubles, Mary Ellen burst out passionately. He had always known how to take the easy way. But the brandy had gone to her head, and she was suffering from shock. She didn't know what she was saying.

For they hadn't any troubles now that Papa had gone, and there wasn't his drinking to worry about. They were comfortably off. Fires burned in all the low-ceilinged dark-paneled rooms. The house was filled with the overpowering scent of hothouse flowers. This was a van Leyden death, and half New York promised to be at the funeral which would be carried out in the style to which a member of such an honored old family was entitled.

Afterward there would be quantities of rich food and more brandy, and Mary Ellen could take satisfaction in knowing that she could legitimately postpone the day when she must go and view her new niece.

Christabel Boydell Spencer, aged two weeks, fair-haired like her father, but with her mother's deep-blue eyes. A little wriggling shrimp of a baby, and how could Mary Ellen ever have known that her heart would go out to the small creature?

It just did. She stood over the cradle, and tears rolled down her cheeks.

She should be mine! she cried silently. Oh, it isn't fair! I was always the one who had things, not Louisa. That was right, because I was the eldest. And I still am, and all this is happening to Louisa, and I am left on the outside. . . .

Louisa looked infuriatingly smug and contented. She lay in her four-poster bed, propped up on snowy pillows, surrounded with flowers and books and hothouse fruit.

"I'm really perfectly recovered, but Harry insists I rest for another week, and the doctor doesn't dare argue. Besides, Serenity is so good with the baby. What do you think of your niece, Mary Ellen? Do tell me."

Louisa's voice was warm and eager, as it used to be when they were still friends. Why did she think having a baby would automatically restore them to this affectionate sisterly state?

"Looks like all new babies to me."

"Oh, Mary Ellen! Surely she's a little different, a little special. Her father certainly thinks so."

"I expect he looks on her as another piece of property."

"Mary Ellen, you get more like Boy every day. And you know you don't mean a word of what you say. It's been a terrible time for you, with poor Papa dying like that, and I was unable to do anything to help. Harry wouldn't allow me even to be told for twenty-four hours. How is Mamma? When is she going to be able to come and see me?"

"You may have to come and see her. She's taken to her bed."

"Oh, not permanently!"

"Dr. Dean doesn't know. Her heart's weak. She could follow Papa any time."

"How terrible!"

"Yes, it's not all who can lie in the lap of luxury and be spoiled like you are."

"I know," Louisa agreed humbly. "I do know. Tell Mamma I'll bring Baby to see her as soon as the doctor says I may take her out."

"You'll have to wrap her up well."

"So you are a little interested in her welfare," Louisa said slyly.

"I'm only saying it's turned as cold as January, and the roads are dangerous. We've had one accident in the family. We don't want another."

"There'll be no accident for little Christabel, I promise you. For one thing, Harry would just about kill me. He's calling her Chrissie, you know. He thinks it's more friendly for such a tiny creature."

She didn't say that that had started after the totally unexpected visit of Mrs. Martha Spencer. Only a grandchild, she said, could bring her to set foot in Harry's grand house. She gaped about her and said it wasn't right that two people should have so much when there were so many poor.

"I've had my share of being poor," said Harry in the tight, hard voice with which he always spoke of poverty. "That's never going to be for my daughter. Or my wife." Already he was mentioning the baby first. Was that of any significance?

"Well, she's a nice little thing," said Martha, looking into the cradle. Louisa wondered if the thin, sharpnosed, chronically hungry face surrounded by a rather grim black bonnet would remain in the baby's subconscious memory until the end of her life.

"Ho!" said Martha, playfully letting the tiny fingers curl around her worn forefinger. "Ho, then, Chrissie! Christabel! That's for grand occasions. You'll be Chrissie to me, my little love.

"And when," she added, looking at Louisa critically, "are you getting out of your bed? I was on my feet the day after the birth, each time. Back at the mangle in a week. Did me no harm. Don't make her too soft, Harry. I can't abide pampered women."

"That's too bad, Ma," said Harry, stroking his little beard, "because you've got two pampered women here, Lou and Chrissie. And I intend them to go right on being that way."

"You don't own 'em," said Martha crisply. "You might think you do, but you don't. They have their own free spirits. That's something all your money can't buy. You mind it, Lou. If you let Harry think he owns you, then you have to go his way all the time."

"I'll mind it," said Louisa, smiling. "I'm going to ring for some hot chocolate. You must be frozen after your drive. And would you like to see baby fed and changed?"

"That I would. You're a nice lass, Lou. But don't think I'm going to be a regular visitor to this royal palace. King Harry, eh? And this is the crown princess, I suppose. She won't be too grand to visit her grandma in the Bowery, I hope."

"Indeed she won't. We'll drive over once a week."

"Not when the roads are bad," Harry said. "I won't risk the horses skidding when the baby's in the carriage."

Harry Spencer had decided that life had now reached one of its peaks. For a man of his nature, there would always be other peaks, but by the age of thirty-six he had certainly reached the summit of three important ones: success, marriage and fatherhood.

He loved his wife. She had all the qualities he had sensed on that first meeting at the opera. Breeding, a quiet distinction in manner and dress, good temper and patience, the ability to run his houses, a great love for her baby and a gentle unfailing concern for himself.

That last attribute, he supposed, was the slight cloud on his otherwise-brilliant sky. He was a practical man and had never expected a young woman like Louisa to fall in love with someone like himself.

However, the mind was one thing, the body another. Dear innocent Louisa would never know the restraint he exercised night after night, taking her gently, one might almost say politely, when he longed to display all his considerable sensuousness and virility. At the beginning of their marriage he had watched hopefully for some response. Could women of Louisa's class never let themselves go? Were they so deeply inhibited by their rigid upbringing? Or was it that nothing in him roused any passion in his quiet wife? Perhaps she even disliked him. Her manners would be much too good to ever let him see that. But she didn't shrink from him. She smiled and welcomed him. She simply never discovered that a man would like his wife to reciprocate passion.

Louisa, he was afraid, in her immaculate white lawn nightgown (he had never again asked her to wear anything of his choosing), her dark hair hanging in neat plaits over her shoulders, her beautiful sapphire eyes serene, was never going to go mad and bite and claw him. And perhaps, deep in his heart, he didn't want her to. She was the woman he had wanted to marry, well bred and calm, a perfect mistress for his house and a perfect mother for his children.

So it was with relief that he could expend noisy and uninhibited affection on Chrissie, plucking her out of her cradle and letting her pull at his beard and toss his white gardenia to the floor. She had begun to shriek with joy when she saw him come into the nursery. Her welcome had all the warmth and excitement that his wife's lacked. He adored her. He thought she was the most beautiful baby in the world.

"I believe he would even sell his precious lots on Madison and Twenty-first Street for Chrissie," said Ephraim de Wynt. "And you know that's his biggest project as yet, building stores and a grand hotel there."

"I know," said Louisa. "He says it will make us multi-millionaires. I personally think we have enough money."

"That's Harry. There'll always be more."

Louisa repressed a sigh. "He says it's for Chrissie. What is all that money going to do to a young girl? And Harry spoils her so already. Serenity will tell you. He overexcites her, and then we have tempers and tantrums. And the toys he brings her would supply a whole orphan-age, except that they'd be far too grand. He's had one of Mr. Bell's telephones installed principally so that he can speak to Chrissie from his office. Serenity has to hold the instrument to her little ear."

"Is she scared out of her wits?"

"No. She recognizes his voice and laughs and gurgles, and of course he's off his head with pleasure."

"You've got to remember his childhood, Louisa," said Ephraim. "It was pretty bleak."

"I know. I do think of that. But all this excess seems just as bad, in its way."

"Only one thing to do, my dear. Have seven or eight more children. Then the spoils and the affection can be divided. Watered down."

"Well, that's fine advice from someone who's a bache-lor."

"An observer, I prefer to call myself," said Ephraim, folding his neat, small hands. "If one recognizes one's role in life, one succeeds in being happier. Take Mary Ellen now. She'd be glad to have eight of Harry's children."

"Not Harry's! She detests him."

"Well"—Ephraim lowered his eyes, discreetly—"eight children anyway. The poor girl didn't ask to be stuck with an ailing mother and a brother with a very uncertain temper."

"I know. It isn't fair. But Mary Ellen is awfully difficult to help. I take Baby there a lot because Mary Ellen is devoted to her. I declare that child gets far too much attention. You're quite right, Ephraim. I hope I have another as soon as possible. Perhaps it will be a boy. Harry would be awfully proud of a son."

The son was born a year later. He was called Henry van Leyden Spencer, and Harry, now a popular member of the best clubs, was said to have bought champagne for a vast number of people for three days of celebration. But he never came home the worse for liquor. He could not risk dropping Chrissie, he said, his eyes getting their merry gleam. Not the new baby. It was still Chrissie who occupied most of his thoughts. She now toddled to the door to meet him, and he thought this the cleverest thing in the world.

Not that he wasn't inordinately pleased with his son and his wife. He gave Louisa another diamond pin and began to worry whether after all he had made Camberwell House too small.

"You're not to alter a brick," Louisa cried.

He smiled, pleased with the love she had developed for his house.

"Well, we can always buy the lot next door and build there. Have you noticed that I was right? This part of New York isn't going to remain a wilderness. People are moving up."

Louisa only knew that she loved the view from her windows over Central Park. She loved hearing the children shouting on their sleds in the snow, the promenaders going by in their spring finery, the chestnut sellers standing over their braziers in the fall. Chrissie was growing so fast she would soon be out there bowling her hoop or demanding to ride on a sled.

"You know those old rat-ridden shanties at the far end of the park," Harry was saying. "I'm trying to get possession of the land so that I can clear away that eyesore."

"What about the people who live in them?"

"They'll have to move. Couldn't find anything worse to live in."

"Isn't that a bit ruthless?"

"Ruthless? When I plan to put up good, clean, modern buildings to house a great many more people?"

"You make it sound like an act of charity when all the time it's making you richer and those wretched people homeless. They'll hate you."

"Perhaps. The rich are always hated. But I can live with some hate better than with poverty. I always remember my grandfather telling how he came down chimneys into those grand rooms. A thin, filthy, starved little boy who was beaten if he made soot marks on the carpet. You just want to take life by the tail and twist it."

"How do you mean?"

Harry gave her a half-sly look under the thick golden fringe of his eyelashes.

"By Chrissie marrying one of those lords with the grand houses."

"In England! You can't mean that, Harry. Just to have revenge on your grandfather's ill-treatment? Anyway, what's wrong with the grand houses in America?"

"You haven't seen the English ones, Lou. Think of those famous names Adam, Inigo Jones, Chippendale, Wedgwood. Creators of the English stately home. There's grandeur and class. I tell you, the Vanderbilts and the Astors don't begin to understand it. They try to be classic and end by being vulgar."

"You've never become American, have you, Harry?"

"I suppose I haven't. I'm like the Irish hankering for shamrocks and peat fires and their bit of bogland. Though I can tell you I'm not hankering for those damp, rat-infested back-to-back houses that are mostly all I can remember of England. I only want to compensate myself and my mother and father and all my ancestors for the squalor and misery they suffered."

"So Chrissie is to be the one to get into those grand English houses?"

"That's right. By the front door."

"Don't get too ambitious, Harry," Louisa begged.

"No, my love. I promise you only to want what is attainable. But that," he added, his eyes getting their diamond bright shine, "will be quite considerable."

Chapter 8

Miss Christabel Boydell Spencer. Miss Chrissie. From an early age Chrissie knew that she was a very important person. Grandmother Spencer, in her funny upstairs sitting room above the store, fed her biscuits, and joggled her on bony knees, and sang her nursery rhymes, and cried merrily, "Ain't you a little lady? Look at your muff and your fur tippet. Too fine for the likes of us, ain't she, Beulah?" Then she would set Chrissie down, bow like a thin branch bent in the wind and say, "Your carriage is waiting, m'lady," and Chrissie, knowing it was a game, would go into shrieks of laughter.

Although the carriage, with Billy on the box, really was waiting, and Serenity was fidgeting. Serenity didn't think Grandmother Spencer had much class. She came on these weekly visits only because she was ordered to.

Every Wednesday to Grandmother Spencer. Every Friday to Aunt Mary Ellen and Uncle Boy. Once there had also been Grandmother van Leyden, a pale sick lady always in bed or on a couch, a shawl around her shoulders, her eyes dark and sad. But last Christmas the angels had taken her away. And Aunt Mary Ellen had said she should not have gone so soon; it was only because she had grieved so much over losing Grandpapa van Leyden. It seemed that Papa had some sort of power over the angels and had arranged these departures. Which didn't surprise Chrissie, because Papa had a great deal of power over everybody and everything.

He had taken away Uncle Boy's desire to work, and now Uncle Boy was always there, in the strange dark old house, with its funny little rooms that led into each other, and the cutest big old bathroom with a tub standing on feet in the middle of the room. The tree of heaven, which had come from China and now filled the little front garden, rubbed against the windows and shut out the light. The house smelled, although Chrissie could not identify the combination of smells. It seemed to be old carpets and dust and lavender water and Uncle Boy's rum.

It wasn't entirely true to say that Uncle Boy didn't work because he was doing what he had always wanted to, writing a book about someone called Lord Byron who had had a lame foot like Uncle Boy's. He enjoyed doing this very much and said it would take him about fifteen years.

"You'll be a young lady by then," he said to Chrissie, his sunny blue eyes smiling. "You can come to my publishing party."

"Chrissie won't be hanging about waiting for that," Aunt Mary Ellen said in her tart way. "She'll be having her own parties."

"Papa says I'm to go to England," Chrissie said importantly.

"Oh, does he? We'll see about that. You're an American, and you'll have your coming-out right here in New York."

Aunt Mary Ellen had a way of talking as if she were responsible for Chrissie's future and would plan it as she saw fit. Mamma said, "Let her have her fancies, if they make her happy. But don't pay too much attention to them. Papa and I know what's best for you."

Aunt Mary Ellen certainly seemed happy. When Chrissie came, she always had a treasure hunt arranged and gave loud shrieks of laughter as Chrissie diligently searched for the treasure: a box of beads to string, a bag of colored marbles, a new hair ribbon or once a darling baby doll with a rosy-cheeked china face. After that excitement was over, there would be tea, with a frosted cake and a jug of lemonade. Aunt Mary Ellen always wore brightly colored dresses with a great deal of trimming, which Mamma said were much too young for her but which Chrissie admired very much. She had a capacious lap and made Chrissie sit on it, to have a story read to her. In such close proximity, Chrissie could see the pale coating of rice powder on her cheeks and the lines around her eyes. She must really be quite old, although not nearly as old as Grandmother Spencer, who must be the oldest lady in the world. She loved Aunt Mary Ellen, with her loud, jolly laugh and her kindness. On the odd occasions when Henry came, too, she was violently jealous, even though Aunt Mary Ellen paid little attention to him. Chrissie was her darling and her pet. This was extremely agreeable, although Serenity grumbled that after a visit to Eighth Street Miss Chrissie was mighty vain and above herself.

The children had a large, light nursery on the top floor of Camberwell House. Their bedrooms were next door, and Serenity's across the passage. Shortly, they were to have a governess who would occupy the other bedroom on the top floor.

Henry had been a delicate baby, difficult to rear, and although now four years old, he had not outgrown his tendency to alarming attacks of croup. This had made Mamma pamper him and coddle him too much. Or so Papa said. He was still very much a baby and therefore an exasperating playmate. He didn't understand the games Chrissie wanted to play, and when she bullied him

—she knew she did and was privately rather ashamed of herself—he burst into loud sobs. He would never make the man his father was, the servants said. Chrissie had a way of overhearing servants' gossip. It was little Madam Christabel who should have been the boy in this family.

Papa said the children must have an English governess. Not only was this fashionable among the richer New York families, but he had deeper motives. He wanted Chrissie to learn the English way of life. When she was older, she would be sent to a school to learn French and dancing and other desirable achievements, but in the meantime Miss Miller, the governess Mamma eventually engaged, could teach her to read and write. Miss Miller was a great prize since she came straight from a titled family who had a large house, and seven children, in Gloucestershire in England. All the children had ridden to hounds. Naturally, Chrissie could not learn to do that, living as she did in the heart of New York and having only her pony at Long Island, but there were many other things she could learn about the way life was lived in a great English house.

Fortunately, Miss Miller was an agreeable person, though rather prim. She couldn't get used to Serenity with her jolly laugh, her dusky face, her colorful clothes. English nannies wore uniforms and were very strict. Serenity laughed with the children and gathered them to her large bosom a dozen times a day. She treated them like puppies, Miss Miller said in amazement. Never mind, she would soon have their manners under control. Especially Miss Christabel's. That child needed some discreet punishment occasionally, though not while her father was about. It was plain to see how the child had become so spoiled and demanding, with an adoring grandmother (common, unfortunately), a slightly crazy aunt, a father who pampered her wickedly and a mother who was wrapped up with the delicate little Henry.

Miss Miller came under Mr. Spencer's spell quite quickly. His visits to the schoolroom were noisy disrupting affairs, which ended in roars of laughter as he plucked the children from their desks and rode them about on his broad shoulders. They clung to his golden beard and shrieked with excitement. It took a long time to settle them to their copybooks again, but Mr. Spencer left an atmosphere of warmth and affection that Miss Miller was sensible enough not to attempt to dismiss. The mother was so different, quiet and self-contained and unknowable. She wasn't even a beauty, although her great grave eyes and her air of fragility had a breeding that even the snobbish Miss Miller recognized. (She had come to New York with the preconceived conviction that all Americans, no matter how rich or clever or charming, were centuries behind the English in culture and breeding.)

Mr. and Mrs. Spencer were simply not made for each other. But what husband and wife were? As an observer in many households she had never yet discovered an entirely happy marriage. It just seemed strange that someone like Mrs. Spencer would marry a man like Mr. Spencer with his noisy extrovert vitality. However, she had done so, and it was clear that he was immensely proud of her. When he wasn't lavishing gifts on Chrissie, he was buying expensive jewelry for his wife, a new picture to hang in her drawing room or a gentle, pretty mare for the phaeton in which she drove herself and the children in Central Park on soft spring days.

Dinner parties at Camberwell House were lavish affairs to which Miss Miller recognized that all the best people came. They always ended with the ladies in the drawing room sipping coffee and boring one another with gossip, while the men remained in the dining room, passing the port and talking business. Mr. Spencer used to pat the shining mahogany table at breakfast the next morning and boast that already he had added considerably to his fortune by deals made around this piece of furniture.

They were mad about money, these New Yorkers, Miss Miller thought. It was religion with them, inspired no doubt by memories of poverty-stricken and persecuted childhoods in European countries. One sympathized, of course, but possessions should not be the only symbol of a successful life. It was essential to teach her small charges this. Nevertheless, Miss Miller's prim spinster heart had twinges of envy and loneliness as she saw how easy and pleasant money made life for Mrs. Spencer and the children. Though that Miss Chrissie, with a wardrobe large enough to clothe a dozen millionaires' daughters, seemed as if her character might be ruined already. Little Master Henry was another matter. He coughed, and was kept indoors, and had curiously spartan tastes for a little boy. His favorite toys were shabby, much-handled ones. He was like his mother, unostentatious and quiet. Miss Miller had uneasy premonitions about him. She kept them to herself. Of one thing only was she sure: if Master Henry lived to grow up, his father was not going to approve of him.

Hannah Miller, daughter of a Scottish minister, brought up to be God-fearing and straitlaced, was going to be thirty years old on her next birthday. She had made the adventurous trip to America because as a governess in England she had found that she was neither fish nor fowl. She lived in an ambiguous world between the drawing room and the servants' basement. She had heard that the class system was much less rigid in America and that even at her advanced age it was possible she would be sought in marriage. She was no beauty, with her sandy eyelashes, her pale-blue eyes, her tilted nose with its sprinkling of freckles, but she was small-waisted and immaculate. Her neat ankles and light step had already attracted Mr. Spencer. She had seen him looking after her. She lay in bed at night and tried not to think how a vigorous man like Mr. Spencer stirred her senses.

There must be many more like him in this great growing city. It was just a question of meeting them, and that could scarcely be done on sedate walks in the park, with a child clinging to each hand. Or in Camberwell House, unless a guest wandered up to the schoolroom by mistake. It was always Serenity who took the children down in the evening, for their hour with their parents and whatever company might be present. This was a feature of the day that was adhered to religiously, even if Mr. and Mrs. Spencer were going out and the hour had to be slightly curtailed.

Miss Miller was about to come to the sad conclusion that it was just as impossible to meet a prospective husband here as it was in England when a new housemaid, Lily, was engaged. She was an attractive young woman, of Irish birth but definitely a cut above the usual Irish emigrant. She had smooth black hair and sparkling black eyes, and she immediately became a favorite with everybody because of her liveliness and good temper. She treated Miss Miller as her friend at once. Weren't they both strangers in a strange land? And weren't they lucky to work in such a grand house with such a lot of treasures? She had told her brother Danny about them, but he didn't believe her. Well, how could he after the sod cottage they had been brought up in with chickens scratching around the hearth and the donkey tethered at the door? Danny worked on the wharves. He was a very pretty fellow, Lily said, much prettier than she was. And she had had the most exciting idea. Couldn't they smuggle him into Camberwell House one night, when the master and mistress were out, and let him have a quick look at its glories for himself?

It would do no harm, would it? said Lily, her bright eyes beguiling. It wasn't fair that the poor were deprived of beauty. Danny would think that marble staircase led right up to heaven.

Miss Miller was definitely uneasy about this plan, although she agreed with all of Lily's arguments about the unfair lot of the poor. Perhaps, if Danny came through the trademen's entrance and was kept out of sight of Dobson, that pompous butler, they could whisk him upstairs when Dobson was eating his substantial meal with Cook in the kitchen. But he mustn't stay long.

Danny came. And Hannah Miller, much against her better judgment, found her senses ravished by his long-lashed deeply blue eyes, his curly black hair, his appealing grin. He was alive with curiosity about the house and wanted to see everything: the first-floor reception rooms, Mrs. Spencer's lovely green drawing room facing the park, the second-floor bedrooms (although Miss Miller flatly refused to allow Lily to open the door of the master's and mistress' suite) and the nursery floor. Danny, with his warm personality, was obviously fond of children and even begged to be allowed to see Miss Chrissie and Master Henry asleep in their beds.

"Don't wake them," he whispered. "Mustn't frighten them with my ugly mug." His fingers felt for Miss Miller's in what might have been a gesture to stop her waking the children. Or something more intimate. Whatever it was, she found her usual dull evening much enlivened and heard herself replying animatedly to Danny's questions about how she spent her day.

"A morning walk in the park," he said. "Always?"

"If it isn't raining or snowing. I don't believe in keeping small children at their lessons for too long at a time."

"And then?"

"Oh, luncheon, and a rest, and then more lessons. Perhaps a drive with their Mamma. Tea. Then the hour in the drawing room with their parents. Then bath and bed."

"But the darky nurse does the bath and bed, doesn't she?"

"Oh, yes."

"And you're free then?"

"More or less. I look after the children's clothes, plan their lessons for the next day."

"Big doings! I never knew anything about a governess' life." His warm gaze rested on Miss Miller. "I'd like to know more, though. Can I come again?"

"Not like this," said Miss Miller nervously.

"What, aren't you allowed callers?"

"Perhaps I would be. I haven't made any friends here yet. But if I mentioned it to Mrs. Spencer—"

"And left the door unlocked for me," said Danny. "Lily'd do that. Well, what I mean is, we're all strangers here, and we don't want to sit moping and getting homesick." His very aware eyes traveled up and down Miss Miller's neat figure. "Me, I'm not going to work on the wharves for long. I'm going to find opportunities. Look at Mr. Spencer and what he's done for himself. Never stops, does he? He's built that grand new hotel on Madison Avenue. Now they say he's going to pull down the shanties at the end of the park and put up more rich buildings."

"Well, the shanties are an eyesore, aren't they? Full of vermin, I hear."

"I don't suppose the people living in them think like that. They'll be homeless."

"I know. One has to be ruthless to make money." Miss Miller's excited eyes searched Danny's face. "Will you be ruthless, too?"

For some reason he laughed, as if he enjoyed the question.

"Oh, yes. I'll be ruthless. Won't I, Lil?"

"Don't mind Danny, Miss Miller," said Lily. "He talks as if he's still chasing Oliver Cromwell with a homemade sword."

Miss Miller laughed, and the funny little moment of tension vanished. "No Oliver Cromwells in America. This could be your country, Danny."

"Yours, too, Miss Hannah."

Now where had he heard her first name?

It seemed that Danny was right about the resentment caused by Mr. Spencer's demolition of the Central Park shanties. But it was a pity that this was manifested on the night when Louisa and Harry were entertaining the Vloordops and the Masons at dinner. Dirk Vloordop was an important banker, and Tom Mason was aiming to be the next mayor of New York City. Even Harry was keeping his noisy high spirits under control on this occasion, and the evening was overformal and, Louisa thought, agonizingly dull.

Until the brick crashed through the drawing-room window. It was followed immediately by another and a third.

Louisa, followed by Harry and their guests, stood staring aghast at the ruin of her lovely room. There was broken glass everywhere. A valuable Chinese bowl had been knocked to the floor and smashed. A pretty Sheraton table, its polished surface scratched, teetered sideways. The cold night air flowed in, and the pale staring faces of passersby loomed wraithlike in the darkness outside.

The culprits seemed to have vanished. Someone was shouting that they had fled across the road and into the park. Two youths, skinny and very fast on their feet.

"Look here," said Mr. Vloordop, "this was tied to a brick."

Harry snatched the piece of paper from his hand and held it under the light. He stared at it for a long time without speaking.

Louisa plucked his sleeve. She was very white and felt a little faint.

"What is it, Harry?"

"Just some abuse."

"What does it say, Spencer?" demanded Mr. Vloordop.

Harry read the note slowly and clearly,

" 'Just so you'll know what it's like having the wind blowing through your house, Mr. Spencer. But you've still got a house. We ain't. You frew us out.' Frew! Frew!" said Harry distastefully. "Illiterate wretch. Wait a minute, there's more. 'We hates you and your money bags, Mr. Spencer. We'll have revenge.' "

"How horrible!" said one of the ladies.

"Aren't you sending for the police, Spencer?" asked Tom Mason. "Surely you've got someone on your staff you can trust."

Harry's blue eyes were suddenly glacial. Not, Louisa

realized, for the culprits disappeared in the darkness, but for the remark his guest had just made.

"Oh, I think so, Mason. I'm accustomed to a trustworthy staff. I'm sorry if you're not so fortunate."

"I didn't say that—"

"Sounded like it." He pulled the bell rope, then realized that Dobson, along with Cook and two or three housemaids, were lurking at the door, goggle-eyed. "Dobson, will you take this note to the nearest precinct at once? I prefer you to do it yourself. Well, folks"—he had pulled himself together and once more wore his customary genial expression—"I'm sorry our dinner has been spoiled. And it's deuced drafty in here. Let us go back to the dining room for coffee, and something stronger. Even the ladies may care for that tonight. Now don't cry, my dear." He had his arm tucked in Louisa's. "We'll have the glass back in the windows tomorrow."

"But will it happen again?" Louisa asked. She wasn't crying, but she was still trembling and cold and much more afraid than she would have liked anyone to know.

It was horrible to be hated. And for money. How could Harry look so unperturbed?

Fortunately the children had not been awakened by the noise. In the morning Chrissie viewed the destruction with awed interest. She privately thought being bad much more interesting than being good, and for such colossal badness as this she had an awed admiration. Imagine those men throwing bricks through Papa's windows. Wouldn't they be put in jail?

"Yes," said Papa. "They'll be put in jail. But you're not to worry your pretty head about it."

Chrissie wasn't worrying about it; she was only wishing that she could help catch the bad men. When Miss Miller took her and Henry for their walk that morning, they didn't go in the park. It seemed that Mamma and Papa had suggested they should not. The men might still be lurking about. It was better to keep to the sidewalks and look in the shopwindows.

Chrissie begged to go past the old apple woman who sat, her long nose sticking out from under her pokebonnet, outside the doors of one of the large stores. She had a basket of rosy apples by her side, and Chrissie was allowed to buy one for herself and one for Henry so long as she rubbed them thoroughly with a clean handkerchief before they were eaten.

When that pleasure had been accomplished, she asked if they might take a hansom cab down Madison Avenue until they came to Papa's big hotel, which was just finished and due to have its opening the following week. There was going to be a very large party, with millions of bottles of champagne. Naturally Chrissie and Henry were not invited, so could they not peep into the lobby with its acres of lush green carpet now?

All in all, it was a much more interesting morning than just walking in the park. When they reached home, they found that Aunt Mary Ellen was there. She had heard the news of the smashed windows and sat in the cozy morning room drinking hot chocolate and pretending to be shocked and sorry. But Chrissie saw how her eyes sparkled, as if she thought it was a great joke. She almost looked as if she would have enjoyed throwing the bricks herself.

"Things like this are bound to happen, Louisa," she was saying. "People like Harry make enemies. It isn't all fun being rich."

"Did I ever say it was?" Mamma said coldly. "Chrissie. Henry. Say good morning to your aunt; then go and take off your outdoor things. Henry, are your feet wet?"

"I'm sure they're not, Mrs. Spencer," Miss Miller said quickly. "We've never been off the sidewalks."

"Yes, I know I fuss too much. It's just that he catches cold so easily."

Mamma had her arms around Henry and held him close, while he struggled petulantly. Chrissie turned deliberately to Aunt Mary Ellen and allowed herself to be kissed lovingly. She didn't care at all for being kissed by grown-ups, but if Mamma was going to go on pretending that Henry was a baby, she could be a bit of a baby, too.

She would far rather talk about the bad men who had thrown the bricks, but as soon as she opened her mouth, she was shushed and told to go upstairs.

She obeyed reluctantly, and lingering a little behind Miss Miller and Henry, she heard Mamma saying, "I just can't help being nervous, Mary Ellen. If they hate Harry this much, what might they do next? We have this big party at the hotel next week. Supposing they make trouble there?"

"Don't be silly, they wouldn't dare. Harry will have too many police around. After all, people jump to do what he says now. You know that. But if you're nervous, let the children come and spend the night with Boy and me."

"Oh, the children will be all right. It's nothing to do with them."

A week later Miss Miller saw the handsome Irishman, Danny Moloney, again. He was strolling in the most casual way across the park when she was taking the children for their morning walk. (They were now allowed to go in the park again but were instructed to keep to the paths near the road where there were plenty of passersby.)

Chrissie was bowling her hoop, and the tall young man caught it and bowled it back to her. He lifted his cap and smiled at Miss Miller.

"Where've you been? I've been looking for you every day. You said you walked in the park in the mornings."

Miss Miller felt herself blushing as if she were sixteen.

"We do, but there was—some trouble. Mrs. Spencer thought we ought to avoid the park for a few days."

"Trouble?" inquired Danny, his black eyes sparkling and inquisitive.

"Some awful ruffians threw bricks through the windows."

"Did they, by Jasus! Why'd they do that?"

"They had a grievance against Mr. Spencer because

he's going to pull those shanties down. But they can't do anything, really. The law is on Mr. Spencer's side."

"The law, Miss Hannah, is on the side of the rich. We know that, don't we? Evictions in Ireland, evictions in Scotland. What do the rich care about the poor?"

"Mr. Spencer used to be poor himself."

"Then he's forgotten."

Miss Miller gave the young man a sidelong look. "I expect you'll forget one day, too."

"When I'm rich? Is that what you mean, Miss Hannah? Is that what you believe?"

Miss Miller gave him a long, considering look, taking in his impudent, attractive vitality. Yes, Danny Moloney would be something. Whatever it was.

Henry was tugging at her hand, whimpering that he was tired. Miss Miller said, "You can't be tired, Henry. We've only begun our walk. Run along with your sister."

Danny looked after the little boy trotting obediently on his spindly legs. "He's a wee bit of a fellow, isn't he? Looks sickly."

"He isn't strong. But please don't talk about that in front of him."

"He's a pampered wee invalid, is he?"

"His mother thinks so. I think she protects him too much."

Danny, without a by-your-leave, tucked his hand under Miss Miller's elbow.

"Are we to talk about someone else's brats all the time? I admire you, Miss Hannah. Come out with me tomorrow night."

"Oh, I couldn't. Not tomorrow. It's the night of the party at Mr. Spencer's new hotel. I always stay in when Mr. and Mrs. Spencer are out."

"I expect the truth is you always stay in."

"Well—"

"Well, tomorrow come out with me. Isn't there that big darky to listen for the children? And Lily's there. She's good with kids. Come on, say yes, Miss Hannah. Just for an hour or so. Am I never to see you alone?"

"Well—"

"That's right, Hannah. You look pretty when you smile."

Miss Miller knew that she shouldn't agree, although Mrs. Spencer had always made it clear that her evenings were her own. But Serenity was inclined to fall asleep in the rocking chair in the nursery, her hands clasped on the soft cushion of her stomach, and Lily was already beginning a flirtation with the knife boy. (He called himself a footman, but to Miss Miller, accustomed to grander houses than this one, he was a knife boy, plain and simple.)

All the same, what harm could an hour do? She would wear her fur-trimmed bonnet and her fur muff. It was so exciting to have a man look admiringly at her. She knew that for the first time in life she was going to forget cautiousness and be plain reckless.

If any bricks were to be thrown tomorrow night, surely they would be through the windows of the grand new Hotel Atlantic.

Chapter 9

Ever since the brick-throwing incident Louisa had been reluctant to leave the house. She knew she was being foolish. Neither her presence nor her absence was going to make any difference. Harry assured her there would not be another attack. The villains had made their protest, and the incident was over. He understood how such people's minds functioned, he said, because once he had known a temptation to behave in a similar way himself. Violent action was a kind of catharsis.

"I don't see how you can be so sure that breaking windows once is going to get rid of all their hate," Louisa said. "Really, Harry, I won't be easy until we know who these criminals are and can make sure they don't attempt some other way of harming you. Or me, or the children."

Harry ruffled her hair with his heavy hand.

"Don't be so fanciful. No one's going to harm you or the children. I'm the object of their hate. But that's a hazard of my life. If I let it worry me, it would inhibit progress."

Louisa raised her eyebrows ironically. "Oh, it's progress, not money."

"Of course it's progress," Harry retorted, slightly irritable. "A few people lose their homes, many more benefit from the new dwellings I will put up, and a great city is gradually built."

"A great deal of money going into your pocket in the process. Don't prevaricate, Harry."

"What ever does that word mean? Don't you remember that I haven't been educated?"

"Then ask Miss Miller." Louisa was seldom like this, tense and with a desire to hurt. That brick-throwing incident had upset her more than she would have believed possible. And she couldn't bear Harry becoming a hypocrite. Building a great city indeed, when his only aim was making the fortune of Mr. Harry Spencer. She chose another subject that nagged at her.

"To tell the truth, Harry, I'm not entirely happy about Miss Miller. I agreed to engage an English governess because you wanted me to, but I really don't find this one very congenial, and Henry dislikes her."

"What about Chrissie?"

"Oh, Chrissie gets on with everybody, you know that. She hasn't Henry's sensitivity."

Harry frowned, giving his complete attention to Louisa's complaint now that it concerned Chrissie.

"Miss Miller had the highest references. She seems all right to me. Not the gadabout type."

"She's certainly not that."

"Well, isn't that better than having someone soft and attractive, as no doubt your son would prefer? Henry has to obey her, not love her."

"Perhaps you're right."

"Of course I'm right. It's time Henry stopped being such a baby for his age."

"You know how badly he still gets croup."

"Another summer on Long Island will cure him of that. Do stop looking so bothered, my love. I want you to sparkle tonight. Wear that new green velvet gown, will you? And your pearls."

"How many people are coming?"

At the mention of his party Harry had lost his irritability and was looking smugly satisfied.

"Everybody. In figures, about three hundred."

Louisa turned away, to hide her reawakened fear. For there she would be, in Harry's proud new hotel, receiving the long line of guests, looking as expensive as Mrs. Vanderbilt in her famous ropes of pearls and terribly conspicuous. Who knew what ill-wishers might slip, uninvited, into so large a gathering?

The children were asleep when Louisa and Harry were ready to leave. Serenity was in the nursery, her moist brown eyes full of admiration.

"My, ma'am, you do look beautiful."

"Thank you, Serenity. We'll be home before midnight. You know where we are, if you need us."

"Sure, but we won't need you, ma'am. Master Henry hasn't coughed since Christmas. And Lily's here. We aiming to play a game of backgammon."

"Miss Miller?"

"She'm reading a good book, ma'am." Serenity gave her deep gurgle of laughter. She had never learned to be anything but her natural Southern easygoing self. No hyprocrisy there, Louisa thought, and turned to take Harry's arm.

He was looking very well groomed and handsome, the gardenia in his lapel, his fingernails manicured, his thick fair hair and his beard neatly trimmed. He was still jolly and genial and loud-voiced, but that touch of uncouthness which had aroused something protective in her had almost gone. She found herself regretting that. Her marriage had begun as such an alarming adventure, and now it seemed her husband was just another rich New Yorker, doing all the correct things. In ten years' time one wouldn't be able to distinguish him from all the rest. Which may have been Ephraim de Wynt's idea of an achievement, but oddly, it was not hers.

She occasionally had a feeling of guilt, as if she had destroyed something natural and honest. But if she had not done it, she supposed some other woman would have. For Harry had been determined to shake off the last traces of the odor of poverty. All the same—building a great city indeed! She couldn't bear it if he became too pompous.

The Hotel Atlantic, named because of the visitors Harry hoped to attract from across the Atlantic, was indeed a fine building, six stories high, lavishly furnished and decorated. Harry had finally obtained the site he had coveted, pulling down old dwelling houses and putting up a row of shops as well as the hotel. People grumbled that this kind of thing was turning Fifth Avenue and Madison Avenue in the Twenties and Thirties into a purely commercial area, but Mr. Harry Spencer's forward-thinking ideas were becoming well known. He intended pushing private houses farther from the center of the city. It was an inevitable aspect of progress, he said. He was employing a larger and larger staff of architects, lawyers and accountants. He seemed to have created a monopoly in the property market.

But people said that if he hadn't married Louisa van Leyden, old Herbert Condon would never have sold those lots on Madison Avenue and Twenty-first Street to him. He wouldn't have dealt with a brash upstart. But a man at whose house one dined—that was another matter.

There was no doubt there would be bigger and bigger deals coming along for the immigrant Englishman who, like all truly successful men, had a touch of the visionary about him. And his wealth carried its own aura. Therefore, people came eagerly to the party at the Hotel Atlantic, making an expensively dressed crowd who talked noisily and drank a great deal of champagne.

Halfway through the evening Louisa's head began to ache, as it did at all large, noisy parties. She suddenly saw her life as a succession of these affairs, ostentatious, impersonal, valueless, and abruptly sat down on a settee beneath one of the opulent potted palms. Her thoughts had brought a wave of dizziness and depression. There was no one here whom she truly wanted to see. The women who greeted her with apparent affection had jealousy lurking in their eyes, the men—well, she wasn't the type who excited easy admiration from men. She was too quiet, too lacking in that witty, brittle repartee in which New York women excelled. She was, boringly, a faithful wife, with impeccable manners. A little intimidating.

Besides, for no reason at all, she kept thinking of Henry tonight. She had thought he had been a little breathless when she had bent over his bed to kiss him good-night. He had flung his bony little arms around her neck. She wished he could put on a little weight and get more color in his cheeks. Perhaps, in the summer, running wild in the big garden at the Southampton house, he would at last outgrow his chest weakness. It seemed so wrong for Harry, monumentally healthy, to have a delicate son.

"Can I get you another glass of champagne, Mrs. Spencer?" came a voice above her.

She moved abruptly, putting the animated smile back on her lips, and looking up at the tall young man who had spoken.

"No, thank you, To tell the truth, I was taking a brief rest."

"I don't blame you. It's awfully hot. Wouldn't you like a little fresh air?"

"I'd love it, but where do we find it?"

"At one of the windows over there. Do you see? There's a little seclusion behind that marvelous herbaceous border."

"I'm not sure the hostess should be looking for seclusion. But just for a minute or two." She took the offered arm. She looked into the young man's face and could swear she had never seen it before because she knew she would have remembered it. Long, fine-boned, intelligent, courteous.

"Now let me see. You're—do forgive me, I've met so many people tonight. My husband always tells me I must remember names, but I'm afraid—"

"How could you, in a gathering this size? I'm Cornelius Peterson. I work occasionally with your husband as an architect. My mother and I moved from Boston to New York about a year ago. We live rather quietly. I confess I detest crushes like this. Now I'm afraid I've said something rude."

"Only the truth," said Louisa, smiling wryly. "I share your opinion exactly. But even small gatherings can get out of hand. The other night—" She checked herself and breathed deeply of the cool air coming in at the open window. "This is nice. I'm revived already."

"What were you going to say about the other night?"

"Oh, only that we had bricks thrown through our windows. It was unpleasant—horrible. I've felt guilty ever since."

"Why should you feel guilty?"

"I suppose for sharing in Harry's success, for being able to arouse this sort of envy and hate. Harry can shrug it off. I can't."

"You're too sensitive, Mrs. Spencer."

"No, just too realistic. I can't live in Harry's world. His

plans grow bigger all the time. Mind you, I didn't enjoy being poor, either, when there was that awful anxious business of keeping up appearances. I don't think I'm very logical."

"Who wants a beautiful woman to be logical?"

"Don't pay me glib compliments, Mr. Peterson."

"I'm not that sort of man, I assure you. I say what I think. You are beautiful."

Louisa fingered her pearls nervously. Anyone with any knowledge could guess what they had cost. Had Mr. Peterson noticed them particularly? She had discovered that wearing valuable jewelry evoked extravagant compliments. She looked at the young man again and was angry with herself for her suspicions, for there was a look of complete sincerity in Mr. Peterson's face. It wasn't fair of her to doubt it.

"Tell me about yourself, Mr. Peterson."

"Me?" He looked faintly embarrassed, as if unused to being questioned about himself. "What can I tell you? I'm twenty-eight, unmarried, and live with my mother in Washington Square. My mother has poor health and is something of a recluse. I'm not very much of a social type myself. I often prefer books and music. I walk a great deal while I can."

"While you can?"

"Manhattan Island is rapidly filling up with bricks and mortar. The open spaces are disappearing, and I do not want to take a five-mile constitutional down muddy sidewalks."

They both laughed. "Do you ever walk in Central Park?" Louisa asked.

"Often."

"Then you must call when you are passing. And I promise it won't be a social occasion."

"I would be delighted."

"We are the same age," Louisa said, almost absently. Then she rose. "And as you appear to be a very eligible bachelor, you mustn't waste the evening with a married lady. Besides, I must look after my guests."

He took her arm again politely, although did his fingers press it a little? She was almost sure they did. She was also now certain that his wouldn't be one of the faces she forgot.

"Don't worry about that unpleasant episode of the bricks through your windows, Mrs. Spencer. Surely it won't happen again."

"No. That's what everyone says. But I have this feeling something else will happen, perhaps worse. Oh, I mustn't bore you with my stupid fears. Harry would be angry with me."

"Harry is fortunate."

She looked at him questioningly.

"Because he has nerves of iron," Mr. Peterson said after a moment.

Louisa was almost certain that it was something else he had wanted to say. Her heart was fluttering slightly. She must be too tired and have drunk too much champagne.

Danny was tapping at Miss Miller's door almost before Mr. and Mrs. Spencer were out of the house. He had slipped up the back stairs, through the door which Lily had left unlocked, and was waiting to take Miss Miller out.

He paced nervously up the passage outside her door, as if afraid of being seen.

She laughed. "It's all right. Mr. and Mrs. Spencer have gone. Anyway, I'm entitled to my evenings."

"Then let's get going before the brats wake up."

"Serenity's here, if they do."

"And you'd be fussing, too."

"Where are we going?"

"Walking. It's sharp out. Put your hands in that fancy muff."

He spoke impatiently, almost as if he regretted his invitation and wanted to get it over and done with as quickly as possible.

But outdoors, under the frosty sky, he was friendlier, tucking his arm in hers and setting out at a brisk pace.

"Ever been inside a saloon?"

"Good gracious, no!"

"Then your education is going to be broadened to-night."

"But—do women go to places like that?"

"In bonny Scotland, no. But in New York, yes. That's what I like about New York. Gives everyone an equal chance."

"Hardly," said Miss Miller. She didn't think she cared much for this hectoring Danny. The streets were too ill-lit for her to see his handsome face and be ravished by it. She only realized that she was being bustled along by a strange Irishman to a saloon.

"You and I don't have equal chances with people who will be at Mr. and Mrs. Spencer's party tonight," she went on. "I believe a certain part of New York society is much more snobbish than English society is."

"What about Mr. Harry Spencer then?" Danny said brusquely. "He was once no more than you or me. He took his chances, that's all."

"Have you something against Mr. Spencer, Danny?"

"Not at all, not at all. Except that he's English, and no true Irishman likes an Englishman."

"How far off is this place we're going to?" Miss Miller asked. She didn't want to spend the evening having an argument with a bigoted Irishman.

"A few blocks. Just off Broadway. The Dog and Duck."

"I mustn't be out too long."

"For Jasus' sake, Miss Hannah, we've only just come out, and already you're talking of going home. Are you afraid of me, for the love of God?"

"Don't be absurd."

"Then enjoy yourself. You will when you get a mug of ale in your hand."

"I don't drink ale!"

"Well, you can't ask for a cup of tay in the Dog and Duck. Don't shame me, Miss Hannah."

Shame him, when it was he who was shaming her! For the Dog and Duck was full of noisy, rough-looking men. There were no more than five or six women, and they of a type Miss Miller recognized at once. Street women with painted faces and overcurled hair. Whatever could Danny be thinking of, to bring her here?

She tugged his sleeve and hissed, "How could you bring me to a place like this? Let us go at once."

He grinned down at her, his eyes full of devilment.

"I wanted to broaden your mind, Miss Hannah."

"My mind doesn't need broadening."

"Sure, it does. You're a wee bit straitlaced. Half a pint of ale inside you will make all the difference."

Miss Miller saw the women staring at her derisively. Street women, she thought again. Danny, from some dreadful Irish sense of humor, must have brought her to observe and enjoy her shocked indignation. She was rigid with anger.

"If you don't take me home at once, I'll go by myself."

The long walk alone would be terrifying, but less terrifying than this place, where now everyone was looking at her, even the bartender. One of the men winked at Danny and addressed him by name.

"So it's you, Paddy," said Danny. "Sorry I can't stay for a drink. The lady isn't happy."

"Thought you knew how to keep ladies happy, Danny boy," someone shouted.

"A man can make a mistake sometimes. Come on then, Miss Hannah, I'll walk you home, since you're insisting. And me with a thirst—"

"Oh, shut up," said Miss Miller rudely. She had got him out into the street and was setting off at a good pace.

"If you thought that was a joke, I don't care for your sense of humor."

"Well, that's a great pity, Miss Hannah, because you yourself now don't seem to have one at all. It's a thing you ought to cultivate."

"Just be quiet, and get me home."

She would never trust another man. She longed for the security of her virginal bedroom, of the children next door and of Serenity dozing in the nursery. She was thankful that Lily had promised to leave the side door open so that she could slip in unnoticed. This time Mr. Danny Moloney would be left on the doorstep. She would make it her business to see that he was never admitted to the house again.

She refused even to say good-night, but he was still grinning as he stood there under the gaslight, still enjoying his senseless joke. She shut the door in his face and hurried upstairs.

Should she look in at the children? No, she would calm herself first. Serenity, as she had expected, was sound asleep in the rocking chair beside the nursery fire. The backgammon board was still beside her, but Lily had disappeared. Which was a good thing, because Danny's sister was the last person she wanted to encounter.

She threw off her outdoor things and, lying on her bed, closed her eyes. She thought she could still hear those awful women in the Dog and Duck calling names at her. There *was* someone calling. Miss Chrissie! And that lazy Serenity sound asleep. Miss Miller sprang up and hurried into Chrissie's room.

The little girl was sitting up, her eyes wide with fright.

"Where are those men?" she was asking.

"What men? There aren't any men in here."

"There were two men," Chrissie insisted. "They looked at me."

"You must have been dreaming. There's no one here but me."

"They said, 'No, that's the girl,' and went out. I wasn't dreaming. I saw them."

Miss Miller's scalp stirred.

"I'll be back in a minute."

"Don't go!"

"I'm just going to see that Henry's all right."

"Please don't go!" Chrissie begged, and began to scream.

That did wake Serenity, who came bustling from the nursery, yawning and flapping her hands.

"Lawd's sake! I'm that sleepy. Whatever is it, Miss Chrissie? All that noise."

"Henry's gone," breathed Miss Miller behind her.

"You mean he's out of his bed, the little rascal."

Miss Miller dragged her out of Chrissie's hearing.

"He's gone! He's been taken. There's a note pinned to his pillow."

"Stolen!" exclaimed Serenity in a high screech, forgetting about Chrissie's listening ears.

"Kidnapped!" whispered Miss Miller, her mouth dry with fear. "The note says they want twenty thousand dollars. Oh, dear God! We've got to send for Mr. and Mrs. Spencer."

The ill-spelled instructions in the note pinned to Henry's pillow said that the money was to be left in the fireplace of the half-demolished shanty on the other side of the park. It was the only one not entirely reduced to rubble.

BE QWIK IF YOU WANT TO SEE YOUR LITTLE BOY ALIVE. WHEN WE HAVE THE MONEY WE WILL LET YOU KNOW WHERE HE IS. YOU CAN TRUST US IF YOU PAY UP AND KEEP AWAY FROM THE PERLICE.

"Monstrous!" Harry muttered. "Monstrous!"

It was so much worse than the broken windows. Louisa had known something else would happen, but nothing as bad as this. She was trying desperately not to faint.

Henry's bedroom, with the gay wallpaper, the white cot, with the shabby rabbit and bear that he cherished tucked at the bottom of it, kept going dark.

"Harry—send them the money at once."

"Be practical, Lou, for heaven's sake. Where can I get twenty thousand dollars in cash at midnight? I'll have to wait until the banks open tomorrow."

"But it's such a cold night and he'll get an attack of croup. You know plenty of bank managers. Wake them up. Make them go and get you the money."

"Calm yourself, Lou. Wait until the police come."

"Oh, God, you haven't sent for the police. They said not to. Oh, God, Harry, you've signed Henry's death warrant!"

"Ssh, love! We've got to question the servants. Someone must have seen or heard something."

"Do that when Henry is safe. Please! It's so cold. He's so little; he can't keep warm by himself. Of what importance is the money? Give it to them and get Henry back."

"I intend to do that. But we also must see that dangerous criminals like this are caught. Otherwise it can happen again."

"Do we have to live with fear like this?" Louisa exclaimed despairingly, and then, mercifully, the room went completely dark.

Chapter 10

The next morning the money, wrapped in a brown paper parcel and tied securely with cord, was left according to the kidnappers' instructions. Harry did this himself, knowing that two vigilant policemen were concealed in a clump of bushes, waiting to seize whoever came to the bait.

No one came.

It snowed a little before midday, only a dry white sugar dusting over the rocks and bare ground, but it was bitterly cold. No delicate child could survive exposure on a day like that.

But there was no reason to think that Henry would be outdoors. He would be being cared for somewhere, since kidnappers would hope to avoid murder.

Fires burned in every room at Camberwell House. Louisa walked from one to another of them, rubbing her frozen hands. She had wanted to go and search the park herself and had had to be forcibly restrained.

"Look after your daughter," Harry said brusquely. "She needs you, too."

This was true enough, for Chrissie had become unnaturally silent, her usually ebullient spirits vanished. She kept saying that the two men who had come into her bedroom had taken Henry. When questioned by the police about what these men had looked like, she only said, "Dirty," and hid her face in her mother's skirts.

It had all come out about the side door being left open for Miss Miller's gentleman friend and how Miss Miller had actually been out of the house when the kidnapping had taken place.

Serenity and Lily had been playing backgammon in the nursery, although Serenity, Lily said, had fallen asleep quite early. She had then gone downstairs to the kitchen and heard nothing. Yes, she said, her pert chin in the air, it had been her brother who had taken Miss Miller out. But it seemed they had quarreled and come home quite early. Danny hadn't come upstairs again. He knew nothing about this. Nor, apparently, did anyone else.

Serenity said she had had a cup of hot chocolate and had then got powerful sleepy. She just couldn't keep her eyes open. She had had the silliest feeling that the chocolate had tasted of Master Henry's soothing syrup, administered to him when his cough was bad. It contained a small proportion of opium.

It was a pity the dregs of her hot chocolate had not been kept, said the police officer. But they hadn't, so nothing could be done about that. Lily said she had not had any of the chocolate. Nevertheless, her room was to be searched. But so was everyone's, Miss Miller's in particular. And Miss Miller had the shaming ordeal of having to repeat everything Danny had said to her. Including his remarks about the English and the Irish, as if those old enmities could have anything to do with this crime. How could he have taken Henry, since he was with her at the vital time?

None of the other servants had heard anything suspicious. They had been in the warm kitchen having their evening meal. Since there had been no dinner to be sent upstairs, they had had plenty of time to gossip, including Dobson, who rather enjoyed dropping his pomposity and leading the women on.

It all came back to that unlocked side door which had provided such easy access for the kidnappers, as if it had been arranged.

Lily was the picture of injured innocence. But her brother Danny could not be found, and she swore that she hadn't the slightest idea where he was.

It came as a deep shock to Miss Miller that Danny (and Lily, too, before she had begun work at Camberwell House) had lived in the shanties in the park before the evictions were made. Lily said she didn't know where Danny was living now. He moved around, she said. Neither did she know all his friends. He had a lot and constantly made new ones, since he was one for company. He was not doing a regular job at present but picked up work here and there.

Anyway, why did the police want to know so much about him, when he hadn't been here last night at the time that the little boy was kidnapped? He had been with Hannah Miller, and if that was deliberate, he doing the planning while his friends did the dirty work, Lily wouldn't be knowing anything about it. She only knew that Danny wouldn't hurt a fly, let alone an innocent little child.

She was allowed to go, on condition that she didn't leave the house, and Miss Miller was sent for.

After a sleepless night her looks had not improved. She knew that the police inspector questioning her was thinking privately that a lively young man like Danny Moloney would not be taking out this plain, prim young woman from preference. But plain unmarried women of a certain age were prone to foolish behavior, and if the kidnapping had been Danny Moloney's diabolical scheme, this silly woman would have been an easy pawn.

"I'm just so ashamed," she kept saying. "I'll have to leave."

"That's between you and your employers, miss. What we want are facts. Now are you sure these men in the Dog and Duck greeted Mr. Moloney by name?"

"Oh, yes, positive. The women, too. That's what was so"—she bent her head—"so humiliating for me."

"Getting this young woman out of the house, in case she heard anything, and providing an alibi for himself," the inspector observed to his sergeant. "I want a man to check on that saloon and its regulars."

He turned again to Miss Miller.

"Last night wasn't the first time Mr. Moloney called on you here?"

"No, he came once before, and I showed him the house. I know I shouldn't have, but he seemed so interested. He said he intended to build one like it himself one day. If Mr. Spencer could, he could."

"I've no doubt," the inspector commented dryly. "Did he seem particularly interested in the layout of the nursery floor?"

"I didn't notice—well, perhaps he was. I didn't think about it then."

"Obviously you didn't."

Miss Miller was deeply distressed. "I thought he had come to see me. I had no idea I might just have been being used. I don't distrust people. Perhaps I'm too trusting. My father is a Scottish minister—"

"You may go now, miss. Don't leave the house."

As the day went on, the wind rose, the air became restless with thickening snow, and Henry had not been found. Neither had the package of money been removed from the fireplace of the roofless house. It seemed that the kidnappers must have suspected the presence of the police. Louisa was convinced that this meant they would kill Henry. She was becoming distraught, and Mary Ellen's arrival did little to help.

Mary Ellen conversed at length on Harry Spencer having some sort of retribution coming to him. Look at the way he threw people out of their homes, even if such homes were only dilapidated shacks. Granted, he was doing his share of building a fine city, but you didn't build people into the bricks and mortar, not even the most wretched and useless. Besides, his main object, whatever pompous attitudes he struck, was to make more dollars.

Henry would be found, of course. Every policeman in New York City was out searching for him. Louisa shouldn't get into such a state. And thank God it wasn't Chrissie who was lost.

"I'm taking Chrissie home with me," she announced in her overbearing manner. "She can't stay here with all those police about frightening her out of her wits. And that mealymouthed governess will have to go. I hope you agree. Keeping assignations with men the moment your back is turned!"

"Yes," said Louisa. "I never did like her very much."

"Then why did you hire her?"

"Harry wanted her. He wanted the children to have an English governess."

"Harry!" said Mary Ellen, with unfeigned contempt.

"There was nothing wrong with that."

"Oh, no, Harry's decisions are always right. Except this
117

time. I'll take Chrissie now. I'll go and get her dressed myself. I really wouldn't trust any of your servants, Lou. Serenity falling asleep, that Lily letting her brother into the house. And what were the rest of them doing, gossiping in the kitchen when they should have been keeping a watch, knowing you and Harry were out, and that you'd had that trouble with those louts breaking windows."

Louisa pressed her fingers to her aching temples.

"Very well, you may take Chrissie for the rest of the day. It's so sad here for her. But she must be brought back as soon as Henry is found."

"I'm not asking your permission, Lou dear. I'm simply taking her. She has eyes like saucers. Boy and I will keep her amused and happy."

After an hour or so beside Mary Ellen's cozy fire in the dark parlor, Chrissie consented to drink a cup of hot milk, the first food she had accepted all day. Then, sitting on Mary Ellen's lap, her head against the cushiony breast, she broke her day's silence and began to talk.

"Why do you smell different from Serenity, Aunt Mary Ellen?"

Aunt Mary Ellen gave her loud, friendly laugh.

"I don't know what Serenity smells of."

"Nigger," said Uncle Boy lazily, from the other side of the fire.

"Soap," said Chrissie. "Mamma smells of perfume from that big glass bottle she has on her dressing table. It has a silver top. It smells like hothouse flowers."

"What do you know about hothouse flowers?" asked Uncle Boy.

"They smell strong, like Papa's gardenia. Lily says that's a wicked waste of money."

"Lily. That's that new girl."

"We don't like her much, Henry and me."

With the inadvertent mention of Henry's name the short outburst of talkativeness came to an end. Chrissie's mouth shut tight.

"I expect they've found Henry by now," Aunt Mary Ellen said comfortably.

"Will he be dead?"

"Good gracious, no. Your Papa simply wouldn't allow that to happen."

"Will those men come again?"

"I shouldn't think so. Anyway, you're safe here." Aunt Mary Ellen gave her jolly laugh. "We might even keep you always."

Aunt Mary Ellen began to happily elaborate on this dream, saying Chrissie could have her mother's old room, with the cabbage rose wallpaper and the long branches of the tree of heaven stroking the windows. There would be no Miss Miller, no Lily, no Serenity, no Henry. At that Chrissie began to shiver again, the unexplained terror on her. When there was suddenly a loud knocking on the street door, she screamed.

But it was only Papa. She flew into his arms, wrapping her arms around his neck, pressing her face into the fur collar of his greatcoat.

"What have you done to her?" she heard Papa asking grimly. "She seems scared to death."

"She was scared to death before she came here. We'd just succeeded in getting her settled when you had to bang on the door, like a band of robbers," Aunt Mary Ellen answered.

"You had no right to bring her here."

"She had to be got out of that house. Who knows what next—"

"Be quiet!" Papa roared, in a terrible voice. "You just stop interfering, you silly woman. I'm taking my daughter home at once."

"What about—"

"You'll hear when there's any news."

"There isn't any yet?"

"Would I be keeping it a secret? And you needn't worry about Chrissie. She'll be watched night and day."

"You can't do that, Harry Spencer."

"I can, and will. Until she's grown up, if necessary."

"But, poor child, her freedom!"

"This is a wicked world. Come along, Chrissie, get your coat on. Billy's waiting outside for us. Mamma needs you."

Uncle Boy followed them to the door.

"Haven't they come for the money yet?"

Papa shook his head. Suddenly his rage had gone. His voice was very tired.

"It's got beyond a matter of money—I'm very much afraid. We scared 'em. Handled it badly. I suppose you could say I've had no practice at this kind of thing. I'll be wiser in future."

"You'll keep that child in a prison," Aunt Mary Ellen shouted.

"If it's necessary."

All the same it might have been wiser to leave Chrissie at Mary Ellen's, for in the space of time that it had taken Harry to drive to Eighth Street and back, Henry had been found. Policeman Fitzgibbon, checking church doorways and hospitals, had discovered that a little boy, wrapped in an expensive rug, had been found on the doorstep of the Founding Asylum on Twelfth Street. He was unconscious and could not be revived. He had died before the doctor had arrived and before his identity could be established. His delicate constitution had been unable to stand up to the long night and day's stress. The cause of death was given as exposure to the elements, but there was another name for it: murder.

Sometime during the ensuing coming and going at Camberwell House, Lily had taken the opportunity to pack a bag with her few belongings and disappear.

Within minutes, she and her brother Danny became the two most wanted people in New York State.

The packet of dollar bills carefully placed in the mouth

of the tumbledown chimney was never claimed. It was brought back to Camberwell House and lay on the table in the library. No one claimed it, even then, not even Harry Spencer, to whom it belonged. It was the price of a little boy's life.

Chapter 11

That summer Chrissie had her portrait painted. She wore a blue velvet dress with a Venetian lace collar, and had Rusty, her spaniel, at her feet. Rusty had been one of the gifts bestowed on her to help to replace Henry, who had been stolen by the wicked men. It was no use Mamma and Papa insisting that Henry had been taken by the angels, because she knew better. They knew better, too, she suspected; otherwise why did Peck follow her everywhere she went? Shopping, walking in the park, playing in the garden or on the beach at Southampton, his tall, watchful form was always somewhere about. He was broad-shouldered and very strong, Serenity said. Quick on the draw, Uncle Boy said, although she didn't know what that meant. He never talked much, but sometimes he gave Chrissie a ride on his broad shoulders, and she quite liked him. It was only rather tiresome that he was always there. She played games, trying to lose him, but she never succeeded. Indeed, deep in her heart, she didn't want to lose him because she knew he was to keep the wicked men away. Lily, too, might be lurking somewhere, and for some reason she also could be dangerous.

Chrissie had overheard just enough to know that Lily and her brother Danny were friends of the bad men and

that although policemen all over America were still looking for them, they had never been found.

Now, a whole six months later, it seemed that they had
disappeared forever, although Chrissie sometimes thought
she saw Lily's snapping black eyes staring at her in a
crowd. She refused to speak to the apple woman on Fifth
Avenue anymore because her black eyes were like Lily's,
grown old.

The world, she realized confusedly, was no longer a
safe place. Even the big wild garden at Southampton that
she had so loved was now slightly menacing. When
Mamma invited children to play with her, because she
suddenly seemed such a lonely little girl, she refused to
play hide-and-seek. The rhododendron bushes crackled,
and shadows moved. The other children thought she was
a scaredy thing, but Papa said in his deep, gruff voice that
she would grow out of it. At present it was a good thing
that she was a little nervous, for that would keep her
safely at her mother's or her governess' side.

All the same he hoped the little girl who now moved
about the house so quietly and sat primly upright in the
landau on the way to church on Sundays, like an obedient
little puppet, hadn't permanently lost her high spirits.

In her portrait she looked like a pretty doll. A very rich
doll, because now that Henry was gone and no other baby
had come (which seemed to disappoint Mamma and
Papa) she was the sole heiress, whatever that meant. That
was a remark she had heard Peck make to her governess.

At least Miss Elizabeth Mansfield, a Philadelphian with
excellent references, was much more likable than Miss
Miller had been. At once she had asked if Miss Christabel
might call her Lizzie, it would make friendship with the
withdrawn child easier. Mamma had thought the intimacy
might affect Chrissie's obedience; but Papa had said bluffly
that it was a splendid idea, and anyway a bit of disobedience would be a healthy sign.

There was no more talk of an English governess.

That fall, when they all moved back to Camberwell House from Long Island, it was arranged that Chrissie should go to dancing classes at Mr. Bilston's Academy, as much to have the company of other children as to equip her for the future. She proved to have a light pair of feet, but she hated most of the children because they taunted her about Peck. Lizzie, with her friendly smile, they could understand since they all had maids or governesses themselves. But a bodyguard! Who did Christabel Spencer think she was, a duchess?

"That's what I am to be one day," she said haughtily, with something of her old spirit. "My father says so."

That did not add to her popularity. Chrissie Spencer was to marry a duke. None of them was good enough for her. They made her dancing and music classes a misery. What was wrong with marrying a duke? It was what Papa wanted her to do, and Papa always knew what was best for her. Anyway, she wouldn't have married any of those horrible American boys even if it meant she was to grow old like Aunt Mary Ellen, petulant, discontented and overdressed.

Mary Ellen thought the duke idea was high-flown nonsense, too, and if she had any say in the matter, her darling child would never leave American shores. Boy, who now smelled constantly of rum and was usually in a flushed and benign state, said that he was all for a sprig of the nobility himself. But it would need to be English rather than European. The English aristocracy were the only people who really knew how to live with style and panache. Look at Lord Byron.

"And look at what happened to his wife," retorted Mary Ellen, who, after listening to Boy discoursing on his favorite literary subject for several years, knew almost as much as he did about the controversial poet. "I won't have that sort of thing happening to my girl."

"She ain't your girl, sis. And a bit of rough and tumble wouldn't do her any harm. She's getting to be a prig. That tame gorilla at her heels doesn't help."

"He isn't at her heels when he comes here. He's down in the kitchen pinching that lazy Sue."

Boy roared with laughter.

"Don't tell Harry. He might find out the man's human and, therefore, vulnerable. He doesn't like vulnerability in anyone around Chrissie."

"I suppose you can't blame him, after what happened. Nor Louisa, either. She's just gone frozen. No wonder she doesn't have another child. It would be like Lot's wife giving birth after she'd been turned into a pillar of salt. A man like Harry Spencer is destructive, I don't care what you say. Poor Louisa. Poor Chrissie, too. But at least we can do things for Chrissie."

If Chrissie found visits to Eighth Street and red-cheeked, jolly Aunt Mary Ellen comforting and enlivening (with the rough bear hugs and the energetic games, she even found herself being an ordinary noisy little girl again), Louisa, to her surprise, was most relaxed with the old lady living in the Bowery. That worn face, carved with a lifetime's anxiety and sorrows, understood more completely than anyone else her fear and desolation.

She had lost her cherished son, all the more beloved because of his delicacy, in a terrible way. But even more than her loss she was obsessed by the fact that the two culprits, Lily and Danny (not to mention their minions who had performed the actual kidnapping), were still at large.

At any time they might reappear. It was no use for Harry to assure her that they wouldn't dare to set foot within a thousand miles of New York. She could never be convinced that the man she saw loitering across the road, cap pulled down over his face, or the woman who brushed by in the new Lord & Taylor's store which everyone was visiting was not Danny or Lily. Dogging her footsteps. Waiting for another opportunity to strike at Harry through his remaining child.

Harry, plunging into bigger and more ambitious schemes, seemed able to forget the tragedy. She was haunted by it every day and night. Grandma Spencer, sitting like a thin, weather-beaten gargoyle beside her small fire, made the only tolerable comments. Even though they were as harsh as winter weather.

"Sorrow doesn't kill. It makes you strong. You'll be a strong woman, lass. It doesn't seem so now, but you'll grow to it."

"I only want to be weak," said Louisa. "I want to cry forever. But I can't cry at all. I just do nothing. Harry tries to be patient with me"—that big bed at night when she turned from him so often, so compulsively—"but Chrissie just goes away. She prefers to spend her time with Lizzie or Mary Ellen. She associates me with Henry not being here, and it freezes her up. It's terrible, Grandma Spencer."

"It will pass, lass. You'll have another boy, and he'll be four rolled into one, like Harry is."

"Not—" Louisa bit her tongue. Not like Harry, she had been going to say. Not another ambitious, powerful man who brought disaster in his wake and then was so well meaning but so clumsy in his attempt to comfort. So patient, too, for an impatient man. She should be grateful. And loving. But she must have more time.

"Life has to go on," said Grandma Spencer. "So somebody said. I don't know on what grounds. Must have been somebody who hadn't lost a son. All the same, you're alive, and you've got a great deal, and I don't like self-pity. What are you doing now you've come back to New York? Can't spend the winter idle."

"Far from it. We have a pile of invitations. Harry says most of them must be accepted. And we'll have to give parties in return. It's perfectly true, people do dislike mourning."

"And quite right. You go and buy yourself some fine dresses, and start living again. There's such a thing as being a victim, and there's such a thing as being a fighter. I was a fighter, and so was Harry's father, and Harry himself. Harry don't want a wife who can't face a big grief. It's time you showed him you're not that sort."

Harry was delighted when the boxes began arriving from Arnold Constable's and Lord & Taylor's.

"Hey, you'll be ruining me, love. What's this? A feather boa? You're going to look like a bird of paradise."

"Not me. You're thinking of Mary Ellen."

Harry grimaced. "Did I say the wrong thing? Well, then, a very charming little wren. No, a bluebird. What's this for, Lou?"

"The van Ruyslers' at home. You haven't forgotten?"

"I had, but I'll fix that. I only have to put off the governor of New York State."

"Harry!"

"Only joking, love. But I would put him off, I promise."

"Your mother talked to me."

"She didn't bully you?"

"Yes." Louisa bent her head. "But I needed it. I didn't mind. Harry"—she was suddenly against his breast—"could we—do you think God would remember us and let us have another son?"

"If only Mr. Bell could get His telephone number—I promise you, I could persuade Him. Don't underestimate my persuasiveness." Harry's hand was ruffling her hair hard. He held her so close her bones hurt. "Or let's just have faith, shall we, love?"

At the van Ruyslers' Louisa met Cornelius Peterson again.

He had written to her after Henry's death, a thoughtful, sensitive letter that she had been unable to answer. She had shied away from all real understanding because it reduced her self-control to nothing. Once he had called and left his card. Dobson had told her about it, but again she had neglected to do anything. She had thought she had forgotten his face. Or had encouraged herself to do so.

But now he was standing beside her, and a sensation of pain so acute shot through her that she swayed.

"What's the matter, Mrs. Spencer?" he asked in alarm.

She saw a chair and sat in it gratefully.

"I'm sorry. The last time we met, I was overcome by the heat. It was at the Hotel Atlantic, wasn't it? The night my little boy was kidnapped."

"Mrs. Spencer, I've so wanted to tell you how deeply I sympathized with you."

"Thank you," said Louisa. "Let's not talk about it. I made a pact with myself only last week to start living again. I've been upsetting my husband and my daughter." She rattled on, hardly aware of what she was saying. "You've never met my daughter, have you? You must come to tea and meet her. She's going to be rather a beauty, I'm afraid."

"Afraid?"

"Harry's determined to make her an heiress. Money and beauty. That's a formidable combination."

"Which I'm sure your daughter will be equal to. Do ask me to tea, Mrs. Spencer."

"Yes, I will."

She had to leave him because she was crying. At last the drought was over, and the tears had come. She sat in the powder room and mopped at her tears with Mrs. van Ruysler's beautiful soft monogrammed towels and crept out what seemed hours later to find Harry.

"Take me home," she whispered. "But I'm all right. Really I am. I just want us to be alone."

It was no use, though. She lay in Harry's arms and saw the long, sensitive, intelligent face of Cornelius Peterson. That was what had brought her back to life, not Harry's overcareful lovemaking, the grunts and breathy whispers with which he restrained himself. He was hoping that to-night they would conceive another son. She had thought that that was her wish, too, but instead, she was thinking that tomorrow, no, Friday, when Serenity took Chrissie to

Mary Ellen's, she would ask Cornelius Peterson to tea. She would say that her sister was ill and had been asking for Chrissie, who was her dearly loved niece. Perhaps Cornelius wouldn't mind that she was alone. She had the greatest desire to talk to him quietly and privately. She thought that he would make a good and sympathetic friend. There was utterly no question of their friendship being anything more, even though she kept remembering his face too vividly.

She had the fire lit in the green drawing room and instructed Bridget to bring tea in there. Although it was a cloudy afternoon bringing early dusk, she didn't want the lamps lit. She preferred the firelight and the etched shapes of the trees in the park. She was almost getting over her fear of the park. One day she would love it again, and love this house, too. Houses were like people; they acquired atmosphere only after deeply emotional events had happened in them. She ran her fingers over her face, thinking that one day it would look like Grandma Spencer's, a lived-in face. In the same way the wallpaper would grow shabby, the carpets worn; people (unborn yet) would say that that was the room where the little boy who had been tragically kidnapped had slept, there was the dining room where Louisa Spencer had held her fashionable dinner parties and the drawing room where she had once taken tea with a good-looking and sympathetic young architect, that was the famous yellow marble staircase which Christabel Spencer, daughter of the millionaire Harry Spencer, had come down in her bridal gown.

Yet her tea with Cornelius Peterson was not a success. She was too tense, and he too stiff. Conversation was formal and artificial. They discussed pictures, books, the opera, new designs for buildings, Louisa apologized for Chrissie's absence and wished she hadn't arranged it, for the child might have reduced the tension. She rang for more tea, since Mr. Peterson was complimentary about it and seemed very thirsty, then for the lamps to be lit. She explained that she didn't care for the modern electricity in her drawing room. If the conversation was difficult, at least he was in no hurry to leave. Finally she suggested that he wait until Serenity returned with Chrissie, which would be at any moment. Harry, too, would be home shortly. Perhaps he would stay on and have a drink before dinner. That was when she and Harry spent an hour with their daughter. It was a family hour, certainly, but he would be very welcome.

Mr. Peterson surprised her by standing up abruptly.

"Could I make a suggestion, Mrs. Spencer? Could we take a turn in the park before it's quite dark?"

He seemed to be watching her closely as she turned suddenly fearful eyes to the darkening landscape.

"Why—if you would like it."

"I would."

"I will have to put on outdoor things."

"Yes, wrap up well. It's getting chilly in the evenings."

"I won't be more than five minutes."

"There's plenty of time."

In her bedroom she put on her fur-trimmed toque and fur-collared coat. She changed her shoes to buttoned boots and chose a muff instead of gloves. Her haste brought animation to her face. A quick glimpse in the mirror showed her that she looked a great deal more alive, as if this flurry of activity had made her shed her stiff armor of uncertainty and shyness. A married lady entertaining a personable young man to tea, then walking with him in the park in the dusk. It was not entirely discreet, and the servants were bound to talk, but oh, God, wasn't it time she shook herself out of that deadly negative state that had been making her wither up? Harry would approve. He would be delighted with her returning vivacity.

When they had walked for some time in silence, Louisa said, "How did you know I was afraid of the park?"

"I saw how you looked. It's always outside your window, isn't it?"

"I used to love it."

"You will again. It's innocent. It's only the people who aren't. And there aren't so many bad ones as you think."

"I know. I just so hope——"

"What? Tell me."

"That my baby didn't suffer too much. He was such a tender little boy, so easily hurt."

She wasn't going to cry again, as she had the other night. Cornelius Peterson, with his understanding, seemed to provoke this weakness in her. But he couldn't know the relief of at last speaking those words, of expressing the nightmare that had haunted her for so long.

"I don't think he did. Take your hand out of that muff."

When she did so, he held it in a firm, warm grip, and the painful ache in her throat subsided. The trees rustled, and they stirred dead leaves with their feet. Children playing with hoops shouted. A few stars had come out. The evening was clear and frosty.

"Thank you for being so sympathetic, Cornelius—may I call you Cornelius?"

"I hoped you would."

"I'm Louisa. Harry calls me Lou."

"I will call you Louisa."

She nodded, smiling. It was nice that he should be different, like sharing a pleasant secret.

"Do you want to be rich, Cornelius?"

"No, not particularly."

"Harry does. Always. No matter what it entails. I think if you had once asked him, would he put his children in danger because of his riches, he would still say he must have wealth. It's a compulsion. He hasn't only been dreadfully poor, he's inherited poverty. I think his ancestors speak through him and remind him of their misery. One has to understand that. But to me, too much wealth seems as bad as poverty. After what has happened, I will always be afraid of it, and I dread it for Chrissie."

"My family has never been either rich or poor. I don't

have anything driving me, which I believe most people think is a lack in a man. I suppose I could be a lot more successful if I worked harder. But I enjoy other things as well as my work."

"What things?"

"Reading. Music. Contemplating. Walking like this on a frosty night."

"Yes," said Louisa eagerly. "That's how it should be. Sometimes I think if you opened my husband's head, you would find it full of neat rows of figures, amounting to thousands and thousands of dollars. No, perhaps that isn't fair. There are other things, too. He adores Chrissie." She paused a moment. "And me, I suppose."

"I'm sure of that."

"What? That he adores me?"

"How could he fail to?"

Louisa bent her head, kicking at drifts of dead leaves.

"We'll have another child, if we can," she said in a low voice.

"I'm sure that's the best thing for you."

"Do you?"

For the first time they were looking fully at each other. She had no idea what showed in her eyes, but she saw something disturbing in his: loneliness, longing, a deep sympathy.

"I think it's the only answer," he said, after what seemed a very long pause.

The compulsion to talk frankly, to confess, came over her again.

"I didn't marry Harry because I loved him. It was for my family. My father drank too much and had ruined us, and my mother was delicate and couldn't stand the shame. She had so much wanted a good future for my sister and me. My brother has a lame foot, and has always been acutely sensitive about it. Even then he had more or less removed himself from life. It was all an enormous problem."

"Which you took on your shoulders?"

"No, Harry took it on his. He's been wonderful. Fair and generous, and all that I could have expected. It was only that I was young and romantic. I had wanted to marry for love. It's no use people saying marriages of convenience can be perfect," she burst out vehemently, "because I don't believe it."

"What marriage is perfect?"

"I don't know. All the same, I guess mine is as good as any." She pressed her hands to her mouth. "How can I be talking to you like this? You've been too understanding, and I've let myself run away. Oh, dear. I have never done this to anyone before."

"Then it was time, wasn't it?"

"The right person, the right place. Yes, I suppose it was time. But I shouldn't have done it. Do forgive me. My marriage is really very happy, and now it's got awfully late. We must hurry."

"What are you running away from all at once? Me?"

Again their eyes were drawn together in a long gaze.

"Yes, it might be you," Louisa said in a whisper. "It might be—oh, do let's go. You can meet Chrissie, and then I really think—"

"I ought to leave? Perhaps you're right. Though I don't know, after this, how I'm ever going to think so."

"Oh, come on," Louisa said, taking his arm and hurrying along the path.

"Louisa, you are a beautiful woman."

"Me! Oh, no, my looks are much too quiet. Compared with—"

"I don't compare them with anybody else. You have a lovely face; it's sensitive, gentle, full of integrity. Too much integrity."

"For what?"

"For my secret hopes."

"No, Cornelius," she said breathlessly, "don't start this kind of conversation."

"Then why did you ask me to tea today?"

"Because—I suppose I thought I could talk to you. As I've proved all too well."

"But we can meet again?"

"Oh—I don't know."

"Of course we can. You look so much better already. Harry should be thanking me."

"He won't if I'm not home within the next ten minutes."

"But we can walk here again? Next Friday, when Chrissie goes to your sister's?"

"On Fridays Chrissie is a van Leyden," Louisa said feverishly. "Mary Ellen insists that she be that at least once a week. She would like it to be much more, to combat the Spencer influence."

"And what is she actually? A Spencer or a van Leyden?"

"She was completely a Spencer at first. Full of life. A spoiled, willful, lively little girl. But after Henry—after the shock of that—we tried to protect her, but one simply doesn't know how much a child senses and absorbs. Anyway, since then, she has been quite different. Quiet and secretive and suspicious. Like me, I'm afraid. But she'll grow out of it. The new governess, Lizzie, is very good, and now that she goes to dancing school she sees more children. She says she doesn't like other children, but that's because she has become accustomed to being the only one. And her father does spoil her and make her too self-important. I've got terrible fears that she'll do exactly as he wants and end up by marrying one of those cold English dukes."

"Cold?"

"I always think of them as being cold and correct and rather stupid. Quite wrong for my little girl. She had such a lot of spirit. It will come back, won't it?"

"Since she's only seven years old, I should think it more than probable."

"Yes. She's going to be so pretty, too. Cornelius, it's getting dark."

"Take my arm. You're nearly home."

Harry met them at the door. He had been watching for them, he said. Bridget had told him they had gone out.

"Cornelius was helping me to get over my silly fear of the park," Louisa said breathlessly.

"Splendid," said Harry warmly. "Thank you, my dear fellow. That's just what Lou needed. I can see she looks a great deal better already."

Louisa put her hands to her flushed cheeks. "That's only because we've been hurrying. We walked too far. Is Chrissie home?"

"Some time ago, I believe. You'll have a drink with us, Cornelius? I wish you would, because I'd like to talk to you about a development scheme I have for a site in Brooklyn. Now that the bridge is being built it's going to become a very valuable part of the city. But, Lou, get Chrissie down first. Cornelius and I can talk later."

"Yes, Harry," Louisa murmured. At the door she paused to look back in some incredulity. Hadn't Harry noticed anything, her flushed cheeks and excited manner or Cornelius' possessive hand on her arm? Because it had been distinctly, if unconsciously, possessive.

But, no. Harry was only glad that his wife seemed brighter and happier, and it was fortunate that her companion was one of his own business associates, so that he could talk about his new Brooklyn scheme to his heart's content. She paused on the stairs to think again. Had Harry really cared, cared agonizingly, about Henry's death? Or was it just a small tragedy incidental to the more important matters in his life? Mind you, had it been Chrissie. . . . Although even Chrissie might have come second to his bricks and mortar, his hunger for more land, more buildings, more affluence.

Or was she misjudging him because suddenly she wanted to?

When she came downstairs again, holding Chrissie's hand and telling her to curtsy nicely to the gentleman whom she was about to meet, she heard Harry saying to

Cornelius, "I've just bought a picture. A Rubens. That Dutch fellow. Paints pink-fleshed women. Can't let those railroad millionaires grab all the old masters. I intend to have a collection that will be talked about."

"Then you must try to buy a Vermeer," said Cornelius so politely that only she, who felt she knew him so well already, could detect the satire.

"Vermeer?"

"He's much the best Dutch old master to my way of thinking. And extremely rare."

"Is that so? Has Vanderbilt one? Or Astor?"

"I doubt it."

"Ha! I shall make a memorandum."

"Neither has either of them a van Leyden wife."

Louisa thought she had misheard Cornelius' careful quiet words, but apparently she had not, for Harry gave his great roar of laughter.

"I can see that you're a preceptive man. Yes, I'm taking great care in furnishing my house. But I can tell you my wife will always be my most loved treasure."

Chapter 12

Louisa sat at her charming small French writing desk and wrote slowly, with many pauses for thought.

MY DEAR CORNELIUS,

I really feel that I owe you an apology for my outburst in the park yesterday. It was quite unintended and must have been embarrassing for you. I want to thank you for being so understanding. And

I would like you to know that today my heart feels lighter, as if that long nightmare is at last receding.

It is true that I have been unable to talk to anybody else, even my husband. But, poor Cornelius, why did I choose to burden you with my troubles? I really do apologize.

Then came the longest pause of all. Louisa chewed at the end of her pen, fiddled with the pretty porcelain inkstand (one of Harry's more imaginative presents), began to write, then stopped again.

She had been going to write, "However, all things considered, perhaps it is better we do not meet privately again."

Impulsively she scratched out the word she had written, "however"—a silly indefinite word. Life must be definite; the chance of happiness must not be evaded.

You have already made me much less nervous about walking in Central Park; indeed I actually ventured out alone today, although only for a short time. So I suggest that our walks on Friday begin at the tea pavilion. Shall we meet there at 4:30? There is no need to answer this letter, unless some business has come along to interfere with your plans. I will understand completely if this is so.

Louisa sat back, read the letter through and decided not to alter a word. She had made it clear that although she, as a married woman, was willing to make a comparatively innocent assignation, she was prepared for him to have doubts about the discretion of it.

Also, it was better that he did not call too frequently at Camberwell House when Harry was not at home. She knew already that their friendship was going to be too valuable and too precious to have it spoiled by gossip.

Several of her friends, she suspected, had vague pleasant liaisons. They had husbands absorbed in business and in making money, as Harry was. A sensible husband,

Harriet Littlebrown had once said to Louisa, would turn a blind eye on a mild indiscretion if it kept his wife happy and contented.

All the same, Louisa intended to behave with the greatest circumspection. She would take this letter and mail it herself.

Do come, Cornelius, she was saying under her breath, as she walked briskly to the nearest mailbox. Do come!

Harry usually breakfasted with Louisa. He quickly glanced over the morning papers, had several cups of coffee and the English muffins which Cook made specially for him. Dripping in butter and maple syrup, the hot muffins melted in his mouth. He frequently apologized to Louisa for his appetite. Memories of childhood hunger had never quite left him. But this kind of indulgence put weight on his already-burly figure. He was a solid, healthy man, almost always good-tempered at breakfast, but sometimes a little too hearty in his appetite for Louisa's taste.

She watched him this Friday morning buttering the muffins, picking up the pieces in his thick, active fingers and popping them into his mouth with relish. She wished he would finish breakfast quickly. Her own appetite had completely left her.

"Not eating, Lou?" he asked.

He had appeared to be absorbed in the newspaper. But she ought to know by now that he never missed anything. Did he notice, for instance, that her hand had trembled slightly as she had poured the coffee? And had there been a hint of hope in his voice as if he thought she might be pregnant? His attentions had been too assiduous lately.

"I have Mary Ellen coming to morning chocolate. I can't eat two meals so close together."

"She's coming for Chrissie?"

"Yes, she had some shopping to do. She asked to have Chrissie for luncheon. I saw no reason to refuse since she'll have finished her morning lessons by then."

"Don't you sometimes think your sister has Chrissie too much?"

"Only on Fridays, Harry."

"That's often enough, for a woman like her. She smothers a child with that strong personality of hers."

"Chrissie is very fond of her."

"That's what I mean. I don't want Chrissie becoming a van Leyden."

Louisa frowned, not sure whether her irritation was caused by the fleck of maple syrup gleaming on Harry's beard or by his implied criticism.

"Is that a fault?"

"Apart from you, my love, I regard your family as slightly macabre. Now I don't intend to apologize for that remark."

Louisa continued to frown, though for another reason.

"I don't neglect Chrissie, Harry. It's only that for a long time I haven't been the brightest company for her. I've wanted her to be with gayer people."

Harry got up and came around to drop a kiss on the top of her head.

"I know, love. I'm sorry I said that. But I do think your sister is a bit of a vampire."

"It's only because she won't flatter you by liking you."

"Oh. Is that what it is?" Harry gave his sudden jolly laugh. "Well, I'm not going to lose sleep over that. By the way, that nice young fellow Peterson seemed to put you in better spirits."

Louisa bent her head, glad that Harry stood behind her, for she could feel the warmth in her cheeks.

"It was only that I was so relieved to get over that stupid fear I had of walking in the park."

"You didn't tell me it had bothered you so much."

"No. I was ashamed of it. And you have so many things on your mind."

"Not too many to have time for my wife, I hope."

"You're much too good to me."

"But you get a little lonely, eh? Then you must get

young Peterson to give you his company occasionally."
He was leaving the room. The remark had been made
over his shoulder. "By the way, just because Mary Ellen
is coming for Chrissie, don't think she can dispense with
Peck. Not that I don't believe your sister would be capable of dealing with several bandits, single-handed."

Young Peterson's company. Had Harry meant that?
Had he guessed something? Or was he joking?

She hastily tried to concentrate on his last instructions.

"Harry, how much longer must we go on having Peck?
I know Chrissie hates him always being there. The other
children tease her about it."

"She'll have to put up with that. Peck remains."

"But for how long?"

"Until she's grown up, I'm taking no risks."

"All those years!" Louisa exclaimed.

"All those years. Until she comes out and we take her
to Europe."

Cornelius was waiting in the tea pavilion. He was holding a punch of white violets, which he tucked into her
muff.

Her gratification was out of all proportion to the modest gift.

"Violets in November!"

"Hothouse. I'm afraid they don't have much perfume."

"They're lovely. I'll put them in my favorite bowl when
I get home."

The way his smile transformed his serious face was utterly charming to her.

"I'd give you a Christmas tree in June if you wanted it.
I'm so glad you came this afternoon."

"Of course I came. It was I who asked you."

"Only because I hadn't managed to do so first."

"No," said Louisa, "because, admit it, you have principles. You hesitated. I did, too. But somehow"— she threw
out her hands—"whoever invented principles anyway?"

"Not us. And we aren't going to talk about them this

afternoon. What shall we do? Have tea? Catch squirrels? Bowl hoops?"

"Everything. I'm suddenly greedy. I feel so alive."

Cornelius touched her cheek lightly with his forefinger.

"You don't need to tell me. It shows. Let's walk. Let's find the most unoccupied part of the park. If I could have my way, I'd like a radius of fifty miles without people around us."

Louisa felt a slight tremble go over her body. For all her flippant talk of principles, she didn't think she had meant things to move so quickly.

"Fifty miles is rather a lot. No people at all?"

"I expect you would want your family."

"Harry and Chrissie? Yes, I expect I would."

He had immediately sensed her change of mood and was formal again. Which was just as well. Though a pity. . . .

"Miss Christabel, you is a bad girl," said Serenity severely.

Chrissie looked at the decapitated doll. The china head had come off in her hands. She hadn't meant it to. She had only picked restlessly at the glue stuck to the rather nasty kid body of the doll until the head had separated itself.

"Is that how you intend to treat your own chillun, Miss Christabel?" came Serenity's remorseless voice.

"Probably," said Chrissie airily. "So they won't be spoiled. I'm not spoiled. Mamma neglects me rather than spoils me."

"Now you is sounding like a parrot. I guess Miss Mary Ellen put that idea in your head."

"No," said Chrissie. "Aunt Mary Ellen only said if I were her daughter, she would make sure to be home when I was."

"Now, you can't mind your Mamma having social occasions of her own. Aren't you happy that she's stopped being sad about Master Henry? I just believe you want all the attention. From me, from Lizzie, from your Papa and Mamma. You is a greedy girl. But never mind. Serenity loves you. Come sit on my lap. Mamma'll be home in no time at all."

It wasn't just that Mamma wasn't home when she returned from visiting Aunt Mary Ellen and Uncle Boy; it was that even when she was there, she was vague and far-off, not really listening to the things Chrissie had to tell her, but just sitting quietly, giving little smiles into the distance.

The servants were saying funny things like, "Mark my words, there's a little stranger coming," but a little stranger was the last thing Chrissie wanted. That would be another crying, peevish baby like Henry who took up all of Mamma's time. And although Papa had assured her that he would love her best, no matter what happened, how could you *know*? Besides, she wanted to be loved best by everybody, not just by Papa and Aunt Mary Ellen with her bear hugs and moist kisses.

She was pretty enough, she knew that. Everyone said, "My, what a pretty little girl," and the abominable boys at dancing school whispered, "Make way! Here comes the beautiful Miss Spencer."

They didn't like her because she was different. She had two arms and two legs and all that the same as they did, but she was always surrounded by watchers. Lizzie, Serenity, that stiff, stupid Peck who scarcely ever spoke, but who was "very quick on the draw," whatever that meant. It was as if she were a rare flower in a hothouse and no one could touch her. She hated it and even planned to run away, but gave up the idea when she remembered that at the end of the day it would get dark and bad men would be lurking.

So she hung about the house waiting for Mamma, although nowadays Mamma always seemed to be in a hurry.

"Chrissie, my darling, what are you doing here alone? Where's Lizzie?"

"I wanted to see you. May I come up to your bed-room?"

"Is there something you want to talk about? Something bothering you?"

"No."

"Then I haven't much time. I stayed out rather long, and Papa and I are going to the Levines for dinner. They live way down Park Avenue. But just for a few min-utes—"

"Can't I watch you dress, Mamma?"

Mamma suddenly swooped and kissed her. She smelled delicious. She had white violets tucked in her muff. Her cheeks were pink.

"Very well. If you promise not to fiddle with things. What shall I wear? You can tell me."

While Mamma took a bath, Chrissie pondered over the rows of gowns in the wardrobe. It was like a dress shop.

"Well, have you decided?" called Mamma.

"I think the pink with the shiny beads."

"No, that's a ball gown, darling. The Levines are very stuffy, very respectable. Old Mrs. Levine wears nothing but black velvet and holds her ancient head on with chokers of pearls. She's a terrible old witch."

"Then why do you go to visit her?"

"Because she owns half of Park Avenue, and that, as Papa says, is something to be respected. No one ever re-fuses her invitations. No one."

"Couldn't you be the first?" said Chrissie, fiddling with the gold-topped bottles on Mamma's dressing table.

"I don't think so. Papa wouldn't care for that."

"Someone has to be the first to do new things," said Chrissie, turning the top off a bottle and spilling some of its precious contents. The smell was lovely, but Mamma was cross.

"Chrissie, I told you not to fiddle! Sit down and be quiet. And you didn't find me a dress. I think it had better be the green lace. That's sober enough for Madame Le-vine's taste."

"Will I have as many dresses when I grow up?" Chrissie asked.

"A great many more, I should think. According to your Papa, you are going to be the best-dressed young lady in Europe, if not the world."

"Oh," said Chrissie.

"You don't sound very pleased."

"I expect I will get rather tired, always changing my clothes."

"Wait till you grow up. You mightn't find it such a chore. Especially if there's a young man you want to impress."

"What's impress?"

"Oh, to make him notice you particularly."

"I shall never want to do that," said Chrissie emphatically. "Those horrid boys at dancing school. I'm sick and tired of them." She sounded just like Mary Ellen. "I'll be glad when I'm as old as you and men don't notice me anymore."

"I'm thirty," said Mamma, giving a faint wry smile.

"That's what I mean," said Chrissie kindly.

"And it sounds as if you've been listening to Aunt Mary Ellen too much."

"It's only polite to listen when she talks to me, Mamma. And she has lots of time. She says it's lucky for me she doesn't live a gay butterfly life."

"Chrissie," said Mamma sharply, "you're becoming a prig."

"What's that?"

"Oh—never mind. Can you button me up? Then I won't need to ring for Ada."

Louisa sat silently at the heavily laden table in the Levines' mansion. This was one of the last strongholds Harry had wanted to conquer, and at last he had done so, although now she was not sure whether it was due to her influence as his wife or to his own growing importance. What was it Chrissie had said? "Someone has to be the first to do new things." Let her be generous and give Harry credit for achieving this new thing tonight. But Chrissie was getting too precocious altogether, and one wasn't helping her by the divided life one was now leading. So thirty was old, was it? Chrissie was wrong about that. It was only the beginning of life.

And it wouldn't be doing a new thing to run away with one's lover. More and more adventurous women, unwilling to submit to an unhappy marriage, were doing that. They had to give up society, of course. But that, to her, was entirely irrelevant.

"Mrs. Spencer," boomed Mrs. Levine in the voice that expected instant and reverent attention, "I asked if you enjoyed the play?"

The play? Louisa saw Harry looking at her across the table, not hiding his surprise at her woolgathering. He was not used to his wife being anything but an impeccable guest, courteous, practiced at small talk, attractive in her quiet, unostentatious way.

"Oh, yes, indeed, Mrs. Levine. You mean *The School for Scandal?*"

"That was the one we were discussing," said Mrs. Levine dismissively, registering a black mark against the inattentive Mrs. Harry Spencer and returning her attention to the absorbing business of consuming peaches in brandy shipped especially to her from Messrs. Fortnum and Mason in London.

Louisa's appetite had vanished. The now-familiar flutter was in her throat, preventing her from swallowing. Had the query about the play, the name of the play itself, been intended as a double-edged remark? Had anyone seen her meeting Cornelius? They had been so careful, arranging all kinds of out-of-way places as their rendezvous. But eventually there was bound to be a catastrophe.

She pulled herself together and made herself talk intelligently for the rest of the evening. She dutifully made admiring sounds about the Levine collection of paintings, tapestries, marble statuary, gilt and rococo furniture, Chinese pagoda birdcages and the rest. It was all too much and in marvelous bad taste. She had a fearful moment of thinking that Harry was envying it, when he only intended to whisper in her ear, "The old lady matches her furniture, don't you think? Overstuffed. When can we go?"

But now Louisa was conscientious.

"After my *faux pas* at dinner—can you endure another half hour?"

He pressed her arm in a gesture of loving and accustomed possession. She felt traitorous and miserable. She had to blink back tears. She thought that Mrs. Levine, with those rather terrible hooded eyes, was looking at her and reading all her thoughts, but it appeared that the old lady was nodding asleep, her head held up by the tight ropes of pearls around her throat.

As a consequence, all the guests began to depart. Apparently this was the usual behavior of their hostess. Handing Louisa into the carriage, Harry said, "When I own Park Avenue, or Madison or Fifth or even Lexington, I guess I'll not worry about falling asleep at dinner, too. Will you mind, love?"

But she wouldn't be there to see that sight of a somnolent husband if Cornelius, gentle, sensitive, loving, but dreadfully persistent, had his way. Strange. Sad. Harry was a comfortable and friendly companion. She had grown so used to looking across a crowded noisy room and seeing his solid, well-groomed figure. He was getting a look of distinction. She was really rather proud of him.

But he had never never succeeded in giving her that stab of wild joy and elation which the sight of Cornelius, dark and quiet and elegant, could do. His caresses and his lovemaking had become familiar and predictable and perfectly tolerable. Harry had never shown any disappointment in her, and until recently she had not realized that he might have had reason to do so. She could understand such a thing now that her imagination conjured up the ecstasy of lying in Cornelius' arms. Their few kisses (the opportunities for such embraces were so limited) had left her trembling for minutes afterwards.

She had had no idea that she could be so sensual and was vaguely shocked by her feelings. Her desire to spend a night, or many nights, with Cornelius obsessed her. But the guilt and furtiveness of taking a lover were not for her, or for Cornelius either.

If only—the refrain kept running through her head—she had been allowed to marry for love.

"No, I don't suppose I will mind too much," she said, at last answering Harry's question.

"You won't even notice if you go on getting as absent-minded as you were tonight. What were you thinking of?"

"Just daydreaming, I guess. They were all such dull people." Louisa had to whip up a little indignation to divert his attention from her unusual lapse in manners. "It's fine for you men, you sit over your brandy and cigars and talk business, which interests all of you passionately, but I can't get passionate listening to those women in the drawing room discussing their new dressmaker."

"I suppose I must be glad you prefer the company of the male sex." Harry's head was against her shoulder. His deep voice rumbled in her ear.

"Yes, you must," Louisa murmured, and knew that it would be some time before she would be allowed to sleep tonight. There would be the hugs, the smothering kisses, the heavy limbs wrapping around hers. And the resentment growing in her, hotter and less controllable as the stark facts presented themselves to her logical mind.

Either she lived with Harry as his wife or she left him. She was too honest for there to be any middle way.

Chapter 13

━━━━━━━━━━━━━━━━━━━━━━━━━━━━━━━━━

They had begun to talk endlessly about ways and means. At least Cornelius talked and she listened hypnotically. They would move to San Francisco, a beautiful city, which Louisa would love. When Harry had divorced her, as of course he would, they would marry and begin a new life. How could they contemplate a life that was not spent together? Harry might even be gentlemanly enough to allow her to divorce him, but this Louisa stubbornly refused to contemplate. The blame would be hers. She would insist on taking it.

Undoubtedly Harry would marry again, but in the interval Mary Ellen would be only too glad to move into Camberwell House and take charge of Chrissie. Her affection for the child would easily outweigh her dislike of Harry.

Louisa always wept when Chrissie was discussed. That was when she could hardly listen to Cornelius' persuasive words.

"But you have to choose, dearest. Her or us."

"She's so little still."

"She's growing every day. Before you know it, she'll be having her coming out, and then she'll be off to Europe and that illustrious marriage her father has planned for her. Come, dearest, you know Harry always carries out his plans. And this one is absolutely top of the agenda."

"It's true that Chrissie has always been more her father's child than mine. Henry was mine."

Cornelius touched the lines of pain on her forehead, saying nothing.

"All the same—couldn't we wait?" Ten years while their love dried up, soured by deprivation? She read the knowledge in his eyes.

"I want children, too," said the quiet voice that was as implacable in its own way as Harry's much louder, aggressive one.

"Then perhaps you should marry someone else."

"Louisa, Louisa!"

"Oh, I know!" she cried, and the clump of young fir trees hid their anguished embrace from passersby.

She practiced writing letters to Harry and tore them up one by one. Coward! At least he deserved to be told to his face.

Time was moving inexorably. It was early spring, and Harry was talking of dates for moving to Long Island.

"Not too early," Louisa said. "Your mother's had that nasty attack of bronchitis. I don't like leaving her. She looks so frail." This was true. The old lady in the Bowery was skeleton thin, and her luminous eyes seemed to look right into Louisa's skull, reading its secret.

"That's thoughtful of you, love, but Ma is saying the same thing about you. Thinks you need some country air."

"I'm as well as can be."

"Are you?"

She couldn't meet his eyes. She had reached the stage lately where it was impossible to allow him to touch her. That was why he was hinting that she needed the freshly blowing spring winds and the quiet of the country. At least she imagined this was so, but how did one know with Harry? He was so shrewd, so aware. His busy brain absorbed everything. There was nothing he didn't know about Chrissie's activities. How could she be sure that he didn't have another Peck following her, observing her walks in the park with Cornelius or their ferry rides on the Hudson or visits to teashops in quiet unfashionable areas?

But she was sure he knew nothing. He was too possessive to keep silent about a thing like the danger of losing his wife. He had bought her, hadn't he? He could be a little miserly about his possessions. He also appeared to love her.

Louisa studied her face in the mirror, trying to decide whether or not its treachery showed. Her lips looked fuller and softer, her eyes brighter. Obviously treachery had a beautifying effect. Or was it just love? She longed and hungered for Cornelius. Her actions now had an inevitability that was almost frightening.

What should she pack, for instance? None of the expensive gowns which Chrissie admired, none of the lovingly bestowed jewelry. Just a simple coat and skirt, a change of underclothing. She would be Louisa van Leyden again, a member of an old but impoverished family, with no possessions of her own.

Harry had arranged their summer move to Long Island for next week. The house was being aired, the furniture uncovered, the curtains hung. It was a little sad, because Louisa loved that big rambling house. She remembered early mornings, full of sun and wind and birdcalls, with nostalgic pleasure. But next week she would be on a train beginning the long overland journey to San Francisco. Cornelius would be holding her hand. She would be crying. That was inevitable.

She didn't dare think of Chrissie. That spoiled child, with her governess, her nurse, her devoted aunt and uncle, her besotted papa. One could not feel pity was needed for Chrissie, who probably would scarcely notice her departure. Even if she did suffer a little, one day she would understand.

The immediate thing was to plan how to get through this evening, when Cornelius had been asked to dinner, a dinner *à trois,* Harry had been told, all unaware of the bombshell that was to be dropped. Or was he unaware?

She had ordered his favorite food and felt more treacherous than ever. She was sure that all the servants were looking at her knowingly, especially the supercilious Dobson, whose self-importance had grown with the mounting fortunes of his employer.

What should she wear? Chrissie, who had been taken out by Lizzie on some long excursion, was not here to choose for her. Something simple and dark, with Harry's lovely pearls. No, not the pearls. Oh, God, what was Harry going to do with all this expensive jewelry, so ungratefully discarded? Give it to another wife?

She had decided on a dark-blue watered silk and was unbuttoning her day dress, wrenching at the tiny buttons with nervous fingers, when there was a flurry outside her door.

"No, Miss Chrissie! Don't disturb your Mamma. It isn't necessary," came Lizzie's voice. "You're making a great fuss over nothing."

But Chrissie was sobbing audibly, and Louisa had barely time to reach the door before she came hurtling in and threw herself into her mother's arms.

"What is it, my darling? Hush! Stop crying and tell Mamma."

It was obvious that Chrissie could not at once overcome her sobs. She was trembling violently, her wet face pressed against Louisa's breast.

"Lizzie, what's happened? Has someone hurt her? Has she been frightened?"

Lizzie's plain freckled face was unusually pale, although she was calm enough.

"We were on the ferry crossing over to Brooklyn, Mrs. Spencer, when Miss Chrissie saw this woman and began screaming."

"Who was the woman?"

"I don't know. I couldn't get Chrissie to say. She just screamed and begged to come home."

"It was Lily, Mamma!" Chrissie cried passionately. "She had come to steal me. I know!"

"Lily," Louisa whispered. "Are you sure?"

"I am, I am! She had on a hat with a feather. She looked at me. Lizzie saw her."

But Lizzie had never known Lily. She could only affirm that the woman had been young and nice-looking and that when Chrissie had begun to scream, she had quickly turned her back and disappeared into the crowd. The gangplank had just been put down, and everyone was disembarking. By the time Lizzie had called Peck, lurking in his unobtrusive way, there was no chance of seeing the woman again. In any case, she had done nothing.

"She looked at me." Chrissie wept. "I was frightened. Mamma, may I sleep with you tonight? Please!"

Louisa hesitated only a few seconds. The train left Grand Central Station at eleven thirty. After the painful evening with Harry she and Cornelius had been going to take a cab and drive to the station. She had vowed to Cornelius that she would have the courage, nothing would stop her.

"My darling, of course you may. I'll tell Serenity to sit with you until I come up to bed. Now dry your tears. Papa won't want to see you looking like that."

Chrissie's hands clung.

"Where are you going now, Mamma?"

"Only to write a note that must be delivered at once. We were having a guest to dinner, but it's better he shouldn't come."

"So you can stay with me?" Chrissie said gratefully.

"So I can stay with you."

She simply scrawled on a piece of paper, "Forgive me! Forgive me!" and then her hand would write no more.

Haunted, guilt-ridden, self-hating, her eyes looked out of the mirror at her. To think she could have so forgotten the innocence and vulnerability of a child. Cornelius was adult and strong; he would recover. So would she, she supposed.

Chrissie was fast asleep, her cheeks rosy, her fears lost

in sleep. Serenity sat beside her, vowing not to stir an inch until the mistress came upstairs. Harry, with calm efficiency, had alerted the police, and a search was being made for a nice-looking woman with the feather in her hat who had crossed on the Brooklyn ferry. But ferries were anonymous conveyances. It was fairly unlikely that she would be traced.

Louisa sat opposite Harry at the dinner table and found that she could not eat.

"I sent a note putting Cornelius off," she said.

"I'm glad you did." Was he looking at her too sharply, or was it only that he, too, was shattered by the return of the nightmare? Although, after reflection, he was sure there was no need for alarm. The woman, if she had been Lily, was probably more frightened than they were. She wouldn't have expected to be seen and recognized.

"She'll be miles from New York by now," Harry said, speaking his thoughts aloud. "Tomorrow you and Chrissie will leave for Long Island. The servants can pack and send your things on after you. I'll come down in the evening."

"Very well, Harry."

"I've given Peck a talking to. Why wasn't he on hand when Chrissie saw this woman?"

"He can't see everything."

"He's supposed to. That's what I pay him for."

After dinner Harry shut himself in the library. Louisa said that she was going upstairs to be with Chrissie. Harry didn't come up later to say good-night. But perhaps he thought they would both be asleep.

The next day Chrissie, having her Mamma all to herself, was in the gayest of moods. She chattered and sang all the way. Long Island was safe. Lily would never find her there. She didn't know the way.

"Truly, you mustn't worry, darling little Mamma." She was gratified that Mamma had been so worried. "We'll all be happy now."

"Yes, my darling. We'll be happy."

"That diabolical woman has slipped out of the net again," Harry said a week later. "There've been reports that she's been seen at various places all the way to the Canadian border. But that's a usual feature of such cases, the police say. By the way, you didn't tell me your friend Cornelius Peterson was leaving New York."

"I didn't know," Louisa murmured.

"He's planning to open an office in San Francisco. Kept rather quiet about it, I must say. Or did he mean to tell us that night you put him off dinner?"

"I expect that was it."

"I hope he does well. I'll always be grateful to him."

Louisa's eyes flew open wide.

"Why?"

"He helped you during the winter, didn't he? Those quiet walks in the park. Got you over your fears."

"You noticed?"

"Watched you come back to life. Admit I was a little afraid you might fall in love with him, but I took the risk."

Don't sound so smug, Louisa screamed inwardly. How could she bear it, his bland, confident possessiveness? Was everyone vulnerable except him?

"I did almost fall in love," she said compulsively.

Harry's eyes were very bright, very blue, very full of pain.

But that revealing look was gone in a flash.

"I know. But it's over now, isn't it? Shall we go down to the beach? I promised to give Chrissie a swimming lesson."

Part Two

Part Two

The Heiress

Chapter 14

Oh, for some freedom! Chrissie thought longingly. She had only been experimenting when she had kissed Ferdie Speight. He was part Spanish and very good-looking, with dewy black eyes and glossy hair. He was also only eighteen, just three months older than she was, and that fact gave them an instant rapport.

She had never known enough people of her own age. Her entire life had been spent being watched and smothered by older people, Mamma and Papa, Aunt Mary Ellen and Uncle Boy, Serenity, Lizzie, that everlasting humorless shadow, Peck, her dancing master, her music mistress, dressmakers, milliners—everyone who cared for the well-being of Miss Christabel Spencer was twice her age.

The few carefully selected young friends she was encouraged to see were stuffy and stupid and nearly, though not quite, as rich as she was.

That was what made Ferdie so interesting. He was poor. Although naturally he didn't intend to remain poor.

He dreamed of discovering and selling a great master-piece, a Raphael, a Titian, a Jan van Eyck. He promised to give Mr. Spencer the first offer, though only if Mr. Spencer allowed him to be friends with his daughter. Chrissie always giggled at this stage and said that Papa would have poor Ferdie drawn and quartered if he suspected them of even holding hands, much less kissing. So couldn't Ferdie offer his great discoveries to Mr. Vanderbilt or Mr. Frick and just tell Papa when he had made enough money?

Though money wasn't important, and, if necessary, Chrissie was quite prepared to run away with a penniless Ferdie.

"Because I can't go on coming into Mr. Solomon's gallery and pretending to like those dreary dark paintings."

"The Claude and the Dürer aren't dreary!"

"I think they are. I believe Papa does, too. He only buys pictures because he wants to impress people with his collection. You know that's true. I would rather grow flowers. And, anyway, what do you know about art; you're only the messenger boy?"

"Mr. Solomon says I have a good eye. How can you be such a Philistine?"

"What's that?"

"It's a word for being ignorant about art," Ferdie said bravely, and Chrissie gave him an indignant slap on the hand, then found she wanted to kiss him again.

Lips were mysteriously soft and alluring. She didn't suppose all men's were, but Ferdie's certainly were, and she thought she might be in love. These surreptitious meetings and snatched kisses were tremendously exciting. It was a game to escape Peck and Lizzie. She slipped out the back door of Miss Foster's millinery shop and met Ferdie at the café on the corner of Sixth Avenue and Forty-fifth Street and sat with him while he had his lunch, a glass of milk and a bun, then slipped back the way she had come, while poor Peck, industriously staring into the distance, thought what a vain creature she was, trying on hats for hours.

She imagined a life surrounded by those dark old Dutch and Italian paintings. It would be as bad as Mamma's life had been, watching Papa put up his higher and higher buildings and being the charming and animated hostess at each official opening.

But it was all a matter of love. Mamma loved Papa in spite of his bricks and mortar, just as she, Chrissie, would love Ferdie in spite of his dull but immensely valuable paintings—just supposing he ever got to owning them. Who could have the good fortune to marry a man with a vocation in which one was genuinely interested? And what would that vocation be? An artist, a great lawyer, an explorer, a priest?

Chrissie thought about it all dreamily. She was so impatient to be grown up because only then would there be a chance of freedom. She thought she might persuade Ferdie to elope with her at her coming-out ball. She had been so good, so painfully good, for so many years, ever since her baby brother had been kidnapped, in fact, that it was time to do something sensational. She felt like a volcano, surging and bubbling and waiting to erupt.

She was almost certain that she loved Ferdie passionately. She might persuade his somber Spanish mother that being a millionaire's daughter didn't make her frivolous and brainless and an unsuitable wife for her son. Though she was very young (as everyone kept telling her) and didn't know that she could be certain of her feelings.

But the dream was pleasant, and it kept her contented until the day Lizzie came into the library and found her halfway up the library steps kissing Ferdie, who had come to hang a picture. They both came scrambling down ignominiously, while Lizzie, her plain freckled face tight with shock, said, "Go up to the schoolroom at once, Miss Christabel."

"The schoolroom!" Chrissie exclaimed, in deep indignation. "I'm eighteen. What do I have to do with a schoolroom?"

"Plenty, if this is your idea of grown-up behavior. I shall have to report this to your father, naturally."

"Lizzie! Don't you dare ruin Ferdie!"

"Chrissie, I can—I mean—I can speak for myself." Scarlet-faced with embarrassment, Ferdie looked about fifteen. It was Chrissie's first disillusionment. She had thought him a man. She made Lizzie the object of her fury.

"Lizzie, if you tell on Ferdie, I will have you dismissed immediately. You know that I can. Papa always listens to me."

"Oh, you're a pair of children. Ferdie had better get on with his work. And the schoolroom for you, Miss Christabel."

One couldn't underestimate Lizzie. She had always known exactly how to prick a balloon. Ferdie, with his enchanting lips, was turned into a schoolboy, terrified of being disgraced. She knew she would never want to see him again and must find an older man, with poise and courage. Perhaps even the English lord Papa kept talking about. He wouldn't be the sort of man who needed defending in an escapade. He would be proud, defiant, determined, ruthless, a daredevil. Lizzie would never dare open her mouth to him.

Papa roared with laughter when he heard about the episode. But, curiously, his eyes lost their twinkle and stayed cool and thoughtful. They had a shrewd, calculating look that Chrissie didn't much care for. It was a look he kept for his secretaries, his servants, his accountants and bankers, not for her.

"Baby, I think it's time for our European trip," he said.

Aunt Mary Ellen came storming into Camberwell House, leaving a scent of eau de cologne and stuffy clothes with the barest overtones of rum in her wake. She had grown very large, but still favored parrot colors, greens, yellows and vivid blues. With her bright wild eyes and red cheeks she was what was known as a character and even commanded a certain respect, especially from young nervous servants, who were terrified of her.

She demanded to see Harry and said that Boy would have been with her, only unfortunately he was a little unwell.

"He had a fall last night coming home from the club," she said, looking at Louisa accusingly. "What can you expect, with too much rum inside him and that poor foot of his? But he was up and working at his desk when I left. He's reached page eleven hundred and fifty of his Lord Byron book. Isn't that a remarkable achievement? He says his book is exactly the same age as Chrissie. And that, Louisa, is what I'm here about. You're not going to let Harry whisk that child off to Europe before she comes out."

Louisa sighed. She had anticipated this fight. Mary Ellen still regarded Chrissie as almost entirely hers. If for no other reason, it would be a good idea to leave New York, to get Chrissie away from the eccentricities of the old van Leyden house, shabby, unaired, redolent of the rich aroma of rum. Boy had become an almost exact replica of their father, with his vague blue eyes, his charming smile, his seedy appearance. To encourage him not to go to the club every night, with the risk of stumbling in badly lighted streets, Mary Ellen had begun to join him in an occasional glass of rum. That was why there was frequently an embarrassing whiff of the stuff about her.

It was ironic that it was not Harry's mother, hidden away, as people erroneously thought, in the Bowery, who had been an embarrassment, but Louisa's own family who had originally been expected to give Harry social prestige. Old Mrs. Spencer had died five years ago, and the whole of the street where she had lived had attended her simple funeral. If Boy fell downstairs and broke his neck, or Mary Ellen expired from lack of breath, as seemed likely when she was in one of her outraged moods, who would voluntarily go to their funerals? Only Harry, whom they hated.

"Louisa," Mary Ellen declared in indignation. "You're not even listening to me."

"Yes, I am. But you know that I can do nothing about this. When Harry makes a decision about Chrissie, that's final."

"You mean you're not going to let her have a coming-out ball in her own home! Why, that's downright wicked."

"She can have a ball when she comes home again," Louisa said serenely. "At present the plans are for her to share Araminta Pepper's coming out in Paris. You remember Millie Pepper?"

"Railroads?"

"George Pepper was. He's retired now. They live permanently in Paris right on the Champs-Élysées. They know all sorts of people. A debutante's ball is called a *bal blanc,* which is rather charming, don't you think? Harry says Chrissie's ball gown must be made by Worth."

"I never thought to live to see the day," Mary Ellen exploded, "when a girl like Chrissie isn't allowed to meet a nice young American because she might fall in love with him. She's being kept for some foreign royalty. Really, Harry's ideas are preposterous."

"Not foreign royalty," Louisa said. "Even I would object to that. But you know Harry has always had this dream of Chrissie marrying into the English aristocracy."

"And you!" Mary Ellen snorted. "Do you encourage this crashing snobbishness?"

"In a way I do, because much as we will miss her, I think Chrissie will be safer in England."

"You don't mean to say you've still got this old kidnapping thing on your brain. I declare, you've brought that poor child up like a prisoner with warders."

"You didn't lose a son, Mary Ellen. That might have got on your brain, too."

"Oh, phut! I'm going to talk to Harry."

"And to what do I owe this honor?" Harry asked, with elaborate politeness, when Mary Ellen was ushered by Dobson into the library. At least, he thought privately, poor old hag, she wasn't going to propose to him this time. They hadn't had a tête-à-tête since that day, both of them having assiduously avoided being alone together.

However, here she was, large, palpitating, overcolored, like a belligerent turkey.

"Harry, I'm absolutely horrified that you're planning for Chrissie to have her coming out in a foreign city. She's a good American girl. She ought to have her ball right here in New York. I'm just surprised at Louisa going along with you. But then Louisa always was too meek to open her mouth."

"I gather," said Harry, his eyes narrowed and flinty, "that you came to discuss my daughter, not my wife."

"That's what I'm doing. And I'm telling you, you're going to ruin Chrissie if you drag her about Europe. Turn her head. Give her all the wrong values. Because those aristocratic young men you prize so highly will only fawn on her for her money. They'll be thinking of an ancient home they want to save. They put their castles before their wives, you know."

"Do they?" Harry observed politely.

"Of course they do. Look at that wretched Vanderbilt girl. Locked in her room on her wedding morning so she couldn't run away from her stuffed-shirt duke. What Chrissie wants is a good honest red-blooded American husband. She doesn't want to eat off gold plate or entertain the Prince of Wales."

"How do you know?"

"Because you only have to look at her and see that she's a nice, ordinary, natural girl without a trace of snobbishness in her."

"I look at her and see a great beauty whom I want to show off to the world."

Mary Ellen hissed in contempt. "Great beauty, indeed.

The ideas you'll put in that child's head. You're only using her to make up for your own miserable childhood."

"And that of my parents and grandparents."

"That's what I mean. You think you can manipulate fate. You can't, you know."

"Can't I?"

"Well, don't do it at Chrissie's expense," Mary Ellen roared. "All you can see is yourself, the boy who climbed out of the gutter and now thinks he can buy a lord for a son-in-law."

"Chrissie won't be forced to marry against her will."

"But she'll only meet those you consider eligible suitors. At the susceptible age of eighteen, what can she do but fall in love with one of them? You and Lou have held her back so much she's bursting with repressed emotions."

"Which is a state of mind I'm sure you know all about," Harry murmured wickedly.

Mary Ellen went scarlet. Before she could answer or look at him, Harry cleverly and shatteringly changed the subject.

"I'm glad you came to see me because I've been wanting to talk to you and your brother about buying your house. I've plans for demolishing most of that block. It's pretty tumbledown nowadays, you must admit. History is one thing, but if buildings aren't constructed to withstand centuries, then they must be sacrificed to make way for better ones. Don't look so horrified. I'm not putting you out in the street. You'll have a year or two to find another house and move. I only want to get negotiations under way while Lou and Chrissie and I are in Europe. I'll pay you a good price, of course."

"I don't believe you!" Mary Ellen gasped.

"Don't you?"

"Well, yes, unfortunately I do, because you're a devil. One thing I can tell you, Boy will never agree."

"I rather think he will. He'll find he can work just as well, even better, in a comfortable modern place. That

house of yours is a rabbit warren, you know. And there will be other inducements."

"If you talk to Boy—if you take advantage of his weakness—"

"That old tree will have to go, which is a pity, but I believe it's now a source of danger. Likely to come down across the road in a gale. I want to put up some apartment houses. That's going to be the style of the future in this city. Do you remember how when I built this house everyone said I was mad to choose a site so far out of town? Look at it now. Houses all around."

"I'm not interested in your reminiscences," Mary Ellen said furiously. "You property men are all the same, plunderers and marauders. But you'll never have the van Leyden house. Even if my brother listens to your inducements, I won't, and Boy can't sell without my consent. You can build all around and over us, but we'll still be there."

"You'll have had time to think about it while we're in Europe," Harry said equably. "I'm sure you'll find it's wise to change your mind."

"Never!" Mary Ellen shouted. "And you ought to remember what happened once before when you evicted people."

"I hope I won't be driven to evicting you, my dear sister-in-law. But it won't be because I'm afraid to."

"No, you're just plain devilish," said Mary Ellen helplessly. She had lost the point of the argument and was defeated. Her beloved Chrissie was going to Europe. Who knew if she would ever come back?

From then on preparations for Papa's advance into Europe, as Chrissie called it, progressed apace.

There were sentimental paragraphs in the social columns of the daily newspapers.

Are we to lose another of our brightest ornaments? Is Miss Christabel Spencer to follow in the footsteps of Consuelo Vanderbilt and May Goelet and become the mistress of an English castle? It is an open secret that this is the wish of her father, the well-known Mr. Harry Spencer, multimillionaire and property king. Mr. Spencer is married to the former Louisa van Leyden, a member of an old and highly respected American family, whereas his own life, as he enjoys recounting, began in a London slum. So which side of the ocean will Miss Chrissie settle for? Which of her ancestors will have the strongest influence? Or will the coveted title be the deciding factor?

"Will we ever know?" Chrissie said derisively, throwing the offending paper away. "Supposing I refuse to marry at all?"

"Don't be ridiculous, dear," said Louisa vaguely. "Now I wonder, should I take these ball gowns? Papa says we're to shop in Paris, that's why we're going there first, but I think we should have a selection of American clothes. Just to show people that we do dress over here."

"If you could have your life over again, Mamma, would you refuse to marry except for love? Oh, you don't need to look at me like that. I know you didn't love Papa when you were married."

Louisa shook out a dress with a sharp crackle of the stiff taffeta.

"Mary Ellen has been talking to you again. Really, I wish she would mind her own business."

"But you love him now, don't you?"

Louisa had trained herself not to think of Cornelius. At first, that had been beyond her willpower, but it had slowly got better. Now she scarcely thought of him at all. If she did, it was with a sad and almost pleasurable nostalgia. There had been a time of richness in her life. That knowledge comforted her.

She nodded in an indeterminate way, in answer to Chrissie's question, and thought that this bright, inquisitive creature was what Cornelius had been sacrificed for.

The sacrifice, as far as Chrissie was concerned, had been justified, for she had grown into a dazzling young woman, well adjusted, full of warmth and spirit. What would she have been like had her mother deserted her as a child? Suspicious and resentful and distrustful? Now the tragedy in her childhood had left only one scar, a fear of the dark. Chrissie still had a night-light. But that was turned into a joke. A candle in the night and Serenity within call. She just loved being a baby. She was going to hate a husband who made her give up her cherished comforts.

"Do you learn to love people when you live with them? Or is that a myth?" Chrissie reflected, and answered her own question. "I suppose that depends on the people. You and Papa are loyal and decent and nice to look at, so you must have got to love each other."

"Chrissie, I think you are being a little indelicate."

"For wanting to know what happens in a marriage? But, Mamma, I've got to be a bit prepared. Papa expects so much of me. I get scared."

Louisa impulsively came and kissed Chrissie's cheek. It was round and soft and had the bloom of a peach.

"You'd like to be swept off your feet, my darling."

"Who wouldn't? But I have an awful fear that Papa and I won't agree about the man who does it."

"Now I've never known you to fight with your Papa."

"The day will come," Chrissie said bleakly. "I know it will."

Chapter 15

Chrissie Spencer and Araminta Pepper liked each other on sight. Araminta was small, dark and vivacious. She was an ideal companion during that first strange week in Paris, when the mornings were devoted entirely to dress fittings, and the afternoons to drives in the little open victoria to the Bois de Boulogne, or Versailles, or just down the Champs-Élysées and around the splendid Place de la Concorde. After that there might be a tea party to meet Araminta's friends, French, English and American (Araminta had been to school in Paris and acted in many ways like a Parisian born and bred), and later a dinner party at one of the grand houses.

This was all leading up to the night of the *bal blanc*. So far Chrissie hadn't met a single young man. They were being kept for that night, she was told.

Louisa and her old friend Millie from the Madison Avenue School for Young Ladies days also found that they got on very well. Louisa was complimentary about Araminta, and Millie was impressed with Chrissie.

"You're going to make a brilliant match there, my dear, if you play your cards right."

"Harry won't let me do anything else, I can assure you."

"You have an entrée into London society? George and I can give you some introductions. We know the ambassador and his wife, to begin with. But you'll be meeting some useful people at the ball. And didn't your mother have English connections?"

"Yes, my grandmother's family come from Feaversham Hall in Suffolk. They've been barons since the time of William the Conqueror, I believe. My old Aunt Abigail kept in touch until she died, and now Harry has asked me to write to them announcing that we'll be in London and giving a party for our daughter."

"You've got to have push," Millie said sagely. "Dollars on their own aren't enough. You don't look as if you're the pushing kind, Louisa."

"No, I'm not, and I frankly dislike all this. But so long as Chrissie has fun and doesn't get badly snubbed—"

"No one's going to snub that girl. They might come prepared to, but they won't when they meet her. She's so delightfully natural. Goodness knows how you've contrived that, with all the barbed wire you had to put up around her during her childhood. You'd have thought she'd have been a nervous little mouse."

"I might be able to have a mouse as a daughter," Louisa said candidly, "But Harry couldn't."

"No, he certainly couldn't. Honestly, Louisa, he's really become something, hasn't he? I admit that an aura of success is irresistible in any man, but he has much more than that. I can only call it a presence. That splendid head, and his lion-colored hair. I can't see him being in the least intimidated by anybody, not even those stuffy aristocratic French families who are too proud to acknowledge anyone who isn't one of themselves. Not even old Queen Victoria. I expect he's hoping to have Chrissie presented at court."

"Money does wonders," Louisa murmured.

"Wives do more. I've always said, whatever would have happened if Harry had chosen Mary Ellen instead of you."

"I've not always been—"

Millie looked at Louisa's bent head.

"My dear, who has? George and I—but that's another story. The awful thing is presenting a picture of complete marital bliss to one's daughters, isn't it? Perhaps that's wrong, but one can't bear to disillusion the pretty things. And one always goes on hoping that their marriages will be perfect, even though one knows such a thing isn't possible. Or rarely."

"Fancy you being so impressed by Harry," said Louisa. She smiled a little. She was pleased.

The budding gnarled old trees bending over the Seine, the artists on the sidewalks, Notre Dame, impressive beyond anything one had imagined, the treasure house of the Louvre, the Rue de la Paix with the discreet elegance of the couturiers' windows, the cafés with their endless cups of coffee or pots of chocolate. Chrissie sipped absinthe and found it so horrible she vowed never to do so again. Lizzie, Chrissie's sober and reliable companion since childhood, had been brought to Europe in the dual role of lady's maid and chaperone. It was better, said Papa, than engaging someone whom one was not sure one could trust. In her neat straw boater and dark brown coat and skirt, she was ordered to accompany the girls everywhere, but this did not prevent their receiving outrageously frank stares from male passersby. Araminta giggled, but Chrissie stared back with unconcealed interest. She had never imagined Paris would be so exciting. She was just beginning to live, she confided to Araminta, and Araminta, giving her a suddenly sober look, advised her to make the most of it.

"They'll have you married in no time, and then you'll have to do what your husband wants. Have babies, run the house, give balls. Mamma has worked like a slave over our ball next week. The flowers, the catering, the extra servants, who takes precedence over who, will the old Comte de Rheims get drunk and have to be discreetly removed, will the Princess Mathilde come, she's well known for changing her mind at the last minute, will any of those wild bluebloods drink too much champagne and try to seduce you or me?"

"Really, it sounds just like a party in New York."

"There's the Honorable Nicholas Paget for you," Araminta said. "I'm not supposed to tell you in case it makes you uncooperative, your mother says."

Chrissie's heart skipped a beat.

"Is he supposed to be *the* one?"

"Oh, I don't imagine so. He's only a younger son, and they don't have much of a chance. But you can practice on him, so to speak. And he might be a lot of use when you're in London. I tell you, parents are the greatest schemers. And by the way, Chrissie, avoid Italian counts like the plague."

"Why?"

"They're the worst tyrants of all. They treat their wives like slaves, and they'd never never allow you to get a divorce because of Holy Mother Church."

"Araminta, do you mean to marry for love?"

"If I'm lucky."

"What do you mean, if you're lucky?"

Araminta put her small head on one side. She looked like a shrewd and dainty little bird.

"Well, I wouldn't run off with the second footman, for instance, even if I loved him to distraction. But if a man has all the right possessions and so on, and loves me, too—" She didn't look at Chrissie as she added, "I believe I'm going to marry Prince Rudolf of Baden Holburg. He's a very minor prince, but I'll be in the *Almanach de Gotha,* and I'll have one of those fairy-tale castles, probably hideously uncomfortable, in the Black Forest. You'll meet Rudolf at the ball. He's blond and blue-eyed and awfully sweet."

"But you don't love him?"

"I—I'm not sure. It's partly language difficulties." Araminta's delectable face crinkled with laughter. "I don't know much German, and he's awfully bad at English. We get into terrible tangles. It's hilarious. But really there are only two essential words. Yes and no." Araminta bent her head. "It's what my parents want. And I expect I'll like him sufficiently to make life bearable. If I decide to accept him. I would dearly like to be a princess," she added ingenuously.

"Really!" Chrissie exclaimed. "I think that's the most cold-blooded thing I ever heard."

Araminta exploded with laughter.

"You are sweet, Chrissie. So naïve. Let's always be friends."

Chrissie paraded in front of her parents in the virginal white tulle ball gown made by the famous couturier Worth. She knew it was a beautiful dress; but the tightly laced waist was making her breathless, and white had never been her favorite color. It made her feel so *jeune fille* in spite of the clever way the hairdresser had piled her hair on the top of her head and pinned into it her only piece of jewelry, the small twinkling diamond clasp Mamma had lent her for the evening. She kept thinking of Araminta, also in white, looking as pure as a snowdrop, and yet with those cold-blooded plans in her head. Where was romance? If it didn't exist in this lovely city, did it exist anywhere?

"You look beautiful, baby," said Papa, his voice suddenly husky, his eyes glistening with sentimental tears.

Mamma gave a small wry smile, and said, "I had my coming-out ball in a cut-down dress of my mother's. I remember your father telling me then that he intended his daughter to be dressed in Paris. I never really thought it would happen, though."

"You know me better now, Lou," said Papa. "When I say I am going to make a thing happen, it happens."

Mamma frowned a little and said that one had to be very sure what one wanted to happen. Very sure, she repeated, and added to Chrissie, "We both hope you are going to have a lovely summer, my darling. But you're very young. Don't be in a hurry to make up your mind about marriage in spite of what your father expects. It's your life, not his."

The gentle reproof was not lost on Papa, who said jovially, "I would certainly put my foot down about her marrying a German princeling. Can't think what Millie and George are about, encouraging such a thing for their girl. You find an English beau, Chrissie. That's all your father is expecting of you at present."

The beautiful long high-ceilinged ballroom, with the windows thrown open to the green gloom of the overhanging trees and the paved garden walks, was lighted by myriads of candles. The air smelled of candle smoke and an elusive perfume that was like a distillation of all the flowers of spring. Of Paris, Chrissie thought intensely. Nowhere else looked like this, nor had she ever seen such an assembly of beautifully dressed people. The men were as elegant as the women. Their manners were so exquisitely formal that she frequently wanted to giggle. Her hand was being raised regularly to receive ardent kisses. She was grateful for the gloves that reached to her shoulders. Her trembling flesh didn't want the imprint of all those kisses.

His Excellency, the American ambassador ("Curtsy!" Araminta hissed), the Princesse Mathilde, the Comte de Rheims, Monsieur and Madame Raoul Pettit, Mademoiselle Antoinette Pettit, the Duke and Duchess of Marlborough, the Earl and Countess of Derby, Lord and Lady Pemberton, the Marquis and Marquise of Duncaster, Mr. and Mrs. Elbur Williams, the Honorable Nicholas Paget (blue eyes, a blank face, a ramrod back), the Prince Rudolf of Baden Holburg (a low bow and smartly clicking heels—oh, lord, would Araminta have to put up with that all the time!), Viscount Monkshood with a long weary face (Monkshood, wasn't that a deadly poison? Had she heard right?).

At last the slow procession up the staircase had come to an end. The music had begun. The first couple, the American ambassador with Millie Pepper on his arm, took the floor.

"When may we dance?" Chrissie whispered to Araminta.

"When we're asked, idiot."

Prince Rudolf, tall, patrician, ever so slightly cross-eyed, was already bowing and clicking in front of Araminta. She flashed a triumphant look at Chrissie and was off, floating in her diaphanous white dress, the nice little American girl who thought it would be such fun to be a princess, irrespective of love.

"Stay beside me," Mamma said to Chrissie. She might have saved her breath, for Papa had swung Chrissie into his arms.

"My dance, baby. Must show off my daughter." He danced energetically, but well, his long tails spinning. "Amazing woman, that Millie Pepper. She's got everyone here. All those titles. Did you hear them?" He lowered his voice. "But the title doesn't always make the man. I'm disappointed. They're a weedy lot, on the whole. That German of Araminta's has crooked eyes. After the Sedan, I didn't think a Frenchman would ever want to speak to a German again. What do you think of young Paget?"

"The young man who looks like a waxworks figure?"

Papa gave his sudden uninhibited roar of laughter. Heads turned. His neatly trimmed golden beard, scarcely flecked with gray, lifted higher, with calculated arrogance. No one here was going to intimidate Harry Spencer.

"Are the English aristocracy all like that, Papa? Do you really want me to marry one of them?"

"No, they're not all like that. My grandfather had stories about them. There was the old gentleman who always gave orders that there were to be buns and milk left on the library table for the chimney sweep's boy. The boy never saw the old man, but the buns never failed to be there. A true English gentleman, my grandfather said, was the finest example of the human species. And that's what I want for my daughter. The best."

The dance was coming to an end.

"Then it isn't going to be the Honorable Nicholas

Paget," Chrissie whispered, and they were both laughing merrily when the music ceased.

She had to swallow her giggles, however, when that young gentleman bowed before her and requested the pleasure of the next dance and perhaps the fourth or fifth. Chrissie fiddled with her program. The gold tasseled pencil was decorative but useless.

"Borrow mine," said someone else, surely the lord with the strange name, Monkshood. "And perhaps I may claim the dance after this one, Miss Spencer."

People must have been watching her dancing with Papa. They must have seen her laughing. Mamma had told her that of all things gaiety in a young woman was what men most admired. She had lacked it herself and had had no beaus until Papa had come along.

Who couldn't help being gay on such a lovely night?

"Do you hunt, Miss Spencer?" asked the Honorable Nicholas Paget.

"No, I don't."

"Pity." A long pause. "I've got a nice little mare. Quiet. Safe jumper. I could teach you to ride."

"How kind."

"You are coming to England?"

"Yes, we are. I didn't say I didn't ride. I said I didn't hunt."

"Oh. You're not sentimental about the fox, are you?"

"I hadn't thought about it. But yes, I think I would be."

"Vermin," said the young man, closing that subject. "I say, you're rather pretty."

"Thank you."

"Jolly pretty," said the Honorable Nicholas Paget with a certain wistfulness. He knew already that he was defeated. How strange. He had no confidence with women, but he was probably like a tiger on the hunting field.

And I'm supposed to marry one of your kind, Chrissie said under her breath, and repressed a sigh of relief when the music stopped.

"Is your waist laced too tight?" whispered Araminta. "I know I'm going to swoon before the night's over. I have a feeling Rudolf will adore that. Chrissie, you don't think his eyes—"

"They're very interesting eyes," Chrissie lied gallantly. "Surely you have to think so when they look at you with that besotted expression."

"You horrid thing, you're teasing."

"My dance, I think, Miss Spencer," said Lord Monkshood.

He danced superbly. His face was long and bony and washed-out, as if he indulged in innumerable late nights. But he had the unmistakable stamp of breeding. His eyes, with their hint of world-weariness and sadness, were bent on Chrissie with a look of deep interest and kindliness. She found this very agreeable. Ever since the ignominious end of her flirtation with Ferdie she had known that she would like older men.

"And how are you enjoying the ball, little Miss New York?"

"Very much. It's wonderful. Don't I look as if I'm enjoying myself?"

"You do, indeed. Everything shows on your face."

"Is that a disadvantage?"

"It depends how much of a coquette you want to be."

"I don't want to be one at all."

His eyebrows lifted.

"Don't decide too soon. You may find it amusing to play games as you get older."

"If I do, I'll learn how to at the appropriate time."

"Whatever sort of a school did you go to where they teach young girls such pompous phrases?"

"It was a very proper school. I didn't learn much about the classics, but you try me walking with a book on my head."

"You were top of the class?"

"When I wanted to be."

"And are you trying to be top of the class tonight?"

"Oh, I guess so. My parents expect it. Anyway, it's so utterly wonderful, a ball in Paris."

After the stiff conversation with the Honorable Nicholas Paget, it was also wonderful to talk in such a frank, easy fashion with this intriguing man. He had a clever way of seeming to hang on every word. She really believed he was listening with interest to her schoolgirl chatter.

"Why Paris? Why not London?"

"Oh, there will be one there, too. My parents are arranging it. Will you come?"

"I would be delighted to."

"Really? I thought you might think me too much of a schoolgirl. This evening is a kind of rehearsal for me, before London. That's where I'm supposed to shine."

"You will."

"Do you think so? I'm very unworldly. I had a very restricted childhood. For reasons I won't talk about on this lovely night. Oh, isn't it a lovely night!"

"Miss Spencer," said Lord Monkshood seriously, "will you allow me to give you some advice? Don't try to copy other women, even if you admire them. Never try to be anyone but yourself. You have a quality of freshness and innocence that is unique on this side of the Atlantic."

"Is that a good thing to have?"

"Oh, beyond price. English debutantes are either mannered and haughty or too bashful to open their mouths."

Chrissie smiled with relief. She was supposed to be pretty, she was certainly very rich; therefore, people expected her to have all the confidence in the world. But she hadn't. She had been secretly scared of all the brilliant English debutantes she would have to meet and compete with. Now Lord Monkshood, so elegant and sophisticated himself, was giving her that much-needed confidence. She wanted to go on talking to him for hours and gladly welcomed his suggestion that they should sit down in a quiet corner, if they could find one, and have a glass of champagne.

They found two chairs under a stiff shiny-leaved orange tree in a tub, and Chrissie, drinking too rapidly, allowed her newly discovered confidence to run away with her.

"Do you live in a castle, Lord Monkshood? One of those dark haunted places, with centuries of history?"

"My house isn't a castle. It isn't even my house until my father dies. I live in one wing, the Elizabethan part. The rest is Tudor, with some renovations made during the Georges."

"The Georges?"

"Kings of England, Georges one, two, three and four, and each one worse than the last."

"Oh, dear, how ignorant I am."

"Not at all. I know next to nothing about George Washington."

"I could tell you all about him in five minutes."

"Splendid. Where will you begin?"

Chrissie shook her head, laughing. "No, no, he simply doesn't go with champagne. I mean all that fuss about never telling a lie. Lies are absolutely necessary at times. How dreary, how impossible life would be without them."

Lord Monkshood nodded slowly, his expression amused. Why did she think that beneath the amusement there was a hint of pain, of suffering?

"You surprise me, Miss Spencer. You're not so innocent after all."

"How could I be? Lizzie—she was my governess, and now she's my companion-chaperone sort of thing—says innocence and money just don't go together. Do you think they do?"

"I'm hardly an authority on that. We've always been poor."

"Poor!"

Again the wry smile. "Well, relatively speaking, I suppose. Old houses and large estates produce their own problems."

"I'd like to have had my great-grandfather listening to

you. He was a chimney sweep's boy. He swept chimneys in houses like yours, and he thought they were paradise."

"No! Are you really descended from a chimney sweep? How irresistible!"

"Are you laughing at me?"

"Not in the very least."

"Lizzie said I shouldn't talk about my forebears. But Papa is absolutely honest about them. He's proud of them. And so am I. Oh, Mamma had some blue blood. But Papa's dominates in me. I want it to. Granny Spencer taught me that. She was alive to the very tips of her fingers. Aunt Mary Ellen—on my mother's side—needs bolstering up with family history and old portraits and a bit of rum, but Granny Spencer could thrive on a crust and be as gay as a robin."

"You really are an unexpected young lady, aren't you?" said Lord Monkshood.

"You yourself told me not to copy."

"Don't, don't, I beg you. And if you want to say those things in a London drawing room, do so. You'll be somebody, at once. Your Grandmother Spencer was right. But I don't entirely agree with your great-grandfather," he added. "Old houses aren't paradise. Far from it."

The shadow had deepened in his eyes. Chrissie was speculating on it when Millie Pepper suddenly stood over them, wagging her finger admonishingly.

"Lord Monkshood, you are very naughty, stealing the belle of the ball like this. I've got to take her away now. Everyone's asking for her."

"My apologies," said Lord Monkshood, springing up and bowing deeply.

"Oh, you're not in the least bit sorry, I can see. Come, Chrissie."

Hustling her back to the ballroom, Millie hissed in her ear. "My dear child, you do not seclude yourself with a gentleman at your first ball. You remain in the center of the stage. And especially not with a gentleman like Lord Monkshood," she added.

"Why? What's wrong with him? Is he a philanderer?" Chrissie was agog with curiosity.

"Look, here's His Excellency longing to dance with you. Go along, you two, and talk about New York."

After her dutiful dance with the ambassador, Chrissie again got Araminta for five minutes alone.

"Araminta, what's wrong with Lord Monkshood? Your mother was cross with me for sitting talking to him."

"I should think she would be. He's divorced. Can't be received by royalty or anything like that."

"Goodness! What happened? Was it his fault? I don't believe it."

"His wife ran off with a lover."

"From a man like that! She must have been mad."

"Oh, you are so gullible, Chrissie. Everything isn't on the surface with men like that. It isn't with my Rudolf, either. That's what I find fascinating about him. American men are so naïve and boyish in comparison. But you have to know what you're doing."

"I certainly know I want to see Lord Monkshood again, divorce or not."

"Well, don't do anything silly. The parents are already whispering. It seems he's been inquiring about your prospects."

"Not my money!" Chrissie exclaimed in deep disillusionment.

"What can you expect? We're heiresses. We've always got to be suspicious. But it doesn't need to ruin things entirely."

"He seemed so nice, so interested. I mean genuinely interested."

"Maybe he is. But it's a fact that Monkshood, which he is due to inherit, needs about half a million pounds spent on it. Well, I won't be going emptyhanded to Rudolf, either. We're pawns, Chrissie. But don't look so miserable. We can be clever enough to do a bit of manipulating of our own.

"And if you marry Lord Monkshood," she added, "you

can't be presented to the queen, but you will be a countess when his father, the earl, dies. Isn't that what your father wants?"

Chapter 16

Papa sat on the padded velvet seat in the center of the Louvre gallery and gazed at the famous Leonardo da Vinci painting of the Mona Lisa.

"I'd like to own that," he said.

"You can't," said Chrissie, who was in a mutinous mood. "Money doesn't buy you everything."

"Oh dear, such wisdom." Papa tugged at her sleeve and pulled her down beside him. It was late afternoon on the day after the ball, and they were both tired. The ball had been a marvelous success, and Millie Pepper was still preening herself about her illustrious list of guests. It was only unfortunate that Chrissie had slightly marred her prospects in society by conspicuously spending too much time with Lord Monkshood, of the flawed reputation. She had danced with him three times and had sat out another entire dance in his company. But being an American, perhaps she could be excused on the grounds of not knowing any better.

This morning, to make matters worse, a charming posy of white rosebuds had arrived for her, and everyone knew at once who had sent them. After all, she had scarcely looked at another man the entire night.

Just before noon the flowers had been followed by a call from Lord Monkshood himself to pay his respects to his hostess and to hope for a glimpse of the delightful

Miss Spencer. He had been told politely but frigidly that Miss Spencer was not yet down. After all, she had not been in bed until dawn. Then tomorrow morning, suggested Lord Monkshood imperturbably. He would like to take her riding in the Bois de Boulogne.

This contretemps was the reason for Harry's talk with his daughter in the anonymity of the Louvre.

"Now, baby, it seems you made a big impression on Lord Monkshood."

"Do you disapprove, Papa?" Chrissie opened her eyes wide. "He's going to be an earl, and you did want me to marry nobody less than an earl, didn't you? Are you worried because he has been divorced?"

"Of course I am," Papa roared. "And don't look at me with those innocent eyes. You're not that unworldly. You know what sort of a reputation you'll get if you're seen about with a divorced man. It will ruin your chances."

"But Lord Monkshood is the injured party, Papa. Why should he be ostracized for something that isn't his fault?"

"Isn't it? How do you know? Why did his wife run off? Maybe she was driven to it."

"By that nice man? Stuff and nonsense!"

"Women do run off from nice men," Papa said, and momentarily his eyes had a sad far-off look that seemed to have nothing to do with Chrissie's problems. "But apart from that, your mother and I can't have you jeopardizing your future by the childish infatuation you seem to have developed for this man. We would prefer you not to see him again."

Chrissie's lower lip stuck out. "Are you forbidding me to?"

"No, not forbidding. You're grown up now, and you have to learn self-reliance and common sense. You can't do that with your parents or Peck or Lizzie at your heels forever. No, we're just asking you to be sensible."

"But I want to see Lord Monkshood again, Papa. He was the only intelligent man I talked to last night. I really badly want to see him again."

That was the formula of any childish demand. I *badly* want this, Papa, and inevitably the object arrived or the desired permission was given.

Chrissie looked at her father's adamant face and recognized that suddenly the indulgent pattern had changed.

"Surely I can see him occasionally and still be sensible," she wheedled.

"No."

"Then I'll have to go against your wishes, Papa. Because I do intend to see him. Really," she burst out indignantly, "you can't cut off my life just as it begins. What is this fuss about, anyway? I'm not going to marry him, I'm only going to ride with him in the Bois de Boulogne."

Papa stood up abruptly.

"We'll leave for London tomorrow. Come along. There's a great deal to do."

"Papa!"

"Come along!"

"Papa," Chrissie said breathlessly, "it isn't only the Mona Lisa you can't have, you know."

When he didn't answer, she followed his broad, stocky figure obediently. She even from habit tucked her arm in his. But her face had exactly the same pugnaciousness as his own.

They sat around the dining table in the chilly dining room of the house in Belgravia which they had rented for the season. It had been raining when they had arrived in England ten days ago, and it was still raining.

Their dinner guests were Lord and Lady Feaversham, Louisa's second cousins from Feaversham Hall in Suffolk. Lady Feaversham was tall and flat-chested, with a long patrician nose and a forbiddingly supercilious expression. Her husband was remarkably similar. They might have been brother and sister or first cousins. And it seemed more likely that it was the English rain rather than warm blood that ran in their veins.

Louisa, with her quiet good taste, might just be accepted, but the "gel" was obviously going to be a high flier, difficult to discipline, as these American girls were, and as for Harry Spencer he was simply commercial, a species which seldom came their way, at least not around a dinner table.

"So you're planning to give the gel a ball," said Lady Feaversham, picking delicately at her chicken.

"Have thought you'd have changed your mind after Paris," said Lord Feaversham.

"I don't understand that remark," said Harry. "Would you be more explicit?"

"Only heard some gossip. Hope you've been warned about that cad Monkshood."

"I don't know what you're talking about," Harry said bluntly.

"Why do you call Lord Monkshood a cad?" asked Chrissie, leaning across the table. What an *awful* couple, gray, stony, appallingly stiff. Now they were looking at her as if she were still a child and should be seen but not heard.

"Because he must be one, m'dear," said Lord Feaversham. "Divorced and all that. Letting his wife run off."

"Should he have locked her in the attic?" Chrissie asked in her clear voice.

Lord Feaversham gave the smallest well-bred splutter. "At that, it might have brought her to her senses. Avoided a scandal."

"The scandal is nothing to do with us, Cousin Reginald," said Louisa firmly. "We do plan to give Chrissie a ball, and we hope you will come."

"Must remember, too, that the gel's a Yankee," said Lord Feaversham, going off in another direction.

"And what's wrong with being a Yankee?" asked Harry, his voice dangerously soft.

"Nothing, my dear fellow. Well, if you want me to be frank, nothing except dollars."

"Which is a bad thing? I don't remember the Duke of Marlborough expressing that particular opinion."

"Oh, him. He had to save Blenheim Palace. National monument, and that sort of thing. Everyone recognized the necessity. The Churchills were always crafty, anyway."

"I thought I was English—" Harry began, in a low rumble.

"Harry!" Louisa beseeched.

"All my life I've cherished my origins. But by God"—he flung his napkin down and pushed back his chair—"from this minute I'm a Yankee. And be damned to all you dried-up superior English who eat my food and drink my wine to warm your cold bones and then think you can patronize me. I'll tell you this," he added, his chin stuck out belligerently. "If my daughter wants to marry a grocer, she'll have my consent. That's true freedom. That's what we have on the other side of the Atlantic. I recommend it to you sir."

He strode out of the room, and Lord Feaversham clapped his napkin to his mouth, making a curious hooting sound to which Chrissie listened with horror. It appeared, however, that he was laughing.

"I say, Louisa, your husband's a bit of a firebrand. I believe I like him. Edith, we must get up a party for this ball. Plenty of suitable young people, though personally I would still draw the line at my daughter marrying a grocer, no matter what particular freedom that represents. Is there a little more of this burgundy? Your husband might say he's a Yankee, Louisa, but he can pick a good wine."

"He'll come back later and have port with you," Louisa said uneasily.

"I doubt it. But we'll get along famously when we meet again. Though I must say, Louisa, if your gel has her father's impetuous nature, she'll be setting the cat among the pigeons. What do you say, Edith? Will you take her on?"

"Only," said Lady Feaversham, fixing her cool gray assessing eyes on Chrissie, "if she behaves herself. What I won't tolerate are secret assignations."

The next morning, over his coffee, Harry kept giving intermittent deep chuckles. Louisa asked whatever he found so amusing.

"Your cousins, my dear. Splendid people. That's what I mean about the English ruling classes, Chrissie. Some of them seem to be as mad as March hares, but they end by making you think you're the one who's lost his wits. Great gift that. Wish I had it."

"Lord Feaversham said nice things about you, Papa. Didn't he, Mamma?"

"Did he, by jove?" Harry was immensely pleased. "Didn't mind me losing my temper then?"

"I'm sure he thought you were behaving exactly like an English gentleman," Louisa said dryly. "Anyway, Cousin Edith is coming this morning to discuss plans. She has agreed to manage Chrissie's Season."

"Presentation at the palace?" said Harry, with satisfaction. "Ostrich feathers and all that lark?"

"I believe so. Chrissie dear, you will be patient with her, won't you?"

Chrissie sighed. "It's such a lovely morning. I wanted to walk in the park."

"There'll be plenty of time for that. You have the whole summer."

Chrissie sighed again. What sort of summer, under Cousin Edith's wing? She imagined a succession of blank-faced, impeccably behaved young men with utterly predictable conversation. Would she ever meet anyone as interesting, as sophisticated, as Lord Monkshood again? Would she ever meet Lord Monkshood again? It seemed all too unlikely, in spite of Papa's brave words about the freedom he was prepared to give her to marry as she chose. She had a strong feeling that she would be reminding him of those words one day.

Letters arrived from Aunt Mary Ellen regularly.

Dearest child, what is all this nonsense about being presented to royalty? What's that got to do with you, a good American girl? Anyway, I thought Queen Victoria was in her dotage. Or is it the Prince of Wales you curtsy to? I hear he isn't to be *trusted* with a pretty woman. It's all a lot of nonsense, anyway. Balls go just as well right here at home, as with all those coronets and flunkies around.

It is my belief that your father is *mad*.

Was there some *trouble* in Paris? Louisa's letter was vague, and yours wasn't much better. You said something about the most interesting guest having disappeared. I don't suppose you meant that *literally*. If he likes you enough, I daresay he will turn up again. Your Uncle Boy sends his love and says you're to visit the great houses where Lord Byron used to go. Between you and me, I don't think I can take much more of that poet. I sometimes think he sits at the table with us.

Dearest child, if you hate England and all this society nonsense, come home. I'll even agree to sell the house to Harry, much as I *oppose* that dastardly scheme, if you need money to run away and come back to America.

What is Cousin Edith like? A *frump*, I'll be bound.

Suddenly homesick, Chrissie sat down at the writing desk in her lavishly furnished bedroom (Papa had taken care that the house he had rented made a grand enough background for the summer's gaieties) and began to answer Aunt Mary Ellen's letter.

I will come home as soon as I am allowed to, darling aunt. I had thought that when I got to London, I was to be grown-up and free, but I am watched over more than ever. Lizzie is my friend, but even she doesn't dare to disobey Papa. So after that very small and silly storm in Paris, I am not allowed to even go shopping in case I make a secret assignation. You see, the only person I was interested in at the ball Millie Pepper gave is someone who is *outside the pale*. Well, that's what people say, but I thought he was the nicest, most charming man I have ever met, who has suffered a great deal for something which was not his fault, and it makes me mad that I am not permitted to see him again. He sent me roses after the ball and asked permission to call on me, but he was sent away. I have been a prisoner all my life, and I am heartily sick of it. At present I am being meek and mild and doing what Mamma and Papa want, but don't think I am beaten. As soon as the opportunity comes, I am going to rebel. I really am. This I am telling you in the greatest confidence because you have always cared about my happiness.

I will tell you more about Lord Monkshood one day, because I just know I will meet him again.

Tell Uncle Boy I have been reading about Lady Caroline Lamb, and that is how I am going to be, bold and self-willed, and determined to find my own Lord Byron.

Luncheon parties with those stiff, well-behaved English girls and their mothers, tea dances, correct sedate affairs when one danced with the well-behaved English girls' well-behaved brothers, two large and glittering balls, one at Lansdowne House and one at Devonshire House, where the dresses and the jewels were dazzling, but the conversation of a deadly dullness. Chrissie sought in vain for the one man she wanted to see. She supposed that he was ostracized from these houses just as he was from royal occasions. Especially since, at the Duchess of Devonshire's ball, the Prince of Wales was a guest. A stout middle-aged gentleman whose pale-blue eyes roved the room in a bored fashion, who occasionally gave a hoot of laughter, but who was more often silent and pouting.

Chrissie couldn't understand what all the fuss was about. She would have found a guest like that a terrible burden and would have breathed a sigh of relief when he departed. However, the game seemed to be that one kept him diverted and amused as long as possible; the longer one succeeded, the greater the triumph.

It looked as if the Duchess of Devonshire was going to be unlucky on this night, for her royal guest was already yawning. Then Chrissie was aware that his eyes rested on her and realized uncomfortably that he had begun to stare.

Cousin Edith, frosted over with gray tulle and diamonds, prodded her, with tense fingers.

"Chrissie, I believe you are to be paid a great honor. I believe the prince wishes to dance with you."

Surely enough, an equerry was bowing before her, and saying that His Royal Highness was requesting the honor of the next dance.

A rich smell of cigars and wine, a flushed face and blearily lecherous eyes, a large stomach thrusting against her, although she appeared to be held at arms' length, in their sedate waltz.

"Can you explain to me," came a gravelly voice, "why American girls are so charming?" He didn't seem to expect an answer. He went on, "Fresh as the morning. I think we drill our girls too much. What do you say? All those damned chaperones sitting around. No wonder the young things sometimes kick up their heels when they escape. Eh? Eh?"

"I've been watched enough in my life," Chrissie said. She rather liked the old gentleman. He seemed tired and rather sad.

"That's because of your father's money, eh? Devilish awkward thing, too much money. Looks and money, eh? I'll give you some advice. Beware of fortune hunters. Though I wouldn't mind being one of them myself." He gave a deep rumble of laughter, then abruptly stopped dancing, handed her over to the watchful equerry, and ambled back to his seat.

Cousin Edith was as animated as she was ever likely to be.

"That's made your Season, my dear. Now you'll be invited everywhere. You haven't a thing to worry about."

Hadn't she? Except for that longed-for face that was always absent.

But not forever. For the morning after her success at Devonshire House, which made Papa roar with delighted laughter, a letter arrived from Araminta in Paris.

Fortunately Chrissie was alone when she opened it, for she discovered that it contained an enclosure, a sealed envelope addressed in a firm beautiful script to Miss Christabel Spencer.

Some sixth sense told her whose handwriting this was.

The words of Araminta's scrawled letter jumped in front of her eyes.

> So sorry we won't be coming to London for any of your festivities, because Prince Rudolf has proposed and I have accepted, and we're to be married almost at once. Royalty doesn't care for long engagements; at least my prince doesn't. Mamma and Papa are in tizzies of excitement. Most of the time I'm just plain scared, but I wouldn't not do this for anything in the world. Imagine the challenge. Princess Rudolf. We're hoping you will be able to come to Paris for my wedding, but we do know it will be in the middle of the English Season, and you will be having your presentation and all these balls in stately homes. I remember them from last year. Utterly exhausting. And that reminds me that I met a certain gentleman quite by chance in the Rue de Rivoli the other day, and he practically fell on me for joy. At last, he said, he would be able to send you a message. He had written twice already, but he was sure his letters had been intercepted because he knew you would have replied if they had reached your

hands. He is leaving for England tomorrow and said that if he did not get a reply to this enclosed letter, he would batter down your front door.

Have fun, my lamb. But take care.

The other letter was much shorter, much more to the point.

My Dear Miss Spencer

I am afraid my previous letters to you have gone astray. I am telling you this only because I did not want you to think I had made no more attempts to see you. I fully understand your parents' apprehension since by this time you will know that I am a more or less branded person. But I would like the decision on whether or not we remain friends to be yours, not your parents. Isn't this the right of an independent woman? So I wondered if I dared suggest a meeting in London, simply to renew our acquaintance. I am arriving on Thursday morning and will be walking in Kensington Gardens that afternoon from three o'clock onward. I take a childish pleasure in watching the children sailing their boats on the Round Pond. Can I persuade you to share this pleasure?

Your friend,
Percival Monkshood

If it had not been for her indignation about those intercepted letters, Chrissie might not have been quite so determined to keep that assignation. But she expected she would have been, for really nothing would have kept her away. The only thing that exercised her was how to get rid of her shadow, Lizzie.

Mamma was easy enough. Never very robust, the late nights were playing havoc with her, and she had taken to resting every afternoon. Papa had many absorbing interests in London, his native city. He had already visited his childhood haunts and found them still as wretchedly poor as he remembered them. He was full of powerful desires to reshape this great sprawling, soot-stained city, one half of it composed of grandeur and unmatchable history, the other half of intolerable, unforgivable slums. As a builder, he wanted to demolish the slums entirely and put up dwellings fit for human beings, not for rats. He talked endlessly about this and offended a lot of people, and at intervals completely forgot his wife and daughter.

If he could be sent on one of his expeditions on Thursday, Chrissie would be left with only Lizzie to cope with.

Lizzie had one weakness, and that was gazing in shopwindows. Neat and nondescript herself, she got a vicarious pleasure from looking at extravagantly trimmed hats and feather boas and other pieces of pretty finery. It would be a great treat for her to be ordered to spend the afternoon walking the perimeter of Bond Street, Regent Street and Piccadilly, dawdling to her heart's content.

Chrissie said virtuously that she would occupy herself writing thank-you letters to hostesses and perhaps taking a nap. There was a dinner party somewhere tonight; she had forgotten its precise whereabouts or who was giving it. How could she think of a dull dinner party when time stopped at the Round Pond at precisely three o'clock?

It was a balmy spring day; the pink and white May trees were out; the air drifted with blown blossom. She would wear her almond green coat and skirt and carry her pink parasol, and look like a fresh little May tree herself. She must slip out of the house by the side door leading into the mews where the carriages of the large houses in this vicinity were kept. With luck, no one would see her go.

Everything went so exactly to plan that Chrissie was certain this meeting was fated. Even while some distance from the Round Pond, she could see the slender, elegant figure of Lord Monkshood, strolling slowly, as if enjoying the sunshine. Her heart began to beat unevenly. She was suddenly shy and nervous. Whatever did this sophisticated Englishman see in her to make him so determined to meet her again? Was he so lonely, so shunned, so hungry for love? No, that couldn't be; there must be a thousand Englishwomen, and well-bred ones at that, who would willingly run to him if he showed interest. Mind you, his wife had run away from him. One had to look at every angle, Chrissie told herself severely, if one was to keep one's head and behave with wisdom.

But when she saw his fine, gray, slightly melancholy eyes light on her and sparkle with pleasure, all thoughts of wisdom vanished. She was so delighted to be with him again, to hear his quiet voice welcome her, to observe that tender look in his face. Who cared for the royal notice of the stout Prince of Wales, for the murmurs of approval from austere ranks of chaperones, for the satisfaction of being a social success, when all that really mattered was this windy spring afternoon and the tall slender man holding out his hands to her?

"You came," he said. "How very good of you."

"Not at all. I wanted to see you again, too."

"Was it very difficult?"

"As easy as could be. Just a little ingenuity required."

Chrissie dimpled with triumph. "I can be quite scheming. I take after my father."

"Shall we walk a little?"

"Yes."

"And you can tell me all you have done since leaving Paris."

"Lord Monkshood——"

"Percival, please."

"Oh, may I? I was only going to say that I was absolutely devastated to hear that you hadn't been allowed to see me and that I never got your letters."

"Oh, that's understandable. I'm not the sort of character who's encouraged to be around young girls. I expect you've heard about that."

"I've heard various things, but I think it's terribly unfair to make you suffer for something that wasn't your fault."

"You're very charitable."

"Well, just knowing you—just looking at you—"

Something flickered in his eyes. "Looks can be deceptive."

"Are mine? Do you see me as anything but a very inexperienced young woman?"

"Chrissie, my dear, how old are you? Nineteen? I see you as young and impulsive and generous. I'm thirty-five."

"And so you're devious and deceitful and blackhearted? I just don't believe a word of that. I think you look a bit like a saint."

"Great scott! I'm no saint."

"Why did your wife leave you?" Chrissie heard herself saying. She was immediately ashamed of her rudeness, but he himself had said that she was young and impulsive, she hadn't learned to be discreet. Besides, she was desperately curious.

"Have they told you scandalous stories about that, too?"

"No. Only that she had a lover."

"True."

"How *could* she have?" Chrissie said intensely.

"Do you mean it might have been because I beat her or starved her? No, I didn't do those things. I neglected her, though. It was my fault, really."

"Didn't you love her?" Chrissie asked in a low voice.

"Not enough," he said tautly. "Not enough."

"But that's no crime! Why should that make you an outcast?"

"I don't know about in New York, but divorce has a pretty nasty stigma here. Apart from the church being against it, it may make other people begin looking into their own marriages and wanting freedom. There's a story that when the Princess of Wales first discovered that her husband was unfaithful—and that wasn't too long after they were married—she packed her bags in a rage to go back to Denmark and her family. But Queen Victoria soon put a stop to that. Marriage is for life, she said, for everybody, but especially for a royal princess. So even the most cruelly unhappy of her subjects are expected to endure. Which is a lot of claptrap. I would never have refused my wife the opportunity to be free to marry again. She's living in Switzerland now, by the way," he added. "You're never likely to meet her."

He smiled again, and the strained, angry look left his face.

"Chrissie, it's a lovely day, and if we're to talk about troubles, let's discuss our own. How am I going to go on seeing you? Because I want to very much."

"We'll manage. Papa never forbids me anything when he knows it's vitally important to my happiness." She blushed, feeling she had committed herself too far too quickly. "I'm not surprised about the Prince of Wales. Being unfaithful, I mean. He looks at women."

"Yes, I hear that he admired you."

"How did you hear that?"

"I read the social gossip columns. I'm jealous of everything you do in which I have no part."

"Is that really true?" Even for Chrissie, who was naturally impulsive, this stride forward into intimacy was a little too quick. He was behaving as if old age and decrepitude were at his heels. Or was he afraid of losing her to someone else? Now that was an intriguing and pleasant thought.

"Yes, it is. I'll tell you frankly that I've been looking for someone like you, though I never expected to be lucky enough to find her. The doctors say my father can't live another year. I'll shortly be the earl. Monkshood needs a mistress and an heir."

"Someone like me," Chrissie murmured, "with money?" The clumsy words leaped out of her mouth.

"That, too. You see, I am being frank. Though we old English families sometimes get our priorities wrong."

"I can see that."

"Chrissie! Your voice is cold."

"Yours was, too."

"But you didn't let me finish. I was putting the practical things first. I was going to add that I hadn't been optimistic enough to expect to fall in love as well."

He took her hand and drew off her glove. The pressure of his warm, dry palm on hers made her blood leap. All the words were blown away, as her body responded with astonishing violence to the physical touch. She believed she could have lain down on the green spring grass and let him take her in his arms there and then.

Was this love or just the dangerous thing Lizzie called sex? "Mind out for getting deceived by sex," she had said once, in a rare moment of communication. "My sister did that. Found she didn't love her husband at all when the mystery had gone. Just don't be too inquisitive about those things, Miss Christabel. You fall in love with your head first. Do you know what I mean?"

She had known what Lizzie meant. But she had also discovered that she wasn't the kind of cool, assessing person Lizzie thought she should be. First, Ferdie's kisses had ravished her, and now the touch of this long, narrow hand on hers was producing the same effect.

Lord Monkshood was aware of her confusion. His eyes, she saw, were wise and tender, as if he were making himself look at her as a beloved child. He wanted to be fair. And yet behind the wisdom there was that puzzling and disturbing sense of urgency, almost of despair.

"You know now why I had to see you by one means or another. But this isn't the best place in the world to choose. We may be seen."

"Does it matter?"

"Indeed it does, because in spite of what I have just said, I'm not proposing marriage to you here and now. You must have time. You must finish the Season, do all the things your father has planned for you—"

"In all those houses where you're not invited!" Chrissie burst out.

He shrugged. "Exactly. And I'll be jealous all the time

194

and terrified that you'll be snatched up by some handsome boneheaded young guardsman."

"Credit me with more intelligence."

"Yes, I do. Otherwise I couldn't take this risk."

"Then why take it?"

"Because you're so young and I must be fair. I want you to grow a little older and be sure of your feelings. I'll just keep in the background in the meantime."

"I'm not to see you again until the end of the summer!"

"We'll contrive something. But not often, and with more discretion than today. It's a great pity. I'd like to send you flowers every day and sweep you off your feet."

"I think you've done that already."

"Oh, you may recover your balance. Though I hope not."

"So, at the end of the summer, you'll come to Papa?"

"If you still want me to."

Chrissie nodded slowly. She had let his hand go, and her rapid pulse had quieted. She saw the sense of his argument. He was an honorable man. But echoing very faintly in her head were his words about money and an heir. That was all part of his honor, this honesty about everything. If he loved her, as well as her money and her young, healthy body, as surely the summer of waiting would prove, then she would simply use every blandishment she knew to get Papa's consent. At this minute, had Lord Monkshood persuaded her, she believed she would have eloped with him. But she was glad not to have to hurt Mamma and Papa so badly. She was really glad to have time.

Later in the afternoon Lizzie looked at her dusty shoes suspiciously.

"You've been out, Miss Christabel."

"N-no."

"Don't you go telling me lies. Where have you been?"

"Only for a very short walk." Lizzie's stern puritan eyes stared at her. "Only in the park," she said reluctantly.

"Not to meet someone!"

"Why do you immediately think that?"

"Because why did you go to so much trouble to get me out of the way? I admit I had my suspicions. I should have paid attention to them. Now, Miss Christabel, you'll get me into a lot of trouble, apart from the trouble you might be getting into yourself. Whom did you meet?"

Now and forever, Chrissie had to protect that wistful, vulnerable figure standing by the Round Pond.

"I only went for some fresh air. I wanted to be alone for once. You know how I feel about always being watched. As if I were the heir to a throne and in danger of assassination."

"It's your Papa's orders. I shall have to tell him about this."

"Don't you dare! I'll never forgive you."

"Now, Miss Christabel, you know I'll lose my position if I deceive your Papa."

This was an argument that never failed. Chrissie knew it well. For a moment she hated the plain, sturdy, stubborn figure of her constant companion.

"Haven't you any loyalty to me?" she asked.

Unexpectedly, Lizzie's face softened.

"Yes, I have, and you know it. It's only that I have to obey orders. But for this once, considering everything, perhaps I haven't noticed the dust on your shoes. However—" Lizzie wagged a stern finger. She was the governess again, speaking to her pupil, not to a grown young lady toying with the thought of elopement. "If you go arranging secret meetings with young men—"

"Lizzie, what a thing to say!" Chrissie declared, impulsively dropping a kiss on Lizzie's cheek. She was so happy from relief. And at least Lizzie hadn't an idea who the man had been. Or had she? Perhaps, in the end, affection for her pupil would come ahead of loyalty to her employer. Perhaps one day poor Lizzie would be required to put that to the test.

Chapter 17

Louisa had an uneasy feeling that something was wrong. Chrissie was behaving too well. She was, thankfully, a success. The highest commendation, Cousin Edith assured Louisa, without a trace of humor, was that one of the duchesses or marchionesses—one got confused about who they all were—had observed that one would never have known Christabel Spencer was an American.

As well as that intended flattery, there had been the famous dance with the Prince of Wales and shortly afterward Chrissie's presentation at court. She had looked sweetly pretty—again Cousin Edith's words—in her long low-cut white dress, wearing the Cartier pearls Harry had given her that morning and carrying the traditional Prince of Wales feathers. Sweetly pretty perhaps, but too subdued. Not the sparkling young lady, given to high spirits and waywardness, who had sailed from New York only two months previously.

The old Chrissie might well have giggled at her presentation when she found herself curtsying to the elegant Princess of Wales, virtually strangled by her high collar of pearls, and to the Prince himself. The Princess was extremely deaf, and Chrissie had been warned that her comments to each debutante were kind but mechanical. The prince, however, with his penchant for noticing a particularly pretty woman, was quite likely to make some unexpected remark. In fact, all he said was, "I'm glad to see you're still decorating these shores, Miss Spencer," but as Chrissie was rising from her curtsy, he gave her a swift unmistakable wink. This made her so sure that he knew of her liaison with Lord Monkshood that she blushed deeply and, stepping backward, tripped on her train. Cousin Edith was deeply disappointed with her clumsiness, after all her careful training, and seemed surprised that such an innocuous remark could have caused her confusion.

Harry thought she had done well in keeping her mouth shut. The naturalness the prince admired in her could have resulted in a long, lively conversation in front of the throne, with a queue of nervous debutantes being kept back by Gold Stick in Waiting in the anteroom. All the same, it wasn't like his Chrissie to be confused and tonguetied. He believed that splendidly dreadful old girl, Cousin Edith, was beginning to intimidate her.

"Nonsense," said Louisa. "I've only known Chrissie to be intimidated once in her life, and that was when she thought she saw that woman Lily on the ferry."

The day she had given up her own happiness, Louisa thought privately, and then wondered if this were true. Had she sacrificed happiness, for Harry had always been a good husband, and over recent years she had found her dependence on him growing. She frequently had headaches, and tired easily, and was glad that he had enough virility for two. She admired, too, the way he refused to kowtow to anybody, even in the most exalted circles. People prepared to humble and snub this wealthy expatriate who came back flaunting his riches, and his attractive daughter, found themselves outwitted. Infuriatingly, Mr. Harry Spencer always had a better quip, which he delivered with the greatest amiability. Then he would tuck his arm in Louisa's and make pleasant farewells. He had in his own way become a personality, and Louisa was surprised at her pride in him. So perhaps this affection and loyalty had been a better thing than the rapture of passionate love. One never knew how that would have worn through the years. Although Cornelius would always remain in her heart as a cherished memory.

She wondered a great deal how she would behave, supposing Chrissie fell in love unwisely. Would she counsel her against it or encourage her to snatch at happiness, no matter how evanescent?

She hoped she would never be put to this test. But Chrissie was a passionately headstrong young woman, and not likely to take kindly to a man whom she did not physically love. People were getting more outspoken about that kind of love and perhaps inflating its importance. The degree of importance was something she herself would now never know.

Which reflection made her reply absently when Harry said that at least that Paris thing had been nipped in the bud.

"Has it been?" Occasionally the thought had occurred to Louisa that Chrissie's wistfulness might stem from that single meeting with Lord Monkshood. It had evidently made a deep impression on her, and one could not assume it was forgotten. "I daresay Lord Monkshood will turn up again one day. He must be in England because I read in the *Times* that his father is seriously ill."

"Well, he'll be *persona non grata* in the royal enclosure at Ascot and at other places. I should think the risk of running into him is fairly remote. Anyway, I have my money on young Lord Farquhar. He's been squiring Chrissie quite a lot, had you noticed?"

"He's only a baron, however," Louisa pointed out, with slight malice.

"Better an unencumbered baron than a divorced earl," Harry said philosophically. "You see, I can make adjustments, if necessary."

"I wish you would make another adjustment and take us back to New York," Louisa said with sudden intensity. "I get urgent letters from Mary Ellen every week. It's going to break her heart if Chrissie marries an Englishman and stays here."

"It's not Mary Ellen's life."

"No."

"I don't want her interfering."

"She will. Nothing will stop that. And to tell the truth, Harry, I'm a little homesick myself. I'm longing to spend the rest of the summer in Southampton. And I'm not altogether sure Chrissie is enjoying all this as much as she pretends to. She isn't like Araminta Pepper, you know, wild for a title. Thank goodness she isn't. But she's being too quiet, Harry. Hadn't you noticed? She isn't like herself at all."

"She's just a little overawed."

"Overawed! Chrissie! She's got as much confidence as you have."

"Then she's aping the English. Being prim."

"That's another thing she could never be. She's far too spontaneous. You know Chrissie. Every feeling shows on her face. At least, it used to."

"Have you talked to her, asked her if she isn't happy?"

"Several times, and she always assures me that she's wildly happy. And then she goes into a dream."

"She doesn't want to go home?"

"That's the last thing. Or so she says."

"Then what the devil are you worrying about?"

"I don't know. I just feel uneasy."

"It's that sister of yours," said Harry. "My advice is, tear up her next letter without reading it. She puts ideas in your head. I expect she's already had Chrissie seduced by some English cad. What that woman has needed all her life is to be seduced herself. But since it's too late for that, you must regard her advice as prejudiced and unsound. Now what finery have you got yourself to wear at Ascot?" He came to kiss her on the forehead. "It isn't only my daughter I'm proud of, you know."

Ascot, and the huge picture hats and parasols, the floating voiles and chiffons, the gray top hats and striped trousers, the misty sunlight that made the trees and lawns swim in a haze, the wild excitement when the Prince of Wales' filly won, and in the burst of cheering and movement, Chrissie finding a hand on her arm, and those well-remembered gray eyes, still slightly haunted, looking into hers. The hurried words, "I'll be driving in Rotten Row tomorrow morning. Nine o'clock," and then the necessity to get back to London that night. She had been supposed to go to a ball at one of the nearby great houses and spend the night. She had to pretend an indisposition, she who was never ill. But she had witnessed enough of Mamma's headaches to be able to give a good imitation of them herself.

"Overdoing it," Mamma said.

"It's not like Chrissie," Papa said, with some anxiety and only the merest hint of suspicion. "Is it the ball you don't want to go to, baby?"

"I'm just a little too tired, Papa," Chrissie whispered plaintively.

"Then it's home and bed for you. We'll miss the last race. Anyway, I haven't won a dime all day."

He drove a phaeton, with two smart grays. He leaned out and whisked Chrissie in before she had time to greet him. "Pull down your veil," he said, and they were off at a thrilling pace, the dust rising, and the lime trees arching above them.

"I don't care if I am seen," Chrissie said.

"That's nice, but don't let's complicate things more than necessary. How did you get out alone?"

"I had a dreadful headache all night. I even managed to look pale. I said the only thing to cure it was a quiet walk in the early-morning air. Alone. I couldn't stand distraction." She sighed a little. "They believed me."

"You don't look pale now," said Lord Monkshood.

After that they talked very little. His father was not expected to live more than two or three weeks, said Lord Monkshood. He was in town only overnight on urgent business. He had gone to Ascot only in the hope of seeing her, which hadn't been difficult, since he had known that at some time she would come out of the royal enclosure.

"Why did you want to see me?" Chrissie asked.

"Just to make sure you remembered me."

She looked at his profile, with the sparse flesh, the proud nose, the firm, disciplined lips. This was what Papa meant about centuries of breeding. This was what he wanted for his daughter. Could he be persuaded to forget Lord Monkshood's unhappy past? Chrissie doubted it. There would have to be scenes, eventually.

"I do remember you," she said. "Too well."

That made the austere profile soften. Lord Monkshood could smile with a kind of radiant tenderness. Chrissie's heart turned over. She was glad of the veil. He might have seen her tears.

"When can I see you again?"

"At the end of August."

"That's when we're supposed to be sailing for New York."

"Not if someone keeps you here. As I intend to. I want to take you down to Monkshood. Your parents, too, if they will come."

"Percival, why me? I mean you hardly know me. It's— it's kind of astonishing."

"Don't you trust me, Chrissie? Really?"

"I just find it astonishing," she repeated.

"I've told you it isn't for your money. Although I admit that will be useful. One inevitably adds up advantages, so let's not deceive each other about that. When you see Monkshood, you'll understand what I mean. It's a completely beautiful place, but it eats up money. All the same, that's nothing to do with you and me personally. If you had been penniless, I would have felt the same about you. You're different from other women. Fresh and natural and honest. No awful female artifices."

"Don't you like them?" He had seemed very emphatic.

"Good God, no! Preserve me from coyness and flirtatiousness and clinging perfumes that nearly strangle me. And tortured hairstyles and feather beds of ruffles and frills."

Chrissie was laughing merrily.

"You sound as if you just don't like women."

"I like you." His voice was oddly harsh. "Haven't I been making that clear?"

Half of June, the whole of July and August. Twelve weeks. How could she keep up the deception for so long? She hated having secrets from Mamma and Papa, and yet the brief furtive meetings and communications gave her relationship with Lord Monkshood an excitement that was almost unbearable. She alternated between a high frenzied gaiety and sudden drooping spirits and headaches that worried her mother and made her father impatient and irascible. He had thought his daughter above those tiresome female weaknesses.

But no one seemed to guess her secret, although Lizzie occasionally gave her a long, thoughtful scrutiny.

Early in July the elderly and ailing Earl of Monkshood died, and the scandal of his son's divorce was briefly revived. If the new earl did not remarry and produce an heir, the ancient title would become extinct. The only other members of the family living were two elderly spinster sisters of the late earl, Lady Kate and Lady Maudie. There was a malicious story going the rounds that it was primarily these two formidable dowagers who had caused the young Lady Monkshood to leave her husband.

They wouldn't scare her, Chrissie thought privately. Not after Grandmother Spencer and Aunt Mary Ellen. She knew all about formidable old ladies.

She couldn't wait until the end of August.

"Well, baby," said Papa, early in August. "I'm going to the shipping offices to buy our tickets home. Your mother's fretting. So am I. This idle life gets deuced boring. I wasn't made for hanging about drawing rooms and ballrooms, and I aim never to drink another glass of champagne once I'm back home. I want to get back to work. I'm seeing a picture dealer about a Canaletto and a Rubens he's getting for me, and your mother has found some Sheraton chairs that she says will look fine in our drawing room." His eyes narrowed quizzically. "But are those things to be the only mementos of our visit to England?"

"If you're talking about a son-in-law—" Chrissie said slowly.

"I was, but you're coming home with us, of course. If any young sprig of the nobility wants to follow you, that's fine. We'll give a great ball in our own house, which is what your mother always wanted anyway. And she also hoped you'd be married in New York. We can get your wedding dress over from Paris. Worth has your measurements, and he can send us some designs."

"Papa!"

"Yes, baby."

"Are you still setting your heart on my marrying a title?"

"To tell the truth I am. I'm not the sort of chap who can easily give up an ambition. And you've seen the way these people live. There's nothing like it in the world. You know I've always wanted the best for you. You've had so many admirers this summer. Now isn't there someone who's made an impression on you? Damn it," he said testily, "if Araminta Pepper can get a prince, surely you can do as well. You've twice her looks."

"Would you like me to be a countess, Papa?" Chrissie asked impulsively, and knew that she had precipitated the storm. But why not? Why wait any longer? She was not going to change her mind, and neither was Percival. She longed with the greatest impatience to go down to Monkshood, and as soon as this matter was made public, she could do so.

Papa was looking at her hard.

"Are you telling me something, baby?"

"Yes, I am. You know when you first saw Mamma at the opera?"

"What's that got to do with it?"

"You said you fell in love immediately and knew she was the only woman for you."

"I did say that, but if you're telling me—"

"I fell in love with Lord Monkshood, in just the same way," Chrissie said steadily. "And he with me. We want to get married, Papa. Please don't object. Please!"

"My dearest girl—" the term he used only when he was stern and upset.

"*Please*, Papa!"

He sprang up and began walking about the room, his jaw thrust out.

"Utterly out of the question," he barked, as if she were a stranger. "Do you mean to tell me you've been seeing this man secretly?" Chrissie nodded, and his face went a strange dark red. "Where's that careless woman, Lizzie? I'll fire her immediately."

"Oh, no, please, Papa. You can't do that and leave her stranded in England. Anyway, it's nothing to do with her. I deceived her, too."

"I'll have that scoundrel Monkshood shown up for the cad he is. Thinks you'll be easy prey because you're young and innocent and rich and a foreigner."

"Papa, you're wrong and unfair. It's none of those things. It's because he loves me."

"Poppycock!"

"Just as you loved Mamma," Chrissie said steadily.

"Now don't you hit below the belt."

"That's what you're doing, Papa. At least you can meet Lord Monkshood and talk to him. You can't be so uncivilized as not to do that."

Papa stopped dead. "What was that word you used?"

"Uncivilized." Chrissie's jaw was sticking out, too, her eyes bright with defiance.

"So you're taunting your own father with having risen from the gutter, with being the descendant of a chimney sweep instead of one of those la-di-da lords who deceives young girls."

"But you want me to marry a lord, Papa."

"Not that kind," he roared. "Not someone who has already got rid of one wife and who people talk about in whispers."

"In whispers! Just because he's divorced. You can't be as old-fashioned as that. You sound like Queen Victoria."

"And you sound like a schoolgirl who hasn't learned manners. We'll sail for New York on the first available ship, and that's final."

"That's what you did from Paris, Papa, and it didn't help. Sailing next week won't help either, because I'd refuse to go with you."

"You'd do nothing of the kind. If you go on like this, you'll find yourself locked in your room until we leave."

"And then how would you get me to the docks? Kicking and screaming? That would really cause a scandal, worse than a man divorcing a wife who ran off with a lover. Now that was justified. But I don't think headlines about an American millionaire forcibly restraining his daughter would be justified. Anyway, you wouldn't care much for them, and neither would Mamma. It would be sort of an ignominious end to our European trip, wouldn't it? And the news would get to New York before we did."

Chrissie ended breathlessly and then was abruptly near tears as she saw the helpless terror in her father's face. In all her life she had never seen that look of defeat, and she found it infinitely distressing. Papa had always been strong, powerful, larger than life. Now suddenly he was just an ordinary man, baffled and unhappy. Had he diminished in these last few minutes, or was it just that she had grown up, casting off all traces of the spoiled, pampered and adoring child?

"We'd better get your mother down," he said at last. "But I warn you, Chrissie, this will nearly kill her."

"No, it won't." Chrissie shook her head stubbornly. "She's stronger than that. Women are."

"Well, my God, I hope so, if you're serious about marrying this dissolute earl."

"It's Aunt Mary Ellen I'm afraid to tell," Chrissie confessed.

"To the devil with her," Papa shouted, and was almost his old self again.

In contrast to Papa, Mamma's worn elegant face showed no anger, only dismay and something that looked remarkably like sympathy.

"We must have a long talk with Lord Monkshood, Harry," she said. "That's the first thing."

"Are you going to take this quietly, Lou? Aren't you going to talk your daughter out of it? It's only an infatuation, of course."

Mamma's slender eyebrows lifted the merest fraction.

"We must be fair. Would you have called it an infatuation if Chrissie had said she was in love with young Lord Farquhar, for instance?"

Papa puffed his lips in and out and blustered. "It's the temptation of forbidden fruits. Of secret meetings and those things. The girl's in love with being daring."

He looked hard at Mamma as he said this, and, strangely, her eyes dropped, evaded his gaze. A very faint flush showed on her cheekbones.

"Perhaps. But I think we ought to give Chrissie the opportunity to test the real state of her feelings."

"And how do we do that?"

"By having Lord Monkshood here, as I suggested. By letting them be seen together. By treating him like an ordinary suitor."

"A divorced man!" Papa expostulated. "Why, they couldn't even be married in a church."

"I know. It's very unfortunate."

"Let me say something," Chrissie broke in. "I don't want a big wedding. I'd rather have the money for other things."

"Money," said Papa bleakly.

"Now, Harry, don't be suspicious," Mamma said. "At least, not yet. Let us get to know this young man."

"Young! He's nearly as old as you!"

"No, I don't think so—"

"He's thirty-five," said Chrissie. "I like older men."

"That wasn't how it seemed when you were found kissing that Spanish boy in the library not so long ago."

"Oh, Papa, I was just learning. Didn't you learn?"

"Maybe, maybe. But it seems to me you're jumping from one extreme to the other."

"No, I'm not. I'm grown up now. I know exactly what I want. Just as Araminta Pepper did. And I might say that I'm far more likely to be happy with Percival, who is gentle and sweet, than with that German prince who probably hides a whip in the wardrobe."

"Chrissie!" Mamma exclaimed.

Chrissie shrugged in a blasé manner. "I want to show Papa I'm not still the schoolgirl he thinks I am. You don't just learn to curtsy during an English Season. You ought to hear the things those innocent debutantes talk about in powder rooms."

"I wouldn't have believed it," Papa said in bewilderment. "Look here, we're sailing for home next week."

"Running away, Harry?" said Mamma, her brows lifted again with that hint of delicate scorn.

Papa threw out his hands in a gesture of helplessness.

"Lou, I expected at least you to be on my side."

"I'm on both your sides. You're my family. I want you to be happy. I shall invite Lord Monkshood to dinner next week. Just ourselves, since he's still mourning for his father. Now if we have a problem, it's how to win over Cousin Edith."

"To whose side?" growled Papa.

"To Chrissie's, of course. When she's entirely sure what she wants." Mamma tucked her arm in Papa's affectionately. "Take me upstairs, darling. What you have to remember is that the world always belongs to the young."

Later Chrissie sat at her mother's bedside and held both her hands.

"Aren't you cross with me, Mamma, for deceiving you?"

"No, my darling."

Chrissie knitted her brows. "How is it you understand so well?"

"I only know that love is a very powerful emotion. That if you've any spirit, you'll defy everything for it, your parents, society, the world. I wish this hadn't happened to you, Chrissie, but since it has, I'd have been disappointed if you hadn't fought for it."

"Oh, Mamma! I love you so much."

"I only hope you are right."

"I am. I know I am."

"Well—only time will tell. You know Cousin Edith will wash her hands of you."

"Who cares?"

"And you'll be deprived of a great deal of society. Your friends will be the slightly raffish kind whose own lives don't stand too much looking into."

"They'll be much more interesting. I'd have *died* if I had married the sort of man Papa wanted me to, who can only talk about horses. Anyway," she added, "Percival and I will spend most of our time in the country. We won't want a lot of friends."

"Don't be too sure of that," said Mamma. "You know you enjoyed meeting the Prince of Wales and all those wonderful balls you went to."

"But I've had all that," Chrissie said with supreme confidence. "I won't want it again."

Mamma kissed her on the brow. "Don't be lonely," she whispered. At least that was what Chrissie thought she said, although she was smiling and her still-beautiful eyes were serene.

Chapter 18

Louisa was right about Cousin Edith. She packed her bags and departed for Suffolk and the country seat of the Feavershams. She declared it a scandal and a tragedy that all the time and trouble she had expended on Christabel Spencer had been wasted. The girl would never amount to anything now. Oh, she would be a countess, if she persisted in this determination to marry the Earl of Monkshood, and her children would be legitimate, even if the great Catholic families such as the Norfolks would maintain she was living in sin. And after all a title was what her ill-bred father had wanted, so perhaps he was happy.

But it was all, said Cousin Edith, a terrible disaster, and she would rather leave London immediately and not have to sit at table with Lord Monkshood when he came to dinner.

"Let the old hag go," said Harry.

Even though deeply opposed to his daughter's actions, he was not going to be disloyal in public. The Spencers presented a united front. And if he had fancied that Louisa's Cousin Edith might have had a heart rather than a book of social etiquette tucked in her bosom, he had been wrong.

So the lovely summer, so full of high hopes, was over. Harry didn't care for defeat. He tried to turn it into success by liking the man who had chosen to steal his daughter. But even this could not be done.

Lord Monkshood, thin, elegant, cultivated, aristocratic

to his fingertips, was not Harry's kind of man. They had nothing to talk about except the rebuilding of Monkshood, and on that question they disagreed sharply. Lord Monkshood said that the roof and the stonework required extensive repair, and he wanted to put in several bathrooms and redecorate the reception rooms, restoring some rare Elizabethan frescoes and generally refurbishing the house. In other words, he wanted the place, which he said was a gem, restored to its original beauty. From photographs Harry could only think that it was a picturesque ruin that should be pulled down and replaced by a solid, comfortable, draft-free house perfectly good enough for the future generations of earls.

He realized at last that he was not English and belonged entirely on the other side of the Atlantic. He could not get home quickly enough. He walked up Piccadilly and down Regent Street, smoking his cigars and sporting his white gardenia, his head held at its usual cocky angle.

But his eyes were bleak.

They had remained so ever since the evening Lord Monkshood had come to dinner and he had seen how it was with Chrissie. She was soft and flushed and starry-eyed and deliciously pretty. She was purely female. Even Louisa turned traitor and allowed herself to be mesmerized by their aristocratic guest's charm. They made cultivated conversation that excluded Harry only because it wasn't his kind of talk.

But later, when the ladies left the table and the port and cigars were brought, he got down to blunt facts.

If, he said, he consented to this unwelcome marriage, what sort of dowry was the noble lord expecting his bride to bring? Supposing, for instance, his daughter had been penniless?

"Then it's unlikely I would have met her," said Lord Monkshood calmly. "But in the event that I had, I would still have wanted to marry her."

"Easy to say," Harry grumbled.

"The truth, nonetheless."

And the irritating thing was that one had to believe the fellow. His gray eyes had a curious luminous sincerity that was convincing and a little disturbing. One could see that he had been through some awkward and painful troubles. Perhaps Chrissie was right, and the failure of his first marriage had been no fault of his own. Must have married a bitch.

The English had them, as well as other countries. One had only to remember Cousin Edith's hasty and heartless departure.

"Well, my girl isn't penniless, as you very well know."

"Monkshood," said Lord Monkshood, "needs about half a million spent on it."

"Half a million! Pounds! Good God, I could build an apartment block on Fifth Avenue for that. That's the latest thing, you know, people living in apartments under one roof. This house of yours—what's it got? Forty bedrooms? Just for two people?"

Lord Monkshood's eyebrows were gently raised. "I hadn't realized you were one of that curious breed, a socialist."

Harry was indignant. "How can a multimillionaire be a socialist? Don't be a fool. We have large mansions in America, too." He seemed to have lost the thread of the argument.

"The restorations to Monkshood would be made for future generations," Lord Monkshood said. "I don't know what you do in America, but we English regard our estates as pieces of history. Preservation is important."

"You don't need to tell me. I was born English. My parents' house hasn't been preserved, however. It has just fallen down, as hovels do."

"Then isn't it rather nice to show your daughter the other side of the coin? I understood this was why you brought her to England."

Harry reached testily for the port. He had a great desire to get drunk tonight.

"All right, all right. I don't mind admitting I made a mistake."

"But you didn't, I assure you. Ask Chrissie."

"Chrissie is exactly nineteen years old and has a head stuffed with romance, as girls of that age do."

"I love her, Mr. Spencer. Is that what you're waiting for me to say?"

"Among other things. I can't decide which you're putting first, her or that pile of ancient stones you call a house."

"Her, naturally," said Lord Monkshood stiffly. "But you must understand that one complements the other. Your daughter is a beautiful young woman and will grace this kind of background perfectly."

"What about your first wife?" Harry said bluntly. "Didn't she do this gracing bit to your satisfaction?"

He hadn't wanted or expected the flash of pain in the composed face. It made him too vulnerable himself, remembering Louisa and that day when he had known she was preparing to leave him. He might have been in the position of Lord Monkshood, innocent and deeply injured. He was suddenly ashamed of himself and thought, all these damned society vultures, waiting hopefully for someone sensitive and gullible to be tripped up by a mistake, so that he could be pecked to death.

Not that Lord Monkshood looked gullible. Far from it.

His expression was haughty and remote.

"I never discuss her," he said briefly.

"Sorry. Guess I shouldn't probe. But I am Chrissie's father, and I want a fair assurance of her happiness."

"I will do everything in my power about that, Mr. Spencer."

"Oh, I guess so, I guess so. I don't disbelieve you."

"And as time goes by, people forget old scandals. I assure you that we will have as many friends as any two people could want."

"I'd like to think that was true, but what does anyone

know about anything? I thought I could plan my daughter's future exactly. I had the money. But here we are. England is going to retain one of her stately homes, and I, I imagine, am going to become the grandfather of an earl."

"Isn't that what you wanted, sir?"

"I suppose it looks all right on paper," Harry grumbled. "But that's all. And you're not the one who has to face my sister-in-law when I get back to New York."

They both laughed. Harry refilled his glass and was just drunk enough to imagine that he had won this encounter.

"But let me say," he declared pontifically. "You've both made your bed, and you'll both lie in it. You'll get the half million, but not a penny more. That applies to my daughter as well as you, and your decaying house, piece of history or not. You can tell Chrissie this, but I also intend to tell her myself. She'll not get another penny. She's been pampered all her life and had her own way. So I have absolutely no intention of supporting her further. She's decided on her road, and she'll stick to it." He stood up, swaying. "My God, what will Lou and I do without her in New York?"

"You were going to lose her some time, Mr. Spencer."

Harry glared at him. The long, intelligent, sympathetic face blurred and refocused.

"Shall we join our ladies, Lord Monkshood?" he said, with elaborate dignity.

"She had better keep Lizzie," said Louisa, in bed that night.

"That dolt! Couldn't see beyond her nose. I blame her for the whole thing."

"She's devoted to Chrissie. And Chrissie will need friends."

"I thought his lordship was all sufficient."

"Harry, you're drunk."

"It's an occasion to be drunk."

"Yes. Well. But I did like him, Harry."

"Reminded you of someone, did he?"

Louisa was very still.

"What do you mean?"

"Nothing, Lou. Nothing. Perhaps I'm paying a debt."

"A debt? Whatever are you talking about?"

"For keeping my wife." Harry threshed over on to his side and put out the light. "Take no notice. I'm drunk. As you observed."

"Then you'd better go to sleep. And, Harry?"

He grunted.

"Let's make the best of it. I, for one, am not going to let Mary Ellen upset me."

"That woman!" Harry burrowed into his pillow, and Louisa knew she had done what she had wanted to, diverted his pain. Dear Harry. He had behaved like a great gentleman tonight, drunk or not.

Chapter 19

It had been expected that Aunt Mary Ellen would be aghast at the news, but not quite so inconsolable as she appeared to be. Letters poured into the Belgravia house. Every ship that sailed from New York carried massive epistles from Aunt Mary Ellen, helpless to do anything but protest. Whatever were Louisa and Harry thinking of to permit such a marriage? Would she ever see her beloved Chrissie again? What would that English rake do to her? Couldn't she at least come home to be married? Everything seemed so rushed and furtive. Were they *hiding* something?

"Tell her we're not hiding anything," said Harry grimly. "Your sister knows as well as we do that we have a willful and headstrong daughter. She's been spoiled, Lou, and now we're paying for it. We could make her wait until she's of age, or course—"

"But you haven't the heart to do it," said Louisa.

"No, I haven't. You know I never could bear to see her looking unhappy."

"Neither can I, for that matter. But I confess I do wonder what an extremely sophisticated man like Lord Monkshood sees in a nineteen-year-old girl, except her money."

"Some men like younger wives. And Chrissie's no ordinary girl."

"Half a million pounds," murmured Louisa.

"Damn it, I won't be called mean." Harry chewed at his cigar. He had a brooding look. "If this had been a marriage I had thoroughly approved of, it would have been a million. But that's between you and me. Spread that sort of news around, and another ceiling at Monkshood might conveniently fall down."

"You forget that apart from her dowry, Chrissie is also a considerable heiress."

"No, I don't forget it, but she'll have to predecease her husband if he expects to get any more, and that isn't likely. He doesn't look as if he'll make old bones. He may not even outlive me. To give him his due, I think he's genuinely infatuated with Chrissie, and he wants an heir. The money comes as a bonus. That's my summing up. Confound it, Lou, you know I'd never consent to the marriage if I didn't consider the fellow to be a gentleman. You can tell Mary Ellen that. And then tell her to shut up."

Chrissie was distressed about Aunt Mary Ellen's unhappiness, although she had known it was inevitable. She tried to soften the blow by writing almost as many letters back to New York, as arrived in London.

I am writing this at Monkshood. We, Mamma, Papa and I, traveled down this morning for our first visit, and I at least am totally enraptured. Indeed, I am jealous. I don't see how Percival can love a wife more than this wonderful old house. All the floors are uneven, and the stairs creak, and there are huge fireplaces, and marvelous old brocade drapes at the windows. The windows are mullioned, which makes the rooms a little dark, but very restful and full of atmosphere. There are family portraits on the stairs and in the dining room and the three drawing rooms. There are about forty bedrooms—dear Percival at the last count said he must have lost one, for he counted only thirty-nine! There is a china room, with the walls lined with valuable old porcelain, a music room, a gun room and a library which must contain every book ever printed. It smells of old leather and woodsmoke, and most of the time the lamps are burning in there. There is no gas or electricity, and personally I adore lamps and candles, but I fancy Percival intends to install electricity when he begins on renovations.

Dear aunt, it gives me the most marvelous feeling to think I am indirectly responsible for preserving such a historic place. Percival has only begun to tell me of the famous people in the past who have walked on these creaking floors and slept in the bedrooms. My bed is a four-poster that requires steps to climb into it!

The garden is what only an English garden can be, lawns like green silk, clipped yews, a sunken garden with a fountain, a lake smudged with water lilies, rose beds and herbaceous borders, and a grassy walk down to an old ruin where the jackdaws nest. You can hear them cawing all the time, it's a melancholy sound that I will always associate with the English countryside. There is also a peacock and two rather dilapidated peahens in the terrace, and in the fields beyond there are fat black and white cows grazing. Can you imagine this idyllic picture?

Percival has two elderly aunts who live in the east wing and who we are to meet at tea. I am a little nervous and hope I won't be tonguetied. What can they think of a brash American girl arriving and capturing their nephew? I have been told they are very outspoken. But they must realize I can't be a worse wife than Percival's first one, so I must be an improvement.

I can see your nose twitching with curiosity about that first wife. Mine is, too, but I have to conceal it. I know her name was Sybil, and that she was very pretty, but with some emotional instability which Percival had not known about when he married her. All the same, he does not make excuses for himself. He is the finest gentleman, and I could swoon like any Victorian maiden with love. How dearly I would like you to meet him. I have made him promise to take me on a trip home next year at the latest. Unless, of course, we have a baby by then, which is our greatest desire.

Imagine, I will be mother to a future earl. It's exactly what Papa wanted, and I must tell you, whatever you say, that Papa has been generous and kind and wonderful in allowing me my wishes. We had to fight a little, of course, but now I believe both he and Mamma are reconciled to my marriage. I truly hope so. It is so ridiculous to say that Percival could be a rake, and I don't care a fig for being ostracized from the stuffier kind of society because he is divorced. We really will scarcely ever want to leave Monkshood anyway.

Now it is time to dress and go down, I will finish this letter later when I have more to tell you. I am going to put on a white lace tea gown with a million yards of ruffles. Dressing for tea in English country houses is quite a ritual. Indeed, one changes one's clothes at least six times a day. Papa is allowing me to keep Lizzie, and she will be my personal maid. He thinks I will need a familiar face, and perhaps he is right, as Lizzie's freckled features have been around in my life for just about always.

I wonder what the aunts will be like. I promise faithfully to tell you. Papa and Percival are busy with the lawyers in the library. I hope they will emerge in time for tea, just in case Mamma and I need rescuing from these two spinster ladies.

It seemed, however, that Chrissie was wrong about Percival being shut in the library with the lawyers, for just as she was completing her toilette, she heard his voice in the corridor outside her door. It was preceded by the sound of running footsteps and a cry of pleasure. Then Percival's voice, surprised, displeased.

"August! I thought you had gone home. I left orders. Why have you disobeyed them?"

"Because I wanted to see you again, sir. Oh, I have missed you. The house has been so quiet. I have kept thinking of the funeral."

A boyish voice, with a foreign accent.

"The funeral! That was over weeks ago. You foolish boy."

"It isn't foolish when one is here alone. I am morbidly afraid of death."

Percival gave his light, amused laugh.

"Morbidly? Your English is getting very good. Then if you were so unhappy, why didn't you catch the steamer from Harwich? I left the ticket for you."

"I know, sir. But I dislike Stockholm very much and I hoped to persuade you—"

"Persuade me?"

"To—to remain, sir."

The voice was so hurt, so young and appealing, that Chrissie could not resist opening her door. A tall boy with blond curls and a milky white face flashed around to face her. A curious shock, which she was totally unable to understand went through her. The boy was distressed at the sight of her. More than distressed. He looked about twelve years old. He undoubtedly had a great affection for

Percival, which was hardly surprising, for no one, whether as host or tutor, could be kinder.

"Who is this, Percival?" she asked with interest. "Introduce me."

"Ah, Chrissie. Did we disturb you? This is my young pupil, August Borg, from Sweden. And this beautiful young lady, August"—Percival took Chrissie's arm in a proprietary way that delighted her—"is Miss Christabel Spencer, whom I am shortly going to marry."

The boy gave a stiff correct bow. The shock—or hostility—in his face was not imaginary. He had haughty features that were suddenly carved in ice.

"August has been here for the last six months," Percival said to Chrissie, speaking blandly as if he were unaware of the boy's distress. "He has been wonderful company for me while my father was dying. The contrast of youth and crabbed age, I suppose. But now he has learned all I can teach him and is ready to go home. I will write to your father tonight, August."

"Percival, you're not sending him away because of me?"

But before Percival could answer, the boy turned and ran off down the corridor, to hide tears, Chrissie was sure.

"He seems touchingly devoted to you. You must have been too kind to him. Does he come from an unhappy home?"

"He comes from a wealthy home, and he will succeed to his father's business if he continues with his English studies and his knowledge of the world. I met his family when I was traveling in Sweden, and this visit was suggested then. Old English families in past centuries have often taken in the sons of other houses, to learn or to be removed from the inhibiting influence of their parents. It's an old-fashioned but very sound method of education and learning maturity. I'm glad to say August has proved to be a splendid pupil. I warrant he's learned more than he would have at Eton. My Latin, you might like to know, is impressive."

"I understand," said Chrissie. "You don't have to go on explaining. I don't even mind if you think the boy should stay a little longer. He won't interfere with us."

"No, no, I've done all I can for him. If he stays here, he faces the risk of getting too attached to English ways. I'm really very displeased with him. He was supposed to have left two weeks ago. I suppose I should have made a point of seeing him on to the steamer myself."

"Yes, you should have, darling. He's only a child."

Percival kissed her forehead. Something flickered in his eyes.

"You're much more thoughtful than I am."

"But not nearly so erudite. I'm afraid the Madison Avenue School for Young Ladies didn't include lessons in Latin."

"Thank goodness. Let's go down to tea. I believe I heard Aunt Kate and Aunt Maudie arriving a little while ago."

They sat in the wing chairs on either side of the fire, two cozy pussycats in their dark dresses and snowy fichus. Mamma and Papa were there, making determined conversation, but it was obvious that the two ladies were interested only in Chrissie. When Percival presented her, Kate, the older one, with flinty, observant eyes set deep in folds of flesh, stared her up and down without apology. Maudie, obviously the milder personality, smiled at her warmly, but presently was unable to restrain her curiosity, and did her staring through a lorgnette with a long tortoiseshell handle. Her eyes had a blurred look, as if she were a little blind. Which could not be too much of a handicap in her case since her sister surely saw enough for two.

"She's only a child," said Aunt Kate at last, her inspection apparently over.

"She certainly looks very young," agreed Aunt Maudie.

"You, sir," said Aunt Kate, beckoning peremptorily to

Papa. "Your daughter looks as if she should still be in the schoolroom."

"More of a companion to August," murmured Aunt Maudie.

"But August is going home, dear," Aunt Kate pointed out. Papa put his arm about Chrissie.

"I'm inclined to agree with you ladies," he said genially. "My daughter is still a schoolgirl in many ways. However, she thinks she is grown-up. I myself was running a business at that age. So I guess Chrissie is old enough to be married."

"There is a great deal of difference between running a business and being a wife and mother," observed Aunt Maudie, who seemed to be able to make pointed remarks in a vague, irrelevant manner.

How old had Percival's first wife been when they had married? Chrissie wondered. The unknown Sybil. Had she, too, been stared at in this uncompromising way?

Mamma, who had been sitting quietly on a sofa a little way from the fireside, said unexpectedly, with a touch of frost in her voice, "Chrissie isn't unfamiliar with large houses or large staffs. Where I was brought up in Virginia—"

"I thought you said she was a Yankee, Percival," Aunt Kate interrupted.

"An American," said Percival. "And I don't think Christabel cares to be discussed as if she weren't here. You are being naughty, as usual, dear aunts." He tugged the rope at the side of the fireplace. "We'll have tea and some less personal conversation."

Papa stroked his golden beard. "Who is this August you said might be a playmate for my girl?"

A maid had come in answer to the bell. Percival ordered tea, then said, "August is a young Swede who has been studying English. It's true he is going home. His father is a friend of mine. After tea, Mr. Spencer, I plan to take you on a tour of the house. I think you'll be interested in the long gallery and my collection of paintings."

"I've been admiring that Gainsborough over the fire-place. By jove, I'd like to own that."

Percival gave a faint smile.

"It's a portrait of my great-great-grandmother. And although I can't say that you will ever own it, sir, your daughter will."

Papa nodded vigorously. He seemed pleased. He had been growing noticeably more mellow ever since arrival at Monkshood. If the Earl of Monkshood was still not the son-in-law he would have chosen, the house was not, after all, the tumbledown ruin he had imagined. He was deeply inpressed.

"You must get Chrissie painted. I had my wife done when we were first married. Nothing enhances a room more than a portrait of a beautiful woman. What have you got in this long gallery?"

"Quite a good collection, I think you will agree. My father and my grandfather liked the English school. There's a Constable and two Reynolds and a very fine study of horses by a man called Stubbs. English to the core. But there are some nice Dutch and Italian things, as well. A very good Canaletto."

"Canaletto! That's a coincidence. I've just acquired one for myself. Admire him immensely. I was lucky enough to get a Rubens, too, and my dealer tells me he's on the track of a Rembrandt. Now that would be something to take back to New York. One gets a peculiar satisfaction from adding to the nation's treasures. Don't you agree? You English aristocrats ought to know. You plundered Europe. But if you want my opinion, you've had your heyday, and it's over to us Americans now. We're pro-ducing some notable collectors."

"As long as you don't ravage England," said Percival amiably.

"Oh, come, old fellow. Fair's fair. You take our daughters; we retaliate as best we can by taking your works of art."

Papa gave his great laugh, and then tea arrived, and

the atmosphere was noticeably warmer. Chrissie waited warily for another broadside from the aunts, but it failed to come. They were temporarily absorbed in demolishing hot buttered muffins and drinking tea out of exquisitely fragile cups. She saw a vista of afternoons ahead, with herself presiding at the tea table, handling the gleaming silver teapot, the sugar tongs, the plates and napkins and fragile cups.

Could it be because Sybil had failed to have a child that the marriage had ended?

It was nearly midnight when Chrissie sat down to finish her letter to Aunt Mary Ellen.

My darling clever Percival has completely won over Papa. They spent ages in the long gallery looking at the pictures, and then they were almost as long in the gunroom examining the collection of weapons which Papa says is superb. There is even a Crusader's sword. It is truly fortunate for Percival and me that Monkshood is exactly the kind of English home Papa has always dreamed of, and it is only regrettable that he and Mama can't be entirely happy about my marriage. But Percival assures them that after Queen Victoria's death things will be different. The Prince of Wales has a much broader outlook, and I am sure will not allow the *innocent* party to a divorce to bear any stigma.

But to return to my account of this long lovely day. We all dressed for dinner, Mamma and I in our finest Paris dresses, and the aunts in black velvet and diamonds, which made them look very regal. Papa—you know how irresistible he can be when he is in the mood—took in an aunt on each arm, and Percival did likewise with Mamma and me. The lawyers had departed for London, as this evening was to be a purely family affair.

Family or not, it was very grand. I wish you could have seen the gold plates, and the masses of candles in beautiful silver candelabra, and the crystal wine-glasses all engraved with the family coat of arms, and the great tureens carried in by a positive retinue of servants. Even Papa knew his money could not buy all this; it takes centuries of inheritance and custom.

And now for the food. We began with two soups, one hot and one cold, then fish, also both hot and cold, after which followed a sorbet, to prepare us for the adventure of the main course, which was *canard à l'orange,* and quite delicious. Percival apologized that the game season has not begun, so we could not have pheasant or grouse. After the duckling came the cook's special confection, an ice cream sweet in the shape of a swan, and flambéed with a great flourish. If you can imagine we could eat more, there was a hot savory and then fresh fruit, peaches, apricots, nectarines, strawberries, grapes. I can't tell you the wines we drank because I am quite ignorant of them, but Papa obviously relished them and could still happily cope with the port when we ladies retired to the drawing room.

Well, the saying that the way to a man's heart, or his friendship, is through his stomach was successfully proved tonight, for when the gentlemen at last joined us Papa was in the mellowest of moods and wanted only to measure the chimney breast to decide whether or not his grandfather, an undersized, soot-stained child, could once have emerged into this room and admired the yellow damask hangings and the beautiful rugs and furniture.

For your information the hangings are considerably faded and frayed, and all the chairs and sofas need re-covering. But by firelight and candlelight everything looks rich and luxurious and exactly right. I think I would rather have it like that, faded and genuinely old, than refurbished with the new things Papa's money will buy.

The aunts, when Mamma and I were alone with them, asked endless questions about where I went to school and what I learned and who my friends were (I was never allowed many, was I? At least, not since Henry's kidnapping). They also wanted to know about you and Uncle Boy, and both Mamma and I made a great deal of Uncle Boy's book on Lord Byron, and how clever he was, and how you lived in one of the oldest and most historic mansions in New York. In the end, I think they were almost reconciled to me, at least Aunt Maudie was, for she patted my hand in quite a friendly way, but Aunt Kate retained her fierce, flinty look. However, I think that is an accident of feature rather than of mood.

We could not discover whether they had approved of Percival's first wife, for when I had the courage to ask what her family had been, Aunt Kate said, "We never speak of her, do we, sister?" and shut her mouth tight. Aunt Maudie merely shook her head and looked sad, almost as if she had been fond of the wicked Sybil.

One thing is certain: they will never have to behave like that about me. I love Percival too dearly. And I am so happy that this visit has been a success. I looked across the dinner table at that fine, serious face, with its centuries of breeding, of my husband-to-be and could scarcely believe my good fortune. Papa has always wanted me to marry an English aristocrat, but I had never been optimistic enough to hope I would fall in love as well.

So please be happy for me, dearest aunt, and stop predicting disasters. What disasters could there be? I will have a beautiful home, an adorable husband and a title. Though I am not like Araminta Pepper —I beg her pardon, the Princess Rudolf—and set great value on titles. It is Percival I want.

And I order you never again to write calling me a romantic schoolgirl, because I am *a grown woman and know exactly what I am doing.*

We return to London tomorrow, and two weeks later Percival and I will be married quietly in Caxton Hall, with only Mamma and Papa and two friends of Percival's present. I will not wear a wedding dress, naturally, but I will carry a posy of white rosebuds because those are the flowers Percival first sent me. Mamma frets about my not having a proper wedding, and I know you do, too, but really what more could I want? I guess God listens wherever the marriage vows are said.

I'm so happy, happy, happy. . . .

In the morning Chrissie stirred in the warm depths of her feather bed and heard the peacock crying harshly on the terrace and someone giving a gasping sob.

She sat up sharply and heard hurried footsteps along the passage down the stairs. Later she thought she heard the wheels of a carriage, but of that she could not be sure, for her bedroom faced over the gardens and the lake and the quiet woodlands.

Percival was late to breakfast. He came in with an apology. He had had to take his young Swedish guest to the railway station. It must have been chilly out, for his face looked hollow with cold.

Chapter 20

Mary Ellen couldn't be told often enough how Chrissie had looked on her wedding day. She even encouraged Harry to add to Louisa's description. She wanted a reason to air her own grievances and thereby ease her desolate sense of loss and anger. It was easier to disagree with Harry than with Louisa.

Harry was making one of his rare visits to the old van Leyden house. To tell the truth, he found his own house appallingly empty, and he suspected that Louisa did, too, although she was a far more disciplined person and accepted that daughters grew up and left home. It was all very well to boast in his club and his favorite eating places that his daughter was now a countess and that the European trip had been a triumph. The way he told the story, Mary Ellen said tartly, crowned heads and coronets were two a penny, and she didn't believe a word of it. Men invariably had base natures, no matter to what splendors they had been born. She didn't suppose the Earl of Monkshood was any more perfect than his butler or his valet or his groom. Only time would tell how successful this marriage would be, but at present the sad fact was that Chrissie had been deprived of a real wedding. Married in this hole and corner fashion without even a wedding gown. Were Harry and Louisa happy about that?

"No, we were not," Harry barked. "I only know of one person whose willpower is stronger than mine, and that is my beloved daughter's. Unless"—he looked balefully at Mary Ellen—"it's yours. Anyway, short of locking Chrissie up and making an even bigger scandal, there was nothing to do but put a good face on it. Was there, Lou?"

"Lord Monkshood is a charming man," Louisa said. "Even you would agree, Mary Ellen."

Mary Ellen grunted.

"Then why couldn't his first wife stick to him? Why had she got to bolt?"

"I gather there was a lover. Wasn't there, Harry? We only know that Lord Monkshood behaved as a gentleman would and took the blame so that the divorce could go through."

"That's his story, I imagine."

"Well, the first lady Monkshood did marry the man concerned," Louisa said mildly. "They went to live in Switzerland, which rather suggests a desire to avoid English society, doesn't it? At least Chrissie won't have the embarrassment of meeting her anywhere."

"Who will Chrissie meet at all now that she'll be cold-shouldered by all those royal sycophants?" Mary Ellen demanded, her highly colored face crumpled and distressed. "All this lark of taking her to England to make a fine marriage. Look how it's ended. Another of your expensive failures, Harry Spencer."

Boy, who was sitting in the wing chair by the fire with the inevitable glass of rum at his elbow, said in his blurred, absent manner, "What sort of cellar does the earl keep?"

"Superb. Superb place altogether, Monkshood." Harry wandered about the room, looking critically at the low ceiling, the shabby wallpaper, the windows darkened by the great spreading tree outside. "And what are my other expensive failures, Mary Ellen?"

"Thinking you can buy this house. Thinking you can wear me down."

Harry trod deliberately on a creaking floorboard.

"Perhaps the house will tumble down first."

"If it does, I'll live in the ruins."

"She will, too," said Boy. "Like a large bloody-minded rat."

"Boy!"

"That's what you can be, sis. Doesn't worry me, so long as I can save my manuscript from the wreck."

"When are you going to get that published?" Louisa asked, hoping to change the subject. A meeting between Mary Ellen and Harry was like the rumbling of two bad-tempered grizzlies.

"Posthumously, old girl. That's soon enough for me."

"They're both crazy," Harry said on the way home. "Crazy as loons."

"You deliberately provoked Mary Ellen."

Harry grinned. "Did her good. Took her mind off Chrissie."

"Is that why you did it?"

"Maybe. I always enjoy a set-to with Mary Ellen. Never do to let her know it, though. She'll go down fighting."

"And so will you." Louisa tucked her arm in his. She

enjoyed driving with Harry, he handled the mare so well, expertly negotiating the tangle and confusion of Fifth Avenue traffic. But then he did most things well. "Did I ever tell you you behaved very generously over Chrissie's marriage?"

"Thank you, Lou. But that's over and done with now. A *fait accompli,* as they say. If it doesn't work, our little girl will have to learn the meaning of adversity."

"You don't mean that. Not with Chrissie."

"I do this time. It would be the only way to make her grow up."

"She is grown up. Look how calm and composed she was at her wedding. Clutching that little posy of rosebuds. No wonder Lizzie cried." Louisa suddenly had to dab at her own eyes.

"That doesn't necessarily indicate a grown-up condition. It could be playacting. She and that Araminta Pepper. They're still living schoolgirl romances. Our mistake was stopping in Paris, Lou."

"I don't suppose everyone would call a princess and a countess in their families mistakes. Anyway, whatever doubts we might have, Lord Monkshood really is a charming man. I didn't just say that for Mary Ellen's benefit. Chrissie is so in love." Louisa dabbed at another tear. "I wonder where they are now. Still in Venice, I expect."

Harry, guiding his horse through the noisy traffic, looked up at the buildings on either side of Fifth Avenue. They were growing higher, as he had always predicted they would. The sidewalks were wide; the big new stores had fine window displays; there was an air of purpose and prosperity and virility that he had not found in any foreign city.

He had rid himself of his lingering hankerings for England.

He knew now that New York was his city. He was immensely proud of it. He would go home and supervise the hanging of his new possessions, the Canaletto, the Rubens and the splendid Rembrandt, which was a rich dark prize.

It had taken centuries to make Monkshood what it was. He had created his home in a mere twenty years. Before he died, it would be fine enough to leave to the nation. He nodded to himself with quiet satisfaction. At the age of fifty-five he had discovered that he was purely American.

"Let's break open a bottle of champagne when we get home, Lou. How would you like that?"

She nodded gently. She was glad to see the aggressive jut to his chin again. He had been a little subdued ever since leaving England and Chrissie. She resolved to keep her own anxieties about Chrissie secret from now on. The child had been allowed the choice that she herself had once longed for and had been denied. One could only be happy about that.

It was, unfortunately, too late in the year to see Venice at its best. They arrived to find a thick damp mist hanging over the waterways and dimming the glories of the architecture. Suddenly Chrissie's optimism left her, and she felt as gray and bedraggled as the pigeons in St. Mark's Square, seeking the vanished lucrative harvest of the summer tourists.

She was tired, that was all that was wrong. It had been such a long journey from Paris. They had had to sleep in narrow couchettes, separately. Even in Paris Percival had insisted that she buy so many clothes, as befitted his wife, and linger so long in the smart couturier salons that by the time she had retired to bed he had declared her too exhausted to want the company of a husband. When she had cried impulsively that she did, his eyebrows had lifted in that delicate, ironical manner she was coming to recognize, though not to understand, and he had pleaded his advanced years and his own exhaustion.

Something had puzzled her. He had looked tired, certainly. But that pale, drawn look was natural to him, and she had always understood that an ardent lover was seldom too tired for the all-important activity into which she had still to be initiated.

That was when her confidence had begun to drain just a little. She had even shed a few tears, then stuck her chin out and told herself there were still many things she had to learn from experience, not from instinct. Percival did love her, as evidence the expensive clothes he had bought her, the sable-lined cloak, the morning gowns and lacy tea gowns, and one fabulous evening gown in heavy cream satin embroidered with thousands of seed pearls, which made her look delightfully sophisticated. It was to wear to the opera at Covent Garden Opera House, Percival said.

It was only natural that they should both be tired after such a day. They hadn't even had time to call on Millie and George Pepper.

Percival, Chrissie consoled herself, was a perfectionist. He would want the ideal surroundings and conditions for their first night together. No doubt he knew exactly where they were to be found in Venice.

Only why didn't he say so, instead of getting more remote and keeping that look of haunted sadness in his eyes? Yes, that was the word. Sadness. And on their honeymoon.

There could be only one explanation. He was thinking of Sybil.

But it surely would be different in Venice, the most romantic city of them all.

They had a suite in a hotel on the Grand Canal. They had been received like royalty, and the rooms were full of flowers. There were two bedrooms, each with double beds. Percival had insisted that she must have the one looking over the canal.

"You'll see the moon shining over the rooftops," he said. "If you can stay awake long enough."

"But, darling—"

He kissed her in his gentle, passionless way. She had

just begun to realize that he almost never kissed her on the lips. Was that unusual? Or just his exquisite courtesy?

"I'll join you later. Why don't you sleep a little? After that night on the train you must be nearly dead."

But I'm young. I'm newly married. I'm in Venice, Chrissie wanted to protest. She was bewildered and edgy and tired and knew that she was going to cry again. She encouraged him to go. He wasn't going to know that he had a weeping bride.

The moon did shine over the jumble of rooftops. She knew, because at two o'clock in the morning she stood looking out of the window at the serene scene. The mist had gone. The water of the canal flowed black and gleaming. The ageless façade of the city spread before her sleepless eyes. She was shiveringly lonely.

So lonely that she tugged her wrap around her and tapped at Percival's door. When no answer came, she opened the door quietly and blinked to clear her vision. A single night-light was burning on the bedside table. The bed itself was empty, the snowy pillows uncrushed, the sheets smooth and immaculate.

So she had an errant husband. Or did she have a husband at all?

Suddenly she was not just lonely; she was frightened as well. Terrified. Deserted. Why had Percival told her he loved her? Why had he married her to leave her alone like this?

For Papa's money, as Papa had suspected? But how utterly awful if that were true, and what a blind besotted idiot she had been. Thinking those catastrophic thoughts, Chrissie flung herself on the bed and sobbed into the immaculate pillows. She sobbed so vehemently and with such relieving abandon that she didn't hear the door open. She didn't know Percival was there until she felt his hand on her shoulder.

"My dear Chrissie?" came his deep, gentle voice.

Trust him to make his sympathy sound not like an

apology but a perplexed question, as if she were the person at fault. Whatever was his wife doing crying her heart out when he had brought her to this beautiful hotel in this unique city, when he had spent a small fortune on clothes for her and given her a title into the bargain?

Oh, no, that sort of courteous English behavior was not going to excuse him this time.

"Why did you leave me? How *dare* you leave me and scare me to death? What have I done? Do you find me so loathsome?"

"Chrissie, Chrissie! Aren't you just a little hysterical?" His long, tender face leaned over her. "You were sound asleep. I didn't want to wake you to tell you I was going for a walk."

"Then you should have. I came in here and thought you had abandoned me."

"What complete nonsense!"

"How did I know I had a husband who must walk about empty streets in the dark?"

"Venice has a subtle beauty at night, quiet and mysterious and a little sinister. I'll show it to you before we go home. It just happened that I couldn't sleep. It's a thing I suffer from. The reason I like separate rooms. My wife isn't to be disturbed by a prowling husband. Now sit up and let me sponge your face. It's hot and wet, and your hair is tumbling down." His fingers curled in her heavy hair. It was true that he had a sleepless look, his eyes strained and slightly red-rimmed. His grip was pulling her hair, hurting a little.

"This is beautiful, darling. Thick and curling. But isn't it a little heavy? Have you ever thought of having it cut short?"

"Short!" She was surprised out of her self-pity. "Like Lady Caroline Lamb? I hope you haven't got my Uncle Boy's obsession for Lord Byron."

"No, I haven't got an obsession, and I sincerely hope you aren't another Lady Caroline Lamb. I was only thinking you would look devastating with a halo of curls.

You'd set a fashion. I'd like that. We Monkshood have never been social conformers, you know. Would you like to set a fashion, my dearest?"

His fingers were still entangled in her hair, and she was aware of a change in his face. It had a deep, inward, rapt look that communicated itself to her and made tremors go down her spine. Her stomach clenched in a spasm of pure excitement.

"Yes—if you wish—I'll have my hair cut."

"Tomorrow." He let her go, and began rapidly divesting himself of his jacket, his shirt, his trousers. "I know a hairdresser. Carlo. He's extremely clever."

With a deft movement he had flung back the sheets and was beside her on the bed. Now, as if she had not been available to him at any earlier stage of their marriage, he seemed to be in the greatest haste, lifting her nightgown in a kind of frenzy and pressing his warm, silky flesh against hers.

Her tears had gone. His kisses had dried them. She was trembling violently, and how could she ever have doubted that her husband loved her? Someone—who had it been? Araminta with her superior knowledge— had warned her that the first time it might hurt. But pain was pleasure, or pleasure was pain, and she only knew that this was her darling Percival, her husband, and if she had any complaint, it was that the absolutely heavenly thing he did to her was over too soon.

There was no doubt that making love was an excellent cure for tiredness and strain and irritation, for in the morning they were both in the best of humor. Indeed, Chrissie was radiantly happy, and Percival had almost, though not quite, lost his haunted look. That Chrissie told herself was probably something he had been born with, a sign of breeding or something. There was nothing sad or wistful about his conversation. It was a brilliantly sunny morning, and they were going to spend the day in gondolas, in exploring the little Adriatic islands dissolving in pearly mist, in strolling around the Piazza San Marco, and in visiting the barber. Unless Chrissie had had second thoughts about his suggestions for improving her already delightful beauty.

Chrissie would have allowed her head to be shaved, had it pleased him. Besotted, she told herself scornfully. Imagine what Lizzie was going to say, let alone Mamma and Aunt Mary Ellen when they heard. Not to mention, also, the formidable ranks of society ladies who were already going to look down their noses at the new, and dubious, Countess of Monkshood. Then let them look harder, at that impudent, shameless little Yankee, who either didn't know better or didn't mind making a laughingstock of herself.

"Indeed I haven't changed my mind," she said. "I can't wait to see how I look. Anyway, I've always been terribly bad at putting up my own hair, and we really didn't want Lizzie on our honeymoon, did we?"

"I should say not."

"Araminta wrote that Rudolf likes her to wear a diamond necklace he gave her in bed."

That inconsequential remark was a mistake. For a second Percival's face tightened. Then he smiled and said, "You will wear the Monkshood diamonds, too, but at the correct time and place."

Chrissie dimpled and flung her arms around him.

"Where? At the opera, when I show off my new curls?"

"A splendid idea. Then come. Aren't you ready? Our gondola is waiting."

The sun is shining. Our gondola is waiting. We are in the most romantic city in the world, with its crumbling pink and chrome palazzos, its gilded church spires, its great campanile, its fluttering pigeons. And I adore being married. Carlo is cutting my hair and exclaiming in alternate anguish and admiration, the thick locks are lying on the floor to be swept up, and Percival is watching with the keenest critical interest while Carlo's clever fingers shape

my new halo of curls. I am afraid to look in the mirror. Then I see a rosy face set inside this frame of glossy brown curls. I think that I look a little like a boyish saint.

And Percival is pleased. He thinks the effect is ravishing. So, after a moment, does Carlo, who waves his hands and talks excitedly, giving sideways glances at what he obviously considers a very eccentric English milord. Whatever else happens I am going to be a talked-about countess, and that's rather fun. I wonder what Percival's aunts will think.

That was the letter that Chrissie was writing in her head to Mamma and Papa and Aunt Mary Ellen. Her lips curved in a smile at their almost inevitable reaction. She would add, placatingly, "I cannot tell you what intense pleasure it gives me to please my husband's whims. I am almost a little afraid. It seems to be tempting fate to imagine that I can ever be so purely happy again."

Chapter 21

Lizzie, bidden from Monkshood to the Ritz Hotel in London where Percival had decided to stay for a short time, gasped with shock when she saw Chrissie.

"Good grief, Miss Christabel, what have you done to your hair?"

"Don't you like it, Lizzie? It's the latest fashion."

"Not one I've ever seen."

"No, because I'm starting it. We're going to the opera tonight, and everyone is going to look at me."

"They'll do that, all right."

"Now, Lizzie, you might have been able to boss me when I was a little girl, but you can't now that I'm married. I have a husband to please."

"You mean it pleased him to cut off your lovely hair and make you look like a freak!"

"It was his suggestion," Chrissie said haughtily.

"Does he want to make you a guy?"

"Lizzie!"

Lizzie had never quite stopped being a governess. "With your permission, Miss Christabel, I'll tell the servants you've had a fever picked up from those dirty canals in Venice and your hair had to be cut off."

"You haven't my permission," Chrissie said. "And if you're not careful, I'll order you to call me 'my lady.'"

Lizzie's plain, honest face crumpled into its first smile.

"That's fair enough, but I'll never remember. You can't teach an old dog new tricks. All the same, I'll grant you this, Miss Christabel, you do look happy."

"Oh, I am, Lizzie," Chrissie cried, her brief annoyance vanishing. "I have the most adorable husband in the world. Wait until you see the things he has bought me. I'm to wear the cream satin with the seed pearls to the opera tonight, so hang it out carefully, will you? And open my jewel box. You'll find the most beautiful little diamond tiara. Percival said I am still too young to wear the heavy family jewels, and anyway I might like my own special jewels to leave to my own daughter. Isn't that the sweetest thought?"

"To be dead," said Lizzie flatly.

"I declare, Lizzie, you would take the romance out of anything. All my life I've been cautioned about this danger and that. I know people die. I haven't forgotten Henry. But let me enjoy my very own tiara and my new husband. And think of the time we'll save this evening since my hair doesn't need to be put up. While you're unpacking, you can tell me how you have been getting on at Monkshood. Don't tell me that you didn't find that heavenly place just the least bit romantic."

Lizzie had never been garrulous, nor had she gossiped. Perhaps it was unreasonable to expect her to talk freely about Monkshood, where she had had to take up quarters while Chrissie and Percival were on their honeymoon. Chrissie hoped that such different surroundings might have loosened her tongue. On the contrary, Lizzie's face closed up in a secretive way, and she merely said that she had managed. It would be better when the mistress was home. She had felt like a fish out of water.

"And those two old ladies, his lordship's aunts—"

"Have they been troublesome?"

"It's not what they say; it's what they don't say," Lizzie burst out.

"You mean they don't approve of me?"

"They didn't say as much."

"What are you trying to tell me, Lizzie?"

Lizzie looked upset and finally admitted that the aunts hadn't seemed to care for his lordship marrying again.

"I think they were fond of the first countess, Miss Christabel."

"But surely—" Could two prim and proper old ladies, jealous of a proud family's honor, be fond of an unfaithful wife? An adulteress, to put it bluntly.

Chrissie closed her mouth. Old friend as Lizzie was, she couldn't discuss these things with her. She mustn't worry, for the aunts' disapproval was not a very large cloud on the horizon. Surely she could dispel it as soon as she wished to. Never in her life had anyone resisted her blandishments, when she cared to use them. All the same, as a millionaire's daughter, her experience had been fairly limited and fairly prejudiced.

She had an uneasy feeling that two elderly aristocratic English ladies might not be too susceptible to an aura of charm, youth and money. They had already looked down their noses at her in the most unmistakable way. If they persisted in their loyalty to the erring Sybil, there was going to be a cool atmosphere in the great house.

But Percival would be there. How could she possibly be unhappy or uneasy when he was so firmly on her side?

The same thing applied at the opera house that evening. Percival held her arm in a closely possessive grip as they mounted the grand staircase. She knew his head was held high and with natural arrogance, so hers rose correspondingly. She knew they were being stared at. She could guess the whispers behind fans.

"That little American heiress—made too much fuss of earlier in the Season—the prince noticing her and giving her ideas of her importance. Just look at her hair! She must have done that to draw attention to herself. A great mistake. . . ."

"I know what they're all saying," she whispered to Percival.

"So do I. Isn't she ravishingly pretty! Lucky fellow, Monkshood. Must tell Caroline to cut her hair like that. Deuced attractive."

Chrissie's lips twitched. "That isn't at all the sort of thing I heard."

"Then my ears must be better than yours."

"Who's Caroline, anyway?"

Percival made a gesture toward the groups of women in their silks and satins, their ostrich feathers and jewels.

"Most of them. It's a very prevalent English name, very boring. Are you enjoying this?"

Chrissie smiled radiantly.

"Enormously! I never thought going to the opera could be such fun. Oh, there's Jane Barron. I stayed at their house this summer. I believe she's actually smiling at me."

"Whyever not? They won't cut you dead. They'll only hold you at arm's length for a little while. Especially if they're people who aspire to entertaining royalty. Or strict mammas who think their daughters might get similar ideas to yours."

"There's only one of you, my darling. And you're

mine. It's not going to be any use any of them envying me."

Percival gave his half smile that even yet wasn't entirely happy. He had a permanent streak of melancholy, Chrissie decided. Although she did not think it was at all beyond her powers to eradicate it.

"Didn't I tell you it would be fun to create a fashion?" he said.

"Oh, it isn't my hair they're envying me for," said Chrissie emphatically.

After the opera they dined in their suite at the Ritz. Chrissie related how it had been at the opera in New York that Papa had first met Mamma and had decided instantly to marry her. She went on at some length because suddenly again Percival's withdrawn quietness had come over him.

Finally she said, "Is there something wrong, Percival?"

He looked at her with his delicately raised brows.

"Would you agree that this steak is slightly overdone?"

"No, I like it like this, and you're evading my question."

His eyes seemed to darken. "Do you always probe at a person like this?"

"When the person is my husband, yes. I don't want us to have secrets from each other."

"You think I have secrets?"

"You shut me out of your thoughts."

"How do you know?"

"If it's me you're thinking of, and not the steak, I don't seem to be making you very happy. You look sad. You look sad too often."

"You're getting too sharp, my darling. I confess I was thinking of you and being angry that you now have to share my tarnished reputation. You should be shining in society."

"Oh, society."

"It's quite important."

"I had enough of it in New York. Those endless dinner

parties, so much too much of everything, and the artificiality and the gossip. I sometimes wished Papa would lose all his money and I would have to become a milliner."

At last Percival laughed.

"I promise you I will never allow you to become a milliner."

"Then let's forget all those soirees and things to which we may or may not be invited and go down to Monkshood. Please, Percival. I want to be with you in our home."

He looked at her intently and seemed to come to a decision.

"Very well. If that's what you want, we'll go tomorrow."

Later they made love quietly and rather too briefly. Her husband, Chrissie decided with both tenderness and regret, was not a very sensuous man. She, unfortunately, seemed to have inherited Papa's virility. She had made that discovery about herself the first time Percival had touched her. Although it was only because she loved him so much.

Now, still wide awake, she would like to have hugged his slender sleeping body to her until she had reawakened his desire. Instinct told her that this would be a mistake. A man liked to take the initiative, especially a man as deeply sensitive as Percival.

It would be better when she became pregnant and her restless body quieted. Perhaps tonight, with the wistful strains of *La traviata* still echoing in her head, her son had been conceived. The new Viscount Monkshood. The future earl.

Dreaming happily, Chrissie fell asleep. When she stirred and woke just before dawn, she found the place beside her in the bed empty.

She knew it was nearly dawn because birds in the park outside the open windows were giving tentative twitters.

The door of the bathroom was open, but no sound came from within. Chrissie, remembering too vividly her

242

fright in Venice, even though it had had a completely harmless origin, sprang out of bed and looked into the adjoining dressing room. There were Percival's pajamas lying on a chair beside his evening clothes. The wardrobe was open, and his Norfolk jacket among other items of clothing was gone.

How long since he had left her? How long had he been on his lonely perambulation of the night streets? What drove him to it?

She stood looking out of the windows over the wide reaches of Green Park, the trees silhouetted against the lightening sky. It was a chilly autumn morning. Presently the mist would rise off the wet grass, and people, early workmen or tramps who had slept rough, would begin to appear. Perhaps some late revelers from a ball in one of the great Park Lane houses might shatter the stillness. No one would notice particularly the solitary figure of the Earl of Monkshood.

When they were at Monkshood, Chrissie didn't think she would mind these nocturnal rambles. But in the cities she had a feeling of utter loneliness and desertion. She was also frightened although she could not have said why.

Go back to bed and sleep, she told herself briskly, and having done so was rewarded later by Percival, dressed in his outdoor clothes, looking bright-eyed and alert, calling her a lazy stay-a-bed, and didn't she remember they had a train to catch?

She said nothing about noticing his absence. He looked too cheerful. She was learning already to encourage and prolong that mood.

But by the time they had reached Monkshood in the late afternoon he was quiet again. The day, too, had lost its brightness. Rags of cloud moved across the sky and made shadows over the lake. The jackdaws were flying restlessly in and out of the old ruin, crying harshly. The house, without the pearly glow of sunlight on it, had a shadowy, deserted look. Not a single window shone with light.

Chrissie felt suddenly too young and too inadequate. She, the Countess of Monkshood, coming home to this gray house. It couldn't be real.

Percival, as aware as ever, had read her thoughts.

"It's our fault for arriving unexpectedly. We'll soon have the place blazing with light. Welcome home, my darling."

"Thank you," Chrissie murmured, and stopped thinking that there should have been a retinue of servants assembled on the front steps to welcome the new bride. The real new bride had been welcomed several years ago. She must seem to be only a substitute.

Anyway, she liked it like this, with Percival holding her hand and Lizzie scrambling off the box beside the coachman to hurry up the steps and ring the bell. She wished that there didn't need to be anyone else in the big house, especially the Misses Monkshood, Lady Kate and Lady Maudie.

Those two ladies stared at her with something that seemed very near horror.

"Percival, what have you done to her hair?" exclaimed Aunt Kate.

"It's a new fashion," said Chrissie gaily. "You should have seen how I was stared at at the opera last night."

"Percival, you didn't take her like this to the opera!"

Percival kissed each aunt with affectionate tenderness.

"Certainly I did. And I'll make a wager that at least a dozen debutantes have short curls today."

"You're shameless," muttered Aunt Kate under her breath.

"Christabel, you poor child," said Aunt Maudie, coming close.

Chrissie stiffened in the soft pussycat embrace.

"I don't know why you're pitying me. I was the cynosure of all eyes last night. Isn't that how it's said? I didn't mind that. I've been used to it all my life." Her touch of hauteur vanished, and she added softly, "I think I pleased my husband."

"Well—"

"Well, nothing, Maudie," said Aunt Kate sharply. "Percival shouldn't inflict his eccentricities on his wife. I disapprove extremely."

Percival's jocularity vanished.

"It's precisely none of your business, dear aunt, how my wife does her hair. Now—shall we talk about the weather? Has Roberts made predictions about the sort of weather we will have? Roberts is my head gamekeeper, Chrissie. He prides himself on predicting how many inches of rain will fall between now and Christmas. Let's hope it's going to be a dry season as I want to get ahead with work on the roof."

"You will excuse us," said Aunt Kate formally. "Maudie, it's time to dress for dinner."

"You will dine with us, of course," said Percival.

The two pairs of faded blue eyes looked from Percival to Chrissie.

As usual Aunt Kate was the spokesman.

"You're a newly married couple. You don't want two old women for company."

"But we do. Don't we, Chrissie?"

Yes, they did. Chrissie read the knowledge in Percival's eyes and hid her hurt that undoubtedly he preferred not dining with her alone on their first night at home.

But that long shining dining table would seem awfully empty with only the two of them. Had he and Sybil dined alone? she wondered inevitably.

The peacock, his splendid tail disheveled with broken quills, squawked stridently on the terrace beneath the bedroom window. Chrissie stood looking thoughtfully out at the darkening garden. Everything, except herself, seemed centuries old. The clipped yews, the stone urns trailing with ivy, the gnarled branches of the climbing roses, even the jackdaws, which must have been exact replicas of previous centuries of hatchings, and that bedraggled old peacock might have been a hundred years old.

How long would it be before she fitted in like a piece of mosaic to these surroundings? Nicely muted by age, with old scandals forgotten.

Judging by Aunt Kate and Aunt Maudie, this was unlikely to happen at all. For, restless and still oddly uneasy, Chrissie took a walk down the many passages of the old house, up small flights of stairs and around corners, looking at the paneled walls, the pictures, the faded curtains, the heavy pieces of furniture with worn tapestry seats—endless passages—and stopped suddenly as voices came from behind a closed door.

She had wandered into the aunts' quarters. For there was a rustling, like mice, behind the door, and the clear voices.

"The roof mended, the frescoes restored and a son. You know that's all our nephew wants, Maudie."

"And money for his self-indulgences."

There was a sigh.

"Imagine getting her to cut her hair." Another sigh. "Let's hope she'll be luckier than Sybil."

"How?"

"By having a child, of course. I don't dislike the girl. I just resent owing these things to a rich American. Besides, she's hardly more than a schoolgirl."

"Percival may like that."

Aunt Kate's voice grew a little sharper.

"That's not what I meant. I was only suggesting she has so much to learn."

"I think she might be a quick learner," said Aunt Maudie softly.

"Perhaps. But I still can't think how she can interest Percival. Still, she looks healthy, at least."

"Yes, healthy," said Aunt Maudie in a voice heavy with doubt.

Chapter 22

The mail was left in a bag in the hall and collected by the postman when he came with his morning delivery.

Chrissie hurried to finish her daily letter to New York. She alternated her letters between Mamma, Papa and Aunt Mary Ellen. Sometimes it was difficult to know how to fill up the crested writing with sufficient news and lighthearted chatter. She had described her daily life too often, and it varied too little.

> Breakfast at nine, downstairs, usually alone, because Percival is up and out so early and the aunts breakfast in their rooms. The sideboard is loaded with silver dishes containing scrambled eggs, bacon and eggs, deviled kidneys, sausages, lamb chops, toast and hot rolls, marmalade and honey, tea and coffee, all just for me. I very often think of the poor and feel fat and greedy. And what a boring newspaper the *Times* is.
>
> After this banquet, I take a long walk and happily never get tired of the beautiful gardens and grounds, especially now that the trees are almost bare and dead leaves rustle, and squirrels flash along the branches.
>
> "Where is Percival?" you are asking. Probably up a ladder supervising workmen because a great many repairs are being made to the house, and we are to have workmen about for a long time to come. My husband, for such a gentle person, is a surprising

martinet and expects a fair return for money expended, which will please Papa. Also, he has a deep love for this beautiful old house. I tell him that Englishmen love their houses (if they are fortunate enough to possess a historic one) more than women, and although he denies this, I suspect that if it were I or Monkshood that had to be saved from disaster, Monkshood would be chosen first. No, I am only joking, and jokes like this don't amuse my darling husband very much.

However—at eleven Percival joins me for coffee or hot chocolate in the morning room, and then we go riding through the autumn woods, and that is the greatest pleasure. Percival likes me to wear riding breeches and ride astride, which occasionally scandalizes people, especially the aunts. They say I will be called the Tomboy Countess and that I look like a stableboy. I don't believe that the previous countess behaved like this, and therefore I suffer from comparison.

After luncheon the day drags for me. I go out and talk to the gardeners or the workmen, or perhaps drive myself in the pony trap to the village and pretend to match silks, or something. I must either start visiting the poor or having a baby. I rather think the latter may be happening already, but I'm not breathing a word until I am sure. I know how much Percival wants a son and couldn't bear to disappoint him with false hopes. So please don't mention this when you write.

To get back to my day, at five o'clock I and the aunts change into tea gowns for tea, even if there are no callers, and the fires are lit, and sometimes Percival joins us, which is the nicest thing of all.

At seven we all go up to dress for dinner, when we do often have guests, people who live in the surrounding district or Percival's friends down from London.

Last night it was the young man who had come to repair the frescoes in the great hall. He is an ar-

tist, and his name is Matthew Smith. He said very little at dinner.

Privately I wish I had friends of my own, but so far I have not met a congenial young person. They are all middle-aged or more. I find myself wishing Araminta lived in England and near to us. She writes regularly, but I fancy her marriage isn't quite perfect. I always thought Prince Rudolf's eyes were set too close together. I must say he had a horrid ill-tempered look. Percival is never ill-tempered. . . .

Only quiet, only much too often unreachable, lost in thoughts, unaware of her, wrapped up in some private emotion.

Or, on rare occasions, looking at her with intensity, really noticing her, but in a way that disturbed her, for it seemed too critical. Once he surprised her by asking her if he had been unfair to her.

"Why do you say that?" she asked carefully. If only he would tell her what he was really thinking, no matter how painful she might find this.

"The aunts think I'm too serious for you. A crusty old man, in other words. You need someone gay who takes you off to balls and parties."

Chrissie pressed her face into his shoulder.

"I only want you. You're not crusty, but you are too silent." Hastily she added, raising her face which was damp with tears, "I'm not criticizing. It's just that it makes me wonder if I'm making *you* happy. Have the aunts thought of that?"

"Never mind what the aunts think. Of course you make me happy, my dear little Yankee. What's the matter? Don't you believe me?"

"I only wondered if it were Sybil you think of when you don't talk. When you're awfully silent at times. No, Percival"—she held his arm—"don't go away. You have to answer this question."

There was a look of relief in his eyes, as if Chrissie's

question had unexpectedly proved to be painless and could be answered without prevarication.

"You're worrying about nothing. I suppose all women are like this. Jealous of—no, curious about their predecessor."

"If they have a predecessor," Chrissie said dryly.

"Exactly. Well, I can promise you that since my first wife left this house, I've scarcely given her a thought. Does that sound callous? But I told you I never loved her enough. I was to blame."

Chrissie's fingers crept into his hair. She pulled his head down.

"I hope you love me enough. Percival? Do you?"

He brushed her cheek with his lips.

"But best on horseback. Come along, lazybones, get your riding clothes on."

The intimacy of their conversation led her to speak before she had intended to.

"Percival! I may not be able to ride much longer. At least, I believe it isn't the wisest thing for young wives. I mean, if what I suspect is true."

He came to her with his arms out, his face shining with joy. All the spontaneity that had been held behind that puzzling reserve was now visible.

The roof, the frescoes, and a son. . . . That was what the aunts had said.

"My darling girl, have you seen a doctor?"

"It's too soon. I didn't mean to tell even you."

"It can't be a minute too soon. I'l send for Dr. Grierson to come up this afternoon. You'll like him. He and his father, before him, have always looked after us."

The uncertainty tore at Chrissie again. So it really was true that this was the thing that animated the Earl of Monkshood, the possibility of an heir. Those gentle protestations of love, charming as they were, had had none of the vital pleasure he was showing now.

"Percival, I will not be pampered," she heard herself saying emphatically. "I will not lie on a couch for nine months. I'm not twenty yet, and I'm as healthy as a young pony. I'll go on doing everything I want to until the last month. You get that clear. You ought to have known my old nurse Serenity. She never could abide a pregnant woman who lay about. 'You walk proud when youse that way,' she used to say to me."

Percival was wearing his charming quizzical look.

"But I'm sure she pointed out that it wouldn't be a sensible thing to fall off a horse. I warn you, Chrissie, what with me and the aunts and Dr. Grierson, you're going to have to do as you're told. And your old nurse Serenity can keep her mouth shut."

Actually, she would dearly have liked Serenity with her. When Dr. Grierson, a rotund middle-aged man with a jolly smile and shrewd eyes, confirmed her pregnancy, she wanted to convince Percival—and the aunts, too, for they were a force to be contended with—that a black nurse, a Southern mammy, was the best thing in the world for a new baby.

But that battle had to be lost before it was begun. For Serenity was too old. She could never make the journey to England, Mamma said. And anyway Chrissie must understand that old English families would want the traditional type of nurse. Chrissie had to remember that she had chosen the English way of life. Of course she knew that Papa was delighted with her news, but Aunt Mary Ellen had wept noisily for half a day. It appeared she had never allowed herself to believe that Chrissie's marriage was real until this news had come. Now she could only hope that when the little viscount—a viscount, wouldn't that kill you!—was old enough to travel, Chrissie would bring him to meet his American family.

In New York Louisa watched the treasures increasing around her in the house and knew that this was Harry's way of compensating for the loss of his daughter. More and more acquisitions as visible proof of his success, a fragment of sculpture by Donatello, a delicious Watteau in almond pinks and greens for Louisa's drawing room, a countess in the family albeit the other side of the Atlantic, a grandchild expected. How could Louisa look wistful? Surely no other woman had so much?

Louisa's discipline, practiced for so long, didn't desert her now. She refrained from reminding anyone that she had long ago lost her greatest treasure, Henry, the little boy whose frail ghostly face still came to haunt her dreams. It was true that Harry's soaring ambition was giving her Watteaus and Donatellos, but he knew as well as she did that they were poor compensation for a house deprived of its youth.

Which was a silly argument, for every family had to part with marriageable daughters. And wanted to. Only, as Mary Ellen said, why wasn't Chrissie just plain Mrs. John Doe living around the corner in New York City?

Those long, slow, uneventful days that Chrissie wrote about and the smothering care she was now getting from her husband and the two elderly aunts disturbed Louisa.

> Really, Mamma, it's as if no one ever before gave birth to a baby safely in this house, and yet there are all those portraits to prove otherwise. I begin to think there is a family curse, or something, all the boy babies stillborn or the young wives barren. I can only say with some exasperation that although I am perfectly well, Percival insists on treating me like an invalid. . . .

Louisa read Chrissie's letters many times. She fought her intuition that for all their liveliness and good humor, they were a little forlorn, a little lost. It had been so wonderful to know that Chrissie had had the good fortune to marry for love, something she herself had so longed to do. Yet was it after all a perfect condition?

Looking across the breakfast table at Harry eating his hot muffins and muttering about the state of Wall Street, Louisa thought with gratitude of his steadiness, solidity and unostentatious kindness to her. He might make a great parade of himself and his possessions and achievements to the world, but never to her. He had always remained simple, direct and, at times, touchingly humble. She realized that the many small ways in which she loved him added up to quite a sum. She was lucky. How was Chrissie, after twenty years, going to look at her husband? Was that languid, wistful charm going to lose its fascination for her?

"You're looking very thoughtful, Lou. What's Chrissie got to say?"

Louisa looked up to answer Harry's question.

"Oh, the usual things. She's not going to enjoy nine months of inactivity. She says Percival's aunts fuss too much."

"Those two tabby cats. Well, I suppose in their view they're awaiting the birth of the crown prince. It had better be a boy, that's all I can say. We'll persuade the earl to bring his wife and child to New York for next Christmas. How about that?"

"Do you think they'd come? I'm sure Chrissie would love to, but she writes already about what a festival Christmas is at Monkshood. The carol singers, the servants' ball, the Christmas tree that touches the ceiling of the great hall."

"Then we'll go there," said Harry imperturbably. "Well, go on. What else does she say?"

"She says Percival is going to Europe to do his Christmas shopping. What a luxurious thing to do."

"Alone?"

"Evidently. Since Chrissie complains that he is treating her like an invalid, he would hardly risk her traveling."

Harry frowned.

"Is she an invalid?"

"Goodness me, no. She emphasizes how well she is."

"Then why the devil is he doing that?"

Louisa saw the inward look in Harry's eye and knew they were both thinking the same thing. Percival, through cautiousness, care or delicacy, was leaving his wife alone at nights. Harry, too, had been careful when she had been pregnant, but not to this extent. He had thought that loving her and caressing her showed his pleasure in her condition. Besides, he would have said bluffly, had he been asked, that nine months of celibacy was not possible for a man in love with his wife.

Was Percival not in love with the girl he had been so determined to marry?

The edginess of exasperation seemed plain in Chrissie's letter. She was going to have to learn discipline and patience and a high degree of understanding if she was going to live happily with that strange, remote, fastidious man, the Earl of Monkshood. Well, that was part of growing up, of becoming a complete, well-balanced woman. She was no longer just a pampered, protected rich man's daughter.

"Said she'd have to lie in the bed she'd made," Harry said in a low growl. "I stick to that. And you stick to it, too, my dear. Don't encourage her to air any complaints. Well, what else does she say, apart from this nonsense about being an invalid?"

"Nothing much. She's been taking long walks, since they won't allow her to ride. That I agree with. The vicar's been to tea. Poor Chrissie! But she finishes, 'Thank goodness for the bearded young man in the great hall. At least he is someone to talk to, although he says very little in reply to my chatter.' "

"The bearded young man. Who the devil does she mean? The butler? No, surely he didn't have a beard? My lord wouldn't have permitted that."

"The frescoes!" Louisa cried. "Don't you remember someone was being brought in to repair them? Those faded amber and blue Tudor figures around the walls."

"Yes, yes, I remember," Harry said testily. "Be better if Lord Monkshood hired a good artist to paint his wife's portrait. He seems to put his damn frescoes first."

"I expect he's waiting until he can have Chrissie painted with her child. That would be charming, wouldn't it? Harry, what's the matter?"

Harry had staggered as he stood up, rattling the china on the table.

"Nothing. Just stumbled."

"Were you dizzy?"

"A trifle—no, I was not!"

The angry roar was the familiar protest against anything that upset him, doubts about Chrissie's happiness or loneliness or whatever emotion it was that had crept into her letters, about the unthinkable thing that a man of his splendid health and energy could have a mild attack of dizziness or could grow old and diminished. He was fifty-five that year.

Ephraim de Wynt had just died. He was found on the floor of his bedroom, fully dressed in the clothes he had worn to the opera that evening. He looked like a thin, elegant bird that had died with all its feathers on. He would leave only a very small void in New York society, for the day of the dandy and the gossip were over, and he had outlived most of his friends.

Nevertheless, Louisa felt his death as a cold shiver down her spine, making her think of mortality. So did Mary Ellen, who huffed loudly and called Ephraim that intefering little jack-in-the-box, but who nevertheless wiped away furtive tears. Boy was scarcely aware of the sad event. Outside events made little impression on his stupefied brain. He spent most of the day at his desk, totally surrounded by papers, none of which must be moved an inch by anybody but himself. They were curling at the edges and gray with dust, the writing on them almost illegible. It was obvious that Boy's great literary work would be buried with him. Perhaps that was what he had always intended.

Harry was becoming more impatient to carry out his plans to develop the block on which the dark, decrepit van Leyden house stood, but Mary Ellen's stubborn opposition increased rather than lessened. Now that Chrissie was to have a baby, she said, there was all the more reason to keep the place standing. Never mind that the boy was going to be born into the magnificent ownership of a Tudor mansion, as well as that smart *nouveau riche* place of Harry Spencer's opposite Central Park. (Mary Ellen had begun to speak of Camberwell House as if she had never seen it, only heard of it.) The new young sprig of the English nobility had American ancestors also and would want to own their historic home. So Harry Spencer had better keep his avaricious hands off it.

One could never imagine an English earl living in that shabby old house under the claustrophobic canopy of the tree of heaven. But neither could one expect anything from Mary Ellen but emotional illogical arguments. To which Louisa thought that Harry responded nowadays with just slightly diminished vigor. Or was she becoming overanxious, since seeing his flushed face as he had stumbled at the breakfast table. He had refused to see a doctor. He worked as hard as ever. He hoped Lou wouldn't mind that their next summer vacation at Southampton would be cut a little short to make up for the long summer spent abroad that year. Anyway, that great rambling house, full of the sound of wind and sea, was a bit solitary for two middle-aged people.

Chapter 23

Percival promised he would be back in plenty of time for Christmas. Why was Chrissie looking so forlorn, he would be gone only three weeks, and she had plenty to occupy her, hadn't she, with her plans for Christmas? She was to promise not to attempt to decorate the tree. The servants would do that according to her instructions. If she dared to mount a ladder. . . .

"Percival, I'm not made of spun glass."

"You are, as far as I'm concerned. Look how your hair's growing again," he added irrelevantly.

"Shall I have it cut?" Chrissie asked, anxious to please him.

"I think not. Aunt Kate and Aunt Maudie are right. You must begin to look like a mother, not a curly-headed —child."

He had hesitated, about to say "boy." He had liked her boyishness but now seemed tired of it. It had been a whim.

"I don't feel in the least maternal," she said crossly.

"You will, my darling. What a pity it takes nine months to make a baby. It's a long, dull time for you. But I promise to find you the most exotic Christmas present while I'm abroad. No other woman in England will have anything like it."

Chrissie smiled, as he expected her to, but felt unaccountably depressed. She didn't want things. She had had every possible variation of every luxury all her life. And Percival seemed too eager to get away.

"All men are selfish," said Aunt Kate. "Your husband is no exception. Don't sulk, child. You'll have to make the best of it. Sensible wives do."

"Did Sybil?"

The two wrinkled faces abruptly took on an identical closed look.

"Sybil was not in your happy condition," Aunt Kate said with asperity.

"But one must say she was very good—about Percival's wandering, I mean," Aunt Maudie murmured.

"You liked her better than me, didn't you?" Chrissie accused them.

"She was English. We understood her."

"What's wrong with being American?"

"You have different ways, which is perfectly natural. We accept that."

"Don't I do things properly?"

"You manage very well," said Aunt Maudie kindly.

"You're just a little belligerent at times. Like your father." Aunt Kate's voice was regretful.

"I want to be like my father."

"But now your hair's growing nicely—that naughty Percival—making you a freak. You mustn't worry if you have a husband who likes to roam around Europe. English noblemen have always done that. You'll have your child. That's why poor Sybil became so unhappy. One couldn't blame her. She was lonely."

"I'm lonely, too," Chrissie burst out.

"But only until the baby is born, dear."

"I'm bored as well. In fact I'm going to London for a day's shopping tomorrow."

"Oh, my dear! That long train journey! Such a tiring day."

"It isn't only my husband who has Christmas shopping to do." Chrissie sprang up, suddenly full of energy and good humor. "I want to buy a dress that will surprise and please him."

"*Buy* one, dear! But Miss Raven—"

"Yes, buy one. Ready-made and modern and ravishing. I don't want Miss Raven sticking pins in me. Papa would have taken me to Worth, but there won't be time for that before Christmas. So the dress will have to be ready-made."

"My dear Chrissie, do remember ladies don't walk alone in Bond Street."

"Goodness me, it's the new century. Hadn't you noticed?"

"Which doesn't make London streets any more respectable," said Aunt Kate frostily.

The two flushed faces looking up at her were genuinely alarmed. Chrissie had a sudden stab of remorse for having displayed again her belligerence.

"I don't mean to go alone. I'm taking Lizzie. Please don't look so disapproving. I have to learn to keep my husband home, don't I?"

But this was not the right thing to say, either, for the aunts' eyes flickered away, almost as if in embarrassment.

Heavens, she wasn't talking of seductive negligees or nightgowns, only of a dress to wear on Christmas Day. A lovely rustling jewel-colored taffeta that would light up the dark rooms and make her look like a real countess. With her short curls and her riding breeches, she hadn't previously been allowed to show off the dignity she knew she possessed. Percival could not help admiring her. And after the festivities were over, he would take her upstairs, and tell her to send Lizzie away, and unhook for himself, and take off her clothes, dress, petticoats, camisole, everything.

"We mustn't stop her, Kate, since the prospect seems to please her so much," Aunt Maudie said in her kind murmur.

What prospect? Oh, of a day in London. Chrissie blushed. For a moment she had thought that Aunt Maudie was aware of her dream.

The young man perched on scaffolding in the great hall answered her good morning in his usual gruff manner. He was becoming as much a part of the place as the butler and the maids. Since the evening of his arrival, he had not again eaten with the family. He preferred to get on with his work and eat at the Swan in the village, where he was staying.

This was a relief, for he had little to say. Percival, accomplished in witty small talk himself, had found Mr. Smith's lack of response irritating, and Chrissie had been a little embarrassed at the way he had stared at her, with very inquisitive brown eyes. Perhaps her short curls had fascinated him. Since then Chrissie, going in and out of the hall, had tossed casual remarks to the broad-shouldered figure perched on the scaffolding. She called him Michelangelo and asked how the painting was coming on and sometimes sat on one of the high-backed Tudor chairs and conversed for half an hour, not minding that the replies from above her head were mostly monosyllabic.

Matthew Smith said that he lived in a suburb of London, and he thought he had more talent for writing than painting. This kind of restoration work was only to buy his bread and butter.

"Are you writing a book?"

"Yes."

"Then don't let it possess you like my Uncle Boy has let his." Chrissie went on cheerfully to relate the saga of the Lord Byron manuscript and then omitted to ask Mr. Smith the subject of his book. But it was doubtful that he would want to tell her. He was not a forthcoming person.

However, the one-sided conversations were a form of release when the days were too long and quiet. But if she were to meet Mr. Smith in a London street, she doubted if she would recognize him. The strong shoulders, the fringe of beard, the inquisitive eyes. He was part of the emerging figures of the frescoes, a dark shape against the lettuce green of the ladies' gowns and the crimson gold of the courtiers.

The great hall was going to be splendid when restored to its former glory. This, however, was going to take some months. They would have a grand viewing when it was finished, Percival had said. A midsummer masked ball, when all the guests could wear medieval fancy dress. "And if the baby isn't born by then, you can hide it under your wimple," he said to Chrissie. She adored him when his eyes were merry.

The trip to London was merely an act of defiance, although Chrissie spent a great deal of money on Christmas gifts and hoped Percival would like the rose-pink taffeta dress she bought for herself. Lizzie thought it immensely becoming, and Miss Chrissie should have her portrait painted in it and look dignified and feminine, like all the previous countesses whose portraits hung at Monkshood.

They reached home long after the early dark had settled over the countryside. Monkshood seemed to brood in the gloom, only chinks of light shining behind drawn curtains. But there was a roaring fire in the great hall and a letter from Percival.

Chrissie told Lizzie to take the packages and boxes upstairs while she herself sank into a chair near the fire and eagerly opened her letter.

The day had been too tiring, as the aunts had predicted it would be. When she read that Percival was remaining abroad another ten days and not returning until Christmas Eve, she began to weep.

She was not a person who shed tears easily. She remembered once bellowing with fright when she thought she had seen Lily, that wicked Irishwoman, on the Brooklyn ferry. Now she wanted to bellow again and might well have done so if a movement hadn't startled her. Someone was sitting in the dark inglenook. Not Lily, but Matthew Smith, dismounted from his ladder and quietly watching her from his corner.

She hastily blew her nose and said aggressively, "Haven't you better manners than to sit there staring at me? And if you're going to ask me if I have had bad news, I have. My husband is delayed in Rome, and I can't stand another day of this dull place without him. So there, now you know everything."

"I expect you're tired, my lady," came his quiet, unemotional voice.

"Now don't you start that, too. Fussing like the aunts. I am not tired, I am only disappointed and hungry and in a bad temper. It's past eight, and the aunts will have dined, so now I'll even have to eat alone. And don't tell me to have a cozy tray in my bedroom. I am not an old lady or a frail invalid."

"I didn't intend—"

"Have you had your evening meal?"

"I've just stopped working. I sat down to warm my hands. It's chilly up near the ceiling. No, I haven't eaten, my lady. I'll get some soup and cold pie at the Swan."

There was nothing subservient about his "my lady," rather a slight sarcasm, although one could not be sure about that. He didn't have a common voice.

"Soup and cold pie doesn't sound much after twelve hours of work. Would you dine with me, Mr. Smith?" The invitation was spontaneous, but she instantly warmed to the thought. Before he could refuse, as he probably intended to, she went on, "If you will, I must give Jenkins orders at once. I'm sure Cook can prepare something adequate, at least something hot, by nine o'clock. And Jenkins can open one of my husband's favorite clarets, the 1892, I think. Don't worry about what you're wearing. We'll be quite informal."

"Why, Countess—"

That sounded better. She liked that.

"I would be honored," said Mr. Smith.

A painter, a writer, an educated man, obviously. Percival would agree with her choice of dinner companion. If he didn't, that was his fault. He should have been here himself.

She knew that Jenkins, the stately butler, was outraged at being ordered to serve the master's best claret and that Cook, thinking she had finished the day's work, was no doubt equally resentful. Lizzie was scandalized and made no secret of it. But who was mistress of this house? She would have no surliness, no disobedience. Dinner was to be at nine. As it was such short notice, she would omit the fish course. Otherwise she expected everything to be perfect.

She had forgotten her weariness. She bathed and put on her simplest tea gown, so as not to embarrass Mr. Smith in his sober working clothes.

Not that, when he had discarded his paint-stained

overall, he didn't look neat and tidy in his dark jacket and colorful cravat. His thick brown hair was glossy, his eyes particularly bright in the candlelight.

She asked him to sit near her. The opposite end of the table was Percival's place, and sacred. Besides, close together, they could converse in lower tones, so that the maid and footman, waiting on table, would have to strain their ears to hear whatever the mistress had to say to a workman.

Not that there was very much to listen to, over the soup and the entrée. Mr. Smith asked questions about New York, and Chrissie was only too ready to talk with nostalgic pleasure of life and customs there. From this distance, it didn't seem that her childhood had been lonely or unhappy or too inhibited by the ever-watchful Peck or that her father's ambitions for her had sat too heavily on her young shoulders.

By the time the claret was half finished, her tongue was loosened, and she said, without resentment, "My darling Papa has always, but always, got what he wanted. He is one of these remarkable people who just has to put out his hands and pluck things from the air. Oh, I know there's a great deal of work and genius behind this, but he makes it look easy. I mean, when he was rich, he went out looking for the right bride, and he found Mamma, and she was exactly right. Then they had me, and I seemed to be what he wanted, too. There was Henry, of course—"

"Henry?"

"Henry was my little brother who was kidnapped and died. Don't let's talk about that. It's terribly sad. Mamma always blamed Papa's money and ambition, and I expect she was right, but it didn't change Papa a bit. He just went right on being more and more successful and putting all his hopes into me, since now he didn't have a son. I got into the habit of going along with him. I couldn't do anything else anyway. I love Papa too much to disappoint him."

"Did you disappoint him by marrying Lord Monkshood?"

Mr. Smith had spoken in a low voice. Chrissie didn't think the maid and the young footman had heard. Nevertheless she told them to take away the dishes and not to come back. She and her guest would drink their coffee at the table.

After a little flurry of activity, the big room, lit only by the candles on the table, was empty except for themselves, and Chrissie said frankly, "Yes, he was disappointed at first. He would have preferred me not to have married a man who was divorced; but I loved Percival, and for once I was as determined as Papa."

"And you got a title."

"Oh, that. I tell you, that night at Millie Pepper's ball, there wasn't a single person without a title. And of course I was going to fall in love that night. It was so utterly romantic. Falling in love was inevitable. All the same, if Percival had been plain Mr. Monkshood, I would still have married him."

The observant eyes of Mr. Matthew Smith were black in the candlelight.

"Would you?" he said.

Chrissie leaned her chin on her hands. "There's a great deal of mystery about my husband. That's what makes him so fascinating."

"And you are very young."

"Are you suggesting mystery won't fascinate me when I am older?"

"Do you think it will?"

"Of course it will."

"And you think a man and woman, living together for years, can still preserve a mystery?"

"Oh, I couldn't, of course, I simply burst out with everything in my head. But my husband—well, you've met him."

Mr. Smith said nothing.

"Aren't you going to comment?"

"He's my employer. A servant doesn't set out to understand his employer."

"Don't call yourself a servant. You're a writer, a student of human nature. You're prevaricating, Mr. Smith."

He made a sudden sharp movement.

"For goodness sake, Countess, do you expect me to sit at your table and criticize your husband?"

"No," said Chrissie slowly, staring at the flushed and suddenly too-alive face beside her. It was very odd, as if she had been touched by his fingers on her flesh.

She must be drunk.

She tried to make her voice cool. "I don't expect you to criticize him, but to admire him. As everyone does."

"Do they?"

"Of course they do. His aunts, the servants, his head groom, his tenants."

"That's nice for the earl," said Mr. Smith.

Chrissie's cheeks were burning. She could feel the purely imaginary creeping, caressing touch on her bare arms.

"And if you're going to say the obvious thing—why did his first wife leave him; why did she fall in love with someone else?—then your curiosity must remain unsatisfied because I can't answer you." She stood up. "And now I think, if you will excuse me, it's late. And you have to begin work early tomorrow. Percival will expect to see great strides made with the frescoes when he returns."

Mr. Smith stood up politely.

"One doesn't make great strides with work of this kind, Countess. It takes time and patience. Ask Michelangelo. But this isn't the Sistine Chapel, so rest assured, I won't be here for seven years. Good night, Countess."

Chrissie stopped at the door and turned back impulsively. Her sharp uneasy display of temper, surely attributable to pregnancy, had gone.

"Do forgive me, Mr. Smith. I was rude."

He watched her, his face shadowy in the candlelight.

"So was I."

"It must have been Percival's wine."

"And we've both had a long day."

"Yes, that's it. Good night, Mr. Smith."

And she hadn't asked him a thing about himself. Not a thing. She had prattled endlessly about herself, and he remained an enigma. Which was just as well, because why should his family or his background interest her? If it were not for the Christmas tree being erected, she would have avoided the great hall over the next few days. As this could not be, she took care that there were plenty of servants employed in the decoration of the tree. The two old aunts came softly in and out. They had heard about the dinner party, and their disapproval showed in their frosty eyes and pursed lips. Nevertheless, that extra ten days of waiting for Percival's return was pleasant in its own way. The aromatic scent of the fir branches, the fire leaping in the cavern of the chimney, the lamps burning from morning until night, the scattered ribbon and tinsel, the cloudy darkness outside, with just a few flakes of snow. One almost wanted the peacefulness to last.

When they had almost given him up, Percival arrived near to midnight on Christmas Eve. He was in the best of spirits. Chrissie thought she had never seen him so gay. He came bursting into the great hall, his cloak flying, and seeing the tree, frosted and bespangled, he clapped his hands like a small boy.

"Oh, bravo! What a splendid sight. No, Jenkins"—he turned to half close the door behind him—"that is not to come in. Around to the servants' quarters with it. Chrissie, my darling, how nice to find you up. Were you waiting for me?"

"Of course."

He folded her in his arms. The night air was still cold on his lips, but the tightness of the embrace compensated for that. Chrissie took a quick glance over his shoulder at Mr. Smith halfway up a ladder against the Christmas tree to see, as she expected, the steady, watchful gaze. Well, let him stare at a loving reunion. If he were envious, he must find a wife for himself.

"I was watching Lizzie and Mr. Smith finishing the tree. Let me look at you, Percival. You seem so well."

"I've never been better. Had a wonderful time, and wait until you see all my Christmas loot tomorrow."

"Never mind about your loot. I only want you."

"I believe you've missed me." His eyes were full of delight.

"What an unnecessary thing to say." She spoke in a low voice. She had a good idea that Mr. Smith's ears were just as keen as his eyes. "I've missed you every minute. It's been so dull."

'It won't be dull any longer. My cousins from Tewkesbury are arriving in the morning, and there'll be all the usual callers, Squire Maxton and his wife, the vicar, of course, the Drummonds and Craighayes and the Pevenseys from Hall Court. Didn't the aunts tell you?"

"They said people would come here after church. Are we all to go to church in the morning?"

"Most certainly. It's the custom. You're an Englishwoman now. How is the heir? More important, how is his mother?"

"Both of us are fine now you're home. And I have a new dress to surprise you with tomorrow. Lizzie and I went to London."

"Did you, indeed? Tiring yourself."

"I was perfectly all right. Don't fuss, Percival. I'm finished with fussing. I intend doing everything I want to— except, to please you, riding a horse."

Percival's eyebrows lifted in the whimsical curve she loved.

"Thank heaven for small mercies. Come and we'll open a bottle of champagne."

"At midnight? I'm not sure how the heir will like that."

"He'll like it very well. We'll drink to our first Christmas together."

It was so wonderful to have Percival home. She could

hardly tear herself away to go upstairs to bed. Especially since she finally went alone. He murmured something about being exhausted and filthy from traveling. She was thankful that she was dizzy from the champagne. Her disappointment was blurred. Tomorrow, she thought hopefully, and fell wearily into bed. On the verge of sleep, a sound aroused her. She sat up, listening intently. It wasn't possible, but she could have sworn she heard a faint girlish giggling from Percival's room.

She lay down and muffled the blankets around her ears. She had imagined it. She would not listen again. If Percival, starved for a woman and fearful of touching his pregnant wife, had got one of the maids in his room, she simply must pretend it had not happened.

Which maid? Betty? Dolly?

No, it just wasn't true. Percival was not that kind of man. He was too fastidious. Overfastidious, oversensitive. She hadn't heard a thing. Go to sleep, and don't remember it when you wake up. . . . Though one couldn't help thinking that carrying the child of a simple man like, say, Matthew Smith (a commoner, as the English so quaintly called untitled people), would be much easier than the heavy responsibility of safely giving birth to the heir of a proud old family.

"You're a nuisance, my little viscount," she muttered into the blankets. "I only hope I'll like you when you arrive. And if you dare to be a girl. . . ."

She made herself smile and instantly fell asleep.

The morning was clear and cold. They walked across the fields to church, she wrapped in furs and arm in arm with her husband, the aunts following, and a gaggle of servants behind them. The Christmas bells rang over the quiet countryside, and Chrissie thought of New York, and snow in Central Park, and Mamma and Papa and Aunt Mary Ellen and Uncle Boy sitting around a heavily laden table trying to enjoy one another's company. And missing her, she hoped, as much as she was missing them.

Percival's profile looked lean and austere, his nose

slightly nipped with cold. She clung to him possessively. She had a feeling of enormous pride in him. She sat in the Monkshood pew and listened absently to the vicar's sermon and thought what a year it had been, travels abroad, a triumphant debut into English society, love, marriage, a title and now a prospective heir. What more could she wish for, except a husband less spartan in his caresses? She must learn more beguilements. She was, after all, still rather naïve and innocent. When the baby was born, six long months away, she would be mature and experienced and irresistible. And this was hardly the time or place to be thinking of lovemaking. Pay attention to the sermon, stop dreaming. . . .

When they got back from church, the cousins from Tewkesbury, Bill and Charlotte Morton, had arrived. Jenkins was ordered to bring champagne, everyone's wraps were discarded, Chrissie was introduced to the middle-aged cousins, a handsome pair, though without Percival's overwhelming look of aristocracy, and they all sat around the roaring fire in the great hall.

It was present-giving time. They could receive and unwrap their gifts before the rest of the luncheon guests arrived. There would be carol singers, too, and, by the look of the darkening sky, a flurry of snow. It was dark enough now to light the candles. Was Chrissie enjoying her first English Christmas?

She thought the interest displayed by the two cousins was deeper than the quite ordinary question warranted. They were looking at her too hard. Were they comparing her with Sybil? And favorably or unfavorably? Did it matter? She was too happy today to care. She shared in the eager unwrapping of gifts. Scarves, books, perfume, bonbons, an antique ring from Aunt Maudie, a Cashmere shawl from Aunt Kate.

But where was the gift Percival had written about, the one he had had to travel Europe to find for her? Involuntarily her eyes sought his face, and he gave her a half smile. His eyes were very bright with suppressed excitement. He was enjoying tantalizing her. All the parcels were unwrapped. Where had she to go to find his gift?

"That's a nice amount of loot you've collected, Chrissie," said Cousin Bill, coming to sit beside her. "What a greedy feast Christmas is. Sometimes I think it should be struck off the calendar."

"No, you don't, Bill," said his wife. "Look at you clinging to your things. That's a nice cravat. Italian silk? Oh, from Percival. He's just back from Europe, isn't he, Chrissie? What did he bring you?"

"She doesn't know yet," came Percival's drawling voice above them. "But she will in a moment. Everyone stay where they are while I bring my wife her Christmas gift."

He went to open the door that led to the library. In the gloom beyond Chrissie saw something shimmer. The object moved. It came toward her, walking on two slim, childish legs. It was a small dark-skinned boy dressed in a glittering brocade turban, a sky-blue jacket and knee breeches. At a sign from Percival the mannikin bowed low before Chrissie and stayed in that position of servitude until Percival tapped his shoulder and told him to stand up. Then he stared boldly into Chrissie's face, rolling enormous liquid dark eyes. He was beautifully made, an exquisite *café au lait* doll, and about ten years old.

"This is Abdul, my darling," Percival said formally. "He is your slave. Abdul, this is your mistress."

The child's eyes rolled up toward Percival, as if for reassurance, although he did not appear to be nervous. Only extremely well rehearsed.

Chrissie found that she had nothing whatever to say. She stared at the perfect child in total disbelief.

"Aren't you pleased? Don't you like him? If you only knew the search I had to find him. I finally sent to Morocco." Percival's luminous eyes watched her anxiously. Chrissie realized his great desire to please her. After all, she had been the daughter of a millionaire all her life, and there was little she had not had. He must have put a great deal of thought into finding a gift that was different, unique, bizarre. She had thought that the days of pampered ladies with little black boys had gone out long ago. She might have been prepared to start a fashion with clipped curls, but with a slave? Wasn't that rather barbarous?

She licked her lips.

"Does he speak English?"

"But, of course. Not quite as well as French, naturally. But he's a clever monkey. Aren't you, Abdul?"

The child grinned widely, showing dazzling white teeth.

"Yes, sir."

"And you will carry things for my lady, and guard her, and amuse her?"

"Yes, sir."

"Percival!" exclaimed Charlotte. "I do think this is the limit. Why, nobody's had a black boy since the days of Queen Caroline."

"Might as well have given her a monkey," muttered her husband.

The look on both their faces was identical, an expression Chrissie couldn't interpret. She had seen something similar once or twice on the aunts' faces. A quick glance at them now showed them looking slightly stunned, as disbelieving as she was herself.

Whatever was she to do with this gaudy animated toy?

But now at least she knew the origin of the girlish giggling she had heard from Percival's room last night. Relief about that made her able, at last, to smile with genuine pleasure.

"Percival, I think this is a quite absurd joke. Whatever am I to do with this child?" She knew that everyone was watching her with an intentness that seemed too exaggerated for Percival's practical joke, and she found herself adding almost placatingly, "When I knew I was going to have a baby, I wanted to send for my old Negro nurse, Serenity. Is that why you thought I wanted someone dark-skinned around, Percival?"

"But Serenity isn't as pretty as Abdul, I'm sure," said Percival gaily. "Now, why don't we all go in to eat. It's all right, child." The little turbaned doll was suddenly clinging to his leg. "Don't be alarmed. You'll soon find what a kind mistress you have. But run off to the kitchen, now. My lady will send for you when she wants you."

Chapter 24

"Now I've been rich enough," Harry said, "but I've never bought you a blackamoor." His voice was incredulous. "I don't think I like the sound of that, Lou. Isn't it a bit decadent?"

Privately, Louisa agreed that it was more than a little decadent, but perhaps this was not unusual among the English aristocracy. One didn't know, and perhaps shouldn't be so uneasy about it. Certainly she had no intention of letting Harry see her uneasiness.

"I expect Percival was just trying to be clever and original. One must appreciate that, when he knows that Chrissie has had everything all her life. I expect he went to a great deal of trouble to find her a present like that little boy."

"Why couldn't he have given her a monkey or a parrot, if it had to be something alive? This Abdul may be a little boy, but I'll wager he's soaked with ancient sins. Someone from the souks of Morocco in my daughter's bedroom!"

"You're thinking of the Arabian nights, dear. And I don't expect Chrissie has him in her bedroom. I hope not. She says he looks about ten years old, but he doesn't know himself how old he is. He's rather endearing and comical and absolutely devoted to Percival, who must have been very kind to him. What else does she say?" Louisa studied the closely written letter again. "Oh, yes, he likes to feed Percival grapes."

"Pah!" said Harry in disgust.

"Just a pretty trick, I expect. Chrissie says everyone always laughs."

"So my daughter is reduced to being amused by the antics of a ten-year-old blackamoor."

"We have to understand this," Louisa said earnestly. "People living in those great English houses are always outdoing each other in finding some new amusement. Didn't we realize that when we were in England?"

"They're all bored and idle, that's the trouble."

"But you always admired them so," Louisa pointed out gently.

Harry rustled his newspaper tetchily.

"Well, maybe I was a bit overromantic. We both know this fellow Monkshood wasn't our ideal choice. All I can say is, don't tell this bit of colorful news to your sister. That's the last thing we want, her rampaging up here, declaring Chrissie is being raped by a blackamoor."

"Darling, your imagination! It's worse than Mary Ellen's. You'll be glad to hear that Chrissie had a lovely Christmas. The carol singers sang around the tree, and the servants came up to receive their gifts. She says the tree touched the ceiling of the great hall, and they had candles burning in every window. It all sounds very feudal. She didn't get to bed until two in the morning, and Percival scolded her for getting overtired. She says it's true she was tired, Lizzie had to undress her and put her to bed. Harry, you must admit she is being thoroughly spoiled."

"If you call that spoiling," Harry muttered. "Sounds to me like being treated like a child." His eyes had an angry gleam. But one had always known he would have been jealous of Chrissie's husband, whoever he was.

The moon hanging over the giant cedar, an owl calling

and its melancholy mate answering, the ivy leaves around the window shivering in the night breeze, creakings in the ancient timbers of the house as the wintry temperature dropped lower, whisperings, muffled footsteps, a stifled giggle. . . .

Chrissie had not been sleeping well lately. She had a habit of waking in the early hours and listening. The house, she told herself fancifully, was hostile toward her. It brought out all its ghosts at three o'clock in the morning. They whispered and giggled. No doubt, if she could see them they would be mopping and mowing at her derisively. She had had to go back to having a night-light. Percival complained that it shone in his eyes and moved back to his own room. She pointed out that she had not had the night-light until after he had moved back, but he was strangely, or deliberately, vague about that.

It all came down to the fact that he was obsessively anxious about her well-being. He thought she would rest better alone.

Privately, she had come to the unhappy conclusion that a pregnant woman gave him some kind of antipathy. This was not a thing she could discuss with her mother or Aunt Mary Ellen, or the two Monkshood ladies, or even practical down-to-earth Lizzie. She had to hide her loneliness and pray for the winter to be over and her baby born.

The baby was quite unreal to her. It was her husband who possessed all her thoughts.

At least Percival now seemed content to be home. He was taking an absorbed interest in the renovations to the house and stayed indoors most of the day, either with the workmen or with Chrissie. He made her examine specimens of wallpapers and fabrics to replace the worn damask curtains in the drawing rooms and wanted her decision on the color of the carpet to cover the creaking stairs. Monkshood was now as much her house as his, owing to the extremely generous dowry she had brought to it. Would crimson silk wallpaper best enhance the pictures in the long gallery? She listened and made suggestions but never succeeded in believing that the old house was hers, even in part. It would be her son's, however, and perhaps that was enough.

Another pleasant thing that happened in the early part of the new year was that Percival frequently took tea in the drawing room with herself and the aunts and afterward sat by the couch where she rested, and talked, or read to her, or was just companionably silent, his face full of gentleness. He was a dear, sweet, complex person. Perhaps one day she would understand him. When this tardy baby was born. . . .

She had insisted that Abdul's spectacular brocade jacket and turban were too outlandish for everyday wear. She had the child put into practical breeches and woolen sweaters, but even then he looked exotic, with his curly black head and beautifully melancholy brown eyes. She had no intention of having him follow her about, carrying reticule and fan. That was too silly for words. She made him do useful tasks, like keeping the log basket full, sweeping dead leaves off the terraces, carrying trays of hot chocolate and other snacks to the aunts' rooms. He was a good-tempered little creature and soon became something of a household pet, even to the austere Jenkins.

He was very willing to sit at Chrissie's feet at any time, respectfully calling her "my lady" and answering her questions. This pleased Percival, who had decided that his bizarre Christmas gift had been a great success. He often gave the curly head an affectionate rumpling, which caused Abdul's eyes to roll adoringly. Really, the child was like a friendly puppy, with his main affections reserved for his master. Chrissie had almost overcome her instinctive distrust of the situation, which she knew had been discussed far and wide in the country. The eccentric earl and his American countess and their unusual plaything.

To overcome this attitude, she sometimes took Abdul to the village with her and had him run errands, while she sat in the pony trap. For his age, he was an astute shopper, recognizing a bargain immediately. But what was his age? Sometimes the gaze he gave Chrissie was disturbingly knowing and adult.

The only people who had remained stubbornly disapproving about the addition of the Arab boy to the household were Aunt Kate and Aunt Maudie. And perhaps Matthew Smith, but it was no business of his.

Chrissie hadn't even wondered about Mr. Smith's private opinion until the day he encountered her getting out of the pony cart while Abdul held the reins. As soon as she had alighted, Abdul whipped up the pony and trotted smartly in the direction of the stables. He adored speed and showing off.

"Thank you," she said absently to Mr. Smith when he took her packages from her. "Isn't Abdul learning quickly? I don't suppose he knew what a pony cart was before he came to England."

"Even a ten-year-old could drive that little beast," Mr. Smith said.

"Why do you say even a ten-year-old? That happens to be Abdul's age or as nearly as he knows it."

"Are you sure?"

"Of course. He's so little."

"Fourteen if he's a day," said Mr. Smith briskly. "Well into puberty, Countess, if you will pardon me using that expression. Don't let him fool you."

"But why should he do that? Are you suggesting that he has deliberately deceived Percival?"

"If your husband is gullible."

But Percival was far from gullible. Or was he? That gentle, ascetic look of his did suggest a vague, dreamy innocence. Yet he also had great sophistication, and did sophistication go with innocence? Perhaps he was just humoring Abdul's mischievous deception.

One remembered the Swedish boy August and his reluctance to return home. Abdul would be exactly the same. Monkshood made a luxurious home for them, and a few wiles exercised on a tolerant master might enable them to stay.

All the same, Chrissie was uneasy. A fourteen-year-old Arab was quite a different proposition from a proportionately more innocent ten-year-old.

Mr. Smith was looking at her with his bright, probing look. Was it also pitying? Surely not.

"Forgive me for interfering, Countess. I just didn't like you being taken in. Perhaps I'm prejudiced. I think all Arabs are scoundrels."

There were gales and rain for most of February. In March the air had a delicate cool clarity, the sky lemon-colored in the evening, the grass emerging from patches of snow, the birds beginning to stir. Presently there were snowdrops and early primroses blooming, and the peacock had begun to scream on the terrace.

Chrissie, Percival said, would love the spring at Monkshood but even more the summer. Summer meant everything; the birth of her baby, release from her bodily imprisonment, freedom to go to parties, to travel, in other words to come to life again.

If the winter had been long and dull, it was only because he had such anxiety for her welfare. But now the time was nearer. April, May, June. . . .

In June the house would be finished, and they would have the midsummer eve party he had talked about earlier. It would be a superb colorful party, such as had not been known at Monkshood since Regency days. Monkshood had never been a house which either Queen Victoria or the Prince of Wales had wanted to visit, and one could count oneself lucky to escape this hugely expensive royal patronage. So the royal circle, which had ignored him since his divorce, could now be ignored in return. It would be enough if all his old friends came. He was certain they would.

He realized that the baby was not due until early in July, but the doctor had assured him that at that stage a moderate amount of gaiety would do Chrissie more good than harm. Perhaps she would like to wear a medieval costume with a high yoke that concealed the heir. Or an Empire gown, not too diaphanous in her delicate condition. "You would make an enchanting Josephine, darling. Although I can't see myself as Bonaparte. Perhaps I could be Talleyrand."

The party promised to be an even more glittering occasion than that of Millie Pepper's *bal blanc* a year ago. Chrissie's spirits rose in expectation. She was too young to have been leading such an elderly life.

"We must ask Mr. Smith."

"By all means. Who is Mr. Smith?"

"He's only been perched on scaffolding in the great hall for the last six months."

"Doing the frescoes, of course. I hadn't forgotten him, my love, only his name. Of course he'll be invited. Perhaps he'd like to dress as Holbein." He clapped his hand to his brow. "Oh, no, I can't be Talleyrand because I had intended to have Abdul as my pageboy. I'll have to be an emperor of some kind."

Chrissie stroked his face. "Darling, you're playing make-believe."

"Fascinating, isn't it?" He looked youthful and happy.

"And Abdul—he'll wear all that nonsense?"

"His turban and knee breeches? Of course."

"He must have grown out of them by now."

"In six months?"

"Adolescent boys grow quickly."

"But he's only a baby. A pickaninny. Isn't that what you Americans would call him?"

"No," said Chrissie coolly. "He'd have been out in the cotton fields long ago."

"But we're not those old Uncle Tom slave drivers, are

we? Why are you suddenly so critical of Abdul? I thought he was your pet."

"I think he has deceived you, Percival. I think he's older than he says. So what is he to be in two or three years? A eunuch?"

Percival winced, too visibly.

"That isn't like you, my dearest. Sarcasm?"

Chrissie hadn't realized until now how much Mr. Smith's suspicions had rankled. But she was glad she had brought them out in the open.

"I don't like you being taken in."

"I'm not as irresponsible as that. I'll take Abdul back to Tangier myself when the time comes. And we'll hope that his years spent in England have been of pleasure and benefit to him. Now shall we discuss who else is to come to our party, besides a painter and your little eunuch?"

His voice was mild, and he was smiling. But the emotion in his eyes was not humor or tenderness. It was, curiously, pain.

The only other disturbing thing that happened that lovely spring was a page of a letter accidentally coming Chrissie's way. Aunt Maudie was sitting at the garden table in the warm sunshine answering her morning's mail. A sudden breeze flicked the sheet of paper out of her reach. It came to rest at Chrissie's feet. She picked it up, and let her eyes rest almost absently on the exquisite but rather large script. The words seemed to leap out of the paper.

> I hear that Percival is getting up to his old tricks again. Does his wife understand? Darling Aunt Maudie, try to protect her.
>
> YOUR AFFECTIONATE SYBIL

"I'm sorry," Chrissie said, coming toward Aunt Maudie ponderously. Her body was now heavy and ungainly. "I read this accidentally. But since I have, can you explain what it means? I didn't know you corresponded with Sybil."

Aunt Maudie was flustered. The pink came into her cheeks and ebbed again.

"My sister and I are very fond of Sybil. We hadn't quarreled with her."

"Then tell me what she means."

"Oh, nothing of any importance, dear." Aunt Maudie was making a great fuss of tidying up her wind-ruffled papers. "Just that Percival has this habit of going off traveling on his own. It hurt Sybil very much. She used to feel rejected, she said."

Rejected. That was the exact word. Chrissie shivered slightly and remarked that for this time of year the wind was a little chilly.

"But it's different for you, isn't it," Aunt Maudie went on brightly, "because you're having your baby. You don't need to be so lonely when Percival—does go off."

"How often?" Chrissie asked bleakly.

"Only two or three times a year. That isn't too much. And really he's been awfully contented at home since Christmas, so perhaps you're changing his ways. Don't look so anxious, my dear."

"I'm not anxious. I shall go with him, in future."

"Your baby?"

"I imagine my baby will have a retinue of nurses. Won't he? The heir to Monkshood." She laughed lightly. "I guess he'll hardly need his mother around.

Chapter 25

The frescoes were finished. The painted figures shone in the gloom like jewels. The great hall looked rich and exotic, and Percival couldn't wait to show it off to the hundred or so guests arriving the following night.

Chrissie came on Mr. Smith packing up his materials and felt genuinely sad that his familiar figure would no longer be working quietly up among the rafters. He had been at Monkshood almost as long as she had.

"Where will you go now?" she asked.

"Back to Hampstead. London. I have a cottage near the heath. I'll finish my book." He looked up with satisfaction. "I can afford to now."

"I'm glad. Artists ought to be encouraged. Do you live alone in this cottage?"

"Yes. I like to be alone to work."

"You're a very self-contained person."

"Am I?"

"You've seemed so. Like a watchdog up there in the ceiling. I'll miss you. But we aren't saying good-bye yet. You'll be at the party tomorrow."

"I'm not coming, Countess, if you'll forgive me."

"Oh, why not? We're expecting you. Don't you want to hear flattering things about your work? Is it because you haven't got a costume to wear? Or don't you like having fun?"

"I like it as much as the next person, but I won't be able to come. Sorry if I'm rude."

"You're honest, at least. You don't want to come."

"I'd be a fish out of water."

"Then what about me? I'm still a foreigner."

Mr. Smith dug into his breast pocket.

"Yes. You're right there, Countess. You are a foreigner." He had produced a slip of paper and handed it to her. "I wrote down my address in Hampstead."

"For me? Why?"

"Just—well, if the roof leaks and makes the paint on my frescoes flake. Or anything."

Chrissie stood squarely in front of him.

"Mr. Smith, what *are* you telling me?"

Challenged, his steady eyes didn't flinch.

"You probably haven't many friends in this country."

"None. Except my husband."

"That's what I'm saying. But you do have one other one. Me. Take it or leave it."

"I'll take it," said Chrissie softly. "I really will miss you, Mr. Smith. We must drink another bottle of wine some time."

"Yes. Let's do that, Countess."

She kept on smiling at him, even after he had humped his equipment on his back and walked off, and even though she felt curiously bereft. When she went upstairs, she carefully put the piece of paper with the address on it in her jewel box. Mr. Smith was a real person, she thought. She would think of him tomorrow night when, anchored by her weight and clumsiness to a chair, she watched the tripping, laughing, posturing ghosts about her.

It had occurred to her that Percival might have postponed his party until after the birth of her baby, so that she could have joined in the merriment. But he had not. His reason was that midsummer eve did not change its date, and this was a midsummer eve party. There was something special about such a night in an English garden. Chrissie would see.

He was right, of course. The evening was fine, the setting idyllic. The air was heavy with the scent of roses and jasmine; not a leaf moved in the still balmy air. The lake glimmered. The splash of the fountain near the terrace seemed to accentuate the quiet. It was still daylight when the first carriages rolled up, but every room was glowing with lighted lamps and candles, and sheafs of flowers cut from the herbaceous borders filled the great hall and the drawing rooms. When the colorfully dressed guests wandered through the rooms, the scene was medieval and brilliant.

Percival, who had finally decided to dress as a cardinal, aptly suggesting chastity while his wife was *enceinte,* looked superb in his scarlet and gold robes. Abdul, dressed to his evident pleasure in his showy brocade turban and jacket, at first lurked close to Percival but was soon the darling of the guests. A cardinal didn't have a pageboy, they said. Why didn't the enchanting little fellow bestow his attentions on other people? Abdul was only too willing, and capered and grinned, and acted like a trained monkey.

Chrissie suddenly began to dislike him extremely. He was too clever altogether. But Percival looked fondly at him, enjoying his success, even if he did seem to be stealing the show from the refurbished house and its new mistress.

Not new altogether, but new to these people. Chrissie smiled and murmured greetings to dozens of powdered, bedizened faces and felt that they were all strangers and would remain so. Ghosts, tricked out in costumes of centuries ago.

Lady Elizabeth Gaye, Lord Somerfond, the Honorable Mrs. Thurston and Mr. Giles Thurston, the Comtesse de Serenac, the well-known actor Mr. Piers Madden, the poet Mr. Aubrey Field, Miss Geraldine Towers, a member of the Covent Garden Opera, several young men who looked as agile and muscular as ballet dancers, the Marquis and Marchioness of Huntleigh, the Irish peer Lord Loverdale. . . . On and on they went, but they weren't real, they were dressed in their curling wigs and their lace fichus and their knee breeches, and she would never recognize one of them again.

Besides, it was dull to have to sit solemnly on a couch while everyone danced. She loved dancing. She would rather be dancing with her husband than sitting here bearing his child.

Gaily dressed people, like butterflies alighting, sat with her briefly, then fluttered on. The two aunts were her most constant companions. They were being very protective of her, and she was grateful, suddenly liking their crumpled faces and anxious eyes. Percival bent over her periodically, offering her champagne, asking her if she was well. She had always wanted to see him gay and lighthearted with none of that melancholy in his eyes, but now that he was so clearly enjoying his party without her active participation, she was less happy.

Don't be so mean and grudging, she told herself. She needed more champagne. Or was it that she had had too much? Or had Percival, with that unfettered, almost wild look?

There was a strange atmosphere—Mr. Smith would have sniffed it out—was it of decadence?

No, she was just fanciful, lonely, left out. She had preferred the much more formal balls in London, with the chaperones, the nervous debutantes, the stiff, correct young men. She hadn't thought she was so old-fashioned. Christabel Spencer, the rich little American girl whom the Prince of Wales had noticed, seemed a more important person than the heavily pregnant Countess of Monkshood who had to behave like an elderly woman while her husband became younger and gayer by the minute.

At midnight Percival sat beside her, and took her hand.

"Dearest, bedtime for you."

She snatched her hand away.

"Really, Percival, you've treated me like a child all evening, and now you're sending me off to bed like a child."

"Yes, my love. Because it's my child I'm thinking of. I

know that you're overtired, or you wouldn't speak like that."

He kissed her cheek, and suddenly she wanted to cry. It was true she was tired. Her head ached from the noise and the candle smoke and the effort of talking to all the strangers who paused beside her politely, then moved on. Mr. Smith would have stayed beside her, she thought irrelevantly.

"The next time we have a party," Percival said gently, "you'll dance until dawn like everyone else. Just be patient."

She leaned her head on his shoulder.

"Sorry I was bad-tempered."

"Not bad-tempered, little one. Only exhausted. The aunts will go upstairs with you. I'll see you in the morning, my dearest."

The soothing words calmed her petulance. She allowed herself to be taken upstairs by Aunt Kate and Aunt Maudie, who seemed eager to escape from the gay scene themselves. Had they only stayed down for her sake? They were more thoughtful than she had realized.

"Thank you," she said, kissing each soft, wrinkled cheek. "Lizzie will help me undress. You go to bed yourselves."

"Yes, I believe we will," answered Aunt Kate. "When Percival is in the mood for a party, he likes it to go on until daylight. We'll happily leave them to their revels."

Revels. That was the word. For although Chrissie fell instantly asleep and slept heavily for several hours, when she stirred and opened her eyes to see daylight in the room, there were still wild cries coming from downstairs. She checked the time. It was five thirty, and the sun was up.

Whatever could the guests look like in their party finery in broad daylight? Drunken and bedraggled, judging by the quality of the shrieks of laughter she could hear. They seemed to be coming from the garden. They were accompanied by a sound like the splashing of water.

Good heavens, some of the guests must have taken a ducking in the fountain.

Chrissie clambered out of bed and went to look out of the window.

The early-morning garden, striped with long shadows, glistening with dew, beautiful and innocent in the pearly light, was completely marred for her. She drew in her breath with shock and disbelief, then opened the window to lean farther out and make sure that what she saw was not a nightmare.

There were two naked figures in the fountain, one small, dark-skinned, agile and slippery, the other tall, pale, with wildly disheveled hair, but unmistakable to her, his wife. She had had that naked body in bed beside her. How could she not recognize it?

Percival and Abdul, his slave boy, in some dreadful bacchanalian romp, diving for each other, slithering and falling, rising again, and giving those wild peals of laughter.

Chrissie began to shiver violently, wrapping her thin nightgown about her. Who else was watching? she wondered in terrible shame. Which of the servants was spying on the naked Earl of Monkshood rioting with his black boy?

Someone touched her. Lizzie, aroused by the noise, her plain face drawn into deep lines of amazement.

"Lizzie—get someone—Jenkins—anybody—to get them in. My husband—must be very drunk."

But not just drunk, she thought in numbed shock. Uncle Boy was often drunk and had never behaved like this.

Percival was more than drunk. Mad, she thought, mad, mad, mad. . . .

She swayed suddenly, as if she had been struck on the head. Abruptly the sun sank, the garden went dark.

When Chrissie opened her eyes again, she was back in bed, and Lizzie and both the aunts were at her bedside.

They must have been aroused by the noise, too. Their faces looked tired and old. They *knew,* she thought. They had always known. They had tried to protect Sybil, and now they were protecting her, the naïve American girl who was to give Monkshood its much-desired heir.

If that incredible scene she had just witnessed were not a nightmare. If she had not dreamed the water glinting on the writhing bodies and the sun gleaming on locks of drenched hair.

"It's true, isn't it?" she said tiredly.

"What is true, dear?" asked Aunt Kate, in her composed voice. "That that wretched little Arab boy drank too much champagne—encouraged by others, I am afraid —and fell in the fountain, and Percival had to rescue him."

Chrissie looked at the ceiling.

"Would he have drowned in two feet of water?"

The watching eyes became furtive. They didn't need to deny or excuse. She was not as innocent as they imagined her. She had heard rumors about the things that could happen between men. She was only angry that she had been too lovesick to recognize the signs long ago. Her reluctant bridegroom. The nights in hotel rooms alone. Her clipped hair and her boyish trousers. Percival's tortured eyes.

Her heart twisted in pain. Percival had tricked her, knowingly and deliberately. It was as people had whispered, he had wanted first an heir and then her money.

Now, fortunate fellow, he was getting both. But what was to happen to her?

"Lizzie!" the pain in her heart had moved to her back and was wrenching her. She could hardly speak. "We must leave here."

"Dr. Grierson will be here shortly," came Aunt Kate's soothing voice. "One of the grooms has gone for him."

"What for? To give—my husband—a sedative?"

"Percival, I am afraid, has taken too much to drink

and has gone to sleep it off. And you, dear child, if I'm not mistaken, are about to have your baby."

"Oh, bother," said Chrissie. "Then Lizzie—we'll have to wait, I suppose."

The next hours became a blur of light and darkness, pain, shapes at her bedside, low voices, the bearded face of Dr. Grierson, a nurse in starched white, the cozy form of a nanny? Did she imagine that? All English families had plump, cozy, rosy-cheeked nannies for their babies. Mothers were necessary only to give birth. What a lucky thing for her, since, having given Monkshood its heir, she could escape.

"Is the—nanny here?" she asked once, as it was getting dark and someone was lighting a lamp.

"Yes, my lamb," came Aunt Kate's bland voice. "She arrived an hour ago."

"That's good. . . ."

"Chrissie! Chrissie, my darling girl. . . ." Percival's low, sad voice, his anguished eyes. . . .

With a great effort she removed her hand from his. She couldn't bear him to touch her.

"I'd like to be alone."

"Remember, I love you."

Love you, love you, love you. . . . Mr. Smith had known. He had tried, delicately, to tell her. Pitied her. . . .

Must get her body free of this baby and get away from here.

Where? Papa had said, you've made your bed. . . . Papa could be very adamant. But she didn't want to go back to New York and didn't want his money. Look what it had already done. . . .

Must keep this secret anyway. It's a criminal secret, isn't it? Men have been put in jail for what Percival was doing.

Oh God, bring this baby quickly!

Just before it was born, she said clearly, "I don't want to see it. Don't show it to me."

Then the merciful darkness of the chloroform, and a

blurred awakening to the sound of vigorous wailing, and someone saying, gladly, "It's a boy."

That was all that mattered in this haunted house, the safe arrival of the new heir.

Chapter 26

For a whole week Harry refused to believe the news in Chrissie's letter.

He was a grandfather, yes, that was fine. His grandson was a future earl. All that had turned out exactly as he had planned. Why not? He was accustomed to the success of even his most long-term plans.

But as for Chrissie's crazy behavior, wanting to abandon her husband and baby, wanting to pour his own investment of half a million pounds down some impossible English drain, no, that he did not believe. His daughter would never be so irresponsible. She must be suffering from the temporary mental lapse that came over some women after the birth of a child. She would soon recover and regret that hysterical letter.

It was no use for Louisa to point out that the letter was not hysterical; it was almost too calm and logical. For some reason, an incompatibility existed between Chrissie and her husband, and that was not going to be overcome in a few days.

"Poppycock!" Harry stormed. "The girl has been too spoiled all her life. Serenity, Lizzie, everyone hanging on her wishes. Me and you, too. We're to blame. I suppose the earl has opposed her. He's probably been spoiled, too. And now it's a battle of wills to see who'll give in first."

Louisa's face was pinched with anxiety.

"Harry, it must be more than that. Chrissie wouldn't leave a newborn baby without some serious reason. She may be headstrong and impulsive, but she isn't heartless."

"You mean the earl's been fooling around with chorus girls or something. They all do it. Take their cue from that prince of adulterers, His Royal Highness. Anyway, would this upset Chrissie so much? She's young, I know, but she's seen the world and she's surely learned how a clever woman handles a situation like this. Dammit, she insisted on this marriage, and now she'll stick to it. I won't have a daughter of mine running away from her responsibilities."

"Don't get so excited," Louisa pleaded, alarmed by Harry's heightened color and protruding eyes.

"I'm not excited. I'm damnably angry. And disappointed. I thought Chrissie would have more integrity. But she will have, eventually. Her next letter will tell us so. She'll go back to her husband. She'd better. And don't you dare drop a word of this to Mary Ellen. I can't stand her descending on us like a ton of bricks with her 'I told you so's.' Take my word for it, Lou, this will blow over."

But it didn't. The next letter from Chrissie, two weeks later, bore the address of a hotel, The Lodge, Bloomsbury, London.

The contents had a liveliness and gaiety that seemed artificial and desperate.

What do you know, Mamma and Papa, Araminta Pepper writes that she has already taken a lover. It is supposed to be a secret, but she is sure Prince Rudolf knows and acquiesces. You might think I should have done this, too, and stayed with Percival. Araminta thinks so. But I'm not like that. I don't want a lover and a husband. That would be too messy for words. And I can't go back to Percival. Don't ever ask me why. I am not in his debt because he has the heir he wanted. This really was all he ever wanted, you must believe me. I don't even hate him. Now I am happy to be free and have a room in this small hotel, which is respectable and deadly dull, and you would approve of it for a young woman alone. I call myself Mrs. Spencer. Lizzie helped me get settled, but now, I am both glad and sorry to say, she has got a position as governess with a family in Surrey. I could not go on paying her wages in my present circumstances. So you see I do mean it when I say I am free even from Lizzie. I have been surrounded with too devoted servants all my life, especially that dreary, prying Peck. I don't think you ever knew how much I hated having him watching me all the time.

I have sold some of my jewelry, but not my lovely pearls, Papa. It will be a really black rainy day before I part with them. And would you believe it, I have a position myself, in a very select milliner's shop in South Audley Street. Some of the debs I met last summer come in, but of course they don't recognize me. It just wouldn't do to admit that your milliner had once been your friend. I helped Arabella Molesley to try on hats for an hour yesterday and finally, deliberately, stuck a hatpin into her thick scalp and made her yelp and nearly got dismissed. She never by so much as a blink admitted she recognized me, the silly snob. This is the other side of the coin, and rather amusing and immensely good for my character.

I know you both disapproved of my marriage and said that if I insisted on going through with it, it would be on my own head. Or was it that I must lie in the bed I had made? Both, I expect, and of course you were right, and I beg you now not to ruin this salutary lesson I am learning by sending a rescue mission. I have been protected too much. Now I truly want to stand on my own feet. I think money buys too many of the wrong things, and too easily. It certainly did for me. I was the plump little partridge asking to be shot down.

But I still do not blame Percival, only the frailties of human nature.

"I shall write to those two old aunts," Louisa said to Harry.

"You won't get far doing that. They'll close ranks. Blame their precious nephew? Not a chance."

"Do you blame him?"

"Certainly I do. Arrogant bastard. Wanting our girl only for breeding. And her money, of course. Laughing up his sleeve. But I blame Chrissie, too. A clever woman can make a marriage."

Louisa had made her own painful decision when Chrissie's first letter had arrived.

"Yes. I do agree with you. Chrissie must find out about herself, and life, without our protection and the trappings of wealth. I wonder sometimes what sort of girl Chrissie would have been without the burden of being an heiress."

"You mean she might not have been the kind of girl who leaves her husbands?"

"She's only had one husband. And there must have been something very wrong. Percival was already a divorced man. We never did know the real reason for his first divorce."

"Precisely." Harry chewed furiously on his cigar. His eyes were angry and miserable. "His wife ran off, as Chrissie has done. But we can't pry. Chrissie says to leave her alone, so we'll do so. She'll grow up."

"Whatever it was, it must have been very bad, for her to leave her baby, too."

"Now don't get sentimental, Lou. The baby is the heir to a noble name, and I know how these old English families feel about that. Chrissie has done what she thought best for him. But she'll go back to him and to her husband when she's had her bit of rebellion. You see if I'm not right. By the way, this has shaken me into making a new will. I signed it last week."

"Oh, Harry——"

"It's all right, love, I'm not about to die. I only wanted you to know that you're taken care of, but for the rest most of it goes to the nation. This house will be called the Spencer Collection. Nice, don't you think? I've made my mark. I've done as well as some of those railroad barons."

But at the expense of both their children, Louisa thought sadly, and could not say so.

"Chrissie understood that she got her share when she married Monkshood," Harry went on in his implacable voice. "I'll have none of this cowardly running away. I'm ashamed of her. She swore she loved the fellow, and that's less than a year ago. You stick by someone you love. Isn't that so?"

His tired, angry eyes fixed remorselessly on Louisa, seeking some truth. She had to nod in assent, although again she was unable to speak.

The scene in Harry's office was a grotesque repetition of one that had happened long ago, although the office was much larger and more expensively furnished, and the protagonists—Harry in his smart striped suit and bow tie, and Mary Ellen, like a vast silk cushion in her red dress and feathered hat—were much older and much more disillusioned.

Once Mary Ellen had attempted to offer Harry Spencer her hand in marriage and had been completely humiliated by his refusal. Now she was being humiliated again.

It wasn't fair. Because on both occasions she had imagined herself to be the benefactor, only to be smartly put in her place, or what that insufferable man deemed to be her place, as a silly and ineffectual woman.

The interview had begun so promisingly, too, with Mary Ellen saying, "Well, Harry Spencer, you've got your way as you always do. I'm prepared to make a deal with you over the house. I want a fair price. Values have gone up since you first made your offer, so bear that in mind."

Then she sat back, mopping her face. It was a very hot day with a high humidity, and she realized she wasn't suitably dressed for such high temperatures. She should have put on a cool blouse. But she had wanted to look her best. She was always happier in vivid colors. They cheered her up.

Harry, on the other hand, for all his show of brisk efficiency looked miserable. It was there in his eyes, the gnawing worry about Chrissie and the ruthless determination not to go back on his word. As if Chrissie's reckless behavior could be her own fault, Mary Ellen thought indignantly. It was entirely due to her upbringing and her blood. She had this impossible man's blood in her veins. Yet now he would let her starve.

"And what will you and Boy do?" he asked now. "You have always said you could never live anywhere but in that tumbledown old mansion."

"We won't live. We'll exist. We'll go into one of those new apartment blocks. In many ways it might be the best thing. I'm terrified that Boy will fall downstairs one day, the way our father did. His eyesight's bad now, and that tree shuts out all the light. Anyway, as you pointed out long ago, Harry Spencer, who's going to be interested in the van Leyden house when we're gone? You sold your daughter to that rascally English Lord. There's no one else."

"And what do you plan to do with the money?" Harry asked suavely.

"Buy an apartment, I told you."

"There'll be a great deal more than the cost of an apartment."

"Then we'll have some luxuries, Boy and I. We might even feel we're not living on your money any longer, since we'll have given a fair exchange. A more than fair exchange. You're getting a piece of American history."

"You're planning to send money to Chrissie, aren't you? Even though you know Louisa's and my wishes."

Mary Ellen started up, the color violent in her cheeks.

"But your wishes are cruel and heartless. Abandoning that poor child. Forcing her to go back to a husband she hates."

"She didn't exactly hate him a year ago. He was the great love of her life."

"Young girls can make mistakes. She should never have been left in England. She should never have been taken there. I want to bring her home. Yes, I do, Harry Spencer, and I only wish to God I could get the money some other way than by appealing to you."

"Chrissie," said Harry, in a slow grating voice, "is just twenty. She's young enough to stand a little hardship. It will, as my wife insists, be the making of her. Louisa, you know, has never enjoyed money, especially since we lost Henry. She thinks it corrupts and destroys. She says there's time to do something about Chrissie's character, so we're doing it. Besides, I won't have a daughter who runs away from responsibilities. Abandoning her son was the thing that Louisa felt particularly keenly." His tired eyes looked at the blowsy overcolored figure of his sister-in-law and grew bleaker. "So leave well alone, Mary Ellen. I absolutely forbid you to interfere."

"And you don't want the van Leyden house?" Mary Ellen said incredulously. "After all that begging and pleading, and talking of the future of New York City and all your development plans."

"Under these conditions, I don't want the van Leyden house."

"Harry Spencer, I declare, I always thought you were a monster but now—"

Harry's tight control snapped.

"Oh, go home, you silly woman, and open another bottle of rum and get drunk."

It wasn't like him to be vicious, but this supremely irritating woman mangled his nerves. How could she be his quiet Louisa's sister? Now he only wanted to catch a train to Southampton and to join Louisa in one of the cool, windy rooms of the seaside house and rest. He was shatteringly tired. He simply didn't dare tell anyone how tired he was. The trouble with Chrissie had been the last straw.

He could only pray that she would not, like her ridiculous aunt, think him a monster.

No one, Chrissie thought, would ever know how difficult it had been to write those cheerful and optimistic letters to her parents. Pretending to be enjoying living alone in this grisly hotel with its antimacassars and pot plants, its seedy residents and its stony-faced proprietress. Assuring Mamma and Papa that she thought selling hats was fun and a delightfully original occupation when it was a humiliation from start to finish. The other girls thought her superior and pretended not to understand her American accent, the customers were rude, haughty or just plain silly, unable to make up their minds, smiling fatuously at themselves in the mirror in unsuitable confections.

She learned patience and diplomacy, it was true. Madame Villiers was quite pleased with her. But she had no idea how long this self-discipline would last or how long she could afford to go on living as she was doing. The hotel cost all her modest salary, and since she couldn't go to work in her elegant Paris clothes, she had had to buy new and horrible garments in black or mousy gray. There was no money left for entertainments. Anyway, she could not go to the opera or the theater alone. She could not dine at the Ritz. She hated the evenings alone in her dingy room, when visions of Monkshood returned to torture her. The green lawns, the terraces, the yew walks, the scent of herbs and roses, the birdsong, the peace. The utterly spurious peace. The paradise with the snake in it.

Her baby, whom she had refused to see, was unreal to her, but again and again Percival's white, tortured face appeared before her; his words echoed endlessly.

"I thought you of all women could have saved me, Chrissie. You were so fresh, so young and hopeful. Believe me, I did think that. But I know now that one is a prisoner of one's nature forever. Nothing changes it. It's a life sentence. I'll go abroad for a year or more. If you do insist on leaving Monkshood, I'll arrange for a divorce at a later date. A little time must go by. My reputation in the divorce court isn't the best. I don't mind about that. I only wonder what the judge might say to another application. But if you could stay here, and love our son—your son, my darling. . . ."

Every word was written forever on her mind.

"No, Percival, I can't stay!" she cried in anguish. There could be no cool, calculated argument for her. She had to speak the entire unhappy truth. "I know I would love my son, but I'm a woman before I'm a mother. I need love myself. I couldn't stand night after night alone, as you've made me do ever since our wedding day. I'd wither up. So there it is. I've given you your son. I don't owe you anything more. Call me selfish, call me what you like. But the little boy will be better with his nurses than with a mother who would get more and more bitter. I have to find life somewhere else. I have to *live,* Percival."

"Chrissie—don't hate me."

"I don't. Truly, I don't. I still love you in so many ways. But not the way a wife loves a husband. I'm just being realistic."

"Yes. I know. You have this refreshing honesty. I discovered it at Millie Pepper's ball. I still love you, too."

He gave a smile that was gone in a moment. "I will look after you. If you will tell me your bank—naturally."

"No, Percival! No! How can I be free if you keep me? I don't want your money. I *beg* you not to give it to me. It will make me feel guilty."

"But how will you manage—oh, your family, of course."

"Yes, my father," said Chrissie unconvincingly.

"I did you a great wrong," said Percival sadly. "Forgive me, if you can."

Forgive. . . . A nice word. She wasn't sure whether she could put it into practice. She hoped she could. The thought of being a bitter woman, neither wife, widow nor mistress, was horrifying. Dear Aunt Mary Ellen, am I to join you with your gaudy brave clothes and your noisy tantrums and your secret glasses of rum? she said to herself.

"You little fool, why didn't you take a lover?" Araminta wrote. "And stay a countess. Are you going to let Percival divorce you and be a nobody? And what about him? Isn't he going to get a reputation for being a Bluebeard? Darling, what *did* happen? You can't shock me. These German princelings and their hangers-on and their sophisticated vices—talk about Grimm's fairy tales. Why didn't our parents prepare us more for the facts of life? Or don't they know them?"

Papa may have, Chrissie thought, but Mamma with her gentle, high-bred face, never!

DARLING MAMMA

I can read between the lines of your letter and you are worrying about me. There is no need. London is of the greatest interest and pleasure to me. I think it's where I belong spiritually. I must be closer to Grandmother Spencer and Papa's other ancestors than I realized. Poverty is part of it. We never really saw this marvelous city when we were going to balls and garden parties. Now I am one of the people who gape in the street at the guests arriving at the grand houses in Park Lane and Mayfair. I think of those poor nervous girls in their tight lacing, wondering who will dance with them, whether their hair will fall down, whether they will be able to breathe, whether they will be a terrible social failure. They say Queen Victoria is dying, so the Prince of Wales may have to be a little more circumspect. I stand in the street and want to shout, "Look at me, I once danced with the Prince of Wales." But is this the sort of thing that really matters?

A letter arrived from Aunt Mary Ellen, enclosing two fifty-dollar bills.

Not a word about this to your parents—they are both *utterly heartless,* and I never want to speak to either of them again. I simply cannot understand them. Your mother seems to think you have been *oppressed* all your life by riches, and it has *depraved* you. I would say, if you had been depraved, it has been done by Harry Spencer, not by his money. But they simply can't let you starve. Tell me, dearest child, whatever did that wicked man do to you? Oh, if only I could carry you back here where you belong. As it is, I am making Boy go without *half* his rum ration in order to send you money. It isn't much, but it might save you from having to go back to your *villainous* husband, as your father thinks you should. Loyalty, integrity, my *foot!* And I expect the new viscount has a *retinue* of nurses, and you would never have got to hold him in your arms, anyway.

Your ever-loving AUNT MARY ELLEN

P.S. That Vanderbilt girl had trouble with her duke, too. You just can't trust those English aristocrats, but can I convince your father? Never!

Aunt Mary Ellen's dollars were welcome, and Chrissie gladly accepted them. They would eke out her wages for several weeks. And if Papa's pearls had to go, they must. She was living from day to day. She dared not look ahead because there surely was no future for her, the disappearing countess, as the gossip-mongering newspapers called her. The truth could never be told for fear of Percival being arrested and committed to prison. So her own reputation must be permanently besmirched.

The only person she could have talked to frankly and safely was that odd, quiet man Matthew Smith, whose address still reposed in her jewel box. But he was writing a book; he needed to be alone. He had been kind to her because he guessed the truth, and was sorry for her. It wasn't fair to involve him in her scandals.

And hadn't she decided she was going to stand entirely

on her own feet to show the world that the pampered millionaire's daughter was not without backbone and pride?

But who was there to notice her brave stand? Madame Villiers had insisted on her anonymity. She didn't want to be accused of harboring a runaway wife or of having her shop besieged by inquisitive newspapermen. It would be bad for business. She would never have employed Chrissie if it hadn't been so difficult to find girls with good manners and some class.

Mrs. Mulligan, the proprietress of that depressing small hotel, was interested only in the payment of her weekly bill. No one in this large city cared two pins about the girl who, all her previous life, had been rich, adored and cherished.

It was a chastening situation that was almost destroying Chrissie. She was desolately lonely. She thought of Percival constantly, but never of her baby, although she dreamed of him. She cried in her sleep and awoke tired and pale.

The summer was over; winter was coming. She wanted to go home.

But Papa was still angry and bitterly disappointed in her, and Mamma's letters held a bewildered, unexpressed reproach that was all too clear. How could Chrissie have done such a terrible thing as abandon her baby? The grave of little Henry haunted them all over again, and Chrissie knew she could not beg to go home. Papa would not refuse to help, he had never refused her anything; but he would be frowning and distant, and Mamma would cry a lot, and it would all be utterly horrible. She would have to accept the rum-odorous embraces of Aunt Mary Ellen, and that would turn her right back into being a little girl.

So the cheerful letters must be sent off each week, and no one must guess her misery.

"You did make that disastrous bed," she said to herself, putting her chin in the air. "Papa's perfectly right."

But she worried about him. She sensed from her mother's letters that he was not well. They were staying at Southampton a month longer than usual because Papa rested more there. Once back in New York, he would be at his desk constantly. Did Chrissie know he had given up the project of buying the van Leyden house, so one day it would be hers after all, since Mary Ellen and Boy were certain to bequeath it to her?

It had nothing of the grandeur of Monkshood, of course, or of Camberwell House. Had Papa told her that he was leaving Camberwell House to the City of New York, as a museum? A wonderful idea, didn't Chrissie agree? It would give Papa his well-deserved niche in the history of New York City. And was Chrissie yet able to contemplate becoming reconciled to her husband, because it would make dear Papa very happy if she could?

No, no, no, Chrissie cried, crumpling the expensive writing paper into a ball, then straightening it out again because the letter would have to be answered. Calmly and cheerfully.

Soon it would be Christmas, and the great tree at Monkshood would be hauled indoors. The baby would be too small to appreciate its glory. Percival would be abroad. The two aunts. . . .

"Good morning, Chrissie," said the two round, cozy bonneted and befurred figures standing just within the doorway of Madame Villiers' shop. "We haven't come to shop, but to take you out to a little luncheon. At Gunters, we thought. Perhaps Madame Villiers wouldn't mind if you are a little late returning."

Aunt Kate and Aunt Maudie!

"How did you—"

"Ssh! We'll talk at luncheon. Do find out, dear, if we can carry you off for a little while."

Madame Villiers frowned but recognized the class of the two small imperious ladies. She said severely, "Just for this one occasion, Mrs. Spencer, since you have relatives up from the country. But you must be back by two thirty at the latest."

"How did you find me?" Chrissie asked, safely in the street and out of earshot of Madame Villiers.

"My dear, that wasn't difficult. Percival has his methods. He would never allow you to be in want, you know. He was so fond of you."

That was Aunt Kate. Aunt Maudie added in her soft monotone, "So unfortunate. We, too, were fond of you, dear. If we didn't seem friendly at first it was because we were afraid for you."

"We felt Percival was not successful at marriage," Aunt Kate explained. "Now that he has his son, he doesn't intend to marry again."

"There's no need," said Chrissie bitterly.

"No, dear. That's perfectly true."

It was typical of her present lonely life that she was genuinely pleased to see the two aunts. She had never imagined she would have so much to talk to them about. How was Monkshood looking? Were the servants all the same? Was the elderly peacock with his two colorless wives still strutting on the terrace, and the jackdaws circling and crying over the old ruin? Was the baby thriving? Not "my baby," but the Monkshood heir. Were Mr. Smith's frescoes still being admired?

That was the thing she had had to remember, Aunt Kate cried in her clear, well-bred voice. Mr. Smith had written asking for Chrissie's whereabouts. He had read in those low-class newspapers of her trouble. One hadn't thought he would read that type of paper; he had seemed quite a cultured person.

"I don't know whether you want us to divulge your address to him, my dear. My sister and I thought we ought to consult you first. But we did think you might be—"

"In need of friends," added Aunt Maudie.

"And you had seemed to find Mr. Smith congenial. We remember the night you stayed up very late dining with him."

"I know where he lives if I want him," Chrissie said shortly.

"But a lady does find it more dignified for the gentleman to make the first approach," said Aunt Maudie. "We thought you would prefer it that way."

The soft, crumpled faces looked at her hopefully.

"It doesn't put you in an awkward position, supposing you no longer find Mr. Smith congenial," said Aunt Kate, in her brisk, sensible way.

"Our sister-in-law, Percival's mother, was not very happy with our brother," Aunt Maudie said with apparent irrelevance. "Consequently she spoiled Percival, her only child, disgracefully. He was seldom allowed to leave his mother's side. So unmanly."

"The boy Abdul has been sent back to where he came from," said Aunt Kate.

Chrissie pushed her food around her plate. She had thought she would be greedy for good food again, but now she was too excited to eat. She was daring to be optimistic, to be happy.

"I have no objection to you telling Mr. Smith where I am," she said offhandedly. "If he's too busy with his book, he doesn't need to see me, does he?"

She saw the concerned and hopeful look in the two almost identical pairs of blue eyes and suddenly leaned across the table to kiss each of the aunts.

"Bless you," she said softly. "Look after my baby for me."

It was the first time she had been able to refer to the new child at Monkshood as hers. The hard knot in her breast was beginning to ease.

Chapter 27

~~~~~~

They faced each other warily over the red-checked tablecloth, the brown pottery teapot, the plate of toasted buns. It was a foggy evening, and the little teashop was almost empty. Chrissie had been intending to hurry home. Bleak as her room was, it was a refuge from the raw, choking, sooty fog and the vaguely menacing streets. But Matthew Smith had materialized out of the black wall of mist and taken her arm firmly and guided her to the warm haven of the teashop.

"Well, Countess, how's life?"

"I'm no longer a countess." She was edgy and stiffly on her guard against emotion. She had no intention of letting him guess how wonderful it was to see a familiar and friendly face. Perhaps especially his face, although that was something she hadn't analyzed. "I'm plain Chrissie Spencer," she said.

"Good."

"Why is it good, my marriage being a failure?"

"It's good that you got out of it."

"But I've ruined my life. Or so my parents think. And I'm still only twenty. As they also point out."

"All the better. Time to start again."

"You sound so glib."

"Just saying what I think. What am I to call you, if countess is forbidden?"

"Chrissie, I suppose. If we're to be friends."

"I accepted that as a fact, when the Misses Monkshood said you wouldn't object to seeing me."

"I was lonely. That was all."

He grinned. "You don't concede much, do you? Well, I don't blame you for being on your guard after the experience you've had."

He was looking at her in his usual intent way. She wondered what he thought of her. Her looks had suffered in the last months. She had lost weight and grown pale, and since she had come straight from the shop, she was wearing her sober working clothes, a very different garb from the couturier gowns to which she had always been accustomed. If it had been the glamor of riches and position that had attracted him previously, he couldn't think much of her now.

He himself was unchanged. His serious, intelligent face gave her the same pleasure. She liked his healthy brown skin, his high, bulging forehead, his broad shoulders. She could identify now one of his attractions for her. It was plain masculinity. She found herself comparing it with Percival's attenuated, overbred elegance and wished briefly and uselessly that it had been Matthew Smith whom she had met at Millie Pepper's *bal blanc*.

"I don't think being a countess was your role in life, anyway," he said.

"Why? Didn't I do it properly?"

"Oh, very properly. You were dazzling."

Chrissie gave a wry laugh. "But no longer."

"I'm terrified of dazzling women. All the same—it was a hard thing to tell you. I blamed myself afterward for interfering."

"About Percival?"

"I couldn't stand what he was doing to you."

"Now, don't you criticize him, Matthew Smith. He was the kindest husband."

"I do criticize him, and I don't apologize."

"It's I who should be criticized for running away. It was cowardly. At least, my father thinks so."

"I expect your father doesn't know the truth."

"No, and he never will. I'll protect Percival until my dying day."

"My dear innocent child, these things may not be shouted from the rooftops, but they're whispered."

"Not in Papa's hearing," Chrissie said stubbornly.

"That noble lord has been luckier in his wives than he deserves."

"It's just a matter of understanding and tolerance," Chrissie said intensely. "One is a victim of one's nature. I simply won't have Percival punished. You're a writer, an observer of human nature. You should understand."

Matthew shrugged. "I wouldn't have given a damn about the earl's morals if he hadn't been your husband. That was when I wanted to take my fist to him."

"Matthew!"

"Give me some more tea, and stop scolding. You're thin. What have you done to yourself?"

"Had a baby. That's a sure way to grow thinner."

"More than that. You look half-starved."

"Oh, no, I eat."

"You suffocate in that hatbox all day, stiffening up your backbone until it's going to crack. Is there anything wrong in asking for help?"

"I haven't needed to."

"You've needed to. You're all tied up with pride and shock and guilt for your previous pampered life. You're trying to find out what you are without your papa's millions and your precious husband's title."

Chrissie's knuckles were dug into her eyes.

"Don't talk like that. It's too much like the truth. Do you realize I had to refuse to see my baby in case I couldn't part with him? He belonged to Monkshood the moment he was born, like one of the stones in those ancient walls. Even if I'd stayed he'd never have been mine. He'd have gone from nannies to tutors to famous schools to famous regiments to that whole tight upper-class circle, which I know now I never want to belong to. So I told myself that I could have more babies, but maybe Monkshood could never have another heir."

"There's something you don't know," said Matthew. "You're one of the stones in the wall, too. When I was doing the frescoes, I painted your face on one of the king's ladies. The slim one carrying a garland of flowers."

"Why ever did you do that?"

"Because I thought you outshone those long, languid, stupid Tudor faces. Why shouldn't you be there, as long as Monkshood stands?"

"My epitaph?"

"Something like that. When does Lord Monkshood plan to give you a divorce?"

"Oh, I don't know. Not too soon. He'd be ruined socially, two divorces in such quick succession."

"Don't waste sympathy on him. Think of me."

"You?"

"You are going to marry me, aren't you?"

"Matthew Smith, this is too absurd!"

"A proposal of marriage over tea and toasted buns? I know you're more used to champagne and moonlight, but I'm not a noble lord or a rich man. I'm not going to be able to keep you in the lap of luxury—"

"Matthew, stop!"

"Nor am I going to be able to buy you diamonds or give you two dozen servants—"

"Matthew!"

"But nevertheless, we do truly belong to each other, and if you deny that, you're the most brazen liar ever to cross the Atlantic."

Under the gaze of a thin little waitress with chilblained fingers who was bringing them a fresh jug of hot water, Matthew took her hand with a serious and touching formality and lifted it to his lips. He held it there so long that the little waitress sputtered into giggles. Chrissie tried to conceal her swift helpless delight. She had got so vulnerable. Her whole body was trembling. She tried to put on her gay social voice.

"Really, I never met such an impulsive man. Even the Prince of Wales, who, goodness knows, demands what he wants, has a little more finesse. He presents his compliments through a second person—"

"Stop that," said Matthew harshly. "I can't stand that artificial voice. You're no longer a countess, or a shining light in society, or even a millionaire's daughter. You're a young woman, whom a perfectly ordinary man like me happens to love and wants to marry. No. Don't answer me now. But think about it. Because I don't intend anyone else to get you."

Tears filled Chrissie's eyes and spilled over. She gave up trying to hide her emotions. She sniffed and clung to his hand, and he smiled and said in his sudden way, "Can you cook?"

"C-cook?"

"You know, stir things in pots. No, of course you can't. You've always had Cook, and six undercooks and ten serving maids and a footman or two. Well, I'm going to teach you something about the English Sunday. No self-respecting family goes without its midday roast beef and Yorkshire pudding. It's an essential part of English life and rated slightly higher than going to church in the morning. So, if you would hire a cab and come out to my house next Sunday, I'll have the fire going and the oven heating, and I'll give you your first lesson in preparing that great feast, the Englishman's Sunday dinner."

"Will there be anyone else there?"

"Only my cat who is a heavy sleeper. She could hardly be called a chaperone."

"I'll come," said Chrissie briskly.

"Oh, that's wonderful. I want to show you my pictures and my books. I want to show you all my life."

On the fourth Sunday of this now firmly established

routine, Chrissie went up the steep, narrow stairway of the endearingly quaint house to the two bedrooms upstairs. She had left Matthew dozing by the fire in the book-cluttered low-ceilinged warm and cozy sitting room. His cat, a large and somnolent tabby, lay curled on the hearth rug. The sitting room was the nicest room Chrissie had ever been in, and she was reluctant to leave it. But the time had irrevocably come.

She undressed slowly, laying her garments tidily on the chair at the foot of Matthew's bed. She looked critically at her naked body in the misty glass of the old mirror. It was not so thin. In four weeks it had got back its healthy roundness. Her breasts, relieved of their aching unwanted burden of milk, were small and firm again. Her waist was hardly its fashionable eighteen inches, but she doubted if it was more than nineteen or twenty. Her stomach was flat, her legs long and slim. Best of all, her hair had grown to its normal length, halfway down her back. She had taken out the pins and let it fall down. When she wrapped herself in Matthew's plaid dressing gown, she flung the thick tresses out over the collar. Her cheeks were bright, her lips soft and inclined to tremble as she went to the head of the stairs and called to Matthew.

He came and stood looking up at her in astonishment.

"Whatever do you think you're doing?"

"Nothing," she said primly, "until you come up."

He bounded up half a dozen steps and stopped.

"Chrissie—"

"I know. I know. But we may have to wait for two years before we can get married, and that's much too long."

"I don't dare to come any closer until you convince me you mean that."

"When did I ever tell you a lie?"

"Never."

"There you are. And if we have a baby, surely you can put a ring on my finger. Can't you? It doesn't need the assistance of a parson. Can't we be Mr. and Mrs. Smith privately, to ourselves? Who else cares? Oh, Matthew stop staring. You're such a starer. Come *up!*"

The light was fading, and the cat, growing chilly by the untended fire, crept upstairs and onto the bed, stretching her soft, heavy body over their feet. They didn't stir. They lay locked in each other's arms. They could stay like this forever, Chrissie thought. The warm, wonderful lethargy following love possessed her. She knew at last who she was and who she was always going to be. Chrissie Smith, Chrissie Smith, Chrissie Smith. . . .

Matthew heard her whispering the name and stirred.

"What, love?"

"Nothing."

"Are you going to live with me here?" His voice was deep in his throat.

"If I'm asked."

"I'll buy you a wedding ring tomorrow. I like eggs and bacon for breakfast. Can you manage them?"

"No trouble."

Then he was clinging to her and trembling, and she thought she felt dampness as if from his tears on her cheek. He was as vulnerable as she was, she realized, and a great engulfing tenderness possessed her. She hoped they would have a baby soon. She thought it would please Mamma and perhaps at last stop her grieving for Henry. One knew she had been appalled by Chrissie abandoning her first baby.

"Chrissie, my darling love, I'm going to make my books a success. We're not always going to be poor—"

She stopped his words with her mouth against his. Money was not going to be mentioned in this house, ever.

Chapter 28

~~~~~~

At the end of the summer Harry had another spasm, worse than the giddy turn he had had at breakfast earlier in the year. There was fairly severe pain in his chest, and he was pale and sweating and breathing with difficulty.

Louisa thought the doctor would never come. If Harry were going to ill, they would have to move back to New York, where Dr. Bates was only ten minutes away. Here Dr. Atkinson had to harness his horse to his buggy and drive four miles. The delay was highly dangerous to someone in Harry's condition, since it seemed all too likely that this was a heart attack.

The doctor arrived at last and administered stimulants. He ordered Harry to bed, where he must stay an indefinite time. Nurses must be engaged.

"It's only a mild attack this time, Mrs. Spencer, thanks be to God. But as you know, there's a fair chance of its recurring and becoming progressively more severe. I'm leaving you some pills. Put one under his tongue the moment he feels discomfort. Will you be sure to do that?"

"Oh course, Doctor. I'll watch him all the time."

"I'm sure you will. But don't let him see you doing it. He's a strong man. I doubt he'll take kindly to illness. Particularly, don't let him get excited."

"When can he be moved to New York?"

"In two or three weeks, maybe. We'll see."

"He'd like to get home, Doctor."

"Isn't this his home?"

"Not in the way Camberwell House is. He built it, you see."

"I understand. Possessions are hard to part with."

"But he's not going to—to die?"

"Not if he behaves himself. I've told him so. It won't do any harm if you tell him, too."

As soon as Harry began to feel better, he fretted to get back to town, he fretted to get to his office, and he fretted for Chrissie. He made a great noise about wanting to be in his own house (he had never regarded the Long Island house, built by someone else, as his own) and to find out what muddles had gone on in the office during his illness. He didn't mention Chrissie in so many words. He only looked hungrily at the letters Louisa brought in each morning and seemed to flatten when he saw that none bore an English postmark. He had forbidden Louisa to tell Chrissie of his illness, although Louisa knew that he was aching for his daughter.

Chrissie continued to write her cheerful letters, relating the pleasures of being in London, the amusing absurd things that happened in Madame Villiers' shop, the unexpected visit of the Monkshood ladies. Louisa wasn't entirely deceived by this prattle, but fortunately Harry was. He admired Chrissie's spirit and was less distressed about the mess she and "that pale overbred fellow" had made of things. He was confident they would have a reconciliation. That was why Chrissie must not be told of his illness and feel it her duty to come home. It was more important that she return to her husband. Hadn't Louisa and he been right not to interfere, but to let things take their course? All the same. . . .

"All the same, what?" Louisa asked gently.

"I keep thinking I've been a bit adamant. How's that girl going to get on without any capital, if she doesn't go back to Monkshood?"

"She's seems to be getting on very well."

"You can make a joke of poverty when you're twenty years old, but how's she going to get on when all her good clothes have worn out or gone out of fashion? She's always been used to the best."

"I know. That's why it's good for her to know a little austerity."

The blue eyes looking at Louisa from the pillow had lost too much of their brilliance. She could hardly bear to look at them, they were so quenched and sad.

"I was only punishing her for behaving like a spoiled child and not facing her difficulties. But you talk as if my money will ruin her. Have you always hated it?"

She could not tell any comforting lies.

"Since Henry was kidnapped, yes. After that I was frightened all the time. And I got so conscious of avaricious and jealous people. And I felt guilty about having too much, and seeing how it hemmed Chrissie in. It isn't her fault she hasn't been able to face life, Harry. It's ours for overprotecting her, suffocating her."

"But she always seemed happy," Harry protested, with some of his old vigor. "She had enough character to overcome that hemming in, as you call it. And look at the compensations she had. Look at that marvelous ball in Paris that I certainly will never forget. Nor will Chrissie."

"I imagine not," said Louisa dryly.

"Look at the people she met, earls, dukes, princes of the blood."

Louisa rubbed her fingers gently back and forth across his forehead.

"If you ask me, all that wasn't for Chrissie at all; it was some fantasy of your own you were living."

She felt the skin tighten under her fingers.

"What poppycock! The whole thing was for our daughter."

A moment later he sat up. "I'll get up tomorrow. The next day we'll go home."

"Now, dear, don't be too impatient. Wait and see what the doctor says."

"That fussing old fool. He'll keep me here forever, embalmed."

"What is it you have to get back to town for?"

"I want to look at my pictures. I want to walk about my house. Another fantasy of your husband's, eh? And," he added, "I want to see my lawyer. I'm going to change my will."

Louisa froze at the bedside.

"But why? You made a very good will. You were pleased with it."

"All that stuff to the nation. Yes, that stays. I'm proud of that. And Chrissie doesn't want my Rubenses or my Canalettos and van Goghs. She's given up a far finer collection than mine. But some stocks and shares—"

"For Chrissie?" Louisa asked sharply.

"—will come in handy. You can't deny that, Lou. A million dollars' worth won't ruin her life, will it? If she wants some extravagance like a palace in Venice, she can have it."

"You can't give up having an influence on her life," Louisa cried accusingly.

"No, that's not true. I've just got to feeling bad about cutting her out. My own flesh and blood. No matter if she is improvident. It's all so damned final once I'm gone," he muttered. "After that, I can't have second thoughts. Nothing can be changed."

The letter came the day after they had returned to Camberwell House.

DEAREST MAMMA

You may not want to show Papa this letter. I am writing it to you because I have a feeling you will understand. Don't mothers, always? Except about leaving my baby, of course, but again I can't explain all the complicated and tragic reasons for that. I can only say that you would forgive me if you knew. And now I am telling you something else that may shock you, although it is the most crazily beautiful thing. I have fallen in love with a more or less penniless writer, and we are living in his house (together with a large agreeable tabby cat) on Hampstead Heath. I am learning to cook and to do the marketing, and honestly you would be proud of me. I realize that all my life previously I have only been a rather nice-looking ornament. Now Matthew tells me I am not only nice-looking but useful.

We can't be married yet because I am not divorced, but I am Mrs. Smith in every way except that "Dearly beloved, we are gathered together" business. Matthew and I feel perfectly reverent without those words being said over us.

You must decide if you want Papa and Aunt Mary Ellen to know about this. At this moment I only want to tell you, because I feel sure that deep in your heart you won't be shocked or disapproving. I have an intuition about it. You know I really was a naïve child when I married Percival. Now I am a grown woman, and Matthew is a grown man. He is *my* man. And if we are lucky enough to have a baby, I can assure you that I will never never never leave it."

In the privacy of her bedroom Louisa cried and wiped her eyes and cried again. She had the strangest conviction that she could smell violets. White violets, too fragile to live for long.

Chrissie's Matthew didn't sound at all fragile or transient. Louisa got a vivid impression of someone robust, humorous and honest. But someone who needed the satisfaction and achievement of making his own way in life and of supporting his wife.

What would a million dollars do to him?

Louisa opened her pretty French writing desk and taking out letter paper and pen, began to write rapidly.

No, my darling child, I don't disapprove. I know you have gone through troubles that you couldn't talk about, but now I am truly so happy for you. I shall tell Papa when he is stronger. He has had a little illness. And Aunt Mary Ellen when *I* am stronger, though her bark is always worse than her bite, and she will be happy if she knows you are.

But now I must prepare you for the fact that Papa has repented of his decision to leave you out of his will, and intends you to have a great deal of money. I am so anxious—

Louisa stopped writing. No, this wouldn't do. She must handle this in some other way. She tore up the letter and walked across to the long windows to look at the darkening park. The trees were leafless, it was getting near Christmastime and midwinter. It was the time of year when she and Cornelius had had those long walks, talking, planning, loving. She pressed her forehead against the windowpane, a strange serenity filling her.

It had been best this way. Harry had been a good husband, and she knew that she had contented him. All the same, she had a deep secret pleasure that Chrissie now had what she and Cornelius had longed for. It was almost as if she had bequeathed this gift to them. She would do everything possible not to have it damaged.

Harry's new will covered two dozen foolscap sheets. Reuben Morrison, his lawyer, brought the draft copy to the house and left it with Harry to study at his leisure.

He stopped to talk with Louisa in her drawing room before he left.

"Don't let Harry ponder on that epistle too long, Mrs. Spencer. I want it back for engrossment."

"Is there any hurry?" Louisa asked carefully.

"Well—when you're making your will, you feel the cold finger is on your shoulder a bit. It's a perfectly natural reaction. Harry will perk up when he's got that document signed."

"Yes, of course. And he is improving a little. The problem is to keep him home."

"He's hankering to see another skyscraper rising, I expect. Well, he'll do that, God willing."

"God willing," Louisa echoed vaguely. She couldn't contemplate the pain of observing Harry's diminished exuberance, of the way he forgot the gardenia for his buttonhole, or went out without his sable-trimmed greatcoat on icy days, or came home straight after lunch because he felt drowsy and wanted to nap by the fire.

Her magnificent Harry with his flair, his panache, his tireless enthusiasm. She was terribly afraid he was going to die.

He wanted her to read the new will.

"You'll live at Southampton, won't you, Lou? That house is yours."

"No, I'll go back to the old van Leyden house," Louisa said. "I'm glad you never had it pulled down. I've always intended to go back if the occasion arose. But I pray it won't."

She took Harry's hands, and he said, "Your eyes are still beautiful, Lou. Deep-blue sapphires. I've always admired them."

"In my old face?"

"Not old. Just nicely worn. Lou! I want Chrissie to come home."

Her heart jumped.

"But she doesn't want to. She doesn't know about your illness. You told me not to tell her."

"I've changed my mind. I want to see her. I won't be here much longer—"

"Oh, my darling!"

"It's true. No use pretending anything else. A man knows when he's getting near his end. Chrissie will come if she's told the truth. What's the matter? What are you hiding from me?" He seized her arms. "Chrissie isn't in worse trouble?"

"No, she's not in trouble at all. She's very happy. She's in love."

"She was in love a year ago, and look where that led her."

"This is different, Harry. A year ago she was an adoring and willful child. Now she's a woman."

He was frowning with fierce suspicion.

"Are you telling me she's living with some man? In sin?"

"Sin isn't the right word for this."

"How do you know?"

"Her letter absolutely breathed happiness."

"And happiness makes it not a sin? Who is this man?"

"A young man who's an artist and a writer."

A little of the belligerence went out of Harry's face.

"Well, I've no objection to those professions," he grunted. "Admire them if they succeed. But they don't usually. This fellow will be penniless."

"Not entirely."

"That means he is." Harry sat up straighter, his eyes beginning to kindle. "Then all the more reason—"

"No, Harry, you mustn't interfere! Please!"

"And why am I not to interfere in my only child's life? When she's living in poverty, in need."

"But don't you remember saying that that would do her good. You can't have forgotten. It isn't long ago. You know this is what I really hate about your money. It makes you meddle with people's lives. You've done it with my parents, and Mary Ellen and Boy, and me. Yes, me. I have to say it. And now you're going to meddle with the happiness Chrissie has found for herself, without your help. Harry, please don't sign that new will. Don't burden her with riches again. Let her be herself, nice, ordinary, happy."

Harry had half started up. His breath caught in a groan. Suddenly he sank back, flaccid and helpless. His face was drawn and ravaged with pain.

"Harry! Oh, darling! Is it another attack? Where are your pills?"

His hand made an ineffectual movement toward his breast pocket. Louisa fumbled frantically, found the little silver box, and in her haste and panic dropped it on the

floor. She had to grope for it on her hands and knees. When she rose again, she saw that Harry's face had a frighteningly blue look, his eyes were closed. He was breathing heavily and very slowly.

If she could open his lips and get the pill under his tongue. On the other hand, if she couldn't, that new will would never be signed. The thought had scarcely formed in her head, she had scarcely hesitated when the heavy hand that had caressed her so often and so lovingly slid down the back of the sofa.

Curled up on the hearthrug, her cheek pressed hard against Matthew's knees, Chrissie read her mother's letter again.

> Papa has bequeathed the house on Fifth Avenue and its contents to the city of New York. The rest of his money, apart from annuities for myself and Mary Ellen and Boy goes to charity. He regarded you as having had your share when you received your marriage dowry. I will go back to live in the old family house and the three of us will be there, Mary Ellen and Boy and I, when you and Matthew come to see us one day. Darling, I hope you don't mind about Papa's will. It was made with the most loving intentions. But tell me that you and Matthew are happy. I badly need to know for my own peace of mind. I miss dear Papa so much. . . .

Chrissie wiped her tears with the back of her hand.

"Are you happy?" she asked gruffly. "Do you mind about the money?"

"My God, no. In fact, if you had got a legacy, I would have made you give it away. You're my responsibility, and that's the way it's always going to be."

His face looking down at her shone red in the firelight. It was intense, possessive, tender.

"Mrs. Matthew Smith," he said. It was a sign of his

thoughtfulness that he frequently called her that, since they were not yet able to marry. "And didn't we agree never to talk about money?"

Chrissie sighed deeply, with sad contentment. She must write and reassure Mamma, who seemed suddenly so anxious, about her absolute happiness.

"But Papa did leave me something, Matthew," she murmured. "Memories."

She looked into the red heart of the fire, and remembered the privileges, the possessions, the expensive clothes, the magnificent houses and the great balls, the debutantes in their white dresses swooping and gliding, the scarlet and gold uniforms of their partners, the company of the great, the famous and the beautiful. The whole bright, glittering, fantastic dream. . . .